ADVANCE PRAISE FOR
THE SUMMER WE FELL APART

"In *The Summer We Fell Apart*, the four children of an indifferent mother and an alcoholic, self-absorbed father stumble into adulthood. The most moving aspect of this very moving novel may be its author's relationship to her characters. By portraying each sibling's muddled life with tenderness, respect, and clear-sightedness, author Antalek proves herself to be the ultimate good parent."

—Martha Moody, bestselling author of *Best Friends*

"*The Summer We Fell Apart* is a bright, bighearted novel about the complexities and heartaches of the way we live now."

—Elizabeth Benedict, author of *Almost* and
*Mentors, Muses & Monsters: 30 Writers on
the People Who Changed Their Lives*

"Reminiscent of *The Glass Castle*, *The Summer We Fell Apart* tells the story of the four Haas kids who are at best neglected, at worst utterly demoralized by their self-centered parents. It's told over the course of fifteen years, point of view shifting from sibling to sibling, as they grow into adulthood. Each perspective is so poignantly etched by Antalek that you can't wait to hear what the next kid knows that the rest don't, what each can tell you about the others, and whether they will succeed in their efforts to rise from the cigarette ashes of their upbringing. With every chapter the story grows richer and clearer, as does your appreciation for the characters' humor, their burdens, and their devotion to each other."

—Juliette Fay, author of *Shelter Me*

"*The Summer We Fell Apart* is a thoroughly entertaining and often heartbreaking romp through the chaos and comforts of a large and extraordinary family."

—Jessica Anya Blau, author of
The Summer of Naked Swim Parties

"Robin Antalek's debut is as haunting as it is gripping—a story of the events, both mundane and dramatic, that tear a family apart and of the often inexplicable love that binds a family together. *The Summer We Fell Apart* is a beautiful, memorable novel."

—Diana Spechler, author of *Who by Fire*

"Sibling love and rivalry take center stage in Robin Antalek's *The Summer We Fell Apart*, the story of the four Haas children, disconnected and adrift in the world, who somehow find their way back to one another in spite of themselves. Full of the best kind of heartache, it's an unforgettable, bighearted debut that will make you want to pick up the phone and call your own brother or sister."

—Will Allison, author of *What You Have Left*

Emma Dodge Hanson

ABOUT THE AUTHOR

ROBIN ANTALEK lives in Saratoga Springs, New York, with her husband and two daughters. *The Summer We Fell Apart* is her first novel.

the summer we fell apart

the summer we fell apart

a novel

ROBIN ANTALEK

HARPER

NEW YORK • LONDON • TORONTO • SYDNEY

HARPER

This book is a work of fiction. The characters, incidents, and dialogue are drawn from the author's imagination and are not to be construed as real. Any resemblance to actual events or persons, living or dead, is entirely coincidental.

HarperCollins books may be purchased for educational, business, or sales promotional use. For information please write: Special Markets Department, HarperCollins Publishers, 10 East 53rd Street, New York, NY 10022.

FIRST EDITION

Designed by Janet M. Evans

Library of Congress Cataloging-in-Publication Data is available upon request.

ISBN 978-0-06-178216-9

10 11 12 13 14   OV/RRD   10 9 8 7 6 5 4 3 2 1

For Frank, Hannah, and Tessa

CONTENTS

part one

Amy

YOU ARE NOT YOU, YET

*T*he summer we took in a boarder my mother started wearing headscarves. They were adorned with elaborate patterns and colors as if a fistful of crayons had melted on her head. Often she wore more than one at a time twisted around each other and tied low at the nape of her neck so a plume of silk cascaded down her back. The scarves swayed from side to side as she walked, like the dragons in the New Year's Parade in Chinatown. They were so odd an affectation that it prompted our boarder, Miriam, to ask me if my mother was sick.

Miriam was from Switzerland and spoke French, with only a minimum of English, so she pronounced the word *sick* as *seeeck* and it took me a few moments to understand what she was asking. I was left to shrug and roll my eyes as if to say: Parents? Who can explain them? Truth was I had no explanation for the scarves, although I guessed they were probably a result of my mother getting home late from the theater with mussed up, dirty hair. She was in a play in New York that required her to wear a wig—some depressing Bertolt Brecht thing. My mother was excited about it because she thought it lent her credibility as an actor. My brother George and I had used her comp opening-night tickets not so much to see our mother as to see the stage debut of a TV actor George thought was hot.

So the weird head scarf affectation could be explained like this: by the time the car she'd hired brought her back from the city to our house in Nyack it was close to dawn. My mother was vain and, frankly, uninterested in the mundane lives of her last teenage children—she was done—*fini*, as the French say—but I didn't know how that would translate, so I gave Miriam the universal shrug. I could tell from the expression on her face that she wanted more than I could give.

I'd caught Miriam more than once studying the dusty family photos that lined the halls of our house and ran up the steps like crooked teeth—her face up so close to some of the old black-and-whites that shreds of cobwebs clung to her chin and nose. In pictures I can see we translate well and so I understand her fascination. Our parents back then were often together, smiling wide, showing all their teeth, and holding cocktails or being hugged by someone famous (if only in their obscure theater circles). The rest of us—we are four in all—looking mildly amused or bored in all the pictures, even when we were babies.

Miriam had not met the rest of us yet since it was only George and me still at home. Miriam occupied Finn's old room with the crew paddles and lacrosse sticks hanging on the wall. Being the only female in the house besides my mother (who was most definitely not participating in the Miriam project), I was the one to get Miriam's room ready and I chose Finn's room because his has a little bathroom tucked under the attic stairs. When I was turning the mattress to freshen it, I found several *Penthouse* magazines and, tucked between the appropriately suggestive pages, love letters from an old girlfriend, Holly, along with an ancient crinkled condom pack.

I pocketed the condom (wishful thinking—I was going to college a virgin) and threw away the magazines, but I kept the love letters. I planned to surprise Finn with them when he came back from Europe at the end of the month.

Finn was off on a backpacking trip with our father and at some point they were supposed to meet up with my older sister, Kate, who lives in Florence and teaches English. Finn was the only sibling actually *invited* to join our father. George suspected Finn was asked because he is the true coward among us and will not question our father on why he has abandoned our family.

When George says things like that, I feel bad that Miriam seems to be idolizing us—at least the "us" in pictures. Our father is responsible for Miriam's presence in our house, which explains everything and nothing. All we know is that she is an exchange student for the year without a place to stay. She would be attending high school with me for senior year. I had no idea my father even knew such a thing as an exchange existed, let alone a single person in town who would even consider allowing my family to take someone in. I thought the whole concept of exchange involved another student participating in the exchange, but in Miriam's case that didn't seem to apply.

Miriam showed up on our doorstep the day our father's bags appeared in the front hallway. Their luggage commingled for a few hours while George (who frequently took our mother's side—because it seemed there was always a side to take) scowled at Miriam from the top landing, vowing to have nothing to do with her (lucky for Miriam his vows usually last all of five minutes), and I destroyed the French language in an attempt at conversation. Our father was, as usual, absent. Our mother was hiding on purpose in her room with the door bolted. I could smell the cigarette smoke from downstairs and I pictured her in her bed, the curtains drawn against the early August heat. She would be smoking furiously, lighting the next cigarette off the last, all the while blinking and applying eyedrops (while she tried not to light her hair on fire) because her eyes watered from the gray cloud above her bed. The day would be no different from the others just because Miriam had arrived. My mother would only rise to shower and emerge from her room moments before the car came to take her into the city.

This is why I know more about Miriam than anyone in the house. She puts double the amount of coffee and half the amount of water in the pot so the coffee is deep and thick and bitter. She prefers baths to showers—when she takes them—and she often wears the same skirt several days in a row, although she always changes her blouse. She eats bread and jam and cheese in her room or standing up at the kitchen sink. Sometimes she cuts the cheese with a knife and fork. She dislikes tomatoes and eggs. She carries an old-fashioned floral handkerchief in her pocket and adores television. I have found her several times sitting in the middle of the den transfixed by the small black-and-white my siblings have long derided because everyone we know has large color televisions where you can identify the actors without the aid of a magnifying glass. Miriam actually cleared off the accumulated detritus we'd neglected so that she could have an unobstructed view of the minuscule screen. Although I had no idea what to think about her viewing choices of the sitcoms—*Roseanne*, *Murphy Brown*, *Home Improvement*, and *Cheers*—it must have given her glimpses of American life that she wasn't experiencing by living with us. After several weeks at our house she surely must have figured out that no television show could accurately portray her existence in our world.

Since I was desperately searching for a way not to be me, studying Miriam became my secret hobby. As soon as I saw her leaning against the newel post in my front hall I'd wished I'd been born a mysterious European. I was tired of being the smart, creative, yet totally nondescript Amy. I was tired of those trite adjectives, period. The night before Miriam arrived, George and I held a bonfire fueled by the journals of my adolescent longings. I'd burned everything because I was sure this would be my last summer at home and I didn't want to take a chance that one of my siblings would take them and use them as fodder for yet another familial drama.

My guidance counselor had assured me I was smart enough to get into college and probably would get a scholarship to pay for some of it. I think he took pity on me—he had seen all of my siblings through this school, guided them all to college despite the apathy my parents displayed. I mean it was seriously all they could do to sign off on the applications. The guy deserved a medal. Before college I planned to spend my last summer traveling— even if I had to earn the money by working the arts-and-crafts table at the after-school camp for overindulged five-year-olds again all year long.

George fought with me over burning my journals—said one day I might want to write a book about our family. He was joking, I could tell. George was just a packrat. Burning the journals didn't bother me. If an occasion ever arose for me to pen my memoirs I was positive my childhood would never, ever leave me.

My summer job consisted of scooping ice cream and making milkshakes at the dairy shack late afternoons and evenings. Usually I spent the time before work sleeping, then fooling around with some fabric or paint, maybe a book (George and I had just gone to the library and the pile between us included: *American*

Psycho, Shampoo Planet, The Kitchen God's Wife, and *How the Garcia Girls Lost Their Accent*), but this August was different. Now in the mornings I led Miriam to the swimming hole at the very back edge of our property. It was actually more than a hole, but that's how our father always referred to it back when he enjoyed playing the role of country dad. Going swimming meant a hike through waist-high weeds and prickly vines all the while swatting away mosquitoes and no-see-ums, but Miriam seemed to take it in stride. The yard and surrounding property, like the house and its inhabitants, were simply worn-out from years of neglect. I liked to imagine that when my parents had purchased this odd crooked house twenty-five years ago they had the best intentions for their young family—when in truth its purchase had been a recommendation from an accountant during a particularly flush period for my father.

Once we got to the water, Miriam stripped down to her underwear and sunbathed topless. Her breasts were small although almost completely overtaken by large brown nipples. Under her arms were thick tufts of dark hair—at odds, it seemed, with her pale pink skin. On the middle toe of her left foot she wore a silver ring. I tried to look sophisticated in my one-piece black Speedo as I spread out on the blanket next to Miriam—but I failed miserably and ended up spending most of the time picking at the suit and redistributing the spandex around my midsection. All I could think was that facing my senior year of high school with Miriam, who was so comfortable in her skin, could only mean I had less of a chance with guys than I currently had.

On the days George joined us I expected Miriam to attempt to cover up, but she barely paid any attention to him except for when he dove into the water. George had been on the swim team all four years of high school. He was tall and thin with broad shoulders and a flat stomach and, with the exception of his time spent in the water, was extremely clumsy. Actually, much to the disdain of my parents, who had assumed their children, like them, would have a penchant for the arts (my collages and fabric creatures were not exactly the Great White Artistic Hope my parents might have dreamed about), all of my siblings excelled in one sport or another. Besides swimming for George, there was crew and lacrosse for Finn. Like my sister, Kate, I was a runner, although I only ran when I was feeling puffy and I exhibited no extraordinary athletic prowess and refused to join the track team as Kate had. I'd say my parents got exactly what they deserved by choosing to live in a small town that, despite its "artsy" reputation and access to New York City, was just like any other cookie-cutter suburb across the country.

When George climbed up to the highest ledge and performed an elegant swan dive—his body sluicing into the water like a knife, barely disturbing the surface—Miriam propped herself up on her elbows and nodded approvingly. "Beautiful," she whispered under her breath. "The boy can fly."

I nodded and was horrified to find water leaking from my eyes down onto my cheeks. George would be leaving for college in New Hampshire at the end of the month and I didn't know what I was going to do without him. There wasn't a moment of my life that I had ever been without George. As family lore goes, my first steps were not to my mother or father but to George. From the ages of three to five I slept curled against him in his twin bed because I was afraid of the monster in my closet. I would have stayed there forever had George not convinced me that he had erected a super-secret monster-detection system in my room that would keep me safe at all times. Miriam reached over and patted me on the thigh—an odd grandmotherly gesture—but she didn't say anything; she was still concentrating on watching George dive.

I closed my eyes and lifted my face to the sun; the dried tears left my skin with a tight feeling high across the cheekbones by the time George got out of the water and came over to us, shaking off like a wet dog.

With my eyes still closed, I lifted my leg to kick George away from me—the water in the pond was spring-fed and felt like pin-pricks of ice. I always waited until the last minute to get wet; I had to be uncomfortably baked before I could be coaxed into the water. George laughed and then dropped down on the other side of Miriam. I knew this because she rolled closer to me to give him more room on the blanket. A few minutes passed in which I could only hear the sound of George's huff-like breathing and Miriam swatting away flies; then Miriam broke the silence.

"Teach me to do that, George?"

"Huh?" It sounded like more of an exhale than George actually answering.

"To dive," Miriam explained. "To fly."

So far I had seen Miriam venture into the water only twice, and each time she did that tiptoe wading-in thing people do when the water is too cold. With her stomach sucked in and her nipples hard and pointy, she patted at the water with flat palms. I can't even remember if she actually swam.

George seemed to be reading my mind because he said, "Do you swim?"

Miriam laughed. "Of course! Do you think I want to perish?"

I was still mulling over her choice of the word *perish* for *die* when I heard George say, "Okay then—let's go."

Miriam hopped up. I opened my eyes and looked at George. He was scrutinizing Miriam and scratching his head. I could tell he knew I was looking at him and that he was purposely avoiding my glare. I never jumped off the ledge. When George first joined the diving team, I couldn't even look at him up there on the board. My palms went sweaty and I felt lightheaded. It had taken years for me to get used to watching George bouncing up and down on the edge of a thirty-foot-high rectangle. Now Miriam was diving? We—I—didn't even know the details of Miriam's exchange. Like who to call in case of an emergency. I only knew how she liked her coffee and what she ate.

She scrambled ahead of George to the rocks and then waited for him to catch up. Along the way he stubbed his toe and skipped around as he cursed in pain. Miriam made appropriate murmuring sounds, a little cluck in the back of her throat. She looked down at his foot when he made it over to her but he shook his head and brushed her off although I could tell he was pleased. George could be a drama queen.

George took the lead—only climbing to the lower ledge that was about four feet above the water. I couldn't even describe this as safer. Miriam stood beside him, peering down into the water as George pointed out the flat sheaf of shale rock to the right that she would want to avoid as she threw herself over the edge. That would be from experience. At one time or another that rock had sheared the skin of every one of my siblings, but not me. And that was not out of prowess—just avoidance. I never dove and in my seventeen years I have heard every word there is to describe my cowardice.

Miriam placed her arms over her head with her palms together, like a beginner ballet student, except her legs were together and her feet pointed out. Without waiting for George to correct her she toddled toward the edge and jumped off. I winced as she hit the water belly-first.

When she came up, she was laughing, although her chest and neck were red from either the cold or the impact or both. She looked at me and waved and I waved back, hoping the pain would dissuade her from any more diving. George stood with his hands on his slender hips—his bathing suit hung dangerously low—and shook his head from side to side.

She yelled up from the water, "Show me, George."

And George, as effortlessly as breathing, made a graceful arc into the water. Miriam waited for him to surface and when he did, she held up her arms in the victory position.

They continued like this for what must have been another hour because I dozed off and when I woke and checked my watch, I had less than thirty minutes to get to work. Before I left, Miriam insisted I watch her dive again. Her form had improved (or maybe *changed* was a better word) so that while she no longer looked like a demented ballerina, she now looked like someone with scoliosis.

George and Miriam's diving lessons continued for the rest of the week. The weather had turned oppressively hot, so much so that even the water felt tepid. When we weren't in the water and I wasn't working, we snuck into the movie theater in town. The back door faced an alley and a boy who had an unrequited crush on George propped open the door for us on the nights he worked. It didn't matter what was playing, because the theater had air-conditioning. We'd eat cheese sandwiches on thick sourdough bread, which Miriam made us, washed down with a huge Coke and some rum that George always provided. For dessert I contributed broken pieces of chocolate-dipped waffle cone that were free for the taking from work.

Sitting like that in the dark with George reminded me of all the hours we'd spent as kids in one theater after another while our parents rehearsed plays. Rehearsing really was a euphemism because in reality my parents spent more time fighting over lines, or fighting over actors or actresses that one accused the other of being attracted to. Not that we always understood it at the time— we only went to the theater when someone forgot to call the sitter and all of the older kids had plans.

By the time I was born my father's career had peaked. Years before he had written a play (about a large dysfunctional family, go figure) that had made it to Broadway and ran for nearly three years, winning several Tonys, including one for my dad, only to follow it up with four more plays that closed after five months, three months, six weeks, and the worst—opening night. That last, particularly painful failure happened the day of my fifth birthday. A day my father hasn't commemorated in twelve years unless you count him locking himself in his study to drink an entire bottle of Jack Daniel's.

After that, the offers were few and far between and so he took to the road, where obscure small towns filled with would-be theater-goers afraid to venture to the big city were more receptive to his work, and he reveled in their attentions, reluctant to relinquish the spotlight.

But an odd thing happened during that time. My mother's career mysteriously revived after she took a role as a crazy inn-keeper in one of those stupid teen slasher movies that (surprise, surprise) made millions of dollars and my mother a "cult" actress. She wasn't quite in the John Waters league of quirky, but she was getting there. All of a sudden she was the one fielding offers and leaving for months at a time. And that was when my dad unex-pectedly took a position as head of the theater department at Skidmore College in Saratoga Springs—about three hours north of where we lived. It meant he was gone, living in some rented room four, usually five, out of the seven days of the week. We were never invited to visit and we never asked. In terms of parental guidance, George and I may as well have been raised by wolves.

On Sunday evening, after we'd sat through a double creature feature of *Halloween* and *Nightmare on Elm Street*, it was close to midnight and still 95 degrees according to the digital time-and-temperature clock on the bank across the street from the theater on Main Street. George suggested swimming. Too lazy to go into the house, we cut through the now well trodden path to the pond and stripped down to our underwear.

Well I did, anyway. George and Miriam pranced like naked toddlers to the water while I, despite my rum buzz, felt like their maiden aunt standing in my bra and panties.

When George yelled, "Take it off for Christ's sakes, Amy, and get in," I shivered but managed to undo my bra and toss it onto the ground along with my underpants as soon as they both disappeared underwater.

The water over my bare skin was . . . indescribable. How could a barrier of Lycra make such a difference in how it felt to swim unencumbered? This was nearly as delicious as the technique I'd perfected in the bath (with the door double-locked) involving the faucets turned on full blast. Almost.

I went under and opened my eyes. Through the cloudy haze of moonlight that spilled through the trees I could make out a flash of leg in front of me. I swam toward it only to have it disappear. When I popped up to the surface, it took me a moment to find George and Miriam. They were standing on the lower ledge, Miriam poised to dive first.

I was sober enough to think "be careful" but not enough to yell out to her. I'd noticed the raw skin and accumulation of deep scratches along her arms and legs from the rock. I'd insisted she put salve on some of the worst and then I had to help her apply it because she couldn't reach them. Her diving had not improved much in a week and so she hit the water with another grand belly flop. When she surfaced, she swam over to where I was treading water and we both turned to watch George dive.

"Goddamn! I haven't seen such a pathetic excuse for manhood in a long time!"

I spun around. The voice came from the bank and belonged to our brother, Finn.

George flipped him the bird and laughed as I called out, "Finn?"

He didn't answer. Just stripped off his clothes and climbed up to meet George. They fake-tussled for a moment—their strong limbs and smooth torsos entangled and made paler than they were by the moonlight—before they fell into the water still holding on to each other.

I swam over to them and then was pulled underneath by a tug on my leg. I hadn't had time to take a breath and I fought harder than usual, kicking someone in the groin; with my toes I felt the curl of pubic hair and tuberous flesh and I instantly recoiled. Growing up with brothers was like living inside a boys' locker room and I was used to seeing (and smelling) a lot, but physical contact was another thing. It wasn't until I came up gagging, my throat and nose burning from inhaled water, that I realized what I'd done.

"Nice to see you too," Finn said, although through his scowl I could tell he wasn't that hurt.

"What the hell are you doing home?" George asked as he filled his mouth with water and spit it at Finn, barely missing his left ear. "It's not the end of August yet, is it?"

Finn shook his head and said without explanation, "I felt like cutting it short."

"Did Dad come with you?" I asked.

"Nope." Finn looked past me to Miriam.

I turned and motioned for her to join us. "Miriam, this is our brother Finn."

Miriam swam closer. "Finn," she said demurely, "hello."

I turned to Finn, "Finn, Miriam."

He flicked water at George before he said, "I know who she is."

I looked at Finn and made a face like "don't be a rude shit," but he didn't get it. He oozed charm without trying, even when he was being a jerk. In that instant it struck me that Finn reminded me a lot of our father. He continued to ignore my pointed stare. Instead he shouted to George, "Race you to the high ledge." And they were off.

"Weird," I said out loud more to myself than Miriam. I had never known Finn to miss an opportunity to impress a girl. Or maybe this was all part of his game. Who knew?

"Weed?" Miriam repeated incorrectly in an attempt to understand the word. She mispronounced it a few more times but I ignored her; I didn't feel like playing translator right now. She gave up and dipped her head back so her face was level with the water. Her hair fanned out around her like seaweed.

I was getting tired of treading water so I swam over to where I could stand on a rock. The water lapped over my breasts as they floated on top of the surface and I folded my arms in an attempt at modesty. Miriam didn't follow me. She was watching my brothers clown around on the high ledge, probably still pondering the meaning of the word *weird*. Let's see, what examples could I give her that she would understand? My life, her presence in our house, or my brothers up on that ledge? George hung back while Finn hot-dogged it, one set of toes curled around rock, his calf muscles taut, while he dangled the other leg over the side like he was going to fall. His arms made windmills while from his mouth came a *whoop-whoop-whooping* sound.

When Finn did finally dive, it was expert but not as elegant as George. I couldn't see the expression on Miriam's face but she clapped. Finn stayed in the water near Miriam and shouted insults to George until he jumped in—a major cannonball that drenched us all. I waited until the water cleared and George and Finn climbed back up on the ledge and then I said good-night to Miriam.

Her mouth turned down into a little pout but she didn't try and stop me from leaving. On the bank I skipped over my bra and underwear entirely and pulled on my T-shirt and shorts as fast as I could. I took a quick look back and felt a little guilty. Finn and George were ignoring Miriam, although either she didn't mind or didn't notice. I hesitated a second and then fatigue settled on me like King Kong himself and I dragged myself back to the house, dropped into bed in my wet clothes, and fell into a hard dreamless sleep.

When I woke, it was almost twelve. There was a dull ache behind my eyes from the heat and humidity. I felt like I did when I had a fever, except I wasn't sick. Under my arms and in the folds of my shorts the fabric was still damp from the night before. I lay there for a little while and then got out of bed. As I got close to my mother's room, I heard Finn's voice and my mother's but I couldn't make out the words. The only thing I clearly heard was when Finn raised his voice and said, "I don't feel bad about a damn thing."

One of my mother's scarves was tied around the doorknob; the tail of another was caught in the door from the other side. I reached out and fingered the silk while I waited. I smelled cigarettes and I imagined the two of them sharing a smoke in silence. Finn was the only one of us, besides Mom, that smoked. I shifted my weight on my feet. I don't know why I didn't just go in and join them; it had to be the youngest-child thing in me that preferred to get my information the sneaky way.

Eventually, tired of waiting and in need of caffeine, I went down into the kitchen. There was an empty pot of coffee and the remains of a jam-smeared English muffin on the counter. On the kitchen table was a pile of mail: mostly junk, a few bills, and on the top something from the University of New Hampshire for George. I wondered who was going to be taking George to school at the end of the summer. I made another pot and was waiting on the back porch steps outside the kitchen door for the coffee to brew when I heard a door slam from upstairs, and then Finn appeared in the kitchen. He was angrily shoving his feet into sneakers as he hopped into the kitchen. When he saw me on the steps he growled, "Move."

"Say *please*." I couldn't resist.

"Say *fuck you*," Finn retorted as he sidestepped around me and took off down the gravel drive in a slow jog. For some reason it reminded me of when he would train for crew in the preseason by jogging with a backpack filled with bricks. Today, he didn't have the backpack but he did have on his old Nyack Lacrosse jersey and a pair of blue, bleach-stained athletic shorts I'd found when I cleared out the drawers in his room for Miriam. I'd dumped everything in the basement laundry. Interesting that Finn should need to find those things. It could only mean one thing: he'd come home without any of his belongings. It certainly wouldn't be the first time.

I had just poured myself a cup of coffee and returned to the back step when Miriam appeared in the middle of the backyard. "You are here," she said, as if I had asked her to point out my location on a map.

I nodded and lifted the mug to my lips. Miriam moved several steps closer and stretched her arms up toward the sun with a little moan. "Everything it hurts today."

"Too much diving," I said, not bothering to correct her English. Miriam smiled, showing all her teeth. "But I'm getting better?"

I nodded as I swallowed my coffee. "Did you guys stay up late?"

Miriam frowned and gave a petite shrug. I wondered if Finn continued being a jerk. I was surprised when she said, "George went to bed—but I stayed swimming with Finn."

"Really?" I said. I shouldn't be surprised. I had never known my brother to go for long without some girl draped all over him. High school had been a revolving door of females in all shapes and sizes. There wasn't what I would call a definitive Finn type before Holly. Yet she of all of them had been really nondescript with long brown hair parted in the middle, flowing paisley tops, and jeans with holes in the knees. Unlike the others, who had a penchant for Love's Baby Soft perfume and Bonne Bell lip gloss, Holly had been bare of any excessive girliness. I remember one time they had given me a ride home from school in Holly's cramped little MG. I had to practically sit on the stick shift wedged between Holly's and Finn's shoulders. To this day I can recall how Holly had smelled like handfuls of dirt from the garden. Not unpleasant, just not flowery. Would he really go for Miriam? Or she for him?

Miriam, who had previously been looking out toward the woods, turned to me and said sharply, "What is it?"

"I'm surprised, that's all. Finn was acting a little . . ." I waved a hand in front of my face. "Forget it." I thought of his greeting to me this morning or using the word *weird* but instead I just added, "He was in no mood this morning—that's for sure."

She looked bored at the mention of Finn's mood. "He's awake?"

"Jogging," I said and pointed in the direction of the driveway.

Miriam pursed her lips and looked up at the sky. "Let's go get the George. I need more practice."

The George? I liked that. It made him sound important. Out of earshot of Miriam I would refer to my brother as *the George*. I rose slowly and Miriam followed me back into the house. I looked at the clock on the wall. I had to be at work in three hours—what else was there to do until then but swim?

In the beginning Finn's arrival had no impact on our daily makeshift schedule of swimming, work (for me), and movies. We barely saw him and so I dubbed him the vampire—only coming out of his room when he knew we'd all gone to bed. The first night Finn was home he had bunked in with George. The next day he moved into Kate's room despite the large hole squirrels had chewed in the baseboard molding (entry had been gained through the porch roof eaves below the window) that was never properly repaired. George and I had cleaned up the squirrel crap, shoved steel-wool pads in the hole (a trick I learned when mice infested the pantry—apparently they won't chew steel wool), and then nailed a two-by-four over the mess and closed the door.

The only reason we knew he'd moved in was because that night when we'd gotten back from the movies there were piles of trash that lined the hall, blocking access to my room. Obviously he had done some house-cleaning. George slouched against the wall and watched silently as I kicked the bags out of the way and slammed my bedroom door. I'd be damned if I was going to have Finn waltz back in here without telling me what was going on. Especially since, out of the blue, Miriam told us that Finn would not be going back to Boston where he lived and worked. As she put it, he told her the night before that he was taking an "absence."

Ever since Finn dropped out of Boston College his sophomore year he had worked construction, but he had a habit of losing jobs. He drank too much and then didn't show up for work. So Finn's "absence" could easily have been a decision made for him, not by him. Even knowing that about Finn didn't make it any better when Miriam told us. George looked like he wished he could be any other place in the world, and even though there were some things I wanted to know, there were more things I didn't want answers for—not yet anyway—and especially not through Miriam.

After a few nights of lying awake and listening to the door across the hall open and close, I decided the time was right to confront Finn. I gave him a five-minute lead before I snuck out of my room. Unusually cool air swept through the upstairs hall, and I shivered in my tank top and shorts. The heat had finally broken at night although from past summers I knew the days would keep the water warm for swimming—at least for now.

As I made my way downstairs I smelled cigarette smoke. Finn must have been meeting my mother every night when she got

back from the city. I walked toward the only source of light in the
house and stopped just shy of the doorway. Finn and Miriam sat
across from each other at the kitchen table, smoking, the chipped
blue willow teapot between them. Finn's head was bowed, his
chin tucked toward his chest, the hand with the cigarette dangled
over the edge of the table. His expression could have gone either
way—boyish shyness or flirting. My money was on the second
option. I stepped back even farther, afraid they would see me.
Although they weren't doing anything wrong, the scene seemed
too intimate, even more intimate than swimming nude in the
pond that first night. Finn said something and Miriam laughed
and then I heard a chair scrape across the floor and I went running back upstairs into George's room.

George slept spread-eagled on the same twin bed he's had since
grade school. His arms and legs hung off the sides. I curled on the
floor next to him and tugged on his hand. "George—wake up."

He moaned. I tugged again. "George, wake up!"

"Go away."

"Not until you wake up."

"Pest—what the hell is it?"

"Finn and Miriam are down in the kitchen."

"Alert the media."

"George!"

"Fuck, Amy—were they naked?"

"No!"

"Well?"

I sighed. "Why do you think Finn left Dad in the middle of the
trip?"

"He finally grew some balls?" He threw an arm across his eyes
and mumbled, "Get me another blanket, would you?"

"Only if you talk to me."

"Why can't you be a moody teenager and go in your room and crank some Nirvana?" He lamely hummed a bar of "Teen Spirit."

"George, I'm warning you! Talk!"

"About what?"

Exasperated, I said louder than I intended, "Pick one: Finn, Finn, or Finn!"

George covered his head with his pillow and I pulled it off and tossed it on the floor. George rolled over onto his side and reluctantly opened one eye. "All that Finn told me was that Dad had other interests and so he just decided to come home."

"You mean a girlfriend?"

"I don't know," George said softly.

George was a horrible liar. "Yes you do! Why are you protecting him all of a sudden?"

He barked, "That's a good one—who the hell do you think I'm trying to protect here?"

"Don't do me any favors, please." More to myself than George I said, "Why didn't Dad stop Finn?"

"What's Dad going to do to stop him?" George touched my shoulder. "Amy, why don't *you* ask Finn yourself if you don't believe me?" He tried to grab the pillow back. "Let me sleep."

I shrugged him off and pulled my knees up to my chest and hugged them tightly. I looked down at the floor where a pile of wet swim trunks and a towel were probably getting moldy. I nudged it with my toe. Soaking wet. I thought about getting in touch with Kate to find out if she'd seen Dad as they'd planned, but I didn't really want to have to go through her. Kate, ever the oldest, would only talk down to me in that way she always did when she thought she needed to impart an important life lesson. I'm sure she could explain away Dad's "other interest" enough to make me feel like a fool. "Have you talked to Mom?" I asked.

"Sort of," he growled. "Yesterday afternoon when I bummed a twenty."

I sighed; money reminded me that we needed groceries. I said this to George and he said, "Now? Seriously Amy, you need to get a life."

Just how was I going to do that? I looked around George's hole of a room and grabbed the olive-green-and-gold-striped afghan from off the desk chair and tossed it on top of George's head. Our grandmother had made one for each of us; mine was orange, purple, and yellow, like Easter dye gone bad. He mumbled something from beneath the pile of acrylic, but I didn't stick around to listen.

I can't remember specifically how the idea of a dinner party came about. We were at the grocery store, Miriam and I, and she came around the corner with a gorgeous pile of deep-purple grapes in her hand and a frozen container of daiquiri mix and the next thing you knew, in our cart we had several steaks, cheese, pears, butter, garlic, leaf lettuce, and a few baguettes, and were planning a party. It was to be a proper dinner, Miriam insisted, one where we dressed up and ate at the table and used napkins.

The afternoon of the dinner party I skipped out on swimming and stayed behind to make a cake even though I was the absolute worst person for the task. I read and reread the directions on the box until I was confident enough to begin. Even if I screwed up it was better than the alternative activity. The novelty of Miriam's diving lessons had finally worn off.

Before she left, Miriam helped clean the dining room. We drew back the drapes and opened the windows. On the sideboard I placed a vase of creamy hydrangeas from the old bushes that circled the foundation of the house. I cleared off the table then washed the dusty lace cloth and hung it on the line to dry in the sun. When the cloth was ready, I planned to set the table with the bone-white china plates and mismatched etched glass goblets I'd found on the top shelf in the pantry.

A week had passed since I'd spied on Miriam and Finn in the kitchen. I tried to ignore the sound of Finn haunting the halls long after we'd all gone to bed. He remained as absent as ever during the day and I had come to the conclusion that maybe George was right—I needed a life other than the one I invented in my head.

The heat was back. Sweat trickled down my back and between my breasts and I regretted my decision not to go swimming. I chewed on ice as I waited to take the cake out of the oven. This last bit of summer made me sad; the days were waning. Soon George would leave, school would start, my mother's play would be over and she would be forced to make an attempt at parenting until her next job came along. And what about Finn?

That evening the purple sunset cast shadows around the room as I lighted candles. Finn teased George relentlessly about his clothes. Under orders to dress up, George had found (God only knows where) a wrinkled pair of herringbone pants and a mustard-yellow button-down shirt topped off with one of our father's old tuxedo jackets. He paired the ankle-length pants with low black Converse sneakers sans socks. He smelled funny but I decided not to say anything since Finn, in pressed khakis and a deep-red bowling shirt that said "Ralph" over the left breast pocket, had greeted him by saying, "You are the least stylish homo I know."

That prompted George to sulk a moment by the drink cart I had set up. He poured himself a glass of the leftover rum from the daiquiris and downed it in a swallow before elbowing Finn in the stomach. Laughing maniacally, Finn grabbed the waistband of George's belt and was about to give him a wedgie when Miriam entered the room. They stopped scuffling and Finn stumbled away from George. I turned around to see Miriam catch Finn by the arm. George yelled, "Let him fall," then he hesitated, suspending us all for a second, before he grinned and I found myself laughing a little too loudly in relief.

Maybe my reaction was because of the high color in Finn's face that hadn't been there before as Miriam let him go. But more likely it was because wrapped around Miriam's torso was one of my mother's scarves. She had tied it twice around and knotted it in the front. It bared a sliver of belly below which she wore a black velvet skirt that touched her ankles. It was the most daringly sexy thing I had ever seen on someone my own age—and it belonged to my mother. On her wrist was a rope of pearls that she had wound around several times, her hair was loosely knotted at the nape of her neck. In contrast, my sleeveless black dress that I had considered to be slightly Audrey Hepburn–like now seemed cheap and constricting.

George began to hum and Finn remained speechless, looking everywhere in the room except at Miriam. It was funny that we all seemed shy now that we were dressed in something other than bathing suits or less. What had once been a sophisticated and fun idea seemed all the more like playacting when I said, "Let's start off with some drinks."

Eagerly we tossed aside dinner-party etiquette and downed the first pitcher of daiquiris and then a second and started on a third. By that time Miriam's legs were propped on the chair next to her and her velvet skirt was up around her thighs. I had kicked off my heels and George abandoned his hideous shirt and wore the tuxedo jacket over his bare chest. Finn, who had drunk copious amounts of alcohol, at a faster rate than the rest of us, was quickly becoming the drunkest of us all. He rested his head on his arms on top of the table.

"Doesn't a dinner party have food?" George asked.

"You look like a rock star," Miriam said to George, ignoring his question.

George did a little air guitar for Miriam's benefit.

Finn lifted his head off the table and enunciated very slowly, "I am hungry."

I stood quickly, too quickly. My vision blurred and my tongue felt thick and awkward in my mouth. I sat back down to wait out the double vision. I wasn't aware that Miriam had left the room but when she returned she had the plate of pears, grapes, cheese, and one of the baguettes. We swarmed the food until there was nothing left but the stems and lightly nibbled innards of the pears.

The bread and cheese had almost an instantaneous effect on me. Maybe it was the booze that gave me courage or maybe I just told myself it did. When I finished chewing and swallowing, I looked across the table at Miriam and said, "I didn't realize you and my mother were close." Out of the corner of my eye I saw that Finn's head swiveled in Miriam's direction.

When Miriam looked confused I gestured with a knife. "Your top," I clarified. "It's her scarf isn't it?"

She nodded quickly. "Is it a problem?"

"Amy," George said quietly.

"Not mine." I shrugged, refusing to acknowledge George. "I mean, you mentioned the scarves before so you must like them, right?" I picked up my glass and set it back down without drinking. "Finn seems to like it."

"Amy, what do you mean?" Miriam's brow was wrinkled and she looked genuinely upset. She glanced at Finn but he seemed unable or unwilling to meet her gaze. I was sorry the words left my mouth but it was too late.

George smiled slowly. "Don't listen to her. She's had too much to drink." Miriam didn't really look like she believed George but she returned the smile anyway.

"How do you know what I do and do not mean?" I asked George. "Weren't you the one who told me to ask Finn?"

"Then ask Finn and stop being a bitch." George had said the word *bitch* so softly I wasn't sure I heard him. Then he stood up and announced to us before he left the room, "I'm going to put the steaks in the broiler."

My heart was thudding in my ears when I turned to Finn. "When is Dad coming home?"

He looked down at his plate.

"Come on Finn, you have to answer me," I cried. "Why did you leave early?"

Miriam shifted in her seat and leaned toward Finn. "Tell her," she said quickly.

Before I really processed that Miriam knew something about my family that I did not, she followed George out of the room.

Finn finally looked at me and said, "He's not coming home."

I watched his face, waiting for something more but there was nothing, so I asked, "Not, as in never?"

He shrugged and twisted his body so his legs were stretched out to the side. I stared at the name embroidered on his pocket while I waited for his answer. My eyes followed the curly script: R—A—L—P—H. Eventually he said, "He'll show up again. At some point."

It seemed, after all of our father's absences, that the information I had pushed Finn for was, at best, anticlimactic. "Mom knows?"

Finn sighed and rolled his eyes at me like I was the stupidest human being in the world. "I don't think he hides anything from her." He cleared his throat. "She was the one who told me that Miriam is the daughter of one of Dad's friends."

My cognitive abilities were obviously shot, because I was totally confused. "What are you talking about? What friend of Dad's?" Finn was silent until it dawned on me what he meant by the euphemism. I leaned back in my chair and stared at my lap. "Shit."

When I looked up again, Finn was rubbing his face with both hands. In a muffled voice he said, "It's not Miriam's fault. Dad . . ." He paused and looked at me like he was in pain. Finn was not your man if you were having an emotional crisis. Finally he mumbled, "Miriam didn't know who we were until she got here." He stalled by loudly clearing his throat. When he was done he said, "Think about it, Amy, we're the same as Miriam. I mean whoever Dad is doing—"

I cut him off. "I get it. Except I don't think Mom is about to ship us off to live with one of them . . ."

Finn laughed. "Don't count on it."

I figured only he could joke about something like that, because he was the one who was closest to Mom. He wasn't in danger of falling out of her graces no matter what he did, and in fact she seemed to care more about him than the rest of us no matter what he said or did.

Secretly I started hoping that Finn had formulated a plan to get rid of Miriam. Because I didn't want to be responsible for showing her the door and incurring the wrath of our father. Even after everything I now knew, I had to admit that I had grown to like Miriam.

"So what do we do now?" I asked.

"You mean with Miriam?"

I nodded.

"Nothing. We do nothing." There was a slight hint of a challenge in his voice.

"How long do we wait?" I asked.

"The thing about you Amy is"—Finn explained like I was a small child—"you need to stop waiting."

I folded my arms across my chest. I could hear Miriam and George laughing in the kitchen, fat from the steaks popping and sizzling in the broiler and silverware clattering in the sink. I thought about how George said that Finn was the coward among us—that he would never challenge Dad—so it was logical that he wouldn't challenge Miriam's place with us. It was obvious I was getting nowhere with Finn. Suddenly I remembered the package of love letters I had found under his mattress. I pushed back my chair and said, "I'll be right back."

I could see Finn tense; he was all coiled up like he might need to spring into action at any minute. In his eyes there was fear and then surprise when I headed upstairs and not in the direction of the kitchen. He must have thought I was going to drag Miriam out here and have it out. When I returned from my room with Holly's letters, he was slumped in his chair with his eyes closed.

"Here." I dumped them in his lap. He opened his eyes and fumbled with the rubber band as he squinted at the handwriting.

As soon as he recognized them, he said, "What the fuck? Where did you get these?" The rubber band snapped as he extricated an envelope and unfolded a letter. He held the paper up close in front of his face; his mouth moved but he made no sound as he read. Finn pulled out several more and continued to read. I realized as I watched a bevy of transparent shifting emotions flit across his face that I had been wrong about love. It was not a linear thing with a beginning, middle, and (sometimes) an end. Perhaps love was just a myth or as simple as the desire not to be alone. That desire could justify anything—what else could explain how my parents lived as they did?

Finn placed the bundle of letters on the table. He looked like an old man beaten down by default; the legacy of our father was his and his alone. His fingers traced the rectangle of the envelope and then he dropped his hands in his lap. "You can't fix everything."

I blushed with embarrassment that he thought I was trying to rekindle a high school romance for him. "That's not what I was trying to do."

He shook his head and shoved the letters away from him. "I mean about Dad, about me and Dad. It's not your problem to fix."

"Tell me what the problem is!" I shouted with frustration. "I don't even know. I know nothing except you went away with Dad and now you're home early." I leaned across the table. "Please, tell me."

His eyes darted around the room as if he was looking for a place to settle where I didn't exist. Finally, he sighed and said, "I had too much to drink."

I slid the remainder of my plate toward him—a crust of bread and a trio of grapes. "Here—eat this."

Finn's lips were twisted together like he'd tasted something sour. "Not tonight, with Dad." Finn got up and grabbed randomly at a bottle on the liquor cart and poured what was left into his glass. Before he screwed the cap on, he offered the empty bottle to me. Confused, I shook my head. I noticed his hand trembled as he set the bottle on the table and finished his drink in a swallow. "I got loaded and told Dad I wasn't going to be his witness anymore. That he could fuck anyone he wanted but I wasn't going to sit there and watch him."

George had been wrong. Finn wasn't a total coward, although apparently he needed alcohol to work as a truth serum. "What did Dad say?"

"He asked me to come outside with him and talk it out like a man." Finn looked into his empty glass, seemed to consider refilling it, and then set it down on the table. "So I did."

"Was the girlfriend there?"

"We were waiting for her to join us," Finn said. "Unfortunately she arrived just as I knocked Dad to the ground. Even though I was trying to help him up, she came over and took his arm and told me if I didn't leave immediately, she was going to call the police."

I exhaled as the enormity of what Finn said washed over me. "You hit Dad? Finn? Really?"

He sank back down into his chair at the table and cradled his head with his hands. "I didn't mean to; I sort of pushed him. He was trying to tell me that he needed to take this chance at love—some shit like that—that he didn't want to lose me, to lose any of us." Finn's face was contorted with anguish. "As if I didn't fucking know that Dad fell in love constantly." He laughed and looked at me for confirmation. "I mean, aren't I right? He's always fucking someone. Why was this time so different?"

I tried to put that information aside. "Did you say that to him?"

By his shrug I guessed that he hadn't shown that much courage. "He wanted me to come back and tell all of you how happy he was. He was using me! It was fucking selfish lying bullshit, Amy; I just wanted him to shut the fuck up. So I pushed him back a little." He demonstrated with his hands palms out. "I thought it was a little, I don't know. He stumbled and Ana Sophia came running over and . . . and the next thing you knew I was fucked."

Physically Finn and Dad were probably evenly matched. What

must it have felt like? The thought of it made me dizzy, I could see it—Finn pushing him down, the panic when he'd realized what he'd done. "Dad didn't stand up for you? Didn't he tell her she had it all wrong?"

Finn squeezed his eyes shut tight and then opened them, blinking several times before he answered, "No." Whatever he had remembered just then he wasn't going to share. After a long pause where I pondered why my father lacked the capacity to be a parent let alone a decent human being, Finn said, "I'm going to stay here for a while with George gone soon . . ." His voice trailed off.

I considered Finn in this new role of provider and protector and it was hard to imagine—then again, people changed. "What will you do?" I asked.

"Hopefully something different."

Finn's answer surprised me. I didn't know whether he meant different from my father or different from what he was doing in Boston. In the end I decided that it didn't really matter which question he answered.

I hadn't realized I'd been holding my breath until George walked back in the room and tossed a baguette like a football at Finn. It bounced off his shoulder and fell to the floor. They were miscreants masquerading as humans. Finn picked it up and threw it back at George, who caught it with one hand. Behind George, Miriam twisted her body shielding a platter of steaks and a bowl of salad.

The savages managed to break the tension and we sat down and ate the dinner. It seemed like the simplest solution. After all, there was nothing else *to* do, was there? While I pushed the food around my plate, I remembered how Miriam studied our family pictures when she first got here. I thought it was envy on her part but now I imagined it was something else.

I should have stopped drinking when I'd sobered the first time around. Instead, along with the berries in amaretto over the cake, I indulged in some Kahlua while the others had cognac. By then, we were so drunk and it was so hot in the house we'd moved to the backyard. I reclined in a lawn chair while I watched Miriam, George, and Finn attempt to play soccer.

I tried closing my eyes but everything spun around so much I was forced to open them. When I did, Finn towered over me swaying from side to side. "Don't drink any more," he said, spittle caught in the corners of his mouth. His eyes were so bloodshot they looked like they were bleeding. "I'm serious, don't drink," he repeated.

I moaned and shielded my eyes from his constant swaying. I didn't know what was worse—eyes closed or open. "Go away," I said and tried to shoo Finn back to the game. Because I suddenly seemed incapable of stringing together a sentence, all I could think was: *Pot. Kettle. Black.*

Miriam had her skirt tied up between her legs as she ran down the yard with the ball. She kicked and missed and fell on her face laughing. Her skirt had come undone from its knot and billowed out around her like an opened parachute. When Finn saw this he ran to her and helped her up. I watched them for signs of something else but I didn't trust my instincts. I had been wrong about so much.

"I'm hot," George announced as he dropped his tuxedo jacket on the ground by my feet. "We need water."

"Swimming!" Miriam sighed as if Jesus had suggested it.

Down at the water everyone seemed to strip without thought—at least down to his or her underpants. However, my sense of modesty in front of my brothers made me keep on my bra. I knew it was different for Miriam; it always would be. Yet tonight she surprised me by keeping my mother's scarf tied around her chest and for once I wished she'd taken it all off.

The water seemed to sober me just enough to know how drunk I really was, but it didn't have that effect on the others. I floated on my back with my eyes closed but it still made me dizzy. When I opened them I saw that Miriam had followed Finn and George to the highest ledge. George dove first. Finn and Miriam stood side-by-side giggling like new friends on the playground. When George popped up I swam over to him. "Can she do that?"

"Now or never," he answered.

"What does that mean?"

George looked up at the sky like he was exasperated by my questions. "It'll be fine, Amy, really."

I stared at George as he taunted Miriam with chicken calls. Finn belted out, "Come fly with me, come fly, come fly away," in a halfway decent Sinatra imitation.

All at once I knew I was going to be sick. I coughed and bile shot up into my mouth. I spit it out into the water and swam to the bank. When I got out, I grabbed my dress and jammed it back over my head and down my hips without doing up the zipper. The fabric clung to my wet skin like tissue paper but I would be damned if I was going to be naked and puking. I broke out in a sweat and barely made it to the bushes before I threw up everything I'd eaten that evening and then some. It was only when I was done coughing and my stomach stopped cramping up that I turned around just in time to see Miriam follow Finn into the water. The tails of the scarf fluttered in the breeze like a fragile pair of wings.

Her execution of the dive sucked but she came up sputtering and triumphant. My legs trembled and I sank down onto the ground and put my head between my knees. I smelled awful, my mouth tasted like pond scum, and there was spittle on the front of my dress, but at least my stomach was settling down. My eyes and nose ran from vomiting and I wiped at my face with the back of my hand, drawing away a long, thin line of mucus.

When I was able, I got up and walked back down to where my brothers and Miriam were playing in the water. There were multiple rounds of high fives and then Miriam noticed me first standing there watching them. She seemed skittish as she avoided looking me in the eye by tucking her chin down and studying the water.

I took the path to the diving spot. As I passed the lower ledge and kept climbing, George and Finn called out to me, but I squared my shoulders back in an attempt at some sort of dignity and refused to acknowledge them. My entire body felt like the morning after when it was still the night before and that was never a good thing. When I stepped out onto the ledge, I had no idea what I was doing and so I kept my eyes focused on the trees and the light from the moon. I had a sudden overwhelming urge to see my mother. It was an odd sensation. I couldn't remember the last time I had purposely sought her out. I was so accustomed to turning to George when I was in need. Now here I was drunk, but not drunk enough that I didn't realize I was about to do something incredibly stupid and I wanted my mommy. My legs trembled again and I took a deep breath and planted my feet farther apart in a power stance while I contracted my muscles. I bent over at the waist and stretched my spine; the metal tines of the zipper scraped against my skin but I wasn't about to take the dress off.

A bat flew out of the trees close to my face and I flinched and pressed back as flat as I could against the shale wall as another and then another and another followed. When they were gone, I gradually inched closer to the edge and felt with my toes until a rock I dislodged went skittering over the side. George and Finn were still yelling something at me, but my heart was thudding so loudly in my ears I couldn't hear them if I wanted to. I did notice that Miriam was now treading water with her head tilted back as she too stared up at me.

I curled my toes around the edge, squeezed my eyes shut so tight I saw sparks, put my arms above my head, and jumped. The wind rushed under my dress and forced it up around my waist when I hit the water. Down I went passing through water that was alternately warm, cold, and then warm again until my toes touched spongy muck. I pushed off from the bottom at the same time reed-like slime twined around my legs. I panicked and groped wildly, spastically at the water as if I could move it out of my way. When my fingers closed around something soft and smooth I opened my eyes and brought my hand up in front of my face. The water was murky from my frantic churning but there was no mistaking the pattern on my mother's scarf. My eyes stung and I ached to take a breath as pinpricks of electric shocks rippled through my lungs and filled my chest. I waited until I couldn't take the pain for a second longer and then I kicked as hard as I could and swam toward the surface.

HOW TO CLEAN HOUSE

*W*hat my mother does admit to me when she calls is that Finn is on another bender and she can't possibly rely on him to help her clear out the house before Monday. She sounds so small and sad on the phone and I am in such a weird state of mind I overlook that I am being manipulated. She needs me. I can tell by the tone of her voice that she would also like me to offer to find him, just like the other times. This time, however, I am going to let him sit and pickle before I drag him back home. Besides, divesting the house of our childhood is enough pain for one weekend.

The house I grew up in, a Victorian that would have made Edward Gorey and Edgar Allan Poe clap hands in glee, was lit up like a birthday cake when I arrived a little after midnight. I actually thought a fire was the only thing that could save the place now. The house had been in sad shape since before I was born, but now it appeared that the entire structure listed to the left. The iron spire on the widow's walk was actually bent. I wiped the traveling crust from my eyes and looked again. Yes, the house definitely appeared as if it were trying to turn its back on the neighbors. How my mother even found a buyer was beyond me. As a restoration project it would seem that the house would fall under the category of "too late."

I picked up my backpack and rummaged around the passenger seat gathering the remains of my fast-food dinner from a rest-area sojourn and then reconsidered before carting more stuff inside. What would be the point? I would only be carrying things out. I dropped everything and got out of the car and stretched, forestalling the inevitable. I was a little queasy and sore all over and the night air, cool for April, felt wonderful. I had been working so hard at school that my whole body hurt from pent-up tension and anxiety and a diet high in sugar and caffeine. A part of me longed to throw myself down in the newly uncovered spring-time grass and gaze at the sky until I fell asleep. Besides, I had no idea what state I would find my mother in; the range of emotions she could cover in a matter of minutes had always been frightening. While there was no doubt that range was what kept her employed as an actress, for a mother it was less of a gift than a handicap. I took a deep breath and gave myself a few extra minutes by slowly ambling around to the kitchen door.

The lights were all on in back as well, illuminating a mountain of large green trash bags that appeared as if my mother opened the back door and tossed them out without thought. Several were blocking the steps and I picked them up and added them to the pile. They were heavy and rattled as if they were filled with broken china wrapped in a miserly layer of paper.

When I walked into the kitchen, my mother met me with two bags in her arms, obviously on her way out the back door for another trash toss.

"Here, take these," she said as she thrust the bags into my hands. As if it had been minutes not months since the last time we'd laid eyes on each other. The bags were awkwardly stuffed with random sharp edges poking through the thin plastic and very heavy. "Just add them to the pile out back. A Dumpster is coming tomorrow."

I took the bags from her but set them down by my feet and didn't move as she turned and walked away. I called after her, "Hi Amy, how are you? I'm fine. How was the drive? Long. How's school? Busy, what with my graduation being next month and lots of projects to finish. Coffee? I'd love some!"

My sarcasm stopped her in the doorway and she rested a hand on her hip. My mother and my older sister, Kate, bore a striking resemblance to each other. In fact, the hand on the hip thing was a mannerism they both shared and employed frequently when challenged. They were each tall and lean, small-breasted with narrow hips and thick dark shoulder-length hair—my mother's gray kept in check by Clairol—and from the back they could be one and the same. It was only when you got up close to my mother that you saw the waddle of skin under her chin and the lines around her eyes.

But while Kate looked like our mother, the similarities stopped there. Kate longed to be a daddy's darling and we all knew it. The only people in my family who had yet to admit the fact were Kate and our father.

When I had my mother's attention, I lamely joked, "What's in the bags? You finally broke all the dishes so you had no choice but to get divorced?" It actually would have been better had my parents physically lashed out at each other like that, but instead their drama had consisted more of head games and sex with strangers. Only once could I remember an airborne ham during a Christmas dinner.

She smirked and shook her head. "Trophies. Medals. Sporting

paraphernalia." She spat the words out like she tasted something bad.

"How do you know the boys don't want this stuff?" I prodded. During their high school years my brothers had racked up an impressive laudatory haul.

She frowned.

"Mom?"

Still frowning, she shrugged and spun on her heel out the door. Over her shoulder she called, "There's coffee in the pot on the counter. Get rid of those bags." When she added *"please"* as an afterthought, I could tell it was because she thought she had to. Welcome home.

I heard her ascend the front hall stairs, the dry wood creaking at the most minimal pressure beneath her light step. Doing as I was told, I dragged the bags across the floor, opened the back door, and rolled them down the stairs. Then I took a mug from the dish drainer and poured myself some coffee. I guessed that sleep wasn't something I was going to get, at least not for a few more hours.

I shuddered when I tasted the coffee. It was swill of the worst kind: hours old. But I drank it anyway. Who was I to be so choosy? I followed the trail of cigarette smoke and found my mother upstairs, collapsed in a chair in the middle of the room that used to be George's, her legs hung over the arm and her feet swung back and forth as she leisurely blew smoke rings into the air. The room had been ransacked: dresser drawers hung open vomiting a trail of clothes awaiting their fate, the shelves and walls stripped of George's swimming medals and trophies, the life-size poster of Greg Louganis I had given him years ago as a joke because I knew George had secretly lusted over him. It was such a familiar mess that if it wasn't for my mother's presence in the room along with the missing possessions and the economy-size box of garbage bags, I could almost trick myself into thinking that George still lived here and that I still slept across the hall.

I bent down to pick up a pile of T-shirts from the floor and hugged them to my chest before I realized that a horrible odor, a combination of mold and cat piss, was coming from the pile.

If I was queasy before, now I was sure to hurl. "Oh my God." I gagged as I quickly dropped the whole lot back onto the floor and pulled at my own T-shirt to shake off the stench.

"You know how George had a habit of putting things away wet. From the smell of things I'd say those drawers haven't been opened since before he went away to college"—she ticked the years off on her hand—"that's a good six years of mold." I noted her voice had a throatier timbre, probably from the smoke. She took another long, deep drag off her cigarette and squinted at me through the haze.

I walked across the room and pushed aside the threadbare madras curtains to open a window. I rattled the old frame, trying to coax the wood up without breaking any of the tiny multiple panes of wavy glass and wedged the first thing I could get my hands on, an overdue library book on South America that was probably the remains of an old school assignment, on the sill underneath the window to keep it open.

I stuck my head out of the window and took a series of deep breaths, slowly filling my nostrils with fresh air. Reluctantly, I pulled my head back inside and looked at my mother. "When is everyone else getting here? Why don't you have George do his own room?"

As I watched her expression it slowly dawned on me that she hadn't called any of my siblings. "I'm the only one coming?" I swallowed back bile.

My mother turned slightly in the chair to face me. "I'm tired of begging the others. I knew you'd at least take pity on me here all alone." She sighed as if she were bored by her own voice before she reconsidered and added, "Well, except for Finn."

I opened my mouth, made a noise of protest, and then stopped. Obviously, this was to be her mantra for the weekend. Poor deserted Marilyn. She was right about one thing: We all left as soon as we could and honestly, it seemed expected of us to do so. The lives of my parents had been full enough without the four of us. I wanted to say that maybe if she'd acted like she wanted us around, maybe we would have stayed, or at the very least come home every once in a while without resentment. Of course now she was moving to a studio apartment on the Upper West Side of Manhattan where there simply would never be enough square footage for anyone but her. A *cachette* she had called it. More than once I wanted to ask her why she'd even bothered with children, but I didn't have the nerve. Just the thought of posing the question made me sad and I felt a little wrench in my stomach when I considered what her answer might be.

She seemed to realize I wasn't going to fight her over her last comment and looked at me with an arched brow. Quietly she went in for the kill, "It's a good thing I have a life because obviously none of you are going to keep me company in my old age." She swung her legs easily off the arm of the chair, limber as a teenager, stood, and walked to the doorway.

"Mom . . ." There was nothing I hated more than a pity party, but we'd already gotten off on the wrong foot and she was filling up the balloons in anticipation of a real blowout.

She waved her hand at me or maybe it was in the general direction of the mess that was George's room. "Bag all this up, will you? I want to have all the rooms cleared out by the time the

Dumpster gets here and then . . ." She yawned and wiped her eyes with the back of her hand. "Then we'll deal with the rest."

I heard her footsteps retreat and then the familiar sound of her bedroom door closing. If there was a sound I associated with my childhood it was that: the lock catching in the latch of my mother's door. I stepped uneasily away from my fresh-air source, afraid for my stomach. I didn't shut the window. I surveyed the mess and my stomach flipped again. Fuck it. I was going to bed.

My room was just as I'd left it the last time I'd been home almost a year and a half ago when Polly and I got the apartment off campus and returned to pack the van with my belongings and take it all back to Providence. I'd left so little of myself behind that the room now had a monastic look to it.

I walked over to my desk and turned the latch on the windows under the eaves. I only had to shimmy the swollen fragile wood gently to swing them open and out. I flopped back onto my bed and surveyed the remains. There was the desk and bed and a random grouping of items I had left behind for no other reason than I ran out of room. On the shelves was a squirrel family I had been inspired to make after squirrels infested the eaves under Kate's old room. There was also a fuzzy llama made from an old bathrobe, and a white terry-cloth cube with a face, which I'd named Tofu.

The walls behind my bed were still collaged with maps torn from a discarded atlas. I'd drawn routes on them with crayon and little pushpin flag markers to denote places of interest along the way. Imaginary road trips I'd planned for the day I'd be anywhere but here.

I rolled over onto my stomach and bit down hard on my lip to quell the pain as my swollen breasts met the mattress. There were other things I would have to deal with before I worried about getting a job. Soon I would have to face the fact that being tired even after twelve hours of recuperative sleep wasn't because I had totally screwed with my body by staying up all night to work on my projects and sleeping all day. Soon I would have to face the fact that the underlying constant nausea I felt wasn't a virus. Soon I would have to face the fact that I needed to go to the drugstore for a pregnancy test.

I closed my eyes and fell into a deep dreamless sleep, woken only by the sounds of an inhuman chattering and the rustling of garbage bags below my window. When I reluctantly rubbed apart my crusted lids, I half-expected it to be morning. But it was an hour before dawn and the raccoons must have crawled from the woods to ravage scraps from the trash bags. I sat up in bed unable to sleep and considered going downstairs for something to eat but given the state of the kitchen I figured there was probably nothing. When it was obvious I wasn't going back to sleep anytime soon, I swung my legs out of bed and padded across the room and out into the hallway. I stopped outside my mother's room and tested the knob and was surprised when it turned. My eyes adjusted to the dark and I could make out a teetering pile of framed photos she'd removed from the walls in the hallway, mounds of clothing, and stacks of books, and distinguish them from the form of my mother sleeping on her back, arms flung off to the side like she was reaching for something. I couldn't remember the last time I had wandered into my mother's room in the middle of the night looking to be comforted. It was George's room I usually sought out, his narrow twin bed and the slim spot of mattress he afforded me as I used to curl up next to him.

So I was surprised when she asked in sleep-thickened voice, "Did you have a bad dream?"

To my amazement my mother moved over and swatted the space next to her with an open palm. I accepted the invitation and adjusted my body into the rippled waves of the already warmed sheets. The bed linens had the combined smell of my mother's perfume and cigarette smoke.

I thought my mother had fallen back to sleep when she asked quietly, "Is everything okay?"

"I've just been going for weeks and not getting much sleep. I think I've confused my internal clock." My voice sounded loud and strange in the dark.

My mother rolled over onto her side so that she was facing me but her eyes were still closed. "You never needed a lot of sleep." She paused. "When you were a baby I would find you lying in your crib with your eyes wide open. You had been so quiet I thought you were asleep, but it turned out you had probably been awake for hours. Watching. Listening." She swallowed. "You never even cried when you were hungry. I was so worried that I would sleep right through and forget to feed you, I had to set an alarm to wake me every three hours when you were a newborn. Your father hated it; he used it as an excuse to sleep in his study until you were eight months old." She pulled the sheet up around her shoulders and tucked it beneath her chin. "You never complained, Amy. Never fussed. It was like you knew something that I didn't."

I held my breath. I had almost no stories from my infancy. If it hadn't been for Kate and a project she was doing for school that had her documenting a family member, which coincided with my birth, there probably wouldn't be any baby pictures of me either. My mother startled me when she said, "Maybe that's why you are an artist, all that watching."

I sighed. Recently I had begun to worry that without any real future plans I was nothing. My degree and four years of projects in a portfolio did not make me an artist. Without school and coursework defining who I was, what would I do? And surprise, surprise, did my mother really think of me as an artist? "I'm scared," I finally admitted out loud.

"Who isn't?"

"What?"

"Everyone is scared, Amy. Everyone. The trick is to close your eyes and look away before the bad part."

"Is that what you do?"

I hadn't been looking at my mother. I had been staring up at the ceiling but I sensed she had opened her eyes and I was right. Her face was inches from mine on the pillow and I couldn't help but wonder if this had been my father's side of the bed. How long had it been since she had shared this bed with anyone? Was I naive to think that she lived a celibate life in this room since he'd left?

"I think that was the difference between your father and me. Richard faced everything head-on. I averted my eyes to the tragedy."

"How long did it take you to figure that out?" I asked the question because I didn't want her to stop talking. I had never had this kind of intimacy before with my mother. I knew it was tenuous at best and might only last until the sun rose and everything reverted back to normal.

She laughed. "I knew it before I married him."

"And you did it anyway?"

"I was looking the other way, remember?"

"And you were pregnant with Kate?"

"I was." She yawned.

I touched my stomach, and in that moment I wanted to tell her my secret but I held back. I was too aware that this kind of sharing wouldn't last, and too afraid of her judgment. "But you were crazy about Dad, weren't you? When you married him?"

"Yes, but it was the kind of crazy that takes over your life. The kind that consumes everything in your path and makes you feel like you have a fever. But when you come out of that kind of crazy, it is, to say the least, disorienting." She closed her eyes again, looking like she was ready to go back to sleep.

She sighed into the pillow and the features of her face settled into a mask of placidity. I was reminded of a series of photographs a friend of mine had done for his senior thesis: a photographic essay of his girlfriend sleeping. He'd photographed her every night for a year without her knowledge. When she found out she broke up with him because she didn't know what else he might do while she was asleep. I thought it was perhaps because he had shown the world a side of her she herself had never seen and that was what she was most afraid of.

"I'm too old for crazy," my mother murmured.

I stroked the slightly swollen pouch of flesh that was my stomach. "What am I going to do?" I whispered.

"You will do what you need to do, Amy." My mother urged, "Now go to sleep."

I didn't want her to stop talking but even as I fought it I felt myself drift off as well. The next thing I knew it was morning and my mother was standing over me with a cup of coffee.

"Amy."

She shook my shoulder and I moaned.

"You slept in your clothes."

I opened my eyes enough to see her frown and then I closed them again. "What time?" I asked.

"Six-thirty. Come on. The junk isn't getting into the Dumpster all by itself."

I tried to sit up but the combination of coffee and my mother's perfume that she thought covered the cigarette smoke conspired against me. My mouth felt all watery and I pressed my tongue against the back of my front teeth before I swallowed. Everything felt tight, including the clothes my mother felt it necessary to point out that I'd slept in.

Eventually I managed to really open my eyes and say, "I need to take a shower."

She sighed in annoyance but released the pressure on my shoulder. Her voice had softened just a little when she said, "Fast, okay?"

She searched for a place on top of the crowded nightstand to put the coffee. As she moved things around to make room for the mug she picked up a framed photo and stared at it for a moment. While she did, the corners of her mouth tugged downward and her lip trembled slightly before she dropped the frame, facedown, into a pile of clothing and books on the floor next to the bed and left the room.

As soon as she shut the door, I reached over the side and picked it up. In the photograph Kate is a toddler squinting at the camera while wielding a shovel, and Finn is still a baby, propped upon a lump of sand at the beach on Long Island by hands I knew to be my mother's. I took a moment to look around her room in the filtered daylight. The heavy violet curtains she had drawn against the sun sagged off the rod and the shadows on the ceiling made the gray circles of smoke damage from years of my mother's cigarettes seem darker and more menacing like ominous spots of cancer on an X-ray. I figured the state of dishevelment the room was in could go either way: she had already started sorting through things for packing and discarding or this was just how she lived.

After the shower I opened windows to let in the fresh air as I towel-dried my hair and brushed it out. My hair was heavy and wet through my T-shirt, but it felt oddly comforting. My stomach had settled enough for coffee and I was just pouring a cup when my mother came into the kitchen from outside.

"Well," she said with an edge of criticism in her voice as she gave me a serious stare, "that's a very familiar look."

Instinctively I stood up straight and sucked in my stomach. "What look?" I asked.

She laughed off my attempt to appear together. "Amy in the morning—wet hair, bleary-eyed, sucking coffee." She moved quickly through the room after that and I heard the front door open.

I followed her just in time to see a truck backing up into the driveway with a large blue Dumpster on the back of a flatbed. I walked out onto the porch and stood next to my mother. The sky was absolutely perfectly blue—not a wisp of cloud anywhere—and the air still held the remains of a cool night. Together, in silence, we watched the Dumpster's slow release into the driveway. It wasn't until it touched ground that I realized it entirely blocked in Polly's car, sealing my fate for the weekend. There really would be no escape until the Dumpster was full.

We worked separately. If my mother felt any differently toward me after the night before, she didn't show it.

A night with the window open made the air in George's room bearable. I finished bagging the clothes and anything else I could fit into a trash bag. I called George seven times and each time I got his voice mail. I was going to kill him when I saw him. I slid his mattress and box spring down the front stairs along with the bags and then hauled them out to the Dumpster. I did the same with the rest of the bedrooms on the second floor except for my mother's. In my room I boxed up what I'd left behind to bring back with me to Rhode Island. That included peeling off some of the collages from the wall. Maybe they'd help me figure out where I was going.

I found a bag of Asian snack mix in the pantry and despite its scary expiration date I was too hungry to care. I figured the salt was enough of a preservative anyway. It was on a shelf next to a piece of molding that had our names and heights on it. I ran my finger down the dozens of marks and dates of my siblings until I found my own. I counted two recorded measurements at age three and five. Kate had always been the one who did the measuring. Considering that she had been thirteen and probably plotting her own escape the last time she measured me, I expected there to be none after that. I noticed that she had even measured our father once while he still was a good six inches taller than both of the boys. I searched for a marking for our mother, but Kate hadn't bothered. I licked my finger and tried to rub out the decade-old exclamation point with a heart for the period that Kate had placed next to Dad's measurements but I only succeeded in creating a smudgy mess.

I took the bag of Asian snack mix off the shelf and ate it as I talked to my mother. She was emptying my father's desk by pulling out drawers and dumping the contents into a large box in the center of the floor. My father, according to his attorney who delivered the signed divorce papers, was on sabbatical from his position at Skidmore College. My mother snorted at the use of the word *sabbatical* and explained that he meant he was on another continent with a benevolent girlfriend. How she knew I could only begin to wonder, but didn't ask. At different times in my life I felt alternately that I knew too much about my parents' private lives and then, at other times, nothing at all. I just wanted to be like everyone else: somewhere in the middle.

I watched my mother. She had some sort of selection system, because every once in a while she would stop and add a random item to a rapidly growing pyramid that included my father's Tony Award for Best Play and Richard Ford's book *Independence Day*, about a man who leaves his family for a fling with a woman in France only to return and try to ingratiate himself back into his family's good graces. Considering our current circumstances it seemed the book was a talisman and an odd reading choice; but I said nothing.

I sucked on a wasabi pea that I found at the bottom of the bag and wondered aloud if a yard sale was worth it. My mother looked up from her pillaging and squinted at me through the dust. "I've seen the crap people buy—are you kidding me?"

Inexplicably, she was saving the furniture for a yard sale on Sunday. She told me about it when I found her in my father's study, repeating her words slowly like she was wasting her time because she claimed she had explained this all before.

"So Dad doesn't want anything?" I felt a bit shy, as if I shouldn't be peeking at any of his stuff. I could count on my fingers the number of times I'd ever been in my father's office. Even after all this time it felt a little sacrilegious.

"I asked. Never got an answer. So I'm going on no." She turned and started on the bookshelves. "But if you'd like to call him you can." It was a challenge I recognized, delivered in the most nonchalant of tones. She pointed in the general direction of the phone but I stayed rooted to the floor. I knew she was paying close attention to me even as she pulled down a leather-bound book.

When she turned it over in her hands I could see it was a copy of Fitzgerald's *This Side of Paradise*. "Get me another box, would you, sweets? I think we can sell some of these."

I probably had earned the affectionate word *sweets* because I hadn't immediately run to the telephone. I wasn't that dumb—maybe I'd try him later when she wasn't around. But even as I thought about calling him, I knew I probably wouldn't bother. When I didn't make a move to leave, my mother stopped what she was doing and frowned. "What is it, Amy?"

I shrugged. "I was just wondering if years from now when I think about home will this be it? I mean, even if it isn't ours anymore?"

My mother's entire body sagged as she leaned back against the desk and considered what I said, still holding the Fitzgerald book to her chest. "I never realized that any of you thought fondly of this house." She sighed. "Who really wanted to be here in this wreck?"

"You must have at one point?" I ventured.

She shook her head. "Not really." She narrowed her eyes at the far end of the room as if the answer was written on the wall. "We were only supposed to be here for a short time and then your father was going to make a triumphant return to Broadway."

"And?"

She smiled, but not happily, and gestured around her at the boxes. "And look where we are today."

Perhaps this was yet another example of what my mother had said last night: she looked away before the bad part and found herself living here. Forever. Or so it seemed.

I cleared my throat. "Well, there are still memories here, none of us can deny that."

My mother straightened up and looked down at the boxes of books. As she rearranged a few in the sell pile I noticed that the veins on the backs of her hands stood out more than usual and her knuckles were thick and knotted. Her hands looked like they belonged to someone else, someone older. Still intent on reconfiguring the books, she said, "You know what they say about memories, don't you?"

There was a lump in my throat and I shook my head in response, even though she wasn't looking at me.

"We always remember things better than they were. Never worse." She smiled and tucked her chin against her chest. "Can you go get me those boxes now?"

"Do you really believe that?" I asked, even though as the words escaped my mouth I knew what she meant. Less than twenty-four hours in the home I'd known my entire life and I was having a hard time recalling the specifics of my discontent. Perhaps time and age had muted the details?

"It helps," she admitted quietly.

*The downstairs rooms had already been stripped of any extra-*neous possessions. The furniture pushed out of place and into the corners in odd configurations looked like the first people at a party huddled in clumps around the edges of the room. In the center of the dining room was a stack of collapsed boxes and a tape gun.

Reluctantly I put down my rice mix and taped together the bottom center seam of the closest box. I tossed it aside and did several others in quick succession. In this one moment I could see the Zen-like appeal in a simple repetitive task and so I continued. It helped to focus on the job in front of me and not to dwell on my mother's curious mood; I was unused to her sharing so much. My concentration was broken only when I heard tires on the gravel drive. I didn't think the Dumpster company was coming back until Sunday. I walked over to the bay window in the dining room and looked out through the overgrown bushes. Lucky for me the lime-green leaves of spring were just beginning to unfurl on the hydrangeas. Before long there would be total obliteration.

My father's ancient red Honda was parked behind the Dumpster. Apparently my mother's source had been wrong. I didn't know whether to run into my father's study to warn my mother or stay here and hide. I held my breath as I watched the driver's side door open quickly, trying to recall the last time I'd seen my father. When Miriam stepped out of the car, I smashed my forehead against the window and said, "fuck," under my breath over and over again. Of course, like a highway strewn with bodies after a wreck, I couldn't look away. She went around to the passenger side and knocked on the window. Again, I held my breath and waited.

She looked annoyed and tired as she gestured at whoever it was through the glass. When the door opened a crack, she stepped aside and looked over her shoulder toward the house. I moved back from the window so I could still see, but so that I wasn't too obvious. I didn't want to start off with Miriam after four years with the accusation of spying hanging over my head.

Finn got out of the car slowly. He was stooped like he'd been punched in the stomach. His hair was long, greasy, and the skin on his face was an unflattering color combination of yellow and gray. When he was fully out of the car, he squinted up at the house. Despite his obvious state of physical deterioration his face lightened when he said something to Miriam. She smiled at him and shook her head then went back over to the car and took an item out of the backseat. A worn and scuffed leather backpack. She slung the pack over her shoulder and waited solicitously for Finn to make the first move. When he ambled unsteadily over the grass in a diagonal line toward the front porch, I skidded across the dining room and ran back down the hall to the study.

I barely waited until I got to the doorway when I said, "Finn's here."

My mother stopped in mid-toss, widened her eyes at me, and said, "Well."

For a second I reveled in the moment—she and I were thinking the same thing, we had a blip of connection—then I blurted out, "With Miriam."

She dropped an armful of paperback books into the bag on the desk and rubbed her hands along the tops of her thighs to rid herself of the dust and dirt. The corners of her mouth turned up, though not enough for a smile.

"Let's go," she said.

We arrived in the front hall just as the door opened. I was behind my mother and I had a moment of déjà vu, of standing in this exact spot years before when I'd first met Miriam. Of course neither my mother nor Finn had been present then. It had only been George and me. Oh, Georgie. I was torn between running to the phone to call him and tell him what was going on and staying put to see what was going to happen.

The last time I'd seen Miriam was four years ago, the weekend after our high school graduation. She was moving upstate. My father had managed to get Miriam into Skidmore College where he taught. He'd also arranged the student visa and a summer job at the racetrack in Saratoga. She would be taking over my father's rented room while he was away on vacation. In the fall she would move into the dorms and he back into his room. It had occurred to me at the time that my father had not assisted a single one of his biological children in their college search, even financially, he'd encouraged (*insisted* is a more accurate word) all of us to take out student loans and work. In other words, to do it on our own just as he had. To get Miriam into the college where he worked, the tuition waived as one of his benefits even though she wasn't his dependent, was never something he'd even offered as an option. Not that I would have accepted.

If I hadn't already spent the better part of my senior year ferreting out information, making sure that Miriam was not my father's fifth child, I would have accused him of this as well. To this day whenever her name came up George maintained his theory was the right one: that our father slept with the wrong woman and taking care of Miriam was payback. A theory I conceded was not without merit. I supposed one misstep in a lifetime of infidelity was bound to happen.

At least this explained why she was driving his car.

What our father never counted on during the year Miriam lived here was that she would fall helplessly in love with my brother Finn. I had thought at the time her love for Finn was unrequited, but now looking at the two of them I wasn't so sure. Of course my experience with love so far was that it was never around when you wanted it, so I could hardly be counted on as an expert.

My mother stepped forward and opened her arms to Finn and he allowed himself to be hugged. Their relationship mystified me. In the sibling lineup Finn came second, born two years after Kate. Family lore had it that he was a fussy baby calmed only by my mother and a bottle. The bottle part still applied. Miriam looked around the clump that was my mother and Finn and smiled unsteadily in my direction. No matter that I'd been out in the world for the last four years, Miriam still seemed exotic to me. Maybe it was my old insecurities. Maybe it was being in this house standing in the exact same spot I'd seen her for the very first time. Maybe it was that despite the warm April air she had a scarf wrapped dramatically around her neck several times. Maybe it was all that plus the love of my brother. Maybe.

When Finn and my mother parted, I fully expected her to say something to Miriam. At least acknowledge that Miriam had returned him to her alive. Instead, she led Finn into the kitchen. I looked at Miriam and sighed. "I'm sorry." Noting with irony that the first thing I said to her after four years apart was an apology for my mother's behavior. It was just like the old days.

She shrugged like she fully expected nothing more from my mother.

Oddly enough I thought to defend my mother who moments before had seemed so fragile and undeserving of my sarcasm. But I didn't, too much to explain and so I let it go. Instead, curiosity forced the words out of my mouth that, really, had I cared about decorum should have waited until at least after I said hello. "What are you doing with Finn?"

Miriam's eyes were downcast. Her eyelashes grazed the tops of her cheeks when she said, "He came up to spend the week with me."

"Ah," I said, alarmed and nauseated; the rice mix was not a great thing to eat on an empty stomach. I was getting the nagging feeling that maybe Finn hadn't been on a bender like my mother implied.

Quickly Miriam rushed on. "It's not like that, I mean, we're not together like that anymore."

Anymore? I tilted my head to the side but didn't say anything. So forget the unrequited part. I suddenly flashed on the picture of all of us skinny-dipping in the pond.

"I'm trying to get him to"—she blinked rapidly and then shrugged—"I'm trying to help him dry out. But it doesn't seem to be working."

"It's not your problem." I realized I sounded a lot like my mother or Kate when I answered Miriam.

In a flat, unaffected voice she stated, "He's going to kill himself, Amy."

In that moment I suddenly knew what was so different about her. Miriam's accent had taken a backseat to her fluent English. I felt Miriam staring at me. She was obviously waiting for a follow-up to her declaration of Finn's suicidal intentions.

So I offered lamely, "He's been trying for a long time. I don't think you have the power to stop him."

Despite her stoic front Miriam paled at my statement and yet I couldn't do anything to take back my words because suddenly I knew I was going to throw up. I ran upstairs and barely made it to the bathroom before I lost it. When I was sure I was done, I slumped against the wall and closed my eyes. I was so damn tired, and now with Finn and Miriam here and the prospect of a yard sale there was going to be too much going on to get to CVS for a pregnancy test. Like I needed one. More like I needed the address for the clinic.

"Are you okay?"

I opened one eye. Unfortunately I'd not had enough time to even think about closing the door. Miriam walked over to the sink, took a washcloth from the towel bar, wet it, wrung it out, and handed it to me.

I pressed it against my mouth and my forehead. "Thanks."

"You're welcome," Miriam said as she put the lid down on the toilet and then took a seat on the edge of the tub. I closed my eyes but I knew she was watching me. I could feel it.

"I'm not drunk," I mumbled.

Miriam laughed a little, like she'd had plenty of experience recognizing drunk from sick. "I didn't think so."

"I'm tired," I said, reluctantly opening my eyes and then added, "and hungry." I winced. "That's weird, huh?"

Miriam shrugged. "Not so much, I guess. Do you want me to go get some food?" She started to stand and I shook my head no so she sat back down. She was trying so hard and I knew it was because somehow I'd made her nervous.

"What's Finn going to do after this weekend?" I swallowed; there was too much spit in my mouth. I dabbed the washcloth at the corners of my mouth. "Can he even work?"

"He's not that bad. He looks worse than he is." Miriam chewed her bottom lip. "I'm trying to get him to stay in Saratoga." She left off the "with me," although I knew that was implied. Miriam continued. "At least I know some people and maybe he could get a job." She plucked at something on her bare knee that I couldn't see.

There was a lot left unsaid as we sat in silence. My mother called upstairs, and I stood shakily, my knees buckling once. Miriam followed close behind not quite with her hand on my elbow. I didn't have the strength to shake her off so I let it be.

With the four of us working, what was left in the house quickly either became trash for the Dumpster or yard-sale merchandise. With the exception of my mother's presence and the absence of George it reminded me of the summer of Miriam. When she had been abandoned by my father on our doorstep and we had reluctantly forged a friendship that was somewhere between stranger and sibling. That summer the unexpected arrival of Finn had changed everything, just as it did this weekend.

Physically, Finn was weak, so Miriam and I hauled most of the heavier stuff and we were able to set up the sale on the lawn in front of the house. We didn't even stop to consider if there was a possibility for rain overnight. My mother just wanted it out of the house and as far as I was concerned, it all could be carried the fifty feet to the Dumpster wet or dry.

Somehow Finn was able to make dinner out of a box of pasta and two cans of beans he'd found in the pantry. We finished with coffee and stale shortbread cookies. My mother barely ate, spoke only when she had something to say to Finn, and otherwise smoked and frowned down at her plate. Unlike my dinner companions, I was starving, and so when she finally pushed her food into the center of the table and excused herself, I finished hers as well. I could have gone on to eat from Finn's and Miriam's untouched plates too, but I refrained.

Finn insisted on cleaning up and while he hunched over the sink, the room filling with warm moist air scented with dish soap, Miriam and I sat at the kitchen counter making signs for the yard sale with drawing paper and crayons I'd salvaged from my desk drawers. I had never been more aware that from the outside, a stranger looking in at the warm glow coming from the kitchen, would easily misinterpret this scene—the truth contained in these walls was never transparent.

Miriam disappeared to get sleeping bags from the car and Finn dried his hands on his jeans as he looked over my shoulder at the posters. He'd taken a shower before dinner and I could smell the same shampoo on him that I'd used that morning. He looked a little better now, some normal color had returned to his face. But his old athletic body was now frail and he held himself like someone recovering from surgery.

We had tried to get close my last year of high school when he'd lived here, but he hadn't taken the place of George, and then I went off to college and he went on drinking. Eventually, the only contact we'd had were the couple of times I found him and brought him back home to dry out. The best conversations we'd had were when he was loaded. I seriously doubted he remembered a single word.

Sometime between then and now Miriam had assumed the role of caretaker, although it was obvious from my mother's absolute refusal to acknowledge Miriam's presence that my mother was trying hard to ignore that fact.

"Nice poster," Finn said as he picked up my recently discarded crayon and read the color on the label. "Good use of cornflower blue against the yellow in SALE."

I laughed and yanked the crayon from his fingers. "Don't you have a dish to wash?"

He picked up another crayon and drew on my poster a circle with dots for eyes and a wide smile. "It's great to see what four years of art school has done for you," he cracked. "What's next?"

I put down my crayon and watched while Finn scribbled smiley face after smiley face until all members of our scattered family were accounted for. "I could ask you the same thing." I raised my eyebrows and waited.

Finn dropped the crayon and shoved his hands deep inside his pockets and studied the kitchen floor. "How about I go back to Providence with you?"

My first reaction was to laugh. Then I saw the expression on Finn's face and I knew he was only half-joking. With that came the realization that Finn was just like me: unsure of the next step. It would seem that my brother and I shared a lack of motivation; a refusal to accept that a future existed seemed to be a common bond. Still, that didn't keep me from stumbling through a litany of excuses: small apartment, roommate, and finals, until I just stopped talking. If I admitted to Finn that I didn't want to be responsible for him, that I was barely capable of being responsible for myself, it would sound trite. I could never put into words that

Finn, when he was with me, reminded me that I was not that unlike him, and it scared me and made me feel like a horrible person for not helping my own brother.

Finn waved me off. "I get it, you have a life."

"Give me a break." I paused and said, "I've worked hard."

"I get it, Amy," Finn repeated as he gathered the trash from dinner, tied the bag tightly, and headed out the back door.

I followed quickly behind him but despite his frailty he was steps ahead of me and had already dumped the garbage and was headed toward the barn. I followed him inside although he didn't turn to acknowledge me. The air was cool but acrid, tinged with the earthiness of the damp dirt floor and mold, and I promptly sneezed. In the center of the barn was a pile of furniture that towered over my head. A mattress shredded and stained, chairs with no legs, chairs with three legs, tables, cabinet doors, paneled doors, and random pieces of lumber. There were things in the pile that I recognized: a metal desk, a floor lamp, and the very first television from the den. At an angle to the pile, like a seat pulled up for front-row viewing, was our old couch: the one with the nubby beige fabric that I used to rub my eczema-plagued arms against, searching for relief when I was under strict orders not to scratch. When I was a child my skin reacted to every emotion by erupting in a raised, angry, itchy mass of water-filled bumps. When my nervous system overloaded I was a walking, oozing mess.

"What are you doing?" I asked Finn as he began to dislodge things from the pile and toss them outside onto the dirt drive.

"What does it look like?" he asked, huffing as he freed a broken desk chair and flung it behind him.

I jumped out of the way just in time. "Hey, let me help you. It will go faster."

"No," he said, more softly than I would have expected, "faster would be to take a match to everything and we can't very well do that, can we?"

Miriam appeared just then in the open door with her arms around two rolled sleeping bags. Finn abruptly stopped what he was doing and moved to help her. Miriam glanced over at me quickly as they left the barn. Either she sensed our exchange or she was just nervous.

I walked over to the pile and half-heartedly tugged on a table leg but I couldn't budge it from beneath the desk. Instead I picked up the chair Finn had tossed into the drive and added it to the Dumpster on my way back into the house. The way Finn mentioned taking a match to everything led me to believe that he was still as angry at our father as he ever was and apparently he was nowhere near letting go of that.

I returned to the kitchen and Miriam reappeared, asking if I wanted to go hang the signs. I had been hoping for another moment with Finn, to make him understand that what I'd said earlier, my reaction to his request, the state of my life, was not so cut-and-dried. I didn't want to disappoint him but at the same time, how could I be his savior when I was incapable of saving myself?

Instead I agreed to Miriam's suggestion and gathered the pile of signs off the counter and walked back through the dining room while Miriam grabbed her keys and leather backpack. In the corner of the room I saw the sleeping bags rolled out on top of the threadbare Oriental carpet. The bags, I noticed, were side by side. I was about to ask her why they didn't just take one of the empty bedrooms upstairs but then I thought better of it.

We got into my father's car. It smelled sweet and sour at the same time, like booze and candy. Miriam turned the key in the ignition and rolled down all four of the windows then glanced over at me as she backed down out of the driveway. "Do you mind?"

I shook my head and stared out the window back at the house. The furniture we'd arranged room-like all over the lawn looked like the house had been turned inside out.

Miriam drove up and down the streets close to the house. Each time she stopped I got out and taped the posters to a lamppost while she waited with the engine running.

As she drove closer to town I said, "I need to stop at CVS."

"Okay," Miriam agreed as she concentrated on the light in front of us. We were the only car at the intersection but that didn't seem to make a difference. I noticed that Miriam was a careful driver—her hands were always in the ten o'clock and two o'clock positions and she rarely took her eyes off the road.

"It's over at that new plaza by the grocery store," I said as I dropped the remaining posters and tape gun down by my feet and folded my arms against my chest.

"I know where it is," Miriam said softly. "Are you cold? Should I put up the windows?"

I turned so my face was to the wind. Despite my eyes tearing up I said, "No."

We stopped two more times to put up signs and then we headed over to the drugstore. Miriam signaled to get into the CVS parking lot. I read the shopping plaza marquee. There was a pizza place as well as a karate studio and a hair salon. The lot was nearly empty but there was a neon sign in the window of CVS that read, OPEN 24 HOURS, right next to a sign that advertised two-liter cola products on sale for 99 cents each. Miriam pulled into a spot directly in front of the door and turned off the engine.

After a few minutes Miriam said, "Are you going to go in?"

"I don't think so."

"What?"

"I really don't need to."

"Oh."

"I thought I did but—really—it would just be a waste of money."

Again Miriam said, "Oh."

I kept my arms folded tight against my chest. I tried to sound casual when I said, "The fath . . ." I paused and swallowed and corrected myself, "The guy doesn't matter, so don't ask me what he thinks about this, okay?"

Miriam unbuckled her seat belt and turned to face me. To her credit she didn't even pretend to look surprised.

"I mean I know him, of course I know who he is, but we're not in any kind of thing you know?" I closed my eyes and leaned back against the headrest. The last time we'd had sex, the time that obviously got me here, we'd done it in his car in the parking lot. It was a car a lot like this, with bucket seats, and even though he'd reclined his seat I'd had bruises from the steering wheel all along my lower back for weeks afterward. It seemed they'd only just faded.

He was the bartender where I went to hide out. It wasn't a college bar and that was why I liked it. I didn't even really go there to drink. I would nurse a beer for an hour or so and sit with my sketchbook. I just liked that the people drinking there weren't doing so on Daddy's gold card. I'd never brought anyone with me, not even Polly. In that sense it would be easy to take care of this. I'd never have to see him again unless I chose. There would be no chance for awkward conversations and hostile glances, no chance we'd run into each other. It was also another reason not to stay in Rhode Island and open a shop with Polly.

"Don't tell Finn?" I asked quietly, ashamed, despite everything, of disappointing my older brother. I opened my eyes and I could tell by the look on Miriam's face that I was failing miserably at appearing unaffected.

Miriam murmured, "I wouldn't," as she righted herself in the seat and buckled her seat belt back up. She put both hands on the steering wheel but waited to start the car. After a few minutes she cleared her throat and turned the key in the ignition but she didn't make a move to drive.

As the engine hummed I asked, "So what's going on with you and Finn?"

She looked startled that I'd actually asked about her life. "You mean . . . ?"

I shrugged. I wanted her to tell me without coaxing.

She gripped the steering wheel hard and then released each of her fingers, flexing them as she did. "I'm so stupid," she said. "Just one of those girls, I suppose." She gave a harsh little laugh and said, "Some people just don't want to be rescued."

By "one of those girls" I assumed she meant the perpetually dumped upon yet hopeful. I turned and looked at Miriam. I wasn't used to this side of her, this vulnerability where guys were concerned. She'd always had more of a relaxed attitude toward guys, whether it be a steady or a date to prom or even marriage. They'd never been a means to an end for her. Miriam had never seemed to possess that tunnel vision that so many of my own peers, despite feminism, had been brainwashed to believe in. Even way back when I had first discovered how crazy she was about Finn, her feelings never took on that psychotic sort of lust. Now she surprised me. I wanted to ask her: Why Finn? But I had enough experience to know that question probably had no answer.

"I just can't help myself," she added.

"My mother knew he was with you this week?" I guessed correctly before Miriam responded.

I noticed that she avoided looking at me when she mumbled, "He tells her everything. If your mother let go a little . . ." She shrugged like she'd said it a million times before and knew it was pointless.

For the second time since they'd arrived I thought to jump to my mother's defense. But then I realized that I was only feeling kind toward her because of the night before. She certainly had not warmed to Miriam, even after all this time; even after all Miriam did for Finn.

"Can I ask you something?"

Miriam gave a little shrug, as if we had no secrets from each other.

"Do you miss going home . . . I mean, to Switzerland?"

She shook her head and answered quickly, "It's better if I don't."

"Why?"

"Then I don't have anything to miss," she said lightly.

"It's really that easy?"

"Of course not," Miriam said. "But you figure that out, Amy. You'll see. One day you wake up and you've been somewhere so long that home becomes someplace you're from, not someplace you go."

We were the same age yet Miriam was talking to me like she had lived a lifetime before me. It didn't strike me until now how invested Miriam had become in our lives. She'd come to stay the year and never really left. It was almost as if my father had made sure of that. For what reason, I was almost positive we'd never know. What was apparent was that Miriam cared more about us than we cared about her. Or maybe she just cared about Finn and the rest was overflow. I felt guilty because in the years since I'd last seen Miriam, I'd barely given her any thought.

If I tried to make up for that right now, it would just seem fake. Instead, I asked, "You're graduating this year?"

She nodded.

"What's your major?"

Miriam peeked at me slyly out of the corner of her eye as she backed out of the parking spot. She paused a moment before she said, "International affairs."

We looked at each other and simultaneously burst out laughing. It felt good. On the way home she blasted Ani DiFranco's latest tape from the cassette deck and we hummed along. At least I hummed. Miriam seemed to know all of the words. Her musical choice surprised me since Finn's taste ran more to The Fugees. As she drove, I tried to spot the signs I'd taped to the lampposts. I counted seven including the one where Finn had drawn the smiling family. Enough, I supposed. The people who knew us, who knew of our family anyway, would surely come to the sale out of curiosity, wouldn't they? When we were growing up in the neighborhood, there hadn't been many families of four children so close in age. It was as if we were a walking advertisement for our parents' inability to keep their hands off each other after a fight, especially since we were four children with such loud, dramatic, and decidedly absent parents. I guess in some regards we were lucky to have been born before the advent of increased child-and-family services.

When we pulled into the drive at home, the headlights flashed on Finn stretched out on the dining room table on the front lawn. When he saw us, he sat up slowly and waved. Despite her recent declaration of stupidity where my brother was concerned, Miriam could hardly wait to turn the car off and get out of her seat belt.

The entire car vibrated as she slammed the door shut. I sat tight and waited. I watched her run across the lawn and slide up onto the table with Finn. In the dark he looked like his old self. Still, his hand trembled as he touched her on the arm and pointed up at the night sky. They lay on the table on their backs shoulder to shoulder. I could tell they were talking, could see the slight movement in Miriam's body as she sidled closer to Finn, thigh touching thigh. Perhaps we had all been wrong about him. Or maybe none of us knew anything in the first place.

On the second floor of the house the only light emanated from my mother's bedroom. Occasionally she moved back and forth across the room, a shadow behind the scrim of a milky-white shade. Maybe she was finally packing her things. Dividing her life into piles: before and after. Or maybe she was tossing it all away, determined not to take anything with her. I decided I would go in and help her. I would wrap the framed photos she refused to look at in the folds of her old scarves. I would seal the box but not label it. Instead I would hide it among the few she was taking with her so that one day when she least expected it she could find us all in there, trapped in another time and place.

I released my seat belt and reclined the seat. And because deep in my heart I knew I was my mother's daughter, despite the fury and protest of my youth, I closed my eyes. In the shadow of the home I'd grown up in, where the walls seemed to barely contain the cacophony of voices clamoring to be heard—of secrets held, of bargains struck, of respect demanded, of love being sought and lost and sought again—I knew what I had to do. Here where there was always noise, there was now a clear and remarkable quiet. And just for a moment I felt absolutely nothing.

KISSING IN CHURCH

$\mathcal{I}$ purchased the pack of cigarettes that may have killed my father five days after he made a miraculous recovery from surgery for a brain tumor. As it often was during the last month of his life, I was the only one out of the four of us present at the hospital, so I had no choice but to honor his request, even though up until his illness we hadn't talked in over two years.

I use the word *miraculous* because he was sitting up in bed joking with the nurses when earlier the doctors doubted he'd live through the surgery. Because of this, the doctors had suggested post-surgery that he get in the wheelchair so I could stroll him around for some air. I found it ironic that after all the cutting-edge treatment ideas the doctors had been spewing since my father's diagnosis of advanced brain cancer, the antiquated notion of fresh air was still offered as an option to aid in his cure.

Since he was given a second chance at life, I waited to hear him atone for years of neglect or even tell me he loved me. Instead what my father said to me on this walk was, "Amy baby, I really need a smoke."

A day later he was dead from a massive seizure and I was scared to admit to anyone that I had given him the cigarettes.

George must have guessed I was sitting on something because when we were in our father's hospital room standing on either side of his bed looking down at his dead body, he leaned over and whispered, "Well done, little sis, well done." And in no way was there an accusatory or malicious tone to his voice. But then again, of all my siblings, I would never expect malice from George.

The doctor who pronounced our father dead told us seizures often happen with patients that have advanced cancer of this type, and he had made sure he pointed out that he had listed this as a possibility before the surgery. He explained this in a way that was totally a veiled warning should we get the idea that he was somehow responsible for our father's death. As if.

The funny thing about my father smoking was that he didn't do it until he was diagnosed with the tumor. My mother on the other hand smoked a pack a day since before I was born twenty-seven years ago and of course was the picture of health. On the single visit that she made to the hospital, a nurse recognized her and asked for an autograph for her teenage son. My mother's recent revival of her role as a still-not-dead psychotic in the third installment of *Dead, Again* was a favorite among teens and video-game geeks. That a likeness of my mother currently existed on GameCubes across America was actually more frightening than her status as a horror queen.

Of course now it would be our job to dispose of our father. Dispose? I didn't mean that. I meant bury. He and my mother had been divorced for five years and so it would be up to my siblings and me whether we liked it or not. Our father had not specified any arrangements other than cremation—he wanted us to direct his final production—his words. This was odd, given that his profession as a playwright and director his entire life was about not ceding control. Ever.

George said it was a trick. I highly doubted that, unless my father left some sort of macabre plan and had friends and the money to bankroll it. Twenty-some-odd years ago he might have commanded that kind of respect or control, but given his status as the man who hadn't written or worked professionally in the last five years, the best bet was that a few pissed off ex-girlfriends might show up and demand that a debt or two be paid off.

When George and I looked down at our father's body, I noticed for the first time that one of the nurses, thankfully, had closed his eyes. George said, "Let's get out of here," and as an afterthought pulled the hospital sheet up under our father's chin as if tucking him in for the night.

As we exited the hospital and walked out into the parking lot I shoved my hands deep into the pockets of my thin red raincoat and shivered. It was cold for September. In my right pocket I found the pack of cigarettes that I'd taken out of my father's drawer when no one was looking. I pulled the pack out and counted. He'd smoked only two. I crumbled the whole thing and tossed it into a trash can as we went by. If George noticed he didn't let on.

I sighed. "Do you think we should have moved him to the city? Maybe he would have had a better chance or gotten better treatment." Even though my mother had sold the house we grew up in right after the divorce and moved into Manhattan, our father had, oddly enough, moved back to Nyack and rented an apartment over a video store on the main street. It was like after all the years of trying to stay away from the town where we were raised he now refused to leave. The local hospital had really not been equipped to handle our father's case, but they also didn't turn him away.

George rolled his eyes. "He had a stage-four tumor the size of a mango, Amy." As an afterthought he added, "And no insurance."

"But . . ." I couldn't shake it—that we, I, never considered doing more.

"But . . ." George echoed. "Woulda, coulda, shoulda, Amy." He slung his arm around my shoulder and pulled me into his chest and said with a shade of sarcasm, "By the way, I like the hair and outfit—it suits the occasion."

My hand flew to my hair. In its natural state it was dark brown but was now short, shredded, spiky, and bleached blond. I'd done it myself at midnight in my bathroom because I'd been inspired by Warhol's photos of Edie Sedgwick, but now I wasn't so sure. I looked down at my red raincoat and the white leather sixties-style boots Owen had bought me in Brooklyn. The boots came up over my knees, like go-go boots. They were Owen's first gift to me when he was pulling out all the stops to prove that Brooklyn was the place to be. What he didn't know was that I had planned on moving there the night I'd met him, I was just waiting for him to ask.

I took notice of George's outfit: navy striped pants, suede tasseled loafers, and a tan trench coat. He did not have much room to mock my ensemble. I nudged him in the ribs and jerked away from his arm. I hated being nestled in anyone's armpit—even my brother's. "When did you start dressing so uptown anyway?" He looked more like a junior executive than a part-time swim coach/ninth-grade English teacher at a private boys' school on the Upper West Side.

He made a face like he didn't care what I thought as he stroked the lapel of his coat. "Jules works at Brooks Brothers, I told you he gets great discounts."

It was my turn to roll my eyes. Jules was George's new lover. An uptight, condescending little prick that worked behind the tie counter, for Christ's sake, and thought he was fucking Christian Dior. Last month, before Owen's band went out on an eight-week tour of colleges in the New Jersey, New York, and Pennsylvania area, I'd invited George to come to the karaoke club for the send-off party. He arrived with Jules. The entire time Jules sat in a booth looking like he smelled shit all because the bar didn't have his special brand of liquor. I couldn't even remember what it was now. What I do remember is George, my big soft-hearted brother George, singing the karaoke version of Olivia Newton-John's "I Honestly Love You" and offering to run to the liquor store they passed by blocks before when they'd exited the subway. Jules simpered but wouldn't allow George to leave. Now that I think about it, he was probably certain someone would beat the shit out of him if George weren't around as his protector. If they had touched Jules, it would have had nothing to do with him being queer—that was for sure.

My brother was an idiot where guys were concerned. He allowed himself to be taken advantage of over and over again. I knew that he was now sharing his four-hundred-square-foot apartment in the West Village with Jules because Jules's roommate kicked him out when he found George coming out of his bathroom naked. Jules had conveniently chosen not to tell George that he and his roommate shared a bed. So now, when maybe George would have gotten tired of Jules after a few dates, he had a new roommate. I wondered just how long it was going to be before George was the one who walked in on Jules.

"So," I said as I maneuvered out of the parking space in the hospital lot, "we're splitting up the calls. Don't even try to get out of it."

George acted like he wasn't planning on doing just that, an expression of mock indignation on his face. "Who is there to call?"

"Well . . . Mom. Kate, Finn." I stopped and thought for a moment. "And someone should call Miriam, don't you think?"

"Really?"

I shrugged and suggested, "Maybe Finn can do that?"

I got on the highway going south before I remembered that we were supposed to go to our father's apartment and get a suit to take over to the funeral home. The nurse at the main desk said that the funeral director would transport the body that night and so we were to just deal with them from now on. From the businesslike way she had recited her spiel I wanted to add, "And don't let the door hit you on the way out."

I glanced over at George. He was looking out the window. Keeping one eye on the road I fished around in my bag between us on the big front seat until I found my cell phone. I tossed it into George's lap.

"Ouch," George cried as he picked up the phone.

"Oh please, it barely hit you. And if it hurts that much you must be over-using it."

"Very funny, very, very funny."

I pointed to the phone. "Call Mom. Tell her about Dad."

"What?"

"You heard me. Call Mom."

George sighed. "Can't you?"

I tapped the steering wheel. "Hey, I'm driving here. Come on, George. Pretend to be a man."

"Fuck you, Amy," he said as he turned on the phone.

"Press one, she's on speed dial."

He looked at me like having our mother not only on my speed dial but as number one was an insult to him. I assumed he thought he should have the number-one slot. Of course this was from the man who as a young boy once dramatically threw his gangly body in between my parents as they were arguing. George could always be counted on to take our mother's side no matter what the argument. To make a point I could have asked to see who was number one on his speed dial, but I didn't.

Finally, he did as I asked and winced in anticipation as he held the phone up in between us. I counted the rings. Our mother picked up on the third.

George didn't seem to think it was necessary to sugarcoat his news. As soon as she picked up he said, "Dad's dead."

Our mother made a little strangled sound, not far from the grunts I'd heard come out of the animated video-game version of her voice, before she said, "Oh, poor man."

After all my parents had done to each other over the years, I couldn't believe that this simple utterance would have made tears come to my eyes, but it did. They'd had four children together. They had, at one time, or so I liked to pretend, an inspiring artistic connection. They married so young that they'd practically raised each other as they raised the four of us. Of course I see that now as part of their problem, but still. I kept my eyes on the road. I didn't want to look over at George to see his reaction. Especially when our mother followed that up with, "I should probably stop smoking."

"Why stop now, Ma?" George joked and I swatted him on the thigh, which prompted him to squeal like a baby and our mother to ask, "Is Amy with you? Did you call the others?"

George raised his eyebrows at me. "Amy's here. We're going to make the calls."

I could hear my mother say again, "Oh, poor man."

George looked at me in disbelief. I shrugged. He rushed off the phone promising to call her with the details and hung up. "Can you believe she feels sorry for him?" he spat out. "Hell, I feel sorry for us. We still have to bury him."

I pulled up in front of the video store next to our father's apartment and parked. The neon was blown in the N so the window advertised EW RELEASES. I looked up at his darkened windows. He'd moved in four years ago but I'd never visited. When he'd called me from the hospital, he claimed that he was reaching out to each of his children to make amends and I was the only one who picked up the phone. Little did I know that all my siblings had caller ID.

"Hey look . . ." George pointed to the sign and whined, "Ewwww releases." He made a face and continued his shtick. "Disgusting, ewwww releases, I don't want any of those." He held his stomach and made gagging sounds.

I opened my door. "Come on, George—out of the car."

"Do I have to?" he asked with his hand on the door handle.

I got out and slammed my door and walked over to the narrow door sandwiched between an alley and the entrance to the video store. I reached into the plastic bag from the hospital that said PATIENT'S BELONGINGS and retrieved my father's key ring. The only other item in the bag was his wallet with five dollars and a credit card. He hadn't even filled in the "in case of emergency" card. There were three keys on the ring, two large: possibly a car key and a house key, and one small, like it belonged to a lock box. I heard George walk up behind me and I turned around and dangled the keys in front of his face.

"Did Dad have a car?"

"How the hell am I supposed to know?"

"Maybe we should have asked him a few questions before he, uh, died," I wondered aloud as I tried the first key in the lock. I turned it upside down thinking I'd put it in the wrong way but it still wouldn't fit so I tried the other key. It slipped right in and I turned it to the left. "We're in," I said to George.

The hallway was dark and smelled like cat piss. I ran my hand lightly along the wall until I located a light switch. A pale yellow bulb illuminated dark-brown-paneled walls and a staircase directly in front of me with carpeting in the same shade, which led upstairs. George was still lingering behind me on the sidewalk. "Come on!" I yelled out to him, annoyed that I had to coax.

I got tired of waiting for George and started up the narrow stairs without him. At the top was a sliver of landing and a door that looked like it was made out of cardboard. I jiggled the knob and the door opened without effort. The stairs were so steep that when I turned to see if George had caught up to me I felt a little dizzy. Then I remembered the only thing I'd had in hours was a sour coffee. "George?" I yelled when I didn't see him.

He poked his head around the doorway. "I was looking for a mailbox," he claimed as he started up the stairs.

"Did you find one?"

"Nope." He shoved his hands deep inside of his coat and took the stairs two at a time. The building felt so fragile I thought for sure the stairs swayed as George ran. "What are you waiting for?" he asked as he reached around me and pushed the door open farther so we could step inside. "Let's get this over with."

I paused on the threshold while George went ahead and looked for a lamp. The streetlight illuminated the room through the curtainless front windows enough for George to locate a switch and turn on a light, but when I could finally look around I said, "We should have left the lights off."

The room was dominated by a brown plaid couch that sagged so much in the middle it looked like someone had tried to fold it in half; a pillow and blanket were balled up at one end and the coffee table in front of the couch was littered with saucers overflowing with cigarette butts. On top of a dresser with one missing drawer was a black-and-white television with the old rabbit-ear antennas perched on top.

George walked into the other room but turned around and came right out. "I think Dad's pet died . . ."

Involuntarily my hand flew to my mouth and I said, "Oh my God."

George shrugged. "Relax, I think it's a mouse." He thought about it for a second and then emended, "Maybe a mouse family. Just take my word for it and skip the kitchen."

I nodded, suppressing the urge to scream and flee. "So that's it then?" I gestured toward the kitchen. "There isn't another room?"

He grimaced. "A bathroom. I've seen better down on the Bowery."

I looked at the couch. "So he slept there?"

"Looks like it."

George looked past me and pointed. "What's that?"

I turned around. "A closet?"

"Open it," George dared me.

"No, you open it."

"No, you."

"Oh for God's sake, George," I said with a sigh. "I'm hungry, I'm tired, and I'm bitchy."

George pretended he was shivering. "I'm scared."

I yanked on the knob and pulled the door back quickly. Hanging on the bar was a black leather biker jacket I remember Dad wearing years ago. The edges of the sleeves were so worn that the leather had gone white in places. Next to that on a few hangers was what could only be termed a very minimal wardrobe.

George pushed the clothes to one side and looked in the back of the closet. "Nothing," he called over his shoulder.

I walked back toward the couch but did not sit down. It was odd to think that my father lived somewhere with no desk, no papers, no books. There wasn't a single personal effect. Not even a pad of paper with a scribbled phone number, no photographs, nothing.

I thought about the garage sale my mother had after my parents divorced. Someone out there right now could be using my father's Tony Award as a paperweight. My father arrived back in the States a year later with the clothes on his back and whatever was in his suitcase. From what I'd seen here, there wasn't much.

I looked around one more time. "Where's his phone?"

"There's nothing we can bury him in, in here." George closed the closet door. I thought he hadn't heard me ask about the phone when he said, "In the kitchen on the wall. Why?" He made a face. "You want to use it? You have a cell."

I shrugged, and felt close to tears. This wasn't the way it was supposed to be when my dad died. We weren't supposed to be standing in some horrible little apartment talking about how there was nothing to bury him in. I felt an indescribable ache for the childhood I never had, for the father who was now, forever, lost to me. But even more, I was angry with myself for never working up enough nerve these last few weeks to tell him how I felt, to ask him if he really loved any of us.

"No. Just wondering." I rubbed at my eyes.

"Ah, Ames." George stepped close to me and fiddled with the collar of my raincoat before he said quietly, "Come on. Let's get out of here."

George stepped aside so I could get out of our father's apartment. I didn't wait for him to turn off the lights and shut the door. I ran downstairs and onto the sidewalk and missed the bottom step, twisting my ankle inside my boot. I stumbled toward the car and took huge gulps of fresh air. I doubted I would wear this coat again without washing it first.

I was in the car with the engine running when George came downstairs. I rolled down the passenger window and tossed the key ring at him so he could lock the door—although really, what did it matter?

When he got into the car he had a brown paper grocery bag in his hands, which he wedged down by his feet.

"What's that?" I asked as I pulled the car away from the curb.

"Don't ask me why, but at the last minute I thought to check under the cushions on the couch. I found this." He kicked the bag.

"George!" I thought of the dead mouse family and made a gagging sound. "Did you look in it first?"

He smirked. "Duh, Sherlock. It's apparently Dad's idea of a filing system. Bank statements, telephone bill, and a bunch of other stuff I haven't gone through yet." He narrowed his eyes at me. "I thought we might need to prove he existed . . . just in case."

I turned down our old street. I doubted George was even paying attention to where we were. "Why do we need proof? He's dead."

He shrugged and looked out the window. "Hey." He pointed at the Carlyles' house as it dawned on him that we were on the street where, for better or worse, we'd grown up. The Carlyles had been our closest neighbors and that made them privy to more of my family secrets than I was.

I slowed the car to a crawl so George and I could take a good long look at our old house. I hoped the new owners had a lot of lights on with no curtains on the windows so we could peek inside. The house was on George's side of the car and I had to crane around and look past his suddenly indifferent posture so it took me a moment to realize that our house was no longer there. In its place was a stone-and-glass monstrosity whose architectural style could only be described as "we've got more money than God and we intend to use it." The big, beautiful oak trees were gone, as well as all the tall pines and of course the ancient pom-pom hydrangeas that had circled the wraparound porch along the foundation. Now, devoid of any greenery, the house had the appearance of an iceberg surrounded by a perfectly manicured, chemically enhanced green lawn.

"What the fuck?" George said, enunciating each word slowly and carefully as he said it again. "What the fuck?"

I was so shaken by the sight of our vanished house that I hit the brakes too hard and the tires squealed angrily against the pavement. George and I jumped at the loud sound on the quiet street and he looked at me quickly before turning back to the house that once was.

George recovered his voice before I did. "I bet we can see all the way down to the swimming hole from here. They probably raped that land as well." He shook his head. "Jesus. This. Sucks."

I cleared my throat but couldn't say anything. The tears that I had been only partly successful at holding back were so very close that I was afraid if I tried to speak I'd never stop crying. And the funny thing was I knew I wouldn't be crying out of nostalgia or even sadness that our father had just died. It was for all the things that now would never be. Things that maybe all of my siblings— and even my mother—had let go of a long time ago. But I obviously hadn't. My inability to articulate any of them, let alone name them, was so frustrating. It was like trying to describe air.

I took my foot off the brake and rolled forward until we were well past the house and we could see around the stone columns at the end of the drive. George was probably right about the woods behind the house being cleared. The path we'd worn trudging back and forth to the water all those years of unending summer days most likely was gone. I squinted into the darkness but couldn't see the water, although I guessed if you stood on the massive back deck that extended off the rear of the house you would probably see the rocky ledges where George perfected his high dive.

"Oh," George moaned with his head cradled in his hands as he slumped in his seat, now refusing to look out the window.

"Stop whining and help me, please. I can't see to turn around," I muttered as I backed up into the spanking-new driveway and turned the car around. The car was so long I misjudged the area I had to navigate. When I did turn, my tire caught the edge of the sod and as I hit the gas and accelerated I could feel the earth churn beneath the wheels. "Shit."

"Floor it," George called from his seat as he pounded the dashboard like we were drag-racing. "Fucking floor it. Let's tear up the yard."

I gave him a look that said he was nuts and turned the wheel slightly so I could get all four tires back on the road. Now the house was on my side as I drove slowly past. I had been wishing for light before so that I could see in, but now I was glad the house, with the exception of a security spot over the garage, was dark.

George's sigh was long, ragged, and painful to hear. When we got to the end of our street he sputtered dramatically, "Now that I've seen that thing I can't remember what the old house looked like!"

We were silent as I drove back through town. It wasn't until I got on the highway headed south that George gave the brown bag he'd taken from our father's apartment another kick and said, "The proof of the existence of our childhood is gone."

"Do you think Mom knows about the house?" I wondered out loud. George couldn't possibly believe that just because the proof of our existence on this street had been eradicated everything else had disappeared as well. I wanted to ask him but I was too overwhelmed to go there now.

"Do you think she cares?" George snapped. "I'd think she'd prefer the house was gone, actually."

I pictured a yawning, cavernous hole that opened up beneath our old house sucking it all in and then magically a newer, better version appeared in its place. I took a hand off of the steering wheel and placed it palm-up on the seat between us. George slipped his hand into mine and squeezed. As much as he would like to think that our childhood no longer existed, I knew he didn't believe it as much as he just wanted it to be true.

George and I did not make a conscious choice to have our father's service at the funeral home; it just seemed easier. The funeral home had collected the body and they had a fill-in-the-blanks kind of service for people just like us, who didn't realize that organized religion was meant for situations like this. But it turned out that our siblings thought the one-size-fits-all funeral that we'd planned was not right. Since his death, Kate seemed to take on the position of literary executress and pointed out that the patriarch of Dad's Tony Award–winning play, who was dying of a (pickled) liver disease, was very insistent on a proper burial, so that must have been Dad's true wish as well.

Then it was my turn to point out to Kate that our father had written that play when he was twenty-five and healthy and probably not thinking of his own demise, but I knew it was too late. Kate had already orchestrated a funeral befitting a minor head of state and convinced Finn to go along with her. Our mother offered no opinion on Kate's funeral plans when Kate called with the details and said instead that we would all understand if she didn't attend. I guessed her cries of sympathy when George had called her were to be the extent of her grieving. With our mother on neutral ground, we were deadlocked two against two for a proper church funeral and so we caved. George and I truthfully were just as glad not to have to make the decisions so we let Kate believe that she'd won. Winning had always been important to Kate. The first game I ever remembered playing with her was Candy Land and she'd hidden the Queen Frostine card under the board so I couldn't beat her. Some things never changed.

While Finn was given the task of finding a church that didn't mind not knowing the deceased, Kate actually used an old friend who was a fact checker at the *Times* to get Dad a proper obit, and George and I went to Brooks Brothers where Jules provided us with a discounted suit, shirt, and tie. I seriously doubted my father had ever worn clothes that fit him as well as those. Our father had been tall his entire life. Even in pictures we had seen of him as a teenager, he had been tall and thin, perennially stooped over. It was as if, at a few inches past six feet, he lived in fear of catching the top of his head on the doorway. Or maybe the stoop in his posture had to do with the head of gray hair he'd had since he was thirty. Either way he always had the air of someone slightly distracted and his manner of dress veered just on the safe side of disheveled, which always lent him an air of charm, even, most disturbingly, in all his Brooks Brothers finery post-death.

The thought that all that money and clothing were literally going up in smoke immediately after the church service at the crematorium seemed outrageous to me. Just this morning I'd been scrounging through the change jar on Owen's dresser for enough money for a MetroCard. But Kate was adamant. She refused to bury him in the ground. And even went so far as to purchase a four-pack of tiny urns so each of us could have a piece of Dad forever. Kate gave many reasons for this, which really, in my eyes, amounted to the same thing: Kate wanted to hold on to Dad. Maybe it was a reminder that she was human. The original idea touted to us was that we could scatter Dad's ashes wherever we wanted, wherever we had a special memory of him. I could not come up with a single memory unless I included his final days in the hospital, which I didn't. For all I knew my conception might have been his last attempt at parenting.

With Owen out of town Kate stayed with me in Brooklyn. She could have put herself up in a sleek hotel with room service and ironed sheets and chocolates on her pillow or she could even have stayed at our mother's place on West 91st Street. Maybe she thought being with our mother on the occasion of our father's funeral was sacrilege—if there was an afterlife and he was watching she might forever lose her chance at favored-daughter status. Whatever the reason, she chose to be with me, and though I didn't really understand why, I also didn't expect an explanation. Kate and I had no sister shorthand. As the oldest, Kate had always acted more like a mother than a sister. And there was this thing that she did with her upper lip that drove me crazy—it stopped just short of outright sneering, but it was there. It was definitely there.

It was there the morning we were dressing for the funeral. I came out of the bathroom to find Kate in a proper black suit with sheer black hose and sling-back pumps. I had on a vintage beaded black sweater and a short houndstooth skirt with my white boots. Kate did one of those up-and-down looks.

"Oh no. No way, Amy."

I knew exactly what she was in a tizzy over but it was more fun to act like I didn't.

"What?" I asked as I widened my eyes in pretend ignorance. But Kate didn't even hear me. She was now too fixated on my head.

"And your hair!" she cried. "What have you done to your hair?"

Kate had been here for twenty-four hours. If she just now realized that my hair was not long and brown but short and blond I felt sorry for the clients she defended. Kate came to her true calling a little late in life—but when she did she pursued it with Herculean force. She graduated college when I was still muddling through seventh grade and moved to Italy with her boyfriend and later fiancé to teach English. She stayed until I was in the middle of my senior year of high school. For reasons I have yet to hear but have long since stopped speculating on, she moved back to the States, alone, applied to law school, graduated first in her class, and took a job in Washington, D.C., working for a lawyer who was frequently interviewed on television. That was the only way I'd known her job was a big deal. He'd had some very high-profile celebrity clients and I was fond of *Entertainment Tonight*.

I smiled at Kate's contorted face and touched a hand to my hair. I'd added a thick black velvet headband right before I walked out. It was cute. It was very sexy. I liked it and I wasn't taking it off.

"Your father is dead," Kate said through a clenched jaw.

"Really? No kidding. I thought that was someone else's bedside I stood by for a month." Despite my repeated phone calls that Dad was really sick, Kate had been unable to extricate herself from her legal briefs and power suits for even one bedside visit. Though she was his most devoted child, I wasn't really surprised at her absence: I understood where she was coming from. She revered our father with a blind adoration that the rest of us did not possess. If she had witnessed the physical ravages his illness had inflicted on his wasted body, his diminishing mental capacities, she wouldn't have been able to cope. In the end, some aspects of living were just so much easier when a real live person wasn't involved. Better to come later to pick out the urns and the church.

She turned away from me and snatched a shiny black clutch off the table, which was cluttered with the contents of the brown bag George had found under the couch cushions. He'd given it to Kate and flattered her by saying she would make the most sense out of what to do with our father's "estate." I'd almost snorted out loud when George used that word. I knew Kate had stayed up late the night before going through everything, but so far she hadn't shared and I hadn't asked. I watched now as she opened the clutch and checked inside. Her lips moved but no sound came out as she pulled out a tube of lipstick, tissues, a folded envelope, and some bills, and then silently named each item before she put it all back inside. When she was done, she asked if I had any mints.

I shrugged.

There was a large vertical crease between her eyebrows when she looked at me and said, "Amy, how do you live like this?"

"Like what? Without mints?"

She looked around at the space. Owen had painted the walls shades of cream in the living areas to a pale Creamsicle-orange in the kitchen. Once I'd moved in we divided the large, bowling alley–like space into separate areas: hangout, music, eating, and most lovely of all: my studio. True to his word, Owen had built a wall and a door, which he painted purple and red. Up above in what used to be the storage loft was our bedroom, where Owen and I slept in a nest of down and pillows. And since the ceilings were high, Owen and his buddies had built another lovely loft where guests, mostly George when he didn't feel like going back to Manhattan (of course this was pre-Jules), occasionally crashed. It was now, much to her disdain, the domain of my sister.

I was about to respond with a nasty comment about how she could have stayed at a hotel if it bothered her so much when the bell saved me. George was downstairs. He had insisted on coming to pick us up and then traveling back together to Grand Central Station. He probably thought I'd kill Kate and dump her body in the East River if he wasn't along to chaperone. I buzzed him up as I gathered my bag. I wasn't sure about what to wear for a jacket and I stood in front of the coatrack making a big deal of deciding between a plastic leopard-print raincoat (mostly because I just wanted to ride Kate a little more) and a black cashmere shawl that I'd picked up out of the latest batch of donations at the used-clothing store where I worked. Kate stood ready and waiting by the door, her black clutch held tight to her chest beneath crossed arms, as if they'd start the funeral without us.

George came in and gave Kate a kiss on the cheek and told her she looked lovely. "You're looking pretty spiffy too," I teased as we walked to the subway station. Kate strode ahead of us even though I wasn't at all sure she knew where she was going. When she heard me compliment George, she glanced over her shoulder.

"He looks like someone going to a funeral should look, Amy."

George's trench coat and shiny shoes screamed *kept man* to me, but somehow I knew the George who perennially smelled like chlorinated pool water was still there beneath the Italian worsted wool. The original *kept man* more accurately described how our father looked laid out in his coffin, and in his case the phrase had actually applied during a great portion of his sixty-two years.

Because we had chosen not to have a viewing and the funeral would be closed-casket, we had all trooped to the funeral home the night before for one last look at Dad dressed nattily for the great send-off. When we got there, everyone filed into the small room but me. I stayed out in the lobby where the air wasn't as suffocating. Instead I sat in a fake gilded chair next to a marble-topped table that held a lone box of tissues. Every time the front door opened bringing people for the wake that was being held in the room next to our father's, I averted my eyes and acted like I needed another tissue. The expectations for grief were too high in a situation like this and I didn't know what else to do.

I had the same suffocating feeling today when we got to the church, except it had nothing to do with a small room and a lot of people. Considering we were on the late side and Finn was already there, the church was embarrassingly empty. I couldn't even look from side to side as we filed up the main aisle toward the casket. I knew the first several benches held a handful of people but I didn't maintain direct eye contact. Instead I concentrated on the way Finn was standing with his hands clasped awkwardly in front of his body, sort of below his waist. He looked like he was wearing the suit from his high school graduation. He smiled when he saw me and made room so I could sit. As I slid in next to him I could smell something akin to Listerine on his breath and I prayed silently that Kate didn't get a whiff. I peeked over at her but she was staring straight ahead, unwilling to make eye contact with any of us. She had not offered a word since we arrived. I made a point of looking around Finn to his other side to see if Miriam had come. Truthfully, I wasn't surprised that the seat was empty.

While a lover purchased George's finery, Kate was entirely a self-made woman down to her fine wool suit and highly polished leather shoes. Kate had ambition that must have come from another branch of the family tree altogether. One of our father's last plays had been about the lazy immigrants in our family. The story had been told from the perspective of his uncle, who had been trying to save enough money to leave his country and come to America since he was sixteen. When he finally booked passage he was in his eighties and managed to live here only one year before he died.

George looked anxious. While I was watching him, I saw him slide back the cuff on his left wrist and check his watch—

twice—before stifling a sigh and affixing his gaze back toward the altar.

I linked my arm through Finn's and he seemed surprised, but then he patted my hand and I knew I'd at least make it through the funeral standing; Finn would not let me fall. Of course if he was too drunk to stand, then I was going down as well. I realized as I glanced at my brothers and sister that this was it. This was our family now. And while I knew that for some family was everything, protection against the cold, cruel world, I only really experienced that with George. With the others, we viewed each other more as obstacles to be negotiated, not shelter. It scared me to think that Finn had yet to hit bottom even though he was trying his hardest and that Kate just didn't give a damn about any of us. I could tell Kate wished that George, Finn, and I (but mostly me) would grow up and get a life. If she would listen to me I would tell her how happy I was, but I doubted she would believe me or, even worse, understand. And while we each had our own issues, Kate made me the saddest of all—she just seemed to view life as one long tangle of disappointments.

As the service began, I was acutely aware that our father currently resided in the pine economy box in his discounted Brooks Brothers suit not six feet away from where we sat and a minister of indeterminate religious affiliation—something called the Congregational Church—was talking about the afterlife. I had no idea what awaited my father on the other side—if indeed there even was one. Every time the minister referred to the other side I thought about England. There was that old saying: "Close your eyes and think of England." It supposedly was the advice Queen Victoria gave her daughter on her wedding night. I hoped if Dad was anywhere he could be in England. He'd always preferred Europe to the States.

Finn stood, and because I was attached at his hip I stood along with him. He shook his head at me and pried my fingers off his arm. When I didn't fully comprehend what he wanted me to do, he pushed me back down onto the bench. I watched my brothers file out of the pew and arrange themselves around the casket. Then, with the help of four other men that I recognized from the funeral home, they carried the casket down the aisle and out the double doors at the front of the church. Kate took hold of my hand and slid me along with her out of the pew. When I realized that she wanted me to follow the casket down the aisle I took a step backward. She refused to let me linger and pulled me out into the aisle, so I stumbled. I kept my head down and walked quickly. I got outside in time to see the hearse drive away. Kate had somehow prevailed upon them to burn our father as quickly as possible. They'd promised an urn pickup by six that evening.

The light outside hurt my eyes and I blinked and squinted until I found my sunglasses and put them on. They were very large and white-rimmed and cost me a dollar on Canal Street. Once I could see I walked over to my brothers. Finn and George were talking to a couple I vaguely recognized. I turned around to ask Kate if she knew whom the boys were talking to, but she was nowhere to be seen. I hovered awkwardly by George's left side, not really wanting to engage in conversation but not knowing what to do with myself. What are you supposed to do after they cart away the body? I wasn't going to stand there and cry—I didn't even have a tissue to dab at my eyes and besides no one else seemed that broken up. Why did everyone else seem to know what to do? I felt a sense of panic rising in my chest and ran back into the church under the guise of looking for Kate.

Inside the vestibule there was a cluster of people who looked up when I entered but then looked quickly away. The double doors to the main church area were still open so I stepped back inside. The altar was empty, as were the pews. I tried hard to remember if we'd ever gone to church as kids. Maybe with my mother's parents once or twice, but I really couldn't come up with anything concrete, just a lot of images of candles and choirs at Christmas, which may actually have been memories I appropriated from watching too many schmaltzy Christmas movies on television.

On either side of the church there were tall, narrow stained-glass windows with a modern flair, no saints or Jesus or Scripture as far as I could tell. The windows appeared as slabs of colored glass pieced together like a quilt. They were actually pretty. I was just standing there getting lost looking at the windows when I heard a noise from behind the altar area, and then my sister exited stage left. Her head was down and she was fussing with her jacket, tugging on it as if it was twisted.

She rushed down the stairs from the altar and headed down the aisle. She hadn't even seen me standing there so I called out her name. She hesitated and looked quickly over her shoulder to see if anyone had followed her before she continued walking out the front of the church. I had to run to catch up to her and when I came up behind her and touched her shoulder on the front steps she screamed. She would hate it if I told her she sounded just like our mother in her latest film.

The boys turned to look at us and Kate shot me a dirty look.

"Why the hell were you sneaking up on me like that?"

I slid my sunglasses down my nose a little and peered at her over the rims. "I called your name but you didn't hear me."

She swallowed hard and her cheeks flushed a shade of burgundy.

"In the church?"

I nodded. "What? Did you have a quickie behind the altar?"

Kate's head snapped back on her shoulders like she'd been slapped. "God, you are so disgusting."

I smiled sweetly at her as George came over and slipped my sunglasses off my face and onto his. He preened a little until I grabbed them and put them firmly back on my face.

Kate groaned, forgetting for a moment that she was superior to all of us. "Come on already. I'm starving."

For once we were all in agreement. Luckily the church was in walking distance to the commercial strip and a Denny's. Kate must really be hungry because she didn't even justify her choice of restaurant. As we walked I noticed Kate glance back over her shoulder a few times so I started to as well. But there was no one behind us.

We were ushered into one of those round booths where everyone had to slide in. I was stuck in the middle of the semicircle between Finn and George. They ordered enough food for a football team. All I thought I wanted was coffee and onion rings but I ended up eating way too much off Finn's plate. Kate kept stabbing at her omelet and sighing until Finn moved it aside so the mutilation could end.

Eating all together like this felt like those rare occasions, when we were kids, when our mother or father (never both of them) would take us to the Howard Johnson's over on Route 9 and we'd all order the Turkey Delight off the children's menu. The meal, which was a quasi-replication of a Thanksgiving dinner complete with an ice-cream-scoop lump of stuffing, came with a free hot-fudge sundae, and Finn would always trade me his if I gave him the thickest slice of my turkey. I glanced around the table at my siblings and wondered if any of them remembered the Turkey Delight. Probably not, they all looked like they just wanted to be far away from here. I ran my tongue over my lips. This was what it would be like if we ever all got together for Thanksgiving or Christmas, everyone disappointed that this was all there was and biding time until they could leave. I sighed and reached for an onion ring. No sense pretending.

As I chewed I realized why the church had looked so stark. There weren't any flowers. Weren't we supposed to have one of those hideous carnation wreaths with a ribbon that said DAD on it? But when I said this aloud Kate started to cry. Not big tears, just the slip-sliding-down-her-cheeks kind that she didn't even make an attempt to wipe away.

I threw a wadded-up napkin in her direction. "It wasn't meant as a criticism; I was just thinking out loud."

"It was just awful," Kate said quietly.

George rushed to say the service was nice so Kate would stop throwing a pity party, while I stayed silent, and I noticed Finn did too.

"No one came," Kate whispered.

I shook my head and stared down at the table. I don't know what Kate had expected.

"Not true," Finn said. "I talked to the bartender from Backstreet Billiards—he came."

"What?" I snorted. And then thought, of course you found the bartender.

Finn nodded. "Seems like Dad spent a lot of time at the bar."

"We should go there," George said.

"Where?" Finn asked. As always, the constant infusion of alcohol had dulled his cognitive abilities.

"Backstreet—shoot some pool and have a drink for Dad." He looked around the table to see who was agreeable to his idea. "Don't we have to hang out and wait for the ashes anyway?"

"About that," Finn said, "why are we waiting—can't they mail them to us?"

Kate's lip did that thing. "Go ahead. Leave. I thought you'd want the ashes right away. I was doing everyone a favor. But obviously if you want to go to your post office to collect your father's remains just let me know and I'll mail them." She looked for the waitress and signaled with her arm for the check. "I'm sure they have special boxes for that sort of thing."

"He was just asking a question, Kate," George said as he reached into his breast pocket for his wallet but Kate was faster. As the waitress approached with the check Kate didn't even look at it—she just handed over her credit card and shooed the girl away.

"I can pay for my own food," I said, quietly hoping I had at least a five somewhere in the bottom of my bag.

Kate turned to me and said, "It's on Dad."

"Dad had money?" I said, surprised.

Kate shrugged like she was the bearer of a big secret she wasn't ready to share. After she signed her credit card she stood. The rest of us, obviously still contemplating the money Dad may have left behind, didn't move. I could almost see the dream on Finn's face. Reality would set in soon. Especially when he remembered how Dad had been living. This was typical of my sister, acting like she had one up on the rest of us even when she didn't. Perhaps that was what compelled her to practice law. Finally Kate stomped her foot and said in an exasperated tone, "Well, aren't any of you coming?"

"Where?" I asked as I reached for a fry from George's plate that I had no intention of eating. My stomach hurt from so much greasy food. We all, even Finn, who was the most solicitous I had ever witnessed, looked to Kate to tell us what our next move would be.

She picked up her bag and flung it over her shoulder. "Come on," she said without an explanation as she marched around the tables and out of Denny's.

* * *

Everyone but me seemed to understand that we were going to make a show of drowning our sorrows at the billiards place. Inside the pool hall our father's friend the bartender recognized us and gave us a greeting like we were his long-lost family. I appreciated that and smiled back, but when I looked at Kate she appeared to be sucking lemons. I slipped onto a stool next to George. Kate stood on his other side while Finn, whose blood alcohol level even when he wasn't drinking was still too high, secured a pool table. The bartender, Mike, set us each up with a shot. Nobody was more surprised than me when Kate lifted it to her lips and tossed it back in one gulp.

George elbowed me in the ribs in case I didn't notice that Kate was tapping her glass on the counter for another. When she got her refill I heard her say, "Start a tab."

Since that was the case, I raised my glass for another as well. And another and another. It was unfortunate that by the time I realized just how much I'd had to drink I needed help getting off the stool and going to the bathroom. I didn't acknowledge that it was Kate who helped me until her face appeared from under the stall next to mine. "Give me some paper."

I blinked at the sight of her head at an odd angle. "What the hell?"

"Amy, damn it, give me some paper."

As only the drunk can do, I hesitated too long and put inappropriate spaces in between words when I finally spoke. "Where's your hand?"

"Oh fuck." Her head disappeared and her hand appeared in its place. "Give me some paper," she demanded.

"What are you going to give me?" I asked as I struggled with the roll, my fingers slipped over the tightly wound roll until I managed to get three pieces of paper. I crumpled it into Kate's hand. "There," I said as I slumped against the side of the stall. My eyes focused on something scratched into the door. Apparently Tiffany gave great head. I yelled this out to Kate above the flush.

A few seconds later she yanked open the door to my stall.

"Ooops, I guess I forgot to lock it."

Kate frowned. "Do you need help?"

"Hey," I said as I realized that she didn't appear to be drunk at all. "How did I drink more than you?"

Kate grabbed me under my arms and lifted me off the toilet. When Kate saw that I was fully dressed she said, "Do you have to go or not?"

My mouth felt funny and I ran my tongue over my teeth and then my lips. "I guess not."

"Then come on—but wash your hands first." She looked at her watch. "It's time to go get Dad."

I took two steps that got me to the sink. "Get Dad?" I shook my head. Why was she trying to confuse me? I looked into the mirror above the sink. It was dark and I said so to Kate.

"Take those stupid glasses off then," she snapped.

I looked in the mirror again and adjusted my glasses without taking them off, but I did remove my headband. The flesh behind my ears ached. I guess I was taking too long at the sink because Kate came over and turned the water on for me and squirted some pink soap into my palm.

"Wash," she commanded.

I did as I was told and rubbed my palms together under the water. "Tell me what you mean about getting Dad," I said.

Kate sighed before she said, "The ashes, Amy, the ashes. We have to go get the ashes." She tapped her foot.

I turned the faucet off and dried my hands on the cashmere wrap from the thrift store before I realized that Kate was holding a paper towel out to me. I looked around for a trash can. "I have no idea where to put him," I said to Kate.

"Paper towels are neither feminine nor masculine," she said as she pointed to the trash can.

I took the unused paper towel and dropped it into the trash. "I meant Dad. I have no fucking idea what to do with Dad."

Her eyes turned to slits and her face darkened. "Goddamn all of you," Kate said as she opened the door with her shoulder. "I tried to do something I thought would be considerate. I see now that maybe I should have just taken him all for myself."

"Will you just stop the freaking drama? He's yours—he's always been yours. Okay?"

Kate paused in the doorway, "What the hell do you mean by that?"

I screamed louder than I intended. "He loved you the best. You should have had that written into the funeral service." I demonstrated by holding my hands above my head like the words were in lights on a marquee. "Dad Loved Kate the Best," I shouted.

With a look of absolute disdain Kate turned and walked away and I ran to catch up to her for the thousandth time that day. I tugged on her jacket. "What?" I said, huffing hard, out of breath from too much greasy food and booze. "You have that many fucking good memories? Take my share then, Kate!" I yelled. "Take my goddamned share and do something with him." I was aware that the few people in the bar at five in the afternoon along with bartender Mike seemed totally unfazed by our familial drama.

George and Finn came toward us, holding their pool cues like weapons cocked and ready.

"What's going on?" asked George with concern.

Kate pushed past him and picked her clutch up off the bar. Finn took a few steps back and turned to her and I saw him put a hand on her lower back and say something into her ear. I noticed that he had taken his jacket off and the whiteness of his dress shirt looked like heavy cream under the dim bar lighting.

I looked at George. "She's pissed because I said I didn't know what to do with Dad's ashes." I sighed. "I told her she could have mine and she got all in my face."

"Looks like you were the one offering a smack-down," George said, trying to make a joke out of it as he put his hand on my shoulder and squeezed. I shrugged him off and headed toward the door. I was sick and tired of the bunch of them. I wanted to go home and crawl into my bed and stay there until Owen came home.

I paced back and forth in the parking lot until my siblings appeared, in their funeral clothes, stumbling and blinking against daylight. Kate barked at Finn, "You drove, right? Give me your keys." She wiggled her fingers, palm up at him. "I know the faster way."

Finn had his suit jacket tossed over one shoulder. He took his time, slipping his arms inside the sleeves and adjusted the lapels, as if the suit were worth a million freaking dollars instead of the cheap polyester knockoff that it was, before he said quietly, "I think it's better if I drive, Kate."

Obediently Kate nodded at Finn and fell into step beside him as we walked back to where Finn had parked his car. It smelled like wet dog and was covered inside with silver tape where the roof obviously leaked. I marveled at how Finn handled Kate and, more surprisingly, how Kate let herself be handled. I did notice, however, that Kate seemed to be slightly ahead of Finn now as we walked, as if she had to get to the car first. I remembered how annoyed I would get when she did the same thing when we were kids, always calling shotgun before anyone else.

I was in the backseat next to George, who was smashed against the door because of the nasty black stain that was on his seat. There was a sleeping bag down on the floor beneath my feet and I felt guilty that none of us had asked where Finn was staying. I wondered if he had slept in the car. Kate was slumped in the passenger seat while Finn drove. We waited quietly like chastised children when Kate went into the funeral home.

"Hey." I leaned forward and tapped Finn on the shoulder. "Why didn't Miriam come?"

I could see the muscles in Finn's jaw working while he considered how to answer me. Eventually he said, "I guess she didn't think the rest of you wanted her here."

I couldn't formulate an argument to his response, so I fell back against the seat and turned toward the window, ignoring George, who I knew was staring in my direction. Twenty minutes later Kate emerged from the funeral home carrying a high square brown box that she placed in the trunk.

When she got back into the car and slammed the door she didn't say a thing and Finn, uncharacteristically, waited to turn on the car. We sat there wordlessly for what felt like forever. Finally, Finn broke the silence.

"I know what we should do with Dad."

It was the first time Finn and Kate had seen that our childhood home was gone. I was relieved that it looked just as dark and deserted as it had a few nights ago. Finn parked down the street so the car wouldn't be visible from the house just in case someone was inside. Kate popped the lock on the trunk and retrieved the box containing Dad's ashes as George and I extricated ourselves from the backseat. It was dusk and still light enough to find the path once we'd circumnavigated the huge stone columns at the end of the drive. We walked single-file but close together, so I kept stepping on the backs of George's fancy shoes.

The last time George turned around and hissed, "Stop with the flat tires."

I mimicked him under my breath. I'd lost my sense of humor as I sobered up. My head was pounding, my mouth was dry, and my stomach was queasy. The triple-header hangover.

Kate, at the front of the line, turned around and hushed us as we passed the enormous back patio. "For fuck's sake, would you all be quiet—what don't you understand about the word *trespassing*?"

I ignored Kate because I couldn't help but stop and stare. There were three levels at least of slate and planters and low stone walls suitable for seating, along with an outdoor fireplace. The back stoop where I'd spent so many early mornings sipping my coffee, the yard where we'd play a stupid pickup game of ball, everything was gone.

Finn was behind me and wasn't prepared to stop when I did. He grabbed me by the shoulders and said in my ear, "Come on— let's get this over with."

I looked ahead of us. George had been right. They'd cleared the land all the way down to the rocks so there was no longer a secret path to the water. I broke rank and walked up next to George. I gave him a sidelong glance and he echoed my look. He had to be thinking of the same thing I was, of the summer before he went off to college when he had taught Miriam to dive and Finn had come home to live. That was the last time I could remember swimming here. Soon after that George left for New Hampshire to go to school. We didn't venture down that winter to skate. Then the following summer I left town as soon as I graduated, before the water had a chance to warm up enough for swimming. And even though I'd been back since then, I never went back to the swimming hole.

We reached the pond and Kate put the box on the ground and opened the flaps. One by one she passed the urns that contained our father's ashes to each of us. The urns were smaller than I expected and I held mine between the palms of my hands like a coffee mug. I tried to pretend that it wasn't pieces of my father and when I couldn't convince myself of that, I became fixated on what part of him I did have. I hated to think he was all jumbled together like a Picasso painting. My heart was racing and all of a sudden I had this tickle at the back of my throat. When I coughed everyone turned to me like I was going to say something. I shook my head and coughed again so hard that my temples throbbed and my eyes ran watery. It was a relief to cry even if it snuck up on me after I held it in all day.

"Are these warm or is it my imagination?" Finn asked.

I shuddered. At its best, when he was alive, my father's presence in my life could be described as ghostlike. Now that he was dead? I honestly didn't know. It couldn't get any worse, that was for sure.

"Should we say something?" George ventured.

Everyone turned to Kate. For once she seemed at a loss for words and shrugged.

I raised my mini-urn up in one hand and offered, "Here's to you, Dad—we hardly knew ya."

The only sound after that was George snorting.

I put my arm down and tried hard to think of something nice

to say. It shouldn't be this hard, should it? We all seemed to be struggling with the same thing.

"I say we just do it," Finn finally announced.

Once Finn said aloud what we'd all obviously been thinking, we walked closer to the water's edge. It was marshy around the bank and I looked down to see thin brown liquid creeping up around my white boots. I stole a look at George's tasseled loafers—they too were sinking into the muck.

Kate was the first to pop the seal on her urn. It actually gave off a little vacuum-pack sound, as if she opened a jar of peanuts. I could have sworn I saw a puff of smoke rise out of the jar. After Kate, we all opened our jars and it was easier than I imagined it would be.

"Ready?" Finn asked, with his jar positioned as far away from his body as humanly possible.

"Ready," George echoed.

I took a giant step closer to the water and without looking at my brothers and sister I flicked my wrist and upended the urn. I watched the puff cloud of smoke and the ashes swirl before landing on the water's surface. They sunk slowly into the water and then disappeared. There were several larger pieces of what I imagined must be bone. Those were the first to go. When I looked down at my boots, I saw that they were covered all over with a gray powder. My father. The first thing that popped into my mind after that was: these boots are made for walking.

As an epitaph, that would have suited him just fine.

part two

George

I'M PRETTY SURE HOLDEN CAULFIELD COULD DATE IF HE WANTED TO

*I*t was four days before winter break and George was teaching this year's freshmen *The Catcher in the Rye*, again. He liked to introduce Holden to the kids at this time of year, since the novel took place in the weeks before Christmas almost directly outside the doors of this very school. He would culminate the lesson plan with a walking field trip. They'd go up a few blocks to the Museum of Natural History where Holden met his little sister, Phoebe, and then they'd go into the park and over to the carousel. Along the way George would encourage conversation and try to get the students to imagine the path Holden took.

This year's boys would be more of a challenge than in years past. They seemed to be a particularly immature bunch, though physically they appeared older; some of them were as tall as George and he was just a hair over six two. And at first glance their clothing styles mimicked George's since he currently wore what his sister Amy called his "frat boy college costume" of wrinkled flat-front khakis, loafers, argyle socks, blue oxford cloth shirt, and a striped tie every single day. At Tate the dress code was such that the boys wore loosely culled uniforms of khaki trousers, white oxford cloth shirts, and a navy tie. So distinguishing teacher from students, in George's class anyway, might take a few minutes for the untrained eye.

Most of the freshmen classes had settled into the routine of high school by this time in the year, but these boys were still grappling with an almost puppylike affection for each other. They gave each other wedgies and yanked each other's pants down several times a day, joked about penis size, and, in the boys' showers after gym class, hypothesized often about which one of their classmates was the serial masturbator. These boys seemed preternaturally aware of each other's sexuality in a way that girls might have been aware of the clothing other girls wore. You couldn't blame it on the same-sex school thing. They had plenty of social interaction with the Tate School for Girls, which was directly across the street on West 68th Street. It was the electrically charged homoerotic air combined with the fact that it just didn't occur to any of them that sex—for most—was not for a public venue. At times all George could think was thank God it wasn't a boarding school. There were also times that George wondered if they acted like this around him because they'd guessed that he was gay. His sexuality wasn't something he had hidden from his colleagues, but it also wasn't something he'd offered up for conversation in the teachers' lounge. Often kids knew these things way before adults, and he sometimes got the uneasy feeling that the boys might be testing him.

Naturally, because of this, George had been more than hesitant to introduce the sexually strangled Holden to them—especially the scene in the hotel where the young hooker gets sent to Holden's room and he can't perform—but in the back of his mind he'd hoped that they might calm down a bit if they saw that sexuality was something everyone struggled with at this age.

Right now George had floated a question to them and was

waiting for a response. He asked why they thought that Holden, while admiring Jane from afar, never had the nerve to ask her out even though his loutish roommate boasted of sleeping with her. The boys seemed to consider this while George waited. Finally, Asa Malik, a recent transfer, at Tate only a month now, raised his hand.

George nodded at him enthusiastically, hoping for a thoughtful comment. Asa's written work had shown a disquieting maturity.

Asa coughed and squirmed in his seat before he said, "I'm pretty sure Holden Caulfield could get a date if he wanted to."

The class erupted into laughter and catcalls, and George raised his hands in the air to hush them because it looked like Asa had more to say. The boy had remarkable composure. His dark-brown, heavily lashed eyes focused on a point above George's head as he waited and there was no flush of embarrassment on his mocha-colored skin. When the class was quiet, he glanced over at Asa and nodded again for him to continue.

Asa looked down at the top of his desk and stumbled through the first few words before he said, "It wasn't about the sex for Holden . . . even if he was, well, you know? He wanted to be with Jane like it was when they were kids. Holden still wanted to be a kid. That was why he wanted to protect Phoebe so much." Asa shrugged. "And of course if Holden was still a kid then his brother would be alive. Holden probably would have liked to freeze time."

"Like a time machine?" some kid yelled from the back row. "Trek me, baby!"

George leaned forward and rested his elbows on top of his desk. He couldn't tell who'd made the lame joke but he was more concerned that Asa had slid down in his seat with his chin buried against the Windsor knot in his navy blue tie. He wanted to applaud

Asa for his intelligent dialogue and was about to when the bell rang, signaling the end of class.

En masse the boys shuffled out with backpacks carelessly over-stuffed and half-zipped slung across one shoulder. George got up from behind his desk and walked over to Asa. The boy was bent over, busily packing his backpack down on the floor and didn't see George. George tapped him on the shoulder and Asa looked up, his face a deep shade of scarlet from his upside-down position.

"Interesting ideas today, Asa."

The boy straightened up and nodded as he stood.

George was not surprised to see that they were eye to eye. "Do you like the book?"

One half of Asa's mouth turned up in a grin when he said, "It's my fourth time reading it." Then he slung his backpack over his shoulder just like the rest of them and ambled out of the class-room.

George was retelling this story to his little sister, Amy, and her boyfriend, Owen, over cheese fondue at their apartment in Brook-lyn. She had invited him for dinner and to help decorate their tree. Though Amy was only sixteen months younger than George, nearly twenty-nine to her brand-new twenty-seven, he sometimes felt much older than her. Like right now.

He wasn't sure that Amy was hearing his story entirely. She was too busy frowning at the lumps in her fondue. She kept swirl-ing it around in the pot with the fork, checking the flame and adding beer to it while George and Owen, totally oblivious to any problems, continued to spear hunks of bread and dip them into the rapidly thinning cheese sauce and then into their mouths.

While he chewed, George contemplated the fact that Amy, who'd gone on scholarship to the Rhode Island School of Design, could make almost anything with her hands—except food.

"It's pretty damn hard to screw up fondue, Amy, maybe you should quit adding beer." Amy held a beer poised above the pot and Owen stabbed the air around it with his sharp little fondue fork. Amy half squealed, half giggled and put the bottle down.

"It's only melted cheese, baby," Owen explained with a smile as he reached for the beer that Amy had been emptying into the pot and put it to his lips for a swig before he leaned over and kissed her on the mouth.

Owen was a musician. Amy, when describing his band to George, said they were a lot like Belle and Sebastian. George hadn't known who Belle and Sebastian were and had to go to the store and listen to a CD so he had a reference point. Owen's band, with a dozen band mates that George had trouble keeping track of, played odd instruments that George had never heard or even known existed, along with the usual guitars, drums, strings, and keyboards. He was initially afraid that their music would be some New Age crap that gave him a headache. Instead, what he found was an incongruous mixture of folk, punk, and pop with a throwback to the early sixties (perhaps the Beatles?) and thought-provoking lyrics by Owen. It might sound trite, but George really did feel like sometimes the songs were poetry set to music. Although he would never say that to Owen; it sounded too—well—faggy. Sometimes when he hung out with his little sister and her friends, he felt like an old man trying to act hip. Being gay didn't even up the coolness ante anymore.

In an attempt to bring Holden Caulfield and Owen's music together, George casually informed Owen that Belle and Sebastian mention *The Catcher in the Rye* in one of their songs. He said this while avoiding Amy's eyes, since she knew she was the one who told him about Belle and Sebastian in the first place. Of course she'd see right through George's feeble efforts to impress her boyfriend and he hoped she wouldn't call him out. It was important to George that Owen liked him and continued to find him interesting, more for his sake than Amy's. He actually counted Owen as a friend and he dared to hope that Owen felt the same way about him, although guys, especially guys past the age of five, didn't go around asking a thing like that so he would just have to take it on faith. He was sure this funk he was in had to do with being left by Jules. Even though he had known Jules wasn't his soul mate, it was humiliating being dumped for the window dresser at Brooks Brothers with a better apartment in Chelsea.

Amy had abandoned the fondue disaster and moved on to the tree—a skinny, long-needled fir desperate for decoration—and was gesturing to him to join her. Owen knelt on the floor by her feet, untangling a pile of tiny pink lights while Amy handed him a square blue box. Inside were miniature bird's nests made out of white feathers swaddled in tissue paper. Inside of each nest was a bird made out of soft wool in a rainbow of colors: lemon yellow, periwinkle, and poppy. Their tiny faces were animated, as though they were winking.

George lifted one out of the box and held it up in front of his face in astonishment.

"Amy, these are amazing."

Amy just shrugged and smiled. She was uncomfortable taking compliments, even though he knew that she thirsted for them. She squeezed a small silver clip that was on the underside of the nest and demonstrated how to attach them to the branches.

Owen stood up to unfurl the jumble of wires. "You have to see the creatures she's been staying up all night to make; she has so many orders she isn't even sleeping."

On cue, Amy yawned and tears appeared at the corners of her eyes. She wiped them away and Owen left the lights and walked to the far end of the loft, where he had portioned off a large chunk of unused space and made a studio for Amy. He returned with an armful of soft-sculpture birds, a larger version of the nesting kind that George was putting on the tree. They were the kind of doll a kid could love just as easily as an adult for whom you didn't know what to buy. Their faces and bodies were all just a little bit different and oddly alive. Attached to the wings of each bird was a storybook, illustrated by Amy, hand-pieced with drawings and paint and brightly colored scraps of fabric that gave a name and told the story of the individual doll.

Owen looked affectionately at Amy before he set the dolls down on the purple velvet couch and ran a hand through her still short and blond spiky hair. Ruffling it so it stuck up even more. Just like the baby birds. She curled into him and he hugged her hard against his wiry chest. Over her shoulder, Owen said to George, "I am so proud of her; they're magic, aren't they?"

George was too choked up to talk. It wasn't so much her successes or even how much Owen obviously adored his little sister, it was that Amy with her whimsical little creatures was re-creating a childhood she wished she'd had. It made George want to cry. He turned away and swiped at his eyes with the back of his hand. God. He felt like a stereotype of a gay man too often lately.

Amy eventually broke away and started humming to herself as she unpacked box after box of her homemade menagerie and placed them on the tree. "I told you we're going out to Long Island to Owen's sister's for Christmas, right?"

"Mmm," George murmured, hoping to avoid the subject entirely.

"So, what are you going to do? Have you talked to anyone?"

George knew that by *anyone* Amy meant either one of their siblings, or their mother. Since he and Jules had broken up right after their father died, Amy seemed to take a proprietary interest in making sure George was never alone. Like tonight. So George recited the familial plans he knew of so far. "Mom is on location in North Carolina." He rolled his eyes. "Kate reluctantly invited me to tag along to Virginia to some Republican bed-and-breakfast with her and her new lawyer friend, but I declined."

"They have Republican bed-and-breakfasts?" Owen marveled out loud.

Amy ignored Owen and laughed. George smiled widely. "I know, right?" He paused. "Frankly, I was surprised she offered. Think she's becoming human?"

Amy made a face at the mention of Kate. She frequently claimed to George that Kate couldn't possibly be related to them. And it wasn't about her job or her money—it was all about the attitude. She had crossed over to the other side, as Amy put it. She hardly laughed, almost never smiled, and she was never ever wrong. How could someone like that be their sibling? George reminded Amy that Kate had always been like that, since she was a kid. He even claimed Kate, despite her hubris, was vulnerable and certainly they knew how to bull's-eye her weak spots. But Amy resisted him where Kate was concerned.

"What about Finn?" she asked hesitantly.

George shook his head. The last he'd heard through their mother was that Finn had lost yet another job after he disappeared on a bender shortly after their father had died in September.

George looked at Owen, who grinned and scratched his head

and said, "Man, you're welcome at my sister's house. It's really casual."

Amy glanced at Owen quickly before she offered, "Or we can come back Christmas afternoon and celebrate together here, have dinner or get loaded at the karaoke bar if that's your mood. Whatever?"

Owen shrugged and nodded. George envied Owen's easygoing demeanor. He actually would have preferred nothing more than taking Amy's suggestion but instead he shook his head. "I went to the Strand and bought myself an early Christmas gift of about fifty books I've been meaning to read. I'm planning to spend the day in my pajamas eating and reading. I'll be perfectly happy."

Amy frowned and bit her lip. "I don't want you to be alone, George."

"I like being alone, Amy."

"You're going to sulk."

"I'm going to read."

"I bet you don't even have a tree," she challenged.

"I do too," George lied.

"So give me a few of these book titles," Amy demanded with her hands on her hips.

George was aware that Owen had long ago collapsed onto the couch and seemed to be enjoying the sideshow that he and Amy provided. When suddenly he stood and grabbed Amy from behind and pulled her down with him onto the couch, George was absolved from coming up with an answer. They tumbled together and he tickled her sides until she shrieked and cried uncle. George looked at them with envy. For a moment he caught Owen's eye and saw there an understanding and empathy for George's position. He smiled tentatively and Owen nodded and George again found himself for the second time that night gulping back tears.

* * *

It was the afternoon before winter break, and Asa Malik and his father were due in George's office for a conference. Every teacher at Tate served as an adviser for ten students. This year George had only seven advisees, and since Asa was a new student he had been assigned to George. Ordinarily they would have had a meeting before now, but this was the only afternoon Asa's father had been available.

Asa was slumped in the chair opposite George's desk. His father was late. He had taken a handheld game out of his backpack and held it up to George and raised his eyebrows. George nodded, pleased with their nonverbal communication and glanced down at the papers on his desk, unable to concentrate. He swiveled in his chair, turning his back on Asa, and looked outside. The window in his office looked out onto a courtyard where several boys tossed snowballs back and forth to each other. Last night had been the first snowfall of the season. George wanted to be anywhere but inside. He wanted to take a walk through the park; maybe he'd see if Amy and Owen wanted to rent some skates. Then again, maybe not. He had to stop appropriating his sister and her boyfriend as his substitute for a social life. He actually needed to get one of his own. He sighed. Was he depressed? Was this what depression was? Maybe after the meeting he'd swim some laps. He needed to get in the pool and get his blood flowing.

The volume of Asa's game was turned up enough that George could hear the music. Every once in a while there was a familiar grunt or scream that he couldn't quite place. Since his knowledge of video games was limited, he couldn't imagine he had a clue as to what Asa was doing.

"Asa, volume," a voice commanded. "Please put that away now."

George swiveled around to face the melodic voice that addressed Asa. It was gentle, full of affection, yet firm at the same time, with a hint of an accent. It was then that George realized why the grunts and screams sounded so familiar. He looked up at the man attached to the voice and smiled. "It's okay, actually, that's my mother." He surprised himself by blurting out what he usually kept secret out of embarrassment.

Asa's head jerked back. George had piqued his curiosity, as well as that of his father. George explained, "My mother is Marilyn Haas— she is the—"

"The innkeeper in *Dead, Again*," Asa filled in for George animatedly as he nearly jumped out of his seat at the mention of her name.

George shrugged. "The one and only, I'm afraid," he added as he caught Asa's father's eye and gestured for him to take a seat next to his son. He did as George asked but not before extending his hand and giving a slight bow in George's direction. He had the same deep-brown, heavily lashed eyes as his son, yet his skin was several shades darker.

"Sam Malik, pleasure to meet you."

George was surprised that the accent he had heard was British. He also noted that Sam Malik didn't apologize for his tardiness. He couldn't make up his mind whether he admired Malik's lack of acknowledgment as honesty or was annoyed by his rudeness.

Asa cut in, "Your mother? Man she is so cool."

Sam smiled indulgently at his son's enthusiasm and then turned to George and said, "I never thought I'd allow these video games. When you're a young idealistic parent, you have other ideas, I suppose." He laughed softly.

George appreciated Sam's self-deprecating humor and laughed too. "I never imagined my mother would actually end up on one of those games, but," George said with a shrug, "that's a story for some other day."

Sam raised his eyebrows at George. For the first time George noticed Sam's brown wavy hair pulled back in a ponytail and his calloused hands resting on the worn knees of his paint-spattered jeans. It looked to George like real paint, not the jeans that would-be hipsters purchased with faux paint and rips scattered throughout. On top he wore a gray hooded sweater, a T-shirt beneath that, and a black jacket over all.

George tried to ignore the little quiver of heat that quickened suddenly in his gut, but still, he stammered a little under Sam's intense gaze when he asked him if anyone else would be joining them. He hadn't noticed a ring on his left hand and there was no record of a mother in Asa's file, but George knew after all this time that student files rarely gave the whole picture.

Asa looked out the window beyond George when Sam said, "It's just Asa and me, I'm afraid."

"That's fine," George assured them, not wanting to pry but finding himself hoping for a little more information. When none was forthcoming, he then opened Asa's file, even though he already knew the meager information that had been provided from his last school in Michigan.

Asa's GPA for the first semester of high school was high. His math scores were a little wanting, but his English scores were off the chart. His entrance exam for Tate supported this as well. That explained of course why this go-around at Holden's tale was his fourth and why his observations had been so keen. Sam expressed some interest in a tutor for the math scores and blamed his own poor math skills for the boy's failings, at which Asa sighed and rolled his eyes.

The meeting ended abruptly when Sam's cell phone rang. George had been in the middle of explaining the tutoring program when Sam excused himself to take the call. He stood outside George's office and argued with someone on the other end about uncrating a painting. From what George overheard, apparently a corner of a canvas had torn when an inexperienced gallery assistant had enthusiastically attacked the packing with the edge of a screwdriver.

George smiled at Asa and tried to appear riveted by the papers in front of him, but the boy's constant sighs couldn't be ignored. Finally, George said, "This happen often?"

Asa shook his head and his cheeks flamed burgundy. "Nah," he said and shifted in his chair. "It's just that this is his first New York show and it's been taking up a lot of time."

"Your father is an artist?" George asked before realizing how stupid he sounded. Way to go, Sherlock.

"A painter," Asa said, then changed his mind. "Well, I don't know what he'd call himself. He used to make these wire sculptures when I was small and then . . ." He frowned and seemed to be considering his next words. "Then he built a model of a, uh, vagina—only it was supersize, like gigantic. It was about the whole process of life. How we all come from that one place." He wrinkled his brow and looked up at George to see if he was getting it.

George bit the inside of his mouth in order to stop from laughing out loud. A supersize vagina? Just then Sam came back into the office and grinned. "What—you're going to leave out John's rocket?" He paused to put his cell phone back in his pocket. "You've gone this far—you should tell Mr. Haas the rest."

Another sigh from Asa. "My dad's partner, John—"

"Ex-partner," Sam corrected Asa as George wondered if they were really using the gay definition of the word *partner*.

"Ex-partner, John," Asa continued after he corrected himself, "built a rocket on wheels that he tried to ride into the . . ." Asa coughed and George remembered suddenly that he was only in ninth grade.

George held up his hand to avoid hearing Asa struggle with the rest of the story. "I think I'm getting the picture." He looked up at Sam. He hadn't taken his seat again and was obviously trying to encourage an end to the meeting. Except George couldn't figure out why he just had Asa tell him that part of the story. Was it for the shock value? Did George seem like he would shock easily? Or was it something else?

Sam tapped Asa on the shoulder. "Get your coat on. We have to go."

George watched as the boy did as he was told. Sam took a card out of his breast pocket and slid it across George's desk. "I'm sorry. I have to take care of an emergency—lately it's one thing or another. My luck?" He shrugged like he couldn't quite figure out if everything was his fault. "This is a card for my show. We open next week. Probably the worst time ever to have an opening—the week between Christmas and New Year's but"—he shrugged again—"but I'll take it."

George picked up the card and looked down at the painting. It was a swirl of angry strokes of red, black, and white. When he looked at it more closely, he saw that it was a portrait of a man's head and shoulders. The expression in his black eyes and slash of a mouth was disconcerting to say the least. He flipped it over. The gallery was in Chelsea—a name he was surprised he recognized, though he didn't know why he did, since he didn't make a habit of gallery-hopping.

"You should come to the opening, bring friends," Sam said as he ushered Asa out the door.

"I'll try," George answered as he stood. "Although I don't know much about art." He was glad their meeting was over. He was looking forward to getting into the pool and clearing his head. He wasn't sure why, but he didn't know if he liked Sam Malik very much. Yet he found himself wanting to know more. What had he been doing in Michigan? Where was Asa's mother?

He realized Sam was staring at him. He looked like he was waiting for a response. George blinked and ran a hand through his hair. "I'm sorry. Did you say something?"

Slowly, Sam repeated, "We'll be in touch about the tutoring?"

George nodded. Then, realizing that he should appear more with it, he said, "After the break good for you?"

Sam nodded, but not before fixing George with the same intense, soul-peering look that earlier caused that quickening in his gut. George closed his office door and waited for them to retreat. He looked out the window and down into the courtyard until he saw the figures of father and son, walking hunched against the cold, shuffling through the snow down the icy flagstone path that led out to 67th Street. Then he turned and grabbed the gym bag that he kept on the floor by his desk and hurried to the pool. He couldn't get in the water fast enough.

On Christmas Eve it snowed again. George thought about going up Amsterdam Avenue to the Cathedral of Saint John the Divine, not for the service but to hear the music. It wasn't that he was religious, just sentimental. It seemed old-fashioned to him. What normal people did on Christmas Eve. He had one such memory of the holiday, and that occurred when he was very young (under five for sure). The entire family went ice-skating on the pond behind the house. There had been cocoa from a red plaid thermos and his father had worn a dingy white beard that he'd stolen from some prop closet along with a red velvet jacket with tails that George and Amy had clung to while he whipped them around the icy pond. After the skating, his father made a big production of choosing and cutting a tree from the woods that they carried back up to the house and decorated with chains made out of tinfoil and sticky pinecones. Years later, as they grew older and details of the holiday had been left to them, he recalled trudging through the snow with numb feet, carrying the saw as he followed behind a very determined Amy intent on the perfect Christmas tree that barely anyone but she would take notice of. Also lurking in his memories was their father's disembodied voice calling out to them from his study. His words sloppy and slurred, he instructed Amy on the proper use of the saw because he was sure George's limp wrists wouldn't be able to handle the physical exertion. Then, he had snickered over his cleverness, whispering the phrase "limp wrists" over and over, chuckling to himself. George had suffered in silence, red-faced and queasy, at thirteen, too afraid to go up against his father. He would have cowered in the shadows forever had Amy not grabbed hold of his gloved hand and pulled him out the front door.

George told Amy his plans when she called to check on him from Owen's sister's house so that she wouldn't feel like she had abandoned him. In the background he could hear the sound of kids opening presents early and squealing with delight. Amy had told him there would be five little girls under the age of ten, and he pictured them in tiny cable-knit sweaters, red-cheeked from excitement, flyaway wispy blond hair in pigtails. George knew that a big family Christmas was the kind that Amy always dreamed of, and he was happy that his little sister's dream had come true, as much as he felt sorry for himself.

Out on the streets there were people rushing despite the snow, despite the holiday. It was freezing and George shoved his hand in his left pocket for his gloves and came up empty-handed. He must have forgotten them. He stood for a moment considering whether he needed them or not. Whether it was worth walking back to his apartment just for gloves. He sighed. When had he become so indecisive?

When he pulled his hand out of his right pocket, he held the folded gallery card for Sam's show. Just to prove to himself that he was still capable of making up his mind quickly, he decided to go there first instead of immediately getting on the subway uptown. Even though the show didn't open until the twenty-sixth, he was curious enough to see the paintings without having to commit to going in. He could probably glimpse something from the window that would allow him to see a little more of what was in Sam Malik's mind.

The gallery was on West 24th Street in an area crammed with galleries. When George crossed over Sixth Avenue at 23rd Street and headed up a block, he realized why the address sounded so familiar to him. Jules's new lover, Bobby the window dresser, lived on 26th Street in a little apartment above a gallery. While George had known from the beginning that Jules and he weren't going to be together forever, he enjoyed the companionship. He liked going over to Union Square Market with Jules on a Saturday morning and buying provisions for the weekend. He liked having someone bring him a cup of coffee in bed and share the *Times* on a lazy Sunday. He liked not coming home to an empty apartment. Although if he was truly honest, he would have to admit those times were rare. Mostly there had been drama and tears and lots and lots of phone calls where, when George answered, the line almost always went dead. He didn't miss that at all. But it did make him wonder if he was always going to choose wrong.

When George got to the gallery, he slowed his pace. There was a spot in the front window that illuminated the sidewalk. He looked up and was surprised to see the painting from the card staring back at him. It was large—it dwarfed him. In the glass he could see his reflection superimposed over the face. He took a step back because it freaked him out so much.

It turned out that all of the lights were on in the gallery, and it wasn't as hard as he'd imagined for him to look past the painting in the window. He stepped off to the side. Directly behind the painting, on the back wall, another face stared him down. Equal in size, it too was of a man from the shoulders up, with a frightening furrowed brow, only in shades of deep blue and gray. There were several variations of this guy, front and back, and the intensity made George wonder if these might be portraits of the ex-partner, John. He glanced back at the painting in the window. What you couldn't tell from the card was that the paint had been applied so thickly that it stood up in stiff ridges—even peaks in some places—almost like frosting that had hardened on a cake. George knew enough about art to understand that in cases like this, the brushstrokes were intentional—that people in the know who looked at this painting and these dried rims of paint would know something of the artist that George did not.

While he was lost in his thoughts, he caught movement out of the corner of his eye. When he peered around the painting, he saw Sam and another man having a discussion in the center of the gallery. Sam was rubbing at his temples and shaking his head back and forth. His ponytail was caught in the collar of his shirt. The other man was attempting to make soothing gestures by stroking Sam's arm through the sleeve of his gray sweater. Sam shook him off, and when he did, he turned in the direction of the window and of George.

George reacted quickly and ducked off to the side. He didn't understand why he actually felt a little foolish. He didn't want to be caught hiding, so he turned and ran without looking back until he was practically to the West Side Highway across from the entrance to Chelsea Piers. He glanced over his shoulder, but he was fairly certain that not only had Sam Malik not followed him but, if he had recognized George at all, he thought George was most likely certifiable. George's shoes were filled with snow, as were the cuffs of his pants, making his ankles numb. He leaned against a building to brush some of the snow off, but of course he didn't have his gloves, and it wasn't long before his hands and fingers were pink and numb as well.

At this point George decided to forget about the music at Saint John the Divine and just go home. He shoved his hands back in the pockets of his coat to keep them warm and headed back to the West Village. After he'd lied to Amy about going to the Strand and buying a stack of books, he'd actually gone and bought a few. On his walk home, he decided he'd reread *The Metamorphosis* and then follow that up with *The Trial*. It seemed there was no one fitting enough but Kafka for his mood. If all else failed, there were always the 104 channels of cable television, which Jules had insisted upon and George had yet to cancel.

Winter break seemed to bring more tension than relaxation. As far as George was concerned, there were too many expectations and too much chance for disappointment in the days between Christmas and New Year's Eve. Three days after Christmas, he'd received in the mail from his mother a DVD of her latest movie and a video-game version of *Dead, Again 2*. The game was a big deal, since it was yet to be released in stores, and Amy told George that she planned to put hers on eBay. George shoved both things back into the box and hid it in the far reaches of his closet.

He was exhausted from all the time he spent alone during the break and found himself deeply relieved to be back at work. The boys seemed to have grown taller and louder in the two weeks of vacation. Some of them had tans from visits to exotic locales— others had windburns where their ski goggles had been. Asa Malik was the only one of them that registered no evidence of where he spent his holiday break.

When George greeted Asa and told him that he'd set up math tutoring to begin the following afternoon, he was relieved that the boy didn't act any differently toward him. George hoped this meant that his father really hadn't glimpsed George spying on him through the glass on Christmas Eve. Although, technically, he hadn't really been spying, had he? How was he to know that Sam would be in the gallery that night, of all nights? Shouldn't he have been at home, celebrating with Asa? Or maybe that was mo-ronic of George to assume that they even celebrated a traditional Christian holiday. Maybe, like for George this year, Christmas had been just another day to get through. The twenty-sixth of December had never been such a relief.

Siddhartha was the next book in George's class. He hadn't assigned any reading over the break—he'd tried that his first year of teaching and found he'd been a laughingstock in the teachers' lounge. Instead, his plan was to discuss the overriding themes of the search for enlightenment and one's own search for self. He could hear the masturbation jokes already as he passed the books out, and he wasn't at all surprised that when he reached

Asa's desk, the boy had his own worn copy sitting atop his note-book.

Over the next two weeks, *Siddhartha* was slow going, painful at times. George found himself lecturing more than he wanted to, even going so far as to find a filmed version from the early 1970s that in the end he couldn't bring himself to show. Eventually, Asa's comments couldn't help the hour go any faster and even Asa seemed to realize this. The boy was preoccupied and on more than one occasion, when George had given the class study hall in order to complete their reading assignments, he had discovered Asa reading a gaming magazine. Granted, he couldn't make the boy reread a book he obviously knew well (his essays so far had been right-on), but he would have appreciated the effort in class. Maybe he was just trying to up his cool factor among his peers. Fourteen-year-old boys were far more complicated than most people gave them credit for.

When Asa's math tutor called George to tell him that in six scheduled visits Asa had shown up only once, George called Asa into his office. This was the part of counseling George dreaded, and he had to admit he was surprised that Asa, of all his advisees, was putting him in this position. The kid was smart and didn't seem like he was trying to jerk George around. He had appeared sincere in his efforts when they had arranged the tutoring and yet here they were.

The boy slumped in his chair and yawned while he waited for George to speak. George rubbed at his temples and sighed. The afternoon was already gray and dark, and it was only half past three. When George had confronted Asa with the no-shows, Asa hadn't denied it. The only thing he wanted to know was if George was going to call his father.

"Don't you think I should?" George asked him now.

Asa shifted in his chair and sat up straighter. "I'm not an idiot," he said.

The boy's hair was a little longer, shaggier, and he looked even more like his father. George leaned back in his chair and swiveled slightly as he considered what to say next. He really didn't believe that Asa was so prideful that he wouldn't attend tutoring to get a better grade.

"You heard what my dad said the last time: I get my poor math skills from him. What does it matter? He's selling paintings; we have money. He has someone who adds it all up for him." He shrugged but George could tell that his bravado was false.

Asa wanted his father's attention, that much was clear. George had been there enough times in his life to recognize it a mile away. Pointing this out to Asa would do no good, so George just went along with the boy's attitude. "Sounds like your father's lucky."

Asa spat, "There's no such thing as luck. He works hard."

George nodded. "I'm sure he does."

"You don't believe me?" Asa's eyes were like slits as he peered at George. "Have you seen his paintings?"

George shook his head slightly. Not quite the truth, not quite a lie.

"Well you should go," Asa said quietly, softening, like a child who was tired after a tantrum.

George tapped his fingers on his desk near his phone. He wouldn't call Sam. Maybe he'd run into him at the gallery. George would suggest the noodle house a few blocks down on Sixth Avenue and then they could have lunch and then the subject of Asa would come up. Casually, naturally, of course. In George's fantasy, the question of whether a teacher's attraction to the parent of a student was wrong or right wouldn't exist.

Suddenly, Asa unfolded himself from the chair and stood up, making George return to reality. "Go to the tutor," George heard himself say. He stopped short of adding *please*.

Asa nodded, but George knew the boy wouldn't go and he would be forced to do something about it. Which was obviously what Asa wanted in the first place.

One week later, when George was grading the final exams from Siddhartha (a book he was close to vowing he'd never teach to ninth graders again), Sam called.

He opened with, "I understand that Asa hasn't been attending tutoring."

George winced and braced himself.

"He told me," Sam added.

"Ah," George sighed.

"I know you were aware of this, so I'm wondering if something has changed? That perhaps you felt that Asa didn't need the assistance?"

George knew from the quarterly reports that, unfortunately, Asa hadn't experienced a miracle in math. He coughed.

Suddenly Sam laughed. "I didn't think so."

Relieved that Sam Malik wasn't about to launch into a diatribe against him, George said, "I should have called you."

Sam laughed again. "I probably wouldn't have picked up. I've been a little preoccupied."

"Asa said your show was successful."

"Successful enough that I can pay back my debts and maybe have enough left over to buy some food, maybe paint—not enough, however, for new video games," he said dryly. "Which seems to be the only thing Asa cares for."

George thought about the video game shoved into the back of his closet. "I can help you with the video-game part." After he made the offer, he removed the receiver from his ear and stared at it like he was crazy.

"A teacher offering to corrupt a child?" Sam teased. "I can't believe what I'm hearing."

"I didn't mean . . ." George stammered. He felt a sweat break in his armpits. "I mean . . ."

"You're reconsidering your offer?" Sam joked.

George felt like he couldn't keep up with this conversation. This was almost like—well, what it felt like was flirting. Or was he just projecting his fantasy? He wiped his brow and pushed the hair off his forehead.

"Are you still there?" Sam asked.

"Yeah—sorry . . . I was grading papers and, you know, twenty essays on *Siddhartha* from uninterested ninth-graders who think it would have been easier on everyone if he'd just stayed home, and my head is buzzing."

"Ah. Have you read Asa's yet?"

"He's number twenty-one and my last hope, I'm afraid." George was starting to feel a little bit more normal talking about the papers when Sam asked to meet him for coffee. He didn't even have time to freak out. He agreed to meet him at French Roast on the east corner of Sixth Avenue and 11th Street in half an hour, and Sam hung up before George had a chance to change his mind.

This time George was late. He half expected Sam not to be there, but he was, sitting at the bar, idly reading the *Daily News*. Before he let himself be known, George watched Sam lazily turn a page, take a sip out of the coffee mug to his left, and then put the mug back down. He had incredible posture for someone sitting on a stool—yet he didn't look stiff. His entire body was relaxed, not at all like a man who had somewhere else he'd rather be.

George walked up and dropped his bag to the floor before he slid onto the stool next to Sam. Sam looked at him and grinned like he saw George every day. By the time George settled himself and ordered a coffee, Sam had closed the newspaper and was waiting.

"Well, where is it?" he asked, looking down at the ground and yanking on the pocket of George's jacket.

George pulled back, confused. "What?"

"The video game?" Sam said, smiling wide.

George felt his heart start beating with relief. The adrenaline rush he'd felt when Sam had tugged on his jacket had almost seriously debilitated him. "Oh, that . . . it's in the back of my closet."

Sam raised his eyebrows and George explained about his mother and her Christmas gift. He was surprised, again, at how much more he wanted to tell Sam. He divulged that his father had recently died, and that he had three siblings with identical gifts, and then he stopped himself.

"So . . ." George said as he received his coffee and pulled it closer to him. "Let me say again I'm sorry you didn't hear it from me—about Asa and the tutor."

Sam shrugged. "I had a feeling Asa was waiting for the perfect moment to tell me. He's been pretty confrontational these days."

George nodded as he lifted his coffee to his lips. He winced from the combination of bitter grounds and intense heat as it traveled down his esophagus when he swallowed. Sam told George about the frequent arguments he and Asa were having ever since the show ended. It was as if the boy had held it in for so long that he was now going to punish Sam every single day.

"Does he want to go home? I mean he probably left friends behind?" George ventured. "This is a tough age for peer change."

Sam frowned. "We weren't in Michigan long. I was visiting artist at the Arts Center in Kalamazoo for a term." He shrugged and looked slightly embarrassed as he elaborated. "Grants, visiting artist, whatever it takes to pay the rent." George saw vulnerability there—not unlike those creatures his sister sewed, warts and all, that begged for someone to take them home and love them.

George tried to play it cool as he continued to dig for clues. He wanted Sam to tell him everything. "Before that?"

Sam looked at George. His motivation was obviously transparent but that didn't appear to bother Sam, who continued to talk. "I was born in Delhi but raised in the UK. London, the East End. That's where Asa was born as well."

"That explains your interesting accent."

"Interesting?"

George blushed and said boldly, "Musical. When you speak you sound like you're singing."

Sam laughed but looked flattered. "I assure you I am tone deaf."

George drank some more coffee to keep something even more idiotic from coming out of his mouth. But it didn't stop him from asking, "Is that where Asa's mother is? London?"

Sam exhaled slowly and played with the corner of the newspaper. "I don't know where she is exactly. We— I . . ." He stopped and looked up at George before he continued, "When I came out I wasn't that useful as a husband anymore, you know?"

George winced with understanding but felt some relief. "But Asa?"

"She pretty much hated anything that reminded her that she had married and slept with a queer. Even Asa." He took another deep breath and exhaled. "Thankfully, he was too young to know at the time . . . although I'm sure some of this anger that's been directed at me is because she recently sent him a letter." He paused. "So to answer your question—she is somewhere in the UK."

"Does she want to see him?"

"Eleven years and she's back." For a moment Sam looked defeated. Up this close George could see thin lines at the corners of his eyes as if someone had sketched them in. There were dark circles as well and his hair was unwashed. He wondered how old Sam was—forty maybe?

Then Sam shook his head and smiled again, and his entire face changed. "I'm not going to project the worst. Asa is curious, for sure. I understand that. But I know he loves me." As Sam lifted his coffee cup to his mouth, George noticed that his hand shook ever so slightly.

George found himself hoping against logic that love was enough when frequently it never was. He thought people put too much faith in the power of love. If only life were that absolute. So far in his twenty-nine years, George had found the idea of love, and that included familial as well as passionate, an enigma. The closest he had been to love was what his sister, Amy, had with Owen, and even that made him scared that she would be disappointed.

Sam brushed against him with his shoulder to get his attention. "I've told my son's guidance counselor too much, I fear."

"No—no, you haven't," George whispered fervently. Then, to dispel a moment that he was afraid was too intimate, he cleared his throat and spoke loudly. "Whatever I can do to help Asa at school, I need to know."

Sam regarded him with that amused smile again—like he knew all of George's secrets. "I know you'll help him, but it's really only Asa who can help himself here."

George smiled weakly. "So I guess I'll tell the tutor to forget it?"

He nodded as his eyes searched George's face. "You said you haven't read Asa's paper yet?"

"No."

"He tells me there is a distinct parallel between Holden Caulfield and Siddhartha. Both were young, alienated, perhaps depressed?" He paused and looked at George for a reaction; George nodded for him to continue. "Each went on a journey. Either way they each had to search for enlightenment, yes?"

"Yes." George exhaled and continued cautiously. "I can't argue with that." He was excited—that a student had actually drawn a continuum from one work of fiction to the next, had understood, at least, what George had been striving for in choosing these works. It was thrilling. But he was also embarrassed. What if Sam thought the connection he'd attempted to draw was sophomoric?

"What about you, George Haas?" Sam continued to probe, "You don't look like you have these sorts of problems in your life, do you?"

George shifted on the stool. His back was starting to hurt and Sam was looking at him intensely. He felt his bowels cramp and he was afraid he'd have to excuse himself to go to the toilet. What would Sam infer from that? That he was trying to hook up with him? Right here? For God's sake! That would be wrong on so many levels. First and foremost, his job would be at stake. He gritted his teeth from the intestinal twist and said, "Believe me, I've searched enough—experienced plenty, I mean I have no children but I've had enough drama. I've just gotten out of a relationship that was . . ." George hesitated, looking for a word to describe exactly what it was he had with Jules when he realized that he had perhaps given Sam more information than he had been looking for. Feebly, he added, "I'm not looking for anything right now." Now why did he say that? Was that what Sam was asking him? Probably not. It was just George projecting his feelings again.

"Ah, no one is ever looking." Sam smiled slowly.

George couldn't tell if he was teasing or not. It was his weakness, a holdover from years of his father's taunts. Either way, it was time for him to leave. He stood and reached into his pocket for his wallet. Sam stopped him by placing a five on the counter in front of them. George smiled and adjusted his jacket and picked up his bag.

As George slung his bag across his shoulder and fixed the strap, Sam leaned over until his mouth was level with George's ear. He could feel Sam's breath as Sam said in a low voice, "Thanks for coming to see the show."

"But I didn't . . ." George started to protest, as his gut twisted and he realized that Sam had seen him through the glass on Christmas Eve. That was when the pain in his stomach turned into something reminiscent of the reaction he'd had to Sam the first time they'd met.

When he looked at Sam, George knew his face must be a startling shade of claret—he could feel it. And that was when George did something so unexpected that he knew later on, when he reconsidered, he would have done it again no matter what. He lifted a hand to Sam's cheek and brushed his fingertips along his jawbone. Just as George moved to press his lips against Sam's, Sam closed his eyes.

That total act of surrender made George hesitate. Sensing this, Sam's eyelids fluttered open.

"It's okay, close your eyes," George said softly, urgently, as he placed his lips against Sam's.

five

YOU SHOULD HAVE SAID HELLO

The first time George slept over at Sam's, he stumbled into the kitchen in the early morning to make himself some coffee. It was a risky endeavor, maybe foolish, but he absolutely needed something to wake him up before class. Since he was half-asleep and he had absolutely no idea where anything was, he swayed back and forth, opening cabinets, until he determined that there wasn't any coffee to be found. The coffeemaker on the counter with the ring of grounds stuck to the lid was obviously a ruse. He was tempted to reuse what was left in the basket, but the gray fuzz around the rim made him shudder and reconsider.

The only thing his search uncovered was an old box of something called Yogi Cleansing Tea. That was not going to be enough to get him going, especially since he and Sam had fallen asleep only three hours ago. The alarm on his watch had woken George with a start. He was aware that he had to be somewhere but foggy on the specifics. Sam's arm had been flung across George's chest possessively while he slept, yet George didn't take a moment to enjoy it. His heart was racing. He couldn't be late for work and he needed to get out of the apartment before Asa woke up and discovered him there. Gently, George lifted Sam's arm and rolled off the futon and onto the floor without waking him. When he sat up, he realized that as he got out of bed, he had taken most of the covers with him, leaving Sam exposed. He grabbed a handful of blankets as he stood up and arranged them carefully over Sam, tucking them in at the lower corners before kicking himself that he didn't have time to linger over Sam's naked back.

His entire body protested being upright and out of the warmth of Sam's bed, but he forced himself from the room for coffee. He had the idea that he would dress while the coffee brewed and leave Sam a note that he'd call later. But then, while he was in the kitchen contemplating the leftover, possibly moldy grounds, he heard the digitally altered screech of his mother's maniacal screams coming from behind the tapestry to his left, which served as a divider for Asa's room. Asa was awake and playing video games.

George ran back into the bedroom for his clothes as silently as he could, cursing the creaking old floorboards along the way. Sam was in the exact position that George had left him moments before, sound asleep. George jammed his arms into his shirt, forgot his socks, and slung his bag over his shoulder. He was out the front door and down onto the street before he realized he hadn't left a note or planted one last kiss on Sam's cheek.

George spent his morning classes in a stupor. He didn't know what was worse: leaving Sam without saying good-bye or hiding from fourteen-year-old Asa. By the time fifth period rolled around and Asa strolled into his English class, George had a serious case of stress-induced sweats. Between the bad coffee from the teachers' lounge that he had guzzled nonstop through the last four classes and the fear of being outed by Asa as having spent the night in his father's bed, his heart roared in his ears as it galloped erratically inside his chest. It would be George's luck if he had a heart attack right now in front of his students. He wondered, briefly, if Asa, whose previous student/teacher relationship with George had been (prior to George spending the night in his father's arms) middling to above average, would call 911 or just let George die.

God, he had to eat something soon or stop drinking coffee.

George coasted through their discussion of Gatsby. He knew most of the boys, with the notable exception of Asa, came from a background of wealth and privilege. Jay Gatsby's yearning to join the ranks of the wealthy along Long Island's North Shore at all costs, was lost on them. These kids yearned for nothing. Had no idea what it was like to be outside looking in. Under normal circumstances, he would have pointed this out, this reversal of fortune. Today he just wanted to get through the class and go to lunch. So he allowed the discussion to veer off to celebrity: how to become one. For these kids, Gatsby's plaintive yearning was somehow analogous to their desire to be rap stars or cast members of *The Real World*.

Asa, uncharacteristically, contributed nothing. He, too, looked heavy-lidded from lack of sleep and George wondered how much the boy had heard. Had they been loud? Sam had assured George that Asa was already asleep when they had entered the apartment in the dark. Sam had muffled George's protests with hard kisses and had led him into the bedroom without turning on any lights. George had been slightly buzzed from the bottle of wine they'd shared at dinner and he allowed himself to be taken by the hand. Since that first kiss initiated by George in the restaurant, they'd had half a dozen dates where they had not so much as brushed fingertips. By last evening, he had been swimming in desire, his cock so hard he thought it would burst through his zipper. George squirmed in his chair as he recalled the persistence of Sam's tongue and the small shudder of his shoulders as he came prematurely while George held him tightly between his palms. That uncontrolled release had endeared him to George all the more. So he wasn't thinking logically, wasn't really registering that his student was on the other side of the apartment asleep in his bed while Sam knelt down on the floor and took George in his mouth. He wasn't thinking about anything but how good it was and how long it had been since he had felt anything for anyone like he felt for Sam.

At lunch George checked his cell and wasn't surprised to find three voicemails from Sam. The dulcet melodic tone of his voice in George's ear was enough to wake his sleeping dick coiled fetally inside his pants. He stood up quickly and rushed out of the lounge and down the front hall until he was outside. Without his coat, the arctic February air was enough to shock his penis back to slumber. He was no better than the hormones with heads housed in the school building behind him. He seriously needed to get a grip.

Dialing Sam, he paced back and forth, mindful of the dwindling minutes of his break and glad his next period was tutoring. Tutoring would keep him focused on the task at hand and he wouldn't be able to wander and descend into this no-man's-land of paranoia and fear.

The last message Sam had left for George said he would be unavailable until after five; so George left him a voicemail loaded with apology and what he hoped sounded like lust instead of desperation before he went back inside the building. He spent the afternoon crashing, coming down off the caffeine high like a novice skier on a black diamond trail, and by the time the final bell rang, he was slumped in the chair behind his desk, wrung out and comatose. He was obviously not cut out for a night of sex, subterfuge, and the subsequent aftermath. His sister Amy jokingly called him the straightest gay man she knew. After last night, he would have to agree.

He ducked out of the faculty meeting with a vague excuse of illness (who wasn't harboring a vicious germ or two this time of year?) and took the back staircase two at a time. He kept his head down and exited the building on Amsterdam Avenue at 68th Street. He was so intent on keeping his focus—get out of the school, to the subway, and safe behind the door of his apartment—that he ran straight into Asa on the corner of 67th and Amsterdam, knocking him off the curb and into the path of a speeding cab.

George yanked the boy safely back onto the sidewalk by his jacket. Asa quickly disengaged and shook himself off. "You should have at least said hello," Asa spat angrily in his face before turning and jogging up 67th Street back toward the park in an attempt to get away from George as quickly as possible.

"Asa!" George shouted after him but did not make a move to follow. He knew it was no use. He guessed that Asa had said all he was going to for now. Of course, it left George wondering if he meant that he could have said hello right then or this morning when he had snuck out of his father's bed. Even though he wished for the former, he had a sinking feeling that it was most definitely the latter.

At home, George fell onto his bed fully clothed and woke only when his cell phone inside his coat pocket vibrated against his side. He opened his eyes as he fumbled for the phone. It was dark except for the clock across the room on the VCR, which read 9:02

p.m. Shit. The vibrating stopped by the time he extricated the phone and flipped it open. He didn't recognize the number, and he was crushed to see that Sam had neither called nor left a voice-mail. Had he really fucked things up that bad?

He took a deep breath and ran his tongue over his teeth. They felt gummy and his mouth tasted horrible. He shuffled into the alcove that housed his airline-style kitchen: mini-sink, mini-fridge, mini-microwave, and a two-burner stove top. He reached for a glass and ran the tap for water. He guzzled three glasses in a row and burped loudly. His gut was empty. Lazily, he pulled up his shirt and scratched his belly as he considered what to do about food when his phone vibrated along the edge of the table where he'd set it down.

He felt weak in the knees when he saw the display. "Hey, hey hello?" George said eagerly into the phone. "Sam?"

"George!" Sam boomed through static.

"Where are you?" George asked. "I can barely hear you."

"Long Island. Train. I'll explain when I see you. Can I come over?"

George smiled. They were the words he had been waiting to hear all day.

George and Sam were naked, lying on their backs shoulder to shoulder on the narrow mattress that was George's bed, eating slices of cold pizza. They were in each other's arms the minute Sam came through the door, removing clothes, sucking, licking, and grunting as they came together quickly, falling down onto the mattress with barely a word exchanged.

The only thing that Sam had insisted upon was light, and he had stopped long enough to turn on the reading lamp next to the bed. He wanted to see George, and so, afterward, as they struggled for breath, they seemed captured inside a golden bubble. Outside of the bed, the corners of George's studio apartment seemed dark and forbidding. He turned on his side toward Sam, trapping him beneath his leg, and Sam breathed into his ear, catching his bare lobe between his teeth. His tongue felt for the hole where an earring would have been, but there was none. George had never marked any part of his body, never cared to, plus he was more than a little frightened of needles. Just add that to the pile of neuroses that George had collected over the years.

He was surprised that Sam had no ink or piercings either, although he was sure that it had nothing to do with a fear of needles. Sam's skin was smooth all over, bearing only the scars from living. And George wanted to discover everything: the topography of Sam's body in the years he'd lived on the earth before George. On Sam's right cheekbone just below his eye there was a small indentation, a chicken-pox crater, where George placed the tip of his index finger. He imagined that if they lived forever he would never tire of running his hands over the multitude of smaller scars and bumps scattered about Sam's body from years spent sculpting wood and metal.

They'd ordered pizza but let it get cold, and now, because neither of them wanted to get out of bed to warm it up, they ate it straight from the box. From the way Sam had gnawed and nibbled his way across George's body, George was pretty sure that his gaffe this morning had been forgiven and so he felt safe to tell him about Asa's outburst after school.

"I'm sick about it," George said as he dropped a crust into the box. "I don't want Asa to be upset."

Sam sat up and looked hard at George. "I swear to you, I had no idea that he knew you spent the night."

"You don't know the things that went through my mind all day. Were we loud? Had he heard us?"

Sam reached out and ran his hand along George's jaw. "Oh, baby. I am so sorry. Asa is a teenager, you know? I mean, how do you think he's going to react to anyone I bring into our family?" He leaned over and pressed his lips against George's and whispered, "I'll talk to him."

George moved back away from Sam. He was torn between asking how many men Sam had attempted to bring into their family before George, and worrying that talking to Asa would only make it worse. Finally, he asked, "Do you think you should?"

"Asa and I have always been open with each other."

"So he knew we went out last night? That we've been out before?"

"He knew I thought you were cute."

"You're not answering my question, Sam. Please. This is tricky, you know? There's my job and . . ." George trailed off, momentarily distracted by Sam's hand stroking high up on his inner thigh. He put his hand over Sam's to let him know he didn't want him to remove his hand but he also wanted Sam to listen to what he was saying. "I don't do anything lightly. You might need to know that about me."

"Really?" Sam said teasingly. "And all along I thought you were some good-time party boy."

"I thought Asa liked me," George said morosely.

"He does, you moron. Why else would he be so angry?"

"Really?" George asked as he released Sam's hand, allowing it the freedom to continue stroking his thigh. "Do you really think so?" George murmured as Sam pushed him back against the pillows. He closed his eyes and reached for Sam. He hoped Sam was right. Ever since his father died a few months ago, George had been unable to shake his fear of dying alone. He wanted a life with some- one that had meaning, more than just a body to hold on to. Was he irrational to think that person could be Sam? Or Sam and Asa?

"Hey." George struggled to get Sam's attention away from his nipples. Between his hand and his mouth, George knew he didn't have long before he was totally gone. "Sam, hey," he said again and tugged on Sam's hair to stop him from doing the incredible thing with his tongue and look up.

Sam obeyed with a slow, lazy smile. George brushed the hair out of Sam's face and said, "You never told me why you were out on the Island."

"Last month, I sold three paintings to this guy and his wife and they invited me out for drinks. She writes cookbooks and he works in finance." He smirked. "The husband is totally in denial. You should have seen him. I thought he was going to soil his fancy suit right there as he looked at the paintings. Why else would he want life-size male nudes hanging in his living room?"

"Maybe they were for his wife?"

Sam cocked his head to the side as though he was listening for something. "No, I got the distinct impression they were for him, you know, his choice?"

George imagined all sorts of scenarios where an elegantly suited Wall Street guy made his sexual intentions known to George's brand-new lover. Sam must have realized what George was thinking because all of a sudden he sat up and said, "When I met you that day in the restaurant," he stopped and shook his head and corrected himself. "When I saw you peering at me through the window in the gallery, you made my insides turn to mush. I haven't felt like that in years. Maybe ever." He stroked George's cheek and hovered over him, staring down into his face.

"I had no idea you would ever feel the same way about me. Do you believe me?"

George nodded, speechless, his throat dry.

"But, baby," Sam continued, "I wish you had been with me to see this house, right on the Sound: with all this private shoreline to themselves. The dark water moving beneath the moonlight; the sand looked silver and the leaves are off the trees and everything was stripped bare, winter-bare—it was practically mystical, you know? The entire back of the house was glass and I couldn't tear myself away from it. I couldn't stop staring the entire time I was there and I don't even think either of them glanced outside, not even once. It was so goddamned beautiful."

"You're just like Gatsby," George whispered.

"No." Sam shook his head, his mouth twisted wryly. "Gatsby was seduced by it all. I'm too much of a realist."

"So I'm the romantic here?"

"You can be anything you want as long as you stop talking, okay?" Sam asked, seeming to enjoy his role as aggressor as he lowered his body back down onto George's. "Okay?" he asked as his eyelashes brushed against George's cheek. "Okay?" he asked a final time, although George knew he really wasn't looking for an answer.

George proposed lunch with Asa and then a trip through the shop Lonely Planet, but Sam nixed the idea.

"You don't have to try that hard, George. I mean it," Sam said by a billboard advocating safe sex on the side of a building on Third Avenue. It was a giant hand in front of a gently bulging button-fly crotch, holding out a condom. Just beneath was the message: COVER UP.

"What is the purpose of that?" Sam asked, pointing and shaking his head. "I mean, really, you want to bone someone you want to bone them. When you're all in, who's going to pull out and say, hold on a sec, I saw this thing over on Third that said I need a rubber." He shook his head again.

"That's the point, Sam. It's supposed to make you think before you're all in," George said more sarcastically than he intended. He was just frustrated. It had been a month since he and Sam had first slept together and he refused to return to Sam's place until the situation with Asa was dealt with. That meant that a pattern had been established where Sam showed up at George's late, usually after Asa had gone to bed and George was half-dead from a day of teaching. They would spend a few minutes talking about the day as they removed their clothing and fell on each other like animals. Afterward they dozed and then Sam would rouse himself around four to make it back to his place so he'd be home to wake Asa for school. George hadn't had a full night's sleep in forever and that was probably adding to his increasingly short temper.

"Waste of space," Sam muttered as he continued down the street.

George sighed. Of course Sam was right about most things. He was probably right about the effectiveness of the billboard. Ever vigilant, and despite all the safe-sex warnings George had ever seen or heard in his life, he and Sam had not been using any protection since that very first time and he passed by this bulletin board almost every day.

He sighed again, loudly. Sam said the best thing to do was to give Asa space to sort everything out and that George was actually making it worse by hiding. Naturally, George didn't think he was hiding from Asa, after all he was his English teacher and he saw him every single day in school. He didn't feel like backing down on this one and so he argued with Sam all the way down to the Bowery. It was the first time that they had really disagreed, and George hated that it had to be about Asa. Was he making more of this than he should? Obviously, he didn't think so or he would have stopped. He wasn't unreasonable.

Sam hesitated in front of a wall of graffiti. A giant painting of a baby suckling at the teat of a beast had been wheat-pasted over a thick quilt of old flyers and caught Sam's eye. He lifted his camera from around his neck and snapped a few frames. "There's really some interesting stuff out here," he called as he walked ahead of George and ran a hand along the wall.

It was the first time they had been together during the daylight hours in a while. Asa was hanging with friends and Sam had suggested George come along with him for a walk so that he could photograph graffiti. He had been playing with ideas for some new paintings incorporating street art and he was gathering inspiration material. George was ashamed that he had instigated the bickering when he and Sam had so little time to spend together. But he couldn't stop. When he had things on his mind, he needed to say them. Sam refusing to see George's point made it all the worse.

George hung back and studied Sam's retreating form. His thick, inky hair was loose from its usual elastic band and hit the shoulders of his bomber jacket, the strong thighs and nearly non-existent ass hidden in baggy jeans, the way he bounced lightly on the balls of his feet as he walked. Tears sprung to George's eyes at the thought of not having Sam in his life, and he quickly wiped them away before he became just another sad, odd queer caught crying on the street. Just as he thought Sam was about to turn the corner without him, he stopped and looked back over his shoulder. George managed a tremulous smile.

Sam extended the hand not holding the camera. "Hey, baby. Are you coming? Are you all right?" He took several steps back toward George, a deep *V* between his brows. "George?"

George inhaled deeply and smiled. "I do know a few things about teenagers, you know? I mean I'm not a parent but I've been a teacher for a while. I'm not just phoning it in with them." He couldn't resist one more attempt, one last stab at credibility where Asa was concerned. "Maybe he's waiting for you or us to talk to him about it. Maybe he just feels out of the loop?"

He caught Sam's darkening expression and steeled himself for what would come next. Instead, Sam said softly, "You are the most brilliant half of the two of us, George. I've never said otherwise. But I know Asa and you just have to trust me on this one. Please." Sam added in a pleading tone although his eyes looked anything but unsure, "Please?"

Reluctantly, George found himself silenced and nodding in agreement as he followed Sam around the corner.

Asa's Gatsby paper was less than stellar. As a matter of fact, it was as close to a failing grade as Asa had ever received. George sat at his desk, tapping his pen against the edge as he waited for Asa to show. He wasn't so sure he would, despite George's scrawl along the top of his paper: *See me,* in bright red ink.

All of George's students knew that *see me* meant to come during sixth period office hours. George got up and checked his watch against the clock on the wall outside the door. Asa had ten more minutes to show.

With less than four minutes before the bell signaled the next class, Asa shuffled into George's office, dropped a pile of books onto the floor, and threw himself against the seat of the chair opposite the desk.

George smiled quickly and said, "Asa."

Asa looked out the window past George and said nothing in return.

George coughed, fumbled, and dropped his pen. Asa looked down at the floor where the pen had rolled, but neither of them made a move to pick it up.

"Soooo, Gatsby. What gives? You read the book, right?"

Lazily, Asa held up one hand with the fingers splayed. George took that to mean he had read it five times.

"And you just didn't feel like writing about it?" He paused, knowing what he said next would light a fire under Asa. "Or you just had trouble comprehending? Fitzgerald may seem like an accessible author in terms of language, but the themes are fairly mature."

Asa snorted. "Maybe I should have written the paper from an immigrant's perspective? You know, the urge to conform. Not to appear foreign but to be American." He spit out the last word like it was an obscenity and shrugged his shoulders. "Gatsby just wanted to fit in, right?"

"Maybe you should have," George agreed. "How about this: you go home tonight and write that paper and turn it in to me tomorrow and I'll consider not marking you off for the first paper?"

"Am I getting special treatment?"

George felt his face redden. "No."

"Really? 'Cause I thought where papers are concerned there were no do-overs with you."

George fought to keep his voice steady. "In the case where a student obviously misinterpreted the assignment, I make exceptions. It seems like perhaps your ideas weren't fully formed the first time."

"Or maybe it's just because I stay awake half the night wondering where my dad is and if he will be coming home." To demonstrate his loss of sleep, he yawned loudly, dramatically stretching his long arms far above his head. "Sometimes I have a hard time concentrating on a little amount of sleep."

The bell rang for the next class. George watched Asa scoop the books off the floor and saunter out of his office without looking back. In that moment, he was more like Sam than George ever realized. He wondered if Asa would share their conversation with Sam. George had no intention of doing so unless Asa refused to turn in the revised paper. Then he would have to take on the role of concerned teacher. Concerned teacher who just happened to have woken up this morning at half past three curled up in the arms of the student's father.

George was astounded when he walked into his office in the morning and dead-center on his desk was a ten-page double-spaced typed paper titled *The Great Gatsby: An Immigrant's Perspective.*

He sat down and rifled through the pages as he sipped his coffee but he was unable to focus. He was beyond exhausted yet again. After Sam left, George had dozed on and off, unable to fully commit to sleep. The little time they'd spent together was unsatisfying: Sam was preoccupied after working eight long hours in his studio, which made any attempt at meaningful conversation obsolete, and he was also in pain, with aching joints and muscles, from building frames and stretching large canvases. It was the first time that neither of them could muster the energy for sex, yet George insisted on working the knots out of Sam's back and legs and arms with his hands. Then, when Sam had fallen asleep, George had stayed awake, watching him. At three he'd woken him up with a kiss and sent him home to Asa.

Instead of the regular class periods today they had an assembly over in the girls' building. It was rare that they brought the schools together during the course of a normal school day, so the halls were buzzing with testosterone. There were minor skirmishes at the lockers and an additional layer of deodorant and cologne over the normal musky odor that naturally permeated the boys' building. These guys were ruled by one thing and one thing only, and they would take whatever opportunity they had to make an impression on the opposite sex, no matter how insignificant.

Being one of the younger teachers meant that George always pulled chaperone detail. After everyone had been herded into place and safely deposited in seats in their assigned rows, George took a spot along the back wall, tucked beneath the shadow of the staircase to the balcony. The balcony was closed off to the boys, and George's standing there made it look as though he were guarding the entrance when in reality there was enough darkness that he could get away with catnapping while the speakers from the association of Ivy Leagues extolled the virtues of their alma maters. As if these kids needed to know something that had been ingrained since infancy.

At the end of the day, he was in his office clearing off his desk, determined to catch a swim in the lap pool before he headed home. George used the water as a sedative all through high school and college and so far continuing into adulthood. As far as he was concerned, it was better than therapy. He was just about to leave when Asa appeared in his doorway.

"Hey," he said as a greeting, his long body wedged against the molding.

George motioned for him to come and take a seat but Asa refused. George shrugged and continued stuffing papers into his bag.

"You got my Gatsby paper?" Asa asked.

George nodded. He was surprised to hear the lack of a challenge in Asa's voice. "I haven't read it yet," he said, then added, "By the end of the week, okay?"

"Sure," Asa answered.

As he began to turn away, George heard himself ask Asa if he wanted to meet his mother. She was in the city, hawking the video release of *Dead, Again 3*, and since Asa was a fan, he thought he might be able to set something up.

Too late to rescind the offer, he watched Asa's face revert from that of a bored, uninterested teenager to that of a six-year-old kid on Christmas morning, and George knew without a doubt that Sam was going to kill him for going behind his back. Was bribery an acceptable form of parenting? He doubted Sam would agree.

That afternoon, he swam fifty laps at the Y pool and stayed extra long under the hot shower. On the way home, he stopped and picked up a few essential groceries and then made himself a grilled cheese sandwich and tomato soup for dinner.

When he couldn't stand it anymore, he called Amy and told her what he'd done.

"You're using Mom to get laid?" she asked incredulously.

"I'm already getting laid," George snapped.

"Then why?"

And George answered, "Because I'm crazy for this guy and I want the kid to like me," even though he knew Amy was going to ream him for it. Which she did. He'd hung up the phone feeling even more certain that his relationship with Sam was doomed and he had no one to blame but himself.

It was only nine o'clock and his eyes were already at half-mast as he struggled to reread Shelley's *Frankenstein* for his ninth-grade seminar class when he heard the click of the key as it turned in the lock. He opened his eyes to see Sam step into the room. He shed his paint-spattered coat, kicked off his sneakers, and dropped into the spot beside George.

Sam slipped the book out of George's hand and looked at the cover. "Ah. What man isn't a monster?" He laughed. "The tale of old lovers?"

George smiled, thrilled and scared to see him. "You're here early."

"Asa's studying at a friend's place near the school and spending the night," Sam announced, as if he and George had won the lottery.

"Really?" George said. "Why didn't you tell me earlier? We could have done something." A weeknight where they actually could have had dinner together, maybe even caught a movie, seemed foreign and exciting compared to what they normally did.

Sam smiled again and clasped George's hand in his. "But this is what I want to do."

"Okay, then let's party," George joked as he rolled away from Sam and got them each a beer from the mini-fridge. He brought them back over to the bed and Sam took his beer and drank half in one long swallow. Instead of resuming his previous position, George sat back down by Sam's feet and sipped his beer. Sissy sips, he thought, in comparison to Sam's enthusiastic guzzle.

Sam put his feet in George's lap and rubbed them lightly over his crotch. George leaned back against the pillows, enjoying the sensation. He looked down at Sam's feet. A deeper brown than the rest of his honey-colored body, his toes were long and elegant, and the nails closely trimmed half-moons of alabaster and mauve. He put his beer down on the floor and took Sam's foot into his hands.

"Ah," Sam said and laughed. "Cold hands."

"Sorry," George said as he rubbed his thumb under Sam's arch. Sam didn't even squirm. "Not ticklish?" George asked.

"Not there," Sam replied. He was relaxed and totally different from the Sam of the night before. He filled George in on his work that day, how the painting was going, how excited he was that his idea was becoming something else on the canvas.

As he spoke, George realized that Sam obviously knew nothing of George's plan with Asa and he wondered, uneasily, why Asa hadn't said anything. All of a sudden he felt suffocated. He needed fresh air. He needed to get out onto the street among other people who surely were as duplicitous as he.

"Want to go for a walk?" George asked.

"Really?" Sam teased. "In your condition?" He curled his toes against George's dick and giggled when he let go and it sprang back against George's stomach.

George glanced down at the straining material of his sweat pants. His own body had betrayed him. "I guess not," he said, taking the beer out of Sam's hand and putting it down on the floor next to his own.

They made love slowly. Sam liked to talk as they touched and George was just now getting used to his erotic narration. At first, this made George feel shy, he wasn't used to someone annotating his body parts. But now he yearned for Sam's voice and his lightly accented whispers in his ear and he was surprised by how quickly it had become an important part of their foreplay. The only problem was that sometimes, when he spoke with Sam on the phone, Sam's voice had that same seductive quality in his ear, and it nearly drove George crazy and made him just a little bit fearful of his body's reaction when he was in a public place. It was like he was thirteen again and prone to a boner as easy as the wind blew.

Afterward, they dressed and went for the walk George had proposed earlier. Only Sam wanted to take George down to his studio to show him the preliminary sketches for the new painting. Sam was excited about his new project and when he talked, he did so with his entire body. The studio was far below Canal Street, in a building that had been taken over by squatters and the landlord didn't seem to care. Or, depending upon the story you believed, the landlord was among them, gathering material for a project of his own, his "tenants" unwitting participants. At least that was the rumor when Sam moved into the back half of the second floor. The idea of the place made George nervous. He didn't understand how Sam could accept on faith that someone wouldn't break into his space and steal his paintings or worse. But Sam seemed fine with everything.

As they made their way through the bowels of Chinatown, every single part of Sam was animated and involved in the moment. The faster he talked the faster he walked, and George practically had to jog to keep up with him. He was just like he'd been earlier tonight in bed and George was envious of his passion and maybe even a little angry that he felt so much for something besides George.

Sam took a flashlight from his pocket and shined the light on the broken staircase so George could see. Nimbly, Sam took the darkened stairs two at a time, but George was more cautious and he thought, in that moment, that the way they approached the stairs could be a metaphor for their relationship. It would probably be accurate except that George had actually skipped up three or more stairs by inviting Asa to meet his mother and then keeping it a secret from Sam.

Sam undid the padlock on the door and went around, turning on the spotlights that hung by nails on the exposed lathe of the crumbling plaster walls. George stood in one place until he could see. When there was enough light, George was touched to see tacked to the wall above Sam's workbench (strewn with rolled tubes of paints, tools smeared with colors, tins of nails, pads of paper, and jars of thick charcoal sticks and pencils of varying leads) a shot Sam had taken the day he'd been photographing graffiti. George was leaning against a chain-link fence festooned with garbage caught in the metal diamonds. Plastic bags, ribbons, dead balloons, shredded paper, vines, and skeletal leaves. And George. Looking grumpy and out of sorts because they had been fighting about Asa moments before. There was a smudge of blue paint to the right of George's head, where Sam's finger must have slipped off the thumbtack when he had adhered it to the wall.

Sam smiled when he noticed George looking at the photograph. George said, "I look like shit."

"You look like you, baby," Sam said.

"So I always look like that?"

"Like shit? No. You are so fucking gorgeous." Sam grinned widely and his entire face changed. "Maybe soon you'll let me paint you?"

George stammered, "Why would you want to do that?"

"Because I love you," Sam stated matter-of-factly.

Something in George's chest squeezed when he heard Sam say the word *love*. How did it come so easily for Sam? And right then, as he considered what to say next, over Sam's left shoulder George noticed a photo of Asa, probably taken a few years ago, his face still had the softness of childhood. He looked more like his mother, in another picture that George had seen, in a photo album, on the only night he had spent in Sam's bed. After they had made love, they had sat up in bed, parceling out their pasts beneath the amber glow of the lamp, when George had spied the album on a shelf across the room. Curious to know everything there was about Sam, he got the album and brought it back to bed. It had wide pages and a ring binder and they had spread it out across both of their laps. While Sam narrated, George turned the pages. He remembered how Sam's hand shook when he pointed to the picture of himself, barely recognizable with short hair, his arm tossed awkwardly around the shoulders of his wife as they squinted into the camera.

From the very first time in the restaurant when Sam had told him about his ex-wife, how she'd abandoned Asa at three and yet was making overtures again, noises that she wanted to all of a sudden be a part of her son's life, Sam had been looking over his shoulder, waiting for her to show up, but so far she had not made an appearance.

Now George couldn't take his eyes off the photo of Asa. This would be the perfect time to tell Sam he had gone behind his back. And then he looked into Sam's open, expectant face and thought: Oh shit. He used the word *love* and I've fucked it up again.

Instead, he said nothing and they went home and got into bed. Sam picked up the copy of *Frankenstein* George had been reading earlier and came to bed with the book and wearing a pair of thick, heavy-rimmed reading glasses on the tip of his nose and nothing else. George flipped through an old issue of *The New*

Yorker and wondered for the thousandth time why he bothered to subscribe. It only made him feel inadequate that he could never catch up and the pile of magazines haunted him. But even as he groused, the magic of the moment wasn't lost on him: he and Sam in bed, reading, like a regular old couple.

If only Asa accepted George as Sam's lover, then they could live like this all the time. Every night and every morning could be even better than this. Maybe reaching out to Asa on his own hadn't been such a bad idea. If it worked, wouldn't Sam forgive him if this were the payoff?

In the morning, while George still slept, Sam made him breakfast. They ate eggs and toast and coffee and followed that with a pretty heavy make-out session in George's tiny shower that made George dangerously late for school—enough to forgo the subway for a cab. But the money spent was worth it. They'd had an extraordinary night followed by an equally wonderful morning, and for the first time in a long time George hadn't brought up Asa's name (because he was scared to) and Sam was relaxed because he didn't have to rouse himself from bed and rush home in the chilly predawn hours.

His hair was still wet, curled against his collar, and he was sure everyone knew what he'd been up to this morning as he rushed into first period. But nothing out of the ordinary happened. As it turned out, sleeping all night made a huge difference in his day, and before George knew it, the time had passed quickly and he was leaving the building when Asa fell into step beside him.

"Did you really mean what you said yesterday?" he asked.

George blinked. Had it really been only yesterday? "Of course," he answered.

"So, like, when?"

"When?" George echoed.

Asa abruptly stopped walking and so did George. A guy behind him kicked the back of his legs and shouted, "Dude, you need to move your ass out of the way," only to scurry off with an apology when he realized that George was a teacher.

"Yeah," Asa challenged. "When?"

"I'll call my mother tonight and find out," George answered.

"Cool," Asa said as he bounded away from George and out the door.

"Cool," George repeated to no one in particular, in an effort to convince himself that it really was going to be okay.

That evening, when George finally reached his mother with news of a young fan that wanted to meet her, he could tell she was flattered, but she wanted more information. Particularly why George was so involved. Was the child sick? Because she knew about the foundation that granted sick children wishes—perhaps it would be better for George to go through them?

George stumbled through the sentence that established Asa as the son of his lover.

His mother sighed, but George could tell she was thrilled to be in the loop of his love life. They agreed to meet at her apartment on West 91st Street at four the following day before she and Saul flew out to Paris that night. Saul was the man behind the *Dead, Again* franchise. He had been the one to pluck their mother out of the actors' graveyard and he was also her lover. Although she had not formally introduced him to George or any of his siblings in that capacity, they all knew it. Saul was a sincere guy and way too interested in them to just be their mother's producer/director. And even though the trip to Europe was due to the wildly popular video release of *Dead, Again 3*, it had the air of a romantic getaway.

Before they hung up, his mother said, "You care about him a lot, George?"

When he didn't answer right away, because he was trying to figure out how to tell his mother he was head-over-heels in love, she laughed and said, "That's all I needed to know."

George squeezed his eyes shut tight. In a panic he called Amy and told her that he was bringing Asa to meet their mother the next day.

Amy was so quiet George thought she'd hung up the phone and he called her name three times before she finally answered.

"What about me and Owen?"

"What about you and Owen?"

"When do we get to meet Sam and Asa?"

George rubbed his forehead. Amy with Owen had become more social than she had ever been in her life. Where before she walked a narrow path of work-school-home, now her world included Owen and his social circle and beyond. Or maybe it was just a response to their father's death. Amy had done most of the hospital duty while the old guy manipulated her from his bed until his last breath. It was something Kate would never give Amy credit for and Finn was too out of it to realize. But George did. His voice could barely hold back his anguish at the thought of losing Sam as he cried, "Aren't you getting ahead of yourself? After tomorrow there might not be a Sam to worry about meeting."

"Ach, you've done stupider things than this, Georgie."

"Maybe, maybe not, but Sam is different."

"Who isn't?" she snapped. "Oh, get over yourself. If you two are still together come over Friday night and we'll make pizza. If you're not, come anyway and we'll get crazy. Deal?"

"Deal," George agreed as he hung up the phone and retrieved Asa's paper from his messenger bag. He might as well read it tonight so that he and Asa had something to talk about tomorrow if conversation veered off on an awkward path. He settled down onto the bed and snorted out loud. How many things could you avoid saying to each other when your teacher was sleeping with your father?

At five the following morning, George sent Sam home with a Judas kiss. He knew he was being dramatic, but now it was complicated by Asa, who, for mysterious reasons of his own, had not shared anything with Sam about meeting George's mother. And if he had and Sam was just playing along to see if George was going to come clean? Well, he couldn't even go there. Sam might be older and wiser by ten years but there were more times than not when George felt the weight of the world rested on his shoulders while Sam acted blissfully unaware. Or maybe Sam's bliss was on purpose so that he could sidestep reality. Sam purposely sought not to go down the dark path where George hid. Instead, he spent all of his time trying to coax George into the light while George resisted.

For instance, he had been thrilled by the invitation for pizza with George's sister and her boyfriend, and for a moment George was happy until he remembered that by the end of the week he might have sabotaged the best thing that had happened to him in forever. And while he could probably get out if it, he wouldn't dare cancel with Asa for fear the boy would hate him even more.

And look where he was now.

On the uptown 1 train, George held on to the bar above where Asa sat plugged into his iPod. At first George was mildly offended, until he realized that it let him off the conversational hook. Asa had barely made eye contact with him, so he was surprised that when an elderly man got onto the train, Asa got up and offered the man his seat. George stepped aside and gave Asa hand-room on the bar and said nothing about his gesture because he didn't want to embarrass him, but he was as proud of Asa in that moment as any father, and equally proud of Sam for instilling his son with such manners. He'd seen men his own age and older refuse to give up their seats. Now this act only made him feel worse that he was encouraging Asa to do something that his father didn't know about and that George hadn't trusted enough in Sam's parenting to abide by the request that he leave Asa to come around on his own.

At his mother's apartment, her suitcases packed and ready for the European trip took over most of the available floor space in the studio. She was gracious and welcoming with Asa and gave him an autographed publicity still along with a DVD and a T-shirt, leaving George to wonder at times like these, when he saw his mother in action, who she had been all those years ago when George was a little boy.

He'd never met this woman who was asking Asa about school and what he did for fun and how he liked living in New York. George had zoned out so it was a little late before he realized she was grilling Asa about Sam. What he did, where they lived, how they had come to be in New York.

And then George heard her ask, "How do you like having George for a teacher?"

"He's great," Asa said. "No matter how dull the book he always seems to relate it to today, you know?" He avoided looking at George when he said, "Everyone likes him."

George's mother laughed. "Everyone has always liked him. George is just that kind of guy, don't you think?"

Unless he's sleeping with your father, George thought miserably as Asa gave a vague nod of agreement and asked to use the bathroom.

As soon as he was out of earshot, George hissed, "Mom, stop the interrogation."

"What?" she asked innocently as she smoothed down her pants. "I just wanted to know a little about him. He obviously knows a lot about me."

"He knows the psycho character you play, not you." He paused. "There's a difference, right?"

"You would think," she said, "but then I've met a few weirdos."

"Asa's not weird." He offered the story of how Asa gave up his seat on the train as if she needed proof that he had been raised well, which in turn would mean that George had chosen well.

"I never meant Asa, George," she said with a slight smile. "You sound like a parent, by the way."

George heard the toilet flush and then the twist of the tap as water hit full-force into the sink.

"Just so you know," his mother said, "I've made a set of keys available to Finn. For while I'm gone. I mean, I don't know if he'll even use the place, but maybe you could come by and check?"

"He's in New York?" George asked, amazed and embarrassed by how little he knew of the lives of his siblings besides Amy.

Asa walked back into the room as she shook her head. "No. Boston still. I just wanted to give him an option, that's all." She smiled at Asa's return. "I have so enjoyed meeting you, Asa. Maybe we can do this again when I come back? I'd love to meet your father as well." When Asa bent down to shove his *Dead, Again* paraphernalia into his backpack, she shot a look in George's direction, which he lamely tried to deflect.

As he looked at Asa, he was surprised to see the boy upright and nodding vigorously in agreement. At that moment, when things could have gone either way, plans made that would only later have to be broken, the doorman called up to let his mother know her car for the airport had arrived. George and Asa helped her into the elevator with the suitcases while Asa and his mother chatted about London. She wanted to know where Asa and Sam had lived, and if he knew of a good restaurant, because she always seemed to pick the worst food and ended up losing weight and getting sick when she was overseas. She made sure to let him know she paid a high price for her B-list fame; she hated these publicity junkets where all she saw was the inside of the hotel and a lot of foreign press who were always surprised she looked younger than she did on film.

They parted at the curb when the driver took her suitcases from them and plopped them inside the open trunk without effort. She gave George a kiss and then leaned over and brushed her lips against Asa's cheek as well.

With one final wave through the window, she was gone and Asa and George were left standing in her absence, wondering what the hell had just occurred. It was a few moments before either of them spoke and then it was George.

"You hungry?" he asked Asa.

"Starved," Asa said.

"Let's go," George said as he pushed him lightly between the shoulder blades down 91st Street toward Amsterdam Avenue. He knew there was a falafel place on the corner of the next block because he had stopped there the last time he had been up to his mother's apartment. When they got there, the falafel place had turned into a pizza joint. It had obviously been more time than he'd thought since he'd visited his mother.

"This okay?" George asked as he opened the door to the heavenly smell of dough and sauce and sharp cheese.

Asa nodded, looking as dazed by the scents as George was. They ordered a pie and took a seat at the counter. George snuck a look at Asa's profile. He couldn't help but be reminded of that first time with Sam at the restaurant counter. He cleared his throat and Asa looked his way.

"Did you tell your dad about today?" he asked.

Asa regarded him wide-eyed and unflinching. "Did you?" he countered.

"No."

"No," Asa parroted.

"Why?" George asked.

Asa shrugged. "I don't know."

George sighed. "Fair enough. I don't know why I didn't tell him either."

The waitress slid their Cokes across the counter with a wordless smile. Asa reached for his and drank. George watched his Adam's apple move as he swallowed, before he took a sip of his own.

"That's a lie, actually," George said as he put his drink back down on the counter.

Asa looked surprised. "What is?"

"Me. I know why I didn't tell him. Because he asked me to give you space and it was bugging me that you really seemed to dislike me all of a sudden. Or maybe you just disliked that I was seeing your father? Either way I wanted to talk to you about it and he wanted me to let you do your own thing."

"Uh-huh."

"That's all you have to say?" George asked. He was at least hoping that Asa would say he didn't hate him.

Asa shrugged. "There's a lot to say but I guess I can't think of the words."

George doubted that, so he took a deep breath and persisted, "Well, what's the first thing off the top of your head?"

"That it's always been me and my dad and I like it that way."

"But your dad had . . ." George knew Sam had been in a long relationship with his last partner before he and Asa came to New York.

"So?" Asa said.

"It's not just me. You don't want it to be anyone," George said, more a statement than a question.

"Do you know about my mom?" Asa asked, evading the question.

George nodded.

"And you know that she wants to see me?"

He nodded again, afraid to speak. Was Asa really thinking that Sam and his ex-wife would be a family again?

"Well, I don't want to see her," he stated simply, as if he'd given it plenty of thought. "I don't want any part of her. I want to leave New York so she can't find us but my dad won't hear of it."

"Why?" George asked, barely able to think of New York without Sam.

"Because of you," Asa said as the pie arrived between them. It was a hot, steamy, bubbly mass of sauce and cheese, and despite the weight of the conversation, George found himself salivating. He watched as Asa pulled a triangle from the pie, plopped it onto the paper plate, and proceeded to sprinkle hot pepper and Parmesan all over the pizza. He folded the piece in half as he opened his mouth to take a bite.

"Careful," George warned. "It's hot."

Asa nodded and waited, the piece of pizza hovering near his chin. He nibbled the triangle off the end and closed his eyes. "Good," he said as he chewed. "Good pizza."

George reached for a piece, put it on his plate but didn't make a move to eat it. "I love your father," he said quietly as he stared down at his plate.

Asa continued taking bites of his pizza as if he hadn't heard what George had said.

So he said it again. Louder. "I love your father, Asa."

Asa's cheeks were so full of pizza that George didn't think he was capable of swallowing, let alone answering George. He mumbled something that sounded like "I know."

"And I think if your mother wants to find you, she will." He paused and lifted his slice to his mouth. "Wherever you are," he said before he took a bite.

Asa reached for another slice of pizza and repeated the hot pepper and cheese steps.

After he swallowed, George said, "So if you don't want me to be with your father just come out and say it. Don't make it about something else, okay? I mean, if you are uncomfortable because I'm your teacher or you're afraid your friends will find out and your life will be hell, well, tell me. Okay?"

Asa's head shot up and he jerked back on the stool. "I'm not ashamed of my dad."

"I never said you were. I thought maybe because I was your teacher the situation would be fodder for, well, you know." George paused, wondering how to broach the subject of the homophobia of a certain segment of teenagers. "Guys your age can be a little protective of their heterosexuality."

"People know you're queer. If you think you're hiding it, you're not." Even though it sounded like the intention of the sentence was mean, George didn't hear that in Asa's voice.

He supposed his sexuality really wasn't a revelation. George was far from flamboyant, but people knew, of course they must. And those people naturally had to include his students. It wasn't like when he was outed in ninth grade by crushing on the oldest Clancy boy who'd worked as a lifeguard at the pool where George practiced. That hadn't ended well, George having been the recipient of his first black eye because he'd been caught staring at Clancy in the locker room and was forever branded *queer boy*. It had been used as a taunt so frequently by Clancy and his group of friends (and once or twice by George's father) that George was convinced it would say that in the yearbook under his picture. It had taken him until freshman year in college before he intentionally and openly looked at another guy in that way. Another six months before he was brave enough to make a move. Until then, he had reserved his longing for the privacy of his room and his poster of Greg Louganis. He looked around the pizza parlor. What an unlikely place to be having this memory, let alone this conversation.

Finally, he said, "I'm not trying to hide from anyone, Asa. Especially you. That's why I'm talking to you now. I want to be with your father . . . and you. I want this to work."

Asa dug into his second slice of pizza as if he hadn't heard George.

"Asa?" George nudged.

When Asa eventually acknowledged George, he had a slick of grease on his chin from the oily pizza. "Huh?"

"I want to be with you and your father," he repeated.

Asa wiped his mouth with the back of his hand before answering. "The permission is not mine to give."

"I don't understand?"

He shrugged. "You guys have been sneaking around for a while."

George winced. He was about to refute Asa's claim but he couldn't. They had been sneaking around. "I guess we thought we were giving you your space."

He narrowed his eyes at George. "You didn't even acknowledge my existence that morning in the apartment. I heard you and my dad come in. I knew you were there. Why couldn't you have just said something?"

"I panicked," George admitted. "It was stupid and I panicked." He hesitated. "When you yelled at me later that day I told your father and he said I should give you space. I didn't want to come to your apartment without your wanting me to."

Asa said nothing. Just continued to eat his pizza. So George followed suit until there was only two pieces left on the tray. The waitress wrapped the leftovers in foil and handed them to Asa as George paid the bill.

They rode the train back downtown in silence, Asa clutching the foil-wrapped pizza to his chest. His stop was first and he hesitated a moment before the door. Silently, he offered the pizza to George. George shook his head no as the doors slid open.

"Thanks for today," Asa said politely as he stepped onto the platform.

Before George could answer him, a crowd of people got on, the doors closed, and he lost sight of Asa at the 23rd Street station. There was a huge lump in his throat, but strangely enough he didn't feel so upset. He was glad they'd talked in the pizza joint. To finally say what he felt out loud, even though he figured it was too late for Asa to hear him, was a relief.

George went home, then turned around and went right back out. There were two things he could do: stay there and wait for Sam to come over or leave the house and go to Sam and tell him everything. The way he saw it now, he really had no choice.

He was out of breath from the combination of fear and jogging by the time he got to Sam's and greeted him at the door. George could see Asa hovering behind him. Sam's body language was welcoming but George knew he was surprised to see him. He smiled warmly and ushered him into the room before closing the door. George looked at Asa but Asa did nothing to indicate that George was even in the room. Instead, he picked up his backpack and headed to the back of the apartment.

"Can you wait?" George called to Asa.

Asa stopped and slowly turned around with a look on his face that said, I can't believe you're going to do this now.

Behind him, George heard Sam call, "George? What's happened?"

He turned around to face Sam. "I took Asa to meet my mother this afternoon."

"You did what?"

"I took Asa to meet my mother," George repeated.

"I see," Sam said as he sank down onto the arm of a chair. He looked at Asa and said, "Why didn't you tell me?"

Asa shrugged in an attempt to appear casual, but George could see tension in his shoulders, the way he was holding himself erect. Asa was more man than boy now, but he still looked awkward with his new body.

Sam shook his head. "I don't understand. Was this planned, unplanned? Can someone explain what's going on?"

George watched Sam's expression change from tired to confused. There was a smudge of vermillion paint on his chin and his hair was pulled back severely from his face, accenting his cheekbones and slightly large ears that stood away from his head. He was still in paint-covered clothes, obviously just having come in the door from the studio. George could detect the underlying odor of paint thinner mixed with sweat. All George wanted to do was take him in his arms and hold him.

"I asked Asa a few days ago if he wanted to meet her and he agreed."

"Just like that?" Sam asked. "Out of the blue? I thought things had been difficult between you." He glanced at Asa for confirmation and Asa bobbed his chin in agreement.

"We were discussing a paper that Asa needed to rewrite and it sort of just came out." He looked imploringly at Sam. "You know how much I want things to work out with Asa."

"Yes," Sam said softly. "But why didn't you tell me?"

"I was scared you'd be angry I went behind your back." He paused, unable to read what was going on in Sam's head. "Once I invited him I couldn't take it back."

Sam made a grunting sound as he shifted on the arm of the chair. "And Asa," he asked, "what was your reason for hiding this visit from me?" Sam's accent sometimes made his manner of speech sound formal, like now. Such a juxtaposition, considering his usual state of dishevelment.

George and Sam turned together to Asa for his answer. Asa's gaze flickered briefly at George as he said evenly, "I didn't want you to think I liked him."

"And do you?" Sam asked his son.

"It doesn't matter what I think," Asa said, shifting his back-pack to his other shoulder. "Listen, I have a lot of work to do." He started to back out of the room.

Sam said sharply, "Stop."

Asa did as he was told.

"I've waited, I think patiently, for you to remember how to behave." Sam got up and walked across the room so that he was standing eye to eye with his son. "George means a great deal to me."

"So I've heard," Asa said.

"Hey," Sam said as he put his hand forcefully on Asa's forearm. "Hey," he said again.

"Sorry," Asa said as he shrugged off Sam's hand and took a

step backward. "But you two can do whatever you want. You don't need my permission. Right?" This time he spun around on the balls of his feet, yanked aside the curtain that separated his room from the main space, and pulled it shut behind him.

In that moment, George felt sorry that Asa didn't have a door to slam. Wasn't that the right of every teenager? Now that he and Sam were alone in the room, he was even more nervous. It wasn't like they could speak privately unless they went into Sam's bedroom and closed the door. George wanted to suggest it, but he was afraid to. He just hoped that Sam would.

Except Sam, when he finally spoke, said to George, "You should probably leave."

George took a step toward Sam, bewildered. "What?'

"Leave. Please, George." Sam stared hard at him with narrowed eyes. "I need . . ." he started to say, then stopped.

"What?" George asked, barely able to breathe. "What do you need?" Panicked at the thought of Sam's answer, George rushed on, "I need you, Sam. I need you and I don't want any of this to go away. Please." How was it that George was able to tell Asa he loved Sam, but when he was faced with Sam he couldn't get the words out? If he could, would it help? Or just make him sound desperate?

Sam came over and stood in front of George. He leaned toward him so their foreheads were touching. "You just need to go home and give me some time to sort it all out, okay?"

"Can we go in your room so we can talk?" George was embarrassed by the pleading tone in his voice but he couldn't stop. "Let me explain."

"Not now," Sam said as he stepped back so they were no longer touching.

Every impulse in George's body was to beg, but he didn't. Instead, he walked slowly to the door, hoping Sam would reconsider and call out to him. When he got to the door and turned the handle, the silence between them was deafening. And no matter what he tried to do for the rest of the evening, the silence hung there, in his ears, mocking him and refusing to go away.

Asa didn't come to school the following day. George had left seven voicemail messages in ascending levels of panic for Sam, but so far none had been returned. By Friday, Asa was back in school. George was surprised that he was talkative in class and met his gaze unflinchingly when he caught George staring at him as he left his classroom. But as far as offering anything on the subject of his father, he was mute.

That evening George dragged his ass to Brooklyn, determined to drown his sorrows with Amy and Owen. He'd lost count of the number of times he'd called Sam's cell phone and hung up without leaving a message. He found it hard to believe that Sam would break up with him this way. He thought at least he would have the decency to tell him face to face.

But perhaps he already had and George had just refused to hear him.

Amy was trying to make pizza from scratch, and for the last few minutes George had been watching her wrestle a lump of gray dough on the flour-covered counter.

George sucked on his second beer and moaned, "Why do you still try and cook?" He was starved.

She looked up at him with a death stare. "I'd give you the finger but my hands are covered in flour and goop."

He considered the dough. She had been stretching and rolling for what seemed like hours and it still looked hard and round.

Nowhere near the size of the pan. "When are you going to surrender and order a pizza instead?"

"Asshole," Amy muttered under her breath.

"Yeah." George sighed. "I am. That's why Sam dumped me."

Amy had been listening to him theorize for days, so she was hardly sympathetic. "Cut it out already."

"She made great broccoli and pasta the other night, George. You should have been here," Owen called as he descended the stairs from the loft. He was carrying a handful of CDs he'd burned for George and passed them off to him as he went around the counter for a beer and to slip his arms around Amy's waist from behind. George flinched at this display of affection and put the pile of CDs in front of him and one by one studied the song lists. Owen was tutoring George in a music scene he never knew existed. For the most part, George enjoyed it, but he never felt like he had anything intelligent to say in response when Owen asked him what he'd thought.

"What are you going to do this summer, George?" Owen asked, stepping to the side of Amy and tipping the beer bottle to his lips.

"Summer?" George asked, confused. As far as he knew, it was marginally still winter.

Owen nodded.

"I don't know," he answered finally.

"We can always use a couple more hands painting. If you want?"

George nodded. Now he knew what he was getting at: Owen and his bandmates ran a house-painting service and they seemed, in between gigs, to have a never-ending supply of jobs.

"I'm not much of a painter, O."

Owen laughed. "Whatever, just floating it out there to you." He took another swig of beer. "I bet you're a quick study."

George nodded forlornly. He wondered what Sam and Asa would do this summer.

Suddenly, Amy lifted the wad of dough and tossed it into the trash, ending the mutilation and admitting defeat. "All right, that's it. Out we go." She washed her hands off in the sink as Owen and George laughed.

"What?" she asked, feigning innocence. "I know when to get out. A lesson you'd be wise to learn, Georgie." She patted him on the shoulder on the way to get her coat.

George ended up getting so drunk he had to spend the night on the couch at Amy's and Owen's. He didn't wake up until after noon, and when he tried to sit up, his head felt the size of a balloon in the Thanksgiving Day parade. Underdog or Snoopy.

Silently, Amy handed him a mug of black coffee and a couple of aspirin. Grateful for both, he got himself into a semi-sitting position and swallowed the pills, chasing them down with the coffee. He waited until his stomach settled before he held a shaky hand out for a refill. Amy obliged him with that and an untoasted sesame seed bagel before she collapsed into the gold velvet chair opposite the couch.

"That chair is so fucking ugly," George said as he nibbled the bagel.

"It belonged to Owen's aunt Tilda," Amy said as she ran a hand up and down the velvet-covered arm.

"Still ugly," George said.

Amy shrugged. "His aunt thought it was pretty at one time, I guess."

"Family," George said. "Mothers and aunts who pretend to be mothers. Fuck them all."

"Hey," Amy said gently. "You can't blame this one on Mom. I thought you said she was great with Asa?"

"She was." George closed his eyes and moaned. "Wait, you're siding with her?" He opened one eye to peer at his sister.

"There's no side to take, Georgie." She leaned forward and frowned. "I'm so sorry you're sad, you know I am."

George nodded.

"But it scares me when you lose control."

"What?" he asked, too hung over to make a connection between words.

"Last night. You: drunk. It scares me because all I could think was how awful Finn looked at Dad's funeral and then there you are trying to blot it all out with beer." She shrugged. "It just scared me."

George rubbed a hand all over his face. Being drunk like that scared him as well, and he couldn't remember the last time he was so totally out of it. "I'm all right, Amy. I mean, I feel like shit, but I'll survive." In response, his intestines clenched ominously from the coffee and the bagel. He sat up straighter to alleviate the sharp pains in his gut but they only seemed to intensify. Man. He did not have the stamina to be a drunk.

Amy nodded and gnawed her bottom lip. "If you want to give this one last shot, I think you're going to have to go to him. Put yourself out there. I mean, George, come on, he's not answering the phone. Track him down if this is what you want. Tell him how you feel. What have you got to lose?"

Thoughts of dying alone in a crappy hospital bed with no insurance and a few family members begrudgingly by his side filled his head again. Maybe that was his fate? Maybe that was the fate of all the men in his family? Amy was right. Finn had looked like walking death at their father's funeral and George wasn't able to get a thing out of him about where he was living or even how he was surviving. Could Finn be very far behind their father? Why not George as well? He certainly didn't have the propensity to drink himself into a stupor, but he was sure another self-destructive behavior would surface if he tried hard enough. Again he thought: Amy was right. Why did he always play it so safe?

"George!" Amy shouted.

He flinched and covered his ear with the hand not holding the coffee. "Ouch."

"Either take my suggestion or forget about him. But do something, okay?" She stood and shook out her skirt. "Do something," she said again as she crossed the room to the coatrack by the door.

"Where you going?" George managed to get out as he watched Amy wind a scarf around her neck.

"Work," she stated. "Owen will be back here for rehearsal in about an hour so you better get up and take a shower. Clear your head, yes?"

"How come you didn't get so drunk?" George wailed as he massaged his temples.

"Who was going to carry you home?"

Horrified, George said, "You had to carry me? How?"

Amy grinned and ducked down to pick up one of his shoes. She dangled it in the air but George couldn't focus. "We really kind of dragged you. Sorry about your shoes." She tossed it toward the couch and it hit the back with a thud before bouncing to the floor.

George peered over the back of the couch and looked forlornly at his shoe. Fuck. The leather along the tops of his black shoes was gray from where it had been torn off.

His head was throbbing and he squinted at his sister. "Tell Owen I said thanks."

"For what?"

"For not leaving my sorry ass on the street."

Amy laughed. Halfway out the door, she stopped and called, "I love you, Georgie."

Lapses in syntax left George unable to formulate a response before Amy slammed the front door. He felt the hollow sound reverberate in his chest as he considered pulling the blankets up over his head and going back to sleep. But then the thought of anyone coming in and catching him like this was all he needed to force him off the couch and take baby steps toward the bathroom.

On the subway into Manhattan, George sat with his head in his hands, staring down at the unbelievably huge scuffmarks on the toes of his shoes. He doubted even polish would fix the gashes in the leather. He tried to imagine what it had been like for Amy and Owen to drag him through the streets of Brooklyn. The thought of it was beyond humiliating.

He rode the line down to the Canal Street stop without going home to shower or change. Sam would have to take him as he was. While the statement was filled with false bravado, George felt empowered, as if thinking it would make it come true. At least he felt pumped up on the sidewalk outside of Sam's studio but not so much as he made his way up the darkened stairs. As his eyes adjusted to the light, he saw that the missing stair treads Sam had so carefully led George past looked like the blackened gap-toothed piehole of a drunk. He felt along the wall on the second floor landing until he came to the door to the studio with Sam's massive padlock secured tightly. George bent down and tried to look beneath the crack under the door but he didn't see any light. Sam wasn't here.

His only other choice was to head to Sam's apartment and he hoped that not only was Sam there but Asa as well. He wanted to plead his case to both of them. No more subterfuge. Everything had to be out in the open, which was the only way it would work. He was convinced of it.

However, his convictions faded fast, along with his courage, as he banged on a door that would not open. Sam and Asa were not here either. George checked his watch: 4:45 on a Saturday afternoon. They could be anywhere.

He shuffled back down the stairs and out onto the sidewalk. He wandered down Sixth Avenue through Chelsea. His temples and a spot behind his left eye throbbed lightly if he walked too quickly; otherwise, he was feeling remarkably clear-headed. He continued on Sixth, reluctant to stray too far from the neighborhood but needing to stay on the move, only stopping when he came to a Food Emporium. His stomach felt hollow and so he ducked in for a quart of milk. Along with that he bought a turkey sandwich wrapped tightly in a womb of cellophane. Back out on the street, he freed his sandwich and took several large bites. As he chewed, he pondered his surroundings. Across the street and down a block was French Roast, where he and Sam had met for coffee.

He tossed the half-eaten sandwich in the trash and tore the safety tab off the milk. He opened his mouth wide and poured, swallowing slowly and evenly so he wouldn't choke. When he had had enough, he put the milk next to the sandwich on top of the trash and started walking.

George hadn't realized how hard and fast his heart was beating until he stopped in front of the restaurant and pressed his face to the glass. He felt his heart slam against his ribs as he peered through the window. He didn't realize until he stood there, breathing hot milky circles on the window, that he fully expected Sam to be sitting at the counter. When it was apparent that Sam wasn't, he felt the weight of disappointment settle on him. Still he scanned the half-empty booths for signs of either Sam or Asa, but there were none.

There was no way he was giving up now and going home. He went back to Sam's apartment building and banged on the door. Again, no one answered. With his back against the door, he slid down onto the floor and shut his eyes. Sam shared the second floor of the brownstone with only one other apartment, in the front of the building. He knew from Asa that the guy was away, because Asa mentioned that he had been feeding the guy's cat. So, as his lids grew heavy, he wasn't worried that a neighbor would discover him there and call the police. Besides, he was only going to rest in the hall for a minute until he figured out what to do.

When George heard someone say his name, he thought he was dreaming. He didn't even try to open his eyes, because being asleep felt so good. Although, as they persisted in calling his name, he became vaguely aware that his body was at an awkward angle, half-sitting, half-lying down. His right ass cheek was asleep as was the hand curled beneath his chin, and his neck throbbed ominously from the way his head rested in the curve of his arm. He tried to tuck back into unconsciousness but it was too late. He was starting to come out of that place that had felt blissfully weightless when he had been asleep.

"George?" Sam said, with a thread of concern. "George, are you all right?"

George blinked as his vision cleared. Hearing the worry in Sam's voice gave him hope. Sam was crouched down before him in the hallway outside his door. His dark hair was loose and fell forward into his face. George tried to raise his hand to push it back away from Sam's eyes but his fingers were asleep. Sam caught his hand where it hovered in front of his face and held it in his own. George's fingers tingled painfully but he did nothing to remove them from Sam's warm grasp.

"Are you all right?" Sam asked again when George didn't answer. "George?"

Behind Sam, George could make out the tall form of Asa stepping through the shadows of the staircase and into the light of the hallway with a look of alarm on his young face as he surveyed the scene before him. Unfortunately, in his mind's eye, George pictured what Asa was witnessing: his teacher slumped against his door, smelling like the remains of last night's bender.

"I'm sorry for this," George said in Asa's direction, his tongue chalky and fat as he sought to formulate his thoughts into words. He added, "For everything," before he turned back to Sam. "But I don't want to live without you." He was aware that, with the hand that wasn't holding onto George's, Sam was stroking his cheek. "Either of you," he added, directing his final comment to Asa. "Whatever it takes, I'll do it."

"Oh, baby, I know," Sam replied. "I know, me too."

George barely heard Sam's admission because he was on a roll. "And this week has been shit and I never want that to happen again. I'm sorry I went behind your back and I'm sorry I worry and make things bigger than they are and that I didn't trust you to know your own kid. This is me and I'm probably never going to change so you should know that right now. I'm insecure and I'm serious most of the time and I get off on climbing the mountains I make out of molehills. But I love you. I love you." He felt water gathering at the corners of his eyes and the clot caught in his throat prohibited him from speaking anymore.

He allowed Sam to help him up. The feeling had returned to his hand and so, as Sam squeezed his fingers, he could now squeeze back. When George was upright, he and Sam swayed together holding on to each other. It was Asa who eventually reached around them and put the key into the lock.

When neither he nor Sam made a move to go inside, Asa said with a hint of youthful exasperation in his voice, "Are you going in, or what?"

George lifted his head and peered over Sam to Asa. "It's okay with you?" he asked.

Asa nodded without hesitation, which, at this very moment, was as good a response as George could have hoped for. It may be that Asa was just trying to get his father and George out of the hall to spare him any further awkwardness. Or not. George would have to wait and see because he wasn't going anywhere anytime soon. Either way, George followed Sam over the threshold and into the apartment while Asa, bringing up the rear, closed the door firmly behind the three of them.

part three

Kate

THINGS I WANT(ED) TO DO TODAY

*J*ust as Kate was ready to leave work for the evening, Benjamin Harris stuck his head in the doorway of her office and asked if they could have breakfast in the morning. Keep it private, he'd requested. Kate's throat closed up. This was it, she was sure, her offer for partner. She agreed, with a nod, and he had smiled and disappeared. After that, she used her nerves as an excuse to have a cigarette. Officially, this meant she was up to ten in one day.

Considering that *before* she found the list written on the back of an envelope offering her father financial freedom from Citibank, *before* his funeral, she only allowed herself two stress-relieving smokes per week—four if she was trying a particularly arduous case—she could hardly believe she still kept count. But of course that was her way of telling herself that she had it all under control. If she could still count, then she wasn't a nicotine addict. Any addictions were a sign of weakness, and as far as Kate was concerned, self-discipline, self-control, and self-deprivation were worthy characteristics in an attorney. Her only allowable excess should be her job.

The first thing she did every night when she came in the door was remove her clothes and put them on the balcony of her tenth-floor Foggy Bottom apartment to air out. She gave the fine Italian wool jacket a good shake before she slipped it onto the padded hanger and then did the same for the slacks. She paused a moment. From the balcony she could see the lights of the Watergate Hotel and always, always, felt a pang of sadness for being born too late. She thought that presently there were too many crybabies in the law profession (and the world in general, but that was another story) and she felt a nostalgia for the seventies, for Deep Throat, for good old investigative journalism, for that buffoon G. Gordon Liddy and, of course, Richard Nixon. The last good political gaffe had been the Clintons'. And yet Ken Starr had made so many litigious bungles with Whitewater and the whole sex thing that he managed to turn it into a tabloid's wet dream; even the *Washington Post* couldn't rise above adding more fuel to the fire against the entire law profession. The First Amendment was a bitch.

She had been courted and courted well. So when Kate joined one of D.C.'s oldest firms fresh out of Columbia Law School, she thought she was choosing to be a part of that distinguished, honorable law profession. She wouldn't admit this to anyone, but she had envisioned herself a female version of Atticus Finch, and the firm, because she was one of three women on staff and the only attorney (the others were paralegals), had dangled the civil liberties—female equality—*Roe v. Wade* carrots in front of her. Kate had been prepared to storm the high courts with her arguments in the name of women everywhere. Instead, within a year of her accepting the offer, the managing partner dropped dead on the golf course and his son, Benjamin, took the reins. He began to woo celebrities after he handled and won a case where a certain Oscar-winning actress now in (forced) retirement had accused her very high-profile senator husband of using the Congressional Pages as his personal escort service.

Soon after that, every wronged B-list celebrity came calling. Kate actually had to write a brief based upon her study of photographs of breast augmentations noting density of tissue due to the level of saline in the implants, cup size, roundness, and nipple size, and she had been forced to use the phrase *silver dollar* and not have it refer to the coin. Soon the big publicity guns had put the firm on retainer. Now they handled legal damage control for any number of actors and actresses that Kate could watch at home on her DVD player if she so desired.

All this celebrity clientele and the possibility that she might have to show up on television at any moment, given the capricious and ridiculous nature of her clients and the advent of twenty-four-hour entertainment channels, meant that Kate had to splurge on her wardrobe. No more perfectly acceptable suits from the sale rack at Ann Taylor or Filene's Basement. Now she had Prada and Donna Karan and several pairs of Ferragamos for her feet, along with a dozen or so form-fitting white dress shirts, cashmere sweaters, and a cache of "good" accessories. Which was precisely why she treated her clothing as though it had a life of its own. Why she held the cigarette away from her body when she smoked, why she put the suits on the balcony for airing the second she took them off. And if the humiliating (albeit necessary) concession to dressing the part along with five years and eighty-hour work weeks wasn't enough to put her in the enviable position of being made partner—an offer she felt was forthcoming over eggs and coffee in less than eight hours, an offer that would make her the youngest partner in the firm—she would be gone in a heartbeat.

Now in old sweats and a faded Columbia T-shirt, she rummaged in the trash can for the bag of chips she'd thrown away in disgust last night. They were right on top where she'd left them, and she quickly picked them up before she had a chance to really think about what she was doing. With the chips, along with the remains of a very expensive bottle of wine sent to her by an appreciative client last month, Kate climbed into her unmade bed and pulled the comforter gingerly up around her. Her veneer was fragile—like a shell whose insides had been blown out and instead held in the qualifying mess she had become since her father's death. She looked at the clock. It was nearly eleven and she had to be up in six hours. She sighed and popped a chip into her mouth and chewed. Before she swallowed, she chased the chip down with a long sip of wine right from the bottle and then put the bottle down on the coaster on her nightstand. The coaster seemed to be the last holdover from her life before the funeral.

Before the funeral, Kate took as much pride in her apartment as she did in herself. Even though most mornings she rose before the sun, she'd always made her bed and rinsed her coffee mug before she left for work. She had a cleaning lady twice a week to change the linens, dust, and vacuum. She'd avoided the Pottery Barn trap and instead acquired things piece by piece from small independent shops in Georgetown and even once on a trip through rural Virginia after a long deposition at a client's house, even if that meant she didn't have a dining table for the first year after she bought the apartment. It wasn't as though she entertained. She took pleasure in the uncluttered space, the carefully chosen pieces, and that everything had its place and no one but she would ever rearrange them. At thirty-four she had officially left her youth behind. She paid a mortgage, chose paint colors, voted, scheduled regular doctor's visits, and paid taxes.

She had no distractions from work—that meant no boyfriend. She had lied to her brother George. Occasionally, she'd invented boyfriends and romantic holiday weekends in a B&B in Virginia, if the occasion arose, when, in fact, she hadn't had a boyfriend since law school. Sex was something Kate didn't really consider anymore, even though it seemed she was surrounded by it. Her clients oozed sex—they were motivated more by sex than money. And it didn't seem to matter to any of them whom they had sex with—gender was no longer an issue. They definitely didn't possess an on/off switch. That, apparently, was Kate's job.

Before the funeral, Kate thought hers had been off so long that it couldn't be turned back on, so it was a shock to find that she had reciprocated Eli's kiss more passionately than either of them expected when he'd surprised her in the chambers of the church. If she hadn't heard someone coming, if she hadn't broken away from his arms, there was no telling what she might have done. And after that Eli had been persistent. He'd left voicemails nearly every day since her father died in September. Eventually, the calls slowed down to a trickle, until a week ago, when they'd stopped.

Eli and Kate had met twelve years ago in the library over Thanksgiving break while they were seniors at an above-average state college north of New York City. With the exception of the foreign exchange students, each had thought they alone were eating ramen instead of turkey and avoiding their families. In Kate's case, there had been no reason to go home. The house was falling apart, no one would remember to defrost the turkey (if they'd even purchased one), and her three younger siblings made her crazy, while her parents (if they were even together under the same roof) fought constantly. The air was tinged with disappointment and angst, and once she'd escaped the house for college, she vowed not to be lured back by guilt. Besides, she had work to do that she couldn't get done at home. At that time she was working toward a degree in translation, and she was in the difficult middle stages where the idea of translating an obscure Italian poetess from the 1600s was becoming tedious and losing its luster. She'd yet to fully grasp the meaning of the poem and she was grumpy and frustrated and wishing she'd not been so ambitious.

Then she came upon Eli in the library, curled up asleep in the Cunningham Collections room. Sara Cunningham had been a trustee of the college, and upon her death her family had donated her books, papers, and enough money to keep said books and papers shelved for eternity. To Kate's knowledge, no one ever went into the room, and she had appropriated the serene space before the break as her own. It was the perfect place to be alone and spread out her work. To see Eli asleep in one of the upholstered chairs, arms folded against his chest, mouth open, sheen of drool apparent on his chin, was disconcerting. She studied him—his shaggy dark curls, his broad chest beneath a rumpled, bleach-pitted blue oxford-cloth shirt, his jeans and stocking feet with the holes in the toes. She did everything she could think to wake him. She coughed. She dropped her books on the table. She sang loudly off-key. Nothing worked. Eli finally woke up an hour later, stretched, grinned, and asked her out for breakfast, even though it was five o'clock in the afternoon.

It seemed Eli was hiding from his family as well—a new step-mother and stepbrother that made Eli, at twenty-one, no longer an only child. He maintained that he didn't mind being usurped; he just didn't want to bond. His plan after graduation was to travel through Europe. His philosophy degree most likely would not net him a job, since he didn't know a damn thing he could do with it.

Kate had boyfriends before, but she never had anyone like Eli in her life. When they were first together, she carried the thought of him inside of her like a secret. She would be going about her normal day: classes, library, a walk to the bank or the market, simple mundane tasks, and all of a sudden her chest would hurt—

physically ache. But it wasn't a painful ache—it was the secret of Eli that she fiercely protected. It wasn't like she had a reason to hide him; she just wanted this new indescribable thing to herself for a while. Even she, in her limited experience, knew that once everything was out in the open, it changed—appropriated by others who claimed to know exactly how you were feeling.

There wasn't a single person besides Eli who could possibly know how Kate felt. And, as she had feared, once her father knew about Eli, she couldn't get that feeling back. Her secret was simplified and tarnished—made tawdry in her father's presence. If it weren't for her father, she would have become Eli's wife, instead of the smiling, ponytailed blonde that she'd seen in a picture in their alumni magazine. She had brought the picture up close to her face in an attempt to see what was behind the eyes of Eli's wife, but her eyes looked unremarkably clear and vacant.

Kate sighed and rolled over and reached for the file folder in the top drawer of her nightstand. When she did this, a gift from her mother, a video game and DVD of her last film, slid off the pile and onto the floor. Kate sighed again. Thankfully, no one she knew in this life would ever connect her to her mother the horror-movie queen. Once she had the file in hand, she sat up, took another swallow of wine, and arranged the contents on the blanket in front of her. There was the note her father scrawled on an envelope that by now she'd memorized.

THINGS I WANT(ED) TO DO TODAY

Call: Kate

         Finn

         George

         Amy *

Kate took note that they were listed in birth order—she and her sister like female bookends for the boys. Kate assumed the star next to her sister Amy's name meant she was the only one he'd talked to that day, although, as usual, she hadn't heard this from Amy but George. Underneath their names was a paltry grocery list:

> Coffee
> Bread
> Cigs
> Aspirin

She shook her head. Had he thought that aspirin was going to help with the headaches from the tumor? Below the list were two other names:

> Miriam
> Elias

And after that, all in caps, was the phrase:

TELL MARILYN !!!!!

Kate hated the exclamation points. Hated that her father had Eli and Miriam's names on the list. What could he possibly have wanted with them? Hated herself for not answering when she had seen her father's number come up on her caller ID, because the last time he'd called he asked her for a loan of a thousand dollars that he'd never repaid. She hadn't wanted to be asked for more money by her father. She never guessed he was calling to say he was dying. She hated that Amy had been the one to answer his call, even though, to Kate's knowledge, she, like the rest of her siblings, had really no relationship with him.

But the most heartbreaking thing of all for Kate, whether she could admit it or not, was that when her father sat down and made that list, he knew before he even wrote a word that he most likely wouldn't live long enough to complete the things on it. The presence of the past tense in parentheses said volumes. She'd never know if the "today" he had written about was one day only or the next however many days he had until he died. She had avoided any visits not because she had been afraid to see him dying but because she knew he wouldn't ever admit responsibility for the role he played in redirecting Kate's life. Truth be told, she was embarrassed by her pedestrian desire for patriarchal approval. Even the thought of Amy being the only one there for him wasn't enough to guilt her into going. If there was one trait she and her father had shared, it was surely stubbornness.

She set aside the list along with a lone key on a ring that, at this point, she figured was a lost cause and rifled through the bills she'd paid with her own money. Not counting the funeral and quickie cremation, her father's death had cost her nearly fifteen thousand dollars. She'd cashed in a 401(k) to do this, which she'd just replenished with her bonus. She hadn't even dealt with the hospital yet, and none of her siblings had even asked about that bill. Amy would never ask, even though Kate had stayed up the night before the funeral going through everything at Amy's dining room table. Certainly not Finn, who drank his money, not George, who would side with Amy even if he did have available cash, and going to her mother was out of the question.

Kate closed her eyes and fell back against the pillows. When she was offered partner tomorrow, everything would be different. With that offer would come more money. Since she really had nothing to spend that money on—a vacation? more clothes? a better apartment?—she might as well let her father be solvent, in death anyway.

When the alarm went off at six, Kate was already awake, her eyes focused on the wine bottle on her nightstand. This wasn't how she expected to feel on the morning she was made partner, and certainly she never imagined that the first thing she'd see was an empty wine bottle.

Kate rose quickly, carrying the bottle and the bag of chips into the kitchen and tossing them in the trash. As an afterthought, she returned to the bedroom and grabbed the video game and DVD. She dumped those in the trash as well and then tied the bag firmly with a giant knot. Over, done. She was finished with the whole business of mourning things she couldn't change. She had to get over the pathetic funeral, her siblings, and the house that she hated growing up in, which now, courtesy of a bulldozer, was no longer there. Erased. Poof. Like magic.

She put the coffee on and then went in to take a shower and dress. She took extra care with her hair, makeup, and clothing selection—the navy Donna Karan suit and a blush-colored cashmere shell underneath, a single strand of pearls around her neck and Tiffany pearl studs in her ears—even though she was fully aware that whatever her fate this morning, what she wore was of no consequence now. Still, she'd learned early that she needed to look the part and she was willing to go there. However, when she saw herself in the hall mirror, she noticed the accoutrements of success didn't really seem to hide the melancholy lurking in her eyes. She squared her shoulders, slipped into her black trench coat, and adjusted the strap of her soft Italian leather briefcase on

her shoulder, but avoided another glance in the mirror on her way
out the door.

The restaurant they agreed to meet at was a hangout for many
who worked on the Hill. Kate, even though her days seemed far
removed from her first year at the firm, when the cases were more
political, was still recognized and greeted as she made her way to
the table where her boss sat perusing a menu.

When he put the menu down and saw Kate, he half-rose from
his chair—an antiquated greeting from another generation—even
though he was only five years Kate's senior. Kate dismissed the
gesture with her hand as unnecessary as she set down her case
and removed her coat. When she was seated, Benjamin looked at
her and smiled.

"You look stunning considering the hour," he said.

Kate tucked her chin against her chest and studied the menu,
even though she knew she'd order what would be her second cup
of coffee, along with a muffin. Her throat felt raw, funny, like she
was getting a cold. She waited until Benjamin remembered that
she wasn't a silicone-filled client that he had to flatter. Soon, she
expected, he'd return to earth and tell her that she'd made partner. Like his manners, his attitudes toward the opposite sex
seemed learned from an old movie starring Cary Grant.

"Well, Kate," Benjamin began as he cleared his throat.

Kate looked up and echoed his opening line, "Well, Benjamin."
She smiled slightly and looked off to the waitress and signaled for
her coffee, so as not to appear too fixated on what he was about to
say. Never look too eager, she reminded herself. They placed their
orders and waited until the waitress was gone.

Finally, Benjamin spoke. "How do you feel about Los Angeles?"

Kate's spine stiffened. *Los Angeles?* "I don't know. Too sunny,
I suppose?"

Benjamin laughed too hard, showing all of his teeth. Kate thought he looked feral. "Ah come on, Katie, you look like you might need a little fun in the sun."

While she and Benjamin had always maintained a strictly business relationship, Kate felt all of a sudden like she had missed something essential that may have happened between them. First of all, he was acting way too chummy; second, no one ever called her Katie. Maybe she should call him Benny. She shook her head slightly. The only bathing suit she owned was a faded red one-piece that she wore to the Y when she swam laps. *Los Angeles?*

Benjamin put his hands one on top of the other on the table in front of him and leaned forward so his face was close to Kate's. The waitress came at that moment and set down their coffees. Kate's coffee sloshed all over the saucer and the waitress reached across Kate, momentarily obscuring her view of Benjamin, to sop it up with a napkin. When she was done, Kate reached for the coffee to stall.

Benjamin continued, "So what do you say?"

"Say?" Kate asked, with the cup to her lips.

"About Los Angeles?"

Kate shook her head. "What are you asking me?"

Benjamin leaned back in his chair and said, "To head up the Los Angeles office, of course, Kate—what else would I be asking you?"

"Does this mean as a partner?"

He cocked his head off to the side and licked his lips. "Well, this is a mega opportunity—we're talking huge." He paused. "You hold the firm's future direction in your hands."

Kate could think of something else she'd like to get her hands around at this moment. She had already let on more than she wanted to when she snapped, "There shouldn't even be any pause in your answer to my question."

"When?" Kate asked.

Benjamin hesitated. "Considering all you've been through"—he stopped before he continued—"is six weeks or eight good for you?"

Kate shrugged.

"Katie," Benjamin conceded in a cloying voice, "of course partner is in your future. You're the best I have. Go to Los Angeles, wow me, and then make partner." He accepted his plate of eggs and sausage and eagerly speared some of each with a fork. He noticed Kate staring as he lifted it to his mouth and he smiled, wolflike, before he shoveled it in.

Kate looked down at her muffin and picked a blueberry off the top. She delicately placed it on her tongue. She decided she would say nothing else until she figured out her plan of action. Let Benjamin sweat it out. Let him guess whether or not she was heading to California. Maybe then, and only then, would she have him by the balls. Kate felt sick to her stomach. She had a feeling that Benjamin's balls in her hand would be precisely the kind of thing that would wow him.

Back in her office, Kate closed the door and told her secretary she didn't want to be disturbed. She sat at her desk, swiveling back and forth in her chair, because if she didn't move she was going to scream. It was the same feeling that, years ago, propelled her to take up running. Her mind never shut down but at least the physical exertion released enough endorphins that she felt calmer. She hadn't run in months, and she told herself she hadn't had the time, when the truth was she hadn't the desire. Her eye had been on the prize for so long, and now she felt like a Miss America contestant forced to strut herself in the bathing suit competition just to prove she was worthy. Her entire body hummed with an electrical energy and she could barely contain herself, but she needed to be in court in thirty minutes and a jog around the monuments just wasn't going to happen.

At the thought of the monuments she laughed out loud. Wasn't the Washington Monument the biggest fucking phallic symbol of all time? Shouldn't that have been a warning to her, when she came to D.C., that only boys with the big ones got to play here?

When she stopped swiveling in the chair, her legs continued to jiggle up and down on their own. She took several deep breaths and pulled out her cell phone. Whom would she call? She dialed her mother, only to realize that would be a terrible mistake. What would Marilyn have to say to make it better? As a child, she had vowed to never be like her. When had she ever made anything more bearable?

Before the call connected, she pressed the cancel-call button and scrolled through the numbers saved until she found Eli's. Without giving herself too much time to think, she hit SEND and then immediately stood and paced the length of her office. When he picked up, she said without indulging in small talk, "Can we meet?"

Kate's agnosticism had fueled her curiosity and later anger at the Roman Catholic Church. Especially when she discovered through the course of her translation research that the Vatican had not only priceless paintings but also manuscripts going back centuries locked in the vaults behind heavily fortressed walls in Rome. Included among those manuscripts was the work of an obscure poetess of the sixteenth century, the subject of Kate's senior thesis: Magdalena Mastopietro, who bore the stillborn child of her father and was subsequently imprisoned for having a child out of wedlock. She committed suicide three days shy of her seventeenth birthday, a day before she was scheduled for execution by the Church. The double sins of sex and suicide ensured that her soul would burn in hell for all eternity.

Kate's obsession with Magdalena's manuscript was what led her to travel to Italy after graduation, where she and Eli were able to get jobs through a program for university grads to teach English in foreign-speaking countries. The pay was nearly nothing, but with both of them working it was enough for a tiny apartment on a crooked, narrow street crammed with shops. Their apartment was above a busy cheese shop that thrummed with noise from dawn till dusk. It was hot in summer and cold in winter, had a bathtub big enough for not quite one person, and no shower. But it didn't matter. They were together, with an ocean between them and anyone who knew them.

They slept on a lumpy, down-filled mattress that came with the apartment, which faced the back of the building where two blue-shuttered windows opened onto a minuscule courtyard. Into their windows wafted the slightly tangy, sour smell of soon-to-be-spoiled milk, while just below, hidden away, was a tiny garden where a tangle of ancient grapevines and their landlady's five prolific chickens lived. Their eggs—the color was a luminous mossy taupe—were fringe benefits of being a tenant and generously provided them with frittatas several times a week.

Eli, a nonpracticing Jew his entire life, was amused by Kate's ire toward organized religion, especially what she saw as the oppression of the Roman Catholic Church and the pope, who she felt was just as bad as Hitler for stealing and hoarding art in the name of God. She claimed religion preyed upon the poor and the weak, who had so little to believe in. Sometimes she got so upset during these tirades against the Church that Eli would cover her mouth with his to get her to quiet down. He liked to tease that she worshipped at the church of Eli, especially when she moaned *oh my God* into his ear as they made love.

They signed up for a tour of the Vatican when they first arrived in Rome and, as students, were able to access what was touted as one of the secret vaults: a manuscript room. But Kate was disappointed to discover that Magdalena's was not among the manuscripts available to the public. Her repeated questioning about other supposed secret rooms only served to arouse the suspicions of their tour guide and have them watched carefully for the rest of the tour. That evening, when they got back to their apartment, Kate had taken the crucifix their landlady had hung above their bed off its nail and placed it in a drawer as Eli hummed the theme from *The Exorcist*.

Kate's father came to Florence for the first time several months into their two-year teaching commitment. Kate had been nervous and shy—anxious for things to go well, since this would be only the second time he had met Eli. But as it turned out, her father stayed only one night of his proposed weeklong visit, and most of that time they spent alone. Although he had been distracted by what he kept referring to as a prior commitment in Naples, and Kate had sent him on his way with a bottle of homemade wine from their landlady's vines along with a wedge of cheese, she was uneasy.

He had been disappointed that she had not succeeded in viewing Magdalena's manuscript and had, in fact, abandoned her idea for a book altogether. While he never said a negative word about Eli, he regarded her domestic life with slight derision. To make it worse, he and Eli had barely exchanged ten words and those were on the morning he left. Eli had been stalled in Rome with a school group, due to a train malfunction. By the time he'd gotten home, it was nearly dawn.

Perhaps that initial disaster had prepared Kate for her father's second visit. He was traveling with her brother Finn on some sort of backpacking trip. They'd already been to England, Ireland, and France, and were making their way to Italy, to Kate.

Kate convinced herself that first visit had been bad because she and Eli had still been getting used to each other and to Florence, and a visitor—especially her father—would be less forgiving of those circumstances. The second time was sure to be better. Living with Eli those past two years was more empowering and passionate than she ever imagined.

With Eli, Kate felt like someone else, in the very best of ways. And that was perfectly fine with her, since all her childhood memories were those of an intense adolescent and angry teen that felt burdened by responsibility—by keeping it all together. Now she reveled in the smallest of things: a bowl of figs, a bath drawn, a dish of marscapone drizzled with honey. She never understood before now how people found their fit with each other, but she and Eli had. She marveled at how easily they fell into their daily life, how they split the domestic duties—she cooked while Eli cleaned—and for once she held no resentment over these tasks. She didn't feel the weight of house and home like she had when she was growing up and caring for her siblings. Then she had likened them to baby birds abandoned in a nest—mouths constantly open and squawking, looking for sustenance. This was different. She was forging a life—her life.

In a short amount of time, she had let go of so much, including the poetess Magdalena, who these days rarely entered her thoughts. She had no desire to spend the next few years researching and writing a book. That idea felt like someone else's right now, even though it had been her own. What did interest her was how few rights women still had centuries later, how the origin of law, really gender-based, created a misogynistic society despite the advances of feminism. Especially in Italy, where myth seemed to be reality: men did want their women to be both Madonna and whore. The women she had gotten to know, their landlady among them (she had taught Kate how to make homemade limoncello), were a wonderfully subversive bunch. They had elevated their subterfuge to a new level that made the men they lived with believe they were in control. Of course the dramas Kate witnessed were mostly familial, in which the real power was in the kitchen with an ancient Nona ruling her large family from behind the stove.

Everywhere in Florence there were informal conversational language exchanges. Signs were posted all over the square— people offering to speak Italian with you and in turn they practiced their English. Their circle of friends was made up of people they met just this way. Eli had participated in more of the exchanges than Kate, as she was at best, socially anyway, a watcher and Eli was a doer. He jumped right into a social life. He made friends easily and was comfortable whiling away the hours after work in a café, animatedly chatting and smoking, sharing a bottle of wine.

When Kate had complained that he was spending so much time away from home, their landlady had opened up her small yard behind the cheese shop to Eli and his exchanges. Long-widowed, she seemed to enjoy the men sprawled out beneath the grapevines, laughing and arguing, chewing on waxy, yellow cheese rinds while they drank. Their voices would drift up into their bedroom windows and Kate would lean over the sill for a look—the hot sun bearing down on her head and the tops of her shoulders.

Sometimes Eli would glance up and wave, but more often than not he would be too involved in some long philosophy discussion, and eventually Kate would close the shutters and retreat to the front of the apartment.

Other than that (and really, could she deny Eli a social life outside of her?), their life together was as close to perfect as Kate could ever imagine. Sometimes she felt giddy, like the besotted teen she had never been, doodling her boyfriend's name in her notebook—dreaming of a long white dress and a walk down the aisle. She had settled into a comfortable life and she couldn't imagine anything disturbing that happiness. She hadn't been back in the States in two years and had only minimal phone contact with her mother and siblings. Their future was a given—Eli wanted to get married as soon as possible and he saw no reason to wait. He was pushing for her to tell her father when he arrived. Kate was confident that her father would see how she had flourished.

So when her father showed up without Finn or an explanation, she was relaxed and off her guard. She had gained weight from the wine and pasta and cheese, which had added softness not only to her face and hips but to her demeanor as well, and it made a difference in how she moved through the world. She didn't bother to pester her father with questions and particulars. Her family had always lacked in execution and follow-through anyway. Besides, in truth, she preferred that her father was here alone—she was proud to show her father the woman she had become, and in the presence of her brother she wasn't sure if she would have the same confidence, or if her life would appear so bright and shiny.

Her father was at his most charming—his mood ebullient and generous. He arrived on a break, so both she and Eli had several days to entertain him before they had to go back to work. It would give Eli and her father time to get to know each other. On the first night, her father gifted Kate with a slim gold bangle bracelet to make up for the birthdays he'd missed in the last few years. Kate saw the slight stiffness in his jaw as he made his presentation and pointedly glanced at Eli—but she tossed it off as nerves. Hers or his she wasn't sure and then she convinced herself they were hers most likely. He joined Eli and his foreign language group friends for a long afternoon of wine. He praised every meal Kate cooked, no matter they were humble affairs of eggs, cheese, bread, and tomatoes, and when finally, on Sunday evening, after several hours in their favorite restaurant, Eli told her father they intended on marrying, soon, her father had reached across the table and, turning her wrist over, had stroked the inside of her arm by running the bracelet up and down while he openly struggled and searched for something to say.

After an awkward moment, Kate had pulled her arm away and put her hand in Eli's lap. Eli took her cold fingers and squeezed them while her father recovered from the shock of his twenty-four-year-old daughter's intentions, smiled broadly, and filled their glasses to the brim in order to toast their happiness. Eli had squeezed her fingers again, as if to say there was nothing to worry about, and they lifted their glasses.

On the surface, it appeared that Eli should not have worried, for her father's campaign was ever so subtle. He started with the most innocuous of questions about their life, their plans for the future. Would they live in Italy for a few more years? Sign another contract to teach? Shouldn't they go back to the States and see if they could handle life there instead of living in this fairy tale?

All together, these questions would have been tantamount to attack. Taken one at a time, over a meal or on a meandering walk through town in search of the perfect espresso, they were just parental nudges about the future. Never mind that her father hadn't been a parent in the most basic of capacity. He was interested now and Kate found herself drawn in and aching to please under his very intense, singular attention. Even though she was the oldest of four—and therefore the only one of her siblings to have ever been alone with their parents as a child—she couldn't remember a time when her father's focus was solely on her, and it was, she was embarrassed to admit, intoxicating.

Soon it was her father and not she who pointed out that Eli seemed to be taking longer and longer to come home after work. And when he did arrive home, he always smelled of wine and smoke and on one occasion had actually stumbled into the dining table long cleared from a supper he did not join them to eat. In bed, he turned his back on her, sullen, like a little boy unused to sharing his favorite toy. Their sex life had suffered as well and had reached an all-time low the afternoon her father's trip to Calabria had been canceled and he surprised them by coming back into the apartment, causing them to jump out of bed and hop around the room scrambling for clothes. Later on, Eli would tell her that he was sure her father planned that—he was trying to drive them apart—but Kate had refused to believe her father was capable of any evil machination.

The night her father had surprised them, Eli was unusually persistent in his quest for her body. His hands were everywhere, as though he had something to prove, until she relented in the dark, beneath the blankets, while her father slept on the cot on the other side of the wall. It was the least satisfying, impersonal sex they had ever had, and neither of them could bear to look at the other in the morning.

Kate begged Eli to be a little more understanding—this was her father and he wouldn't be here forever. When he was gone, she thought, they would go back to the way things were before. Eli responded by staying away. He explained that he was trying to salvage what they had, and while he knew he was being unreasonable, he didn't trust himself to not make the situation worse. Kate was scared and eventually confided in her father, naively believing that he would offer her some guidance on the male psyche—she didn't want to drive Eli further away.

On his last evening in Florence, she and her father went to dinner alone. Before he said anything, he placed his hands on either side of her head. He touched her hair and gathered it loosely in his fingers until he formed pigtails. He smiled and tugged on them, as if to say, *Remember?* Kate had squirmed in her seat. Finally, he told her she was too young to marry. That neither she nor Eli were to blame; they just needed to grow and experience life without each other. He hinted that Eli was directionless and too weak for someone like her. While he might make her happy now, he would never be capable of keeping her happy. When Kate confronted him and asked if he had shared his opinion with Eli, he played coy, but she knew that he must have suggested as much.

Instead, in an abrupt change of subject, he claimed that it pained him to see Kate settling into becoming a housewife when she had a brilliant mind—a mind that could make a difference and change the world. After he tried flattery, he urged her to go back to school—to consider law, politics even. He knew she had taken the LSAT test before she had graduated from college because, before Eli, a secondary degree had always been her plan. He said he couldn't force her to do anything—she was an adult—but if she married Eli now, he would be tremendously disappointed.

Her father left at dawn the next day. He'd been with them a little over ten days. She heard him shuffling around in the other room as he gathered his things. She waited until she heard his footsteps retreat and the courtyard door latch strike against the post as he swung it shut behind him before she went in search of Eli. She found him asleep, curled on his side, snoring under the arbor in the backyard.

Alone for the first time in weeks, they didn't make love; they didn't even really talk. They just lay next to each other, shoulder to shoulder, with their fingers loosely twined as the sun came up. Kate had pictured how they must look from above the bed: like corpses side by side. Her father's presence had colored everything. When she examined her life with Eli, where there had once been nothing but light, there was now a web of tiny dark fissures.

To start over, Kate and Eli went on holiday to Greece. He surprised her with a ring one morning when she was waking from a dream, sliding it onto the ring finger of her left hand. Drowsy, through half-open lids, Kate had allowed him to remove the bracelet her father had given her and place it on the table next to the bed. It wasn't until a week later, when they returned to Florence, that she remembered she had left it there. By then it was too late to call and ask the hotel if someone had found it and turned it in. She imagined it on the wrist of a deeply tanned, thin-armed girl with long, dark hair. Occasionally, she would make a circle around her wrist with her thumb and forefinger where the bracelet once was. She would feel sad for a moment, and then her eyes would catch the carved silver band that Eli had placed on her finger.

Soon after their trip, when the equilibrium had been delicately restored and plans for their future seemed more real than ever, Kate received a package from her father. Inside, there was no note, just a thick sheaf of applications from a collection of the best law schools in the United States. Kate took the envelope and shoved it into an empty suitcase on top of the wardrobe. She didn't want Eli to find it and yet she couldn't bring herself to throw it away. Even if they did decide to return to the States, going back to school seemed an indulgent and frivolous idea.

During this time, Kate began tutoring a student after school hours. She wasn't grateful so much for the money as she was for the time it filled in her head. Time she didn't have to think about what to do next. Their teaching contracts ended in August and Eli was in the process of training his replacement while Kate was waiting for hers to arrive. She had not taken the option to renew the contract for another two years because it seemed like too much time, but now she wasn't so sure. Eli was incapable of committing to one thing—he just wanted to marry and travel and pick up work where they could. He didn't think about the practical things like travel visas and where to live. She felt too old for a hostel and not old enough for a real home.

The worst times were when she couldn't get rid of her father's voice in her ear, when she would take out the applications and sit cross-legged on the bed while she idly fantasized about going back to school. She even went so far as to write an essay, request a transcript with her grades and LSAT scores, and fill out the applications to Columbia and NYU. When she posted them, she told herself it wasn't so much about going back to the States as it was about having a plan, a plan she wouldn't really follow through with.

When Kate's replacement arrived, she had even more unstructured time. After training, she was supposed to let the girl take charge of the class while Kate was available only in an observatory position. So when the father of her tutorial student asked Kate to assist him with his English—just a little conversation over coffee, as he put it—Kate had obliged. She was trying to put a little space between herself and Eli. They'd recently rehashed a bitter fight and parted with angry words hanging like ghosts in the air, waiting for them to resume the argument when they returned.

The argument had started when Eli offhandedly told her that their landlady had stopped and asked him when they were moving out. Eli had told her they'd be gone in six weeks. When Kate asked him where they were going, he had smiled and shrugged and kissed her hard on the mouth and said they'd figure something out. Of course Kate couldn't let that go, and before long there was yelling and doors slammed. Hinges held in place by century-old hand-hewn pins shuddered and Eli was gone.

Coffee with Dominick was just what she needed to get her mind off the turmoil with Eli. Dominick told her in English (which was far better than she expected) that he and his daughter, Pia, were planning a visit to relatives who lived in northern California. They had a winery, the family business, he explained almost shyly, and he didn't want to be an embarrassment. He was refreshing—humble and charming yet not at all salacious in the way desire and sex oozed from most Italian men, and so Kate agreed to meet him again after Pia's next lesson. As she walked home from the café, she realized for the first time in weeks that she felt light and nearly relaxed.

She continued to meet Dominick and Pia, separately, twice a week. One afternoon, she was early and she sat going through the mail she had just retrieved from the post office, with a coffee and a thick dark chocolate pastry on the table in front of her. She had hoped to share the pastry with Dominick but had eaten most of it already when she came upon the acceptance letter to Columbia Law School. Foreign post being what it was, the deadline to reply was in two days. When Dominick arrived, she was in a panic.

Without really thinking—without talking to Eli—she made the decision to accept Columbia's offer. She allowed Dominick to give her a ride on the back of his motorbike to his office, where he had a fax machine. When the fax had been sent and received, she looked up at Dominick and started to sob as she realized the gravity of her decision. When Dominick put his arms around her and hugged her tight against his chest, she didn't back away. She found herself grateful to be crying against his shoulder while he massaged the tension from her neck.

Soon it seemed that Kate and Eli were always starting a fresh argument on top of an unfinished argument. Even the most innocuous words strung together escalated rapidly into a full-blown debate of which there was no end and no winner in sight. Kate didn't set out to destroy what she had left with Eli, but that was precisely what she did. Any hope of quietly slipping out the back door of the life they'd made had gone by the wayside the moment she had told him what she had done. It was not that he was opposed to Columbia or law school, if that was what she really wanted; it was the subterfuge. That the applications had come from her father made it all the worse, proving the point that Eli had tried in vain to make to her before and that she adamantly refuted: her father was trying to drive them apart.

Since the hug that afternoon in his office, Dominick slowly revealed his true nature. His advances were more overt, and oddly, Kate rationalized, by succumbing to Dominick it was she and she alone that would drive Eli away. It would have nothing to do with her father, as Eli had insisted. Certainly not the ideal father that had finally materialized in Italy, the father Kate had been waiting for her entire life. Kate would prove to be the unreliable one, not as steadfast as she had led Eli to believe. If there was blame to place, it should be with her. Years later, she would regret this one rash decision that altered the course of her life. But caught in the moment, she couldn't find her way back to the Kate she had been before her father had visited.

When Dominick kissed her and removed her clothes, she cried. He mistook it for a bubbling-over of emotion at their passion for each other and responded with vigorous sex that left her sore and bruised as she made her way back to Eli and their apartment. She supposed that Eli might have forgiven her a single indiscretion, so she made sure that he wouldn't, by returning to Dominick several more times.

By that last night with Dominick, she was diminished. Shame didn't even begin to cover what she felt as she dressed and left his flat. As she walked quickly down the narrow side streets, she bowed her head and refused to meet the eyes of anyone, and yet her Italian was good enough to understand what the old ladies hanging out their laundry in the early morning hours whispered behind her back.

The extent of what she had destroyed was only just becoming evident. Peeling back a minuscule corner on the life they'd shared was absolute torture. Still, she ran the reel over and over in her head, back to the beginning, when every day with Eli had been amazing and she had felt impossibly full, engorged by the unexpected bounties in her life. On the plane leaving Florence and Eli behind, she felt small and hollow in her bottomless grief. Even the silver band—once so tight against her plump finger that a ridge of flesh puffed above and below the thick edge—slid effortlessly from her hand somewhere between their apartment and the airport, leaving behind pinched, hard, calloused skin as a reminder. She was so empty, in fact, that if the seat belt hadn't held her down in her seat, Kate was sure destiny would have sucked her out the window, hurtling her through space for an eternity. As the engines of the plane had roared beneath her during the ascent, Kate prayed to God for forgiveness, knowing full well it was unlikely that either really existed.

For only the second time in her professional career (the first having been for the funeral of her father), Kate cleared her schedule. She drove north the next morning to a small town along the river in Pennsylvania, the purported halfway point between D.C. and Eli's home in Beacon, New York. There was snow here and plateaus of ice that floated on top of the water. She stopped once to go to the bathroom and get a cup of coffee. While she was in the bathroom, she took her hair out of its ponytail and shook it out all over her shoulders, only to secure it again once she got back in the car.

When she reached the coffee shop off the interstate that Eli had given her directions to, she was surprised to see that it was a restaurant and a gas station attached to one of those low-slung seventies-style motels. In the parking lot were several tractor-trailers as well as minivans and SUVs. The sun was bright and made it hard for her to see as she parked and walked toward the glass doors, unsure where to go and why she had come so far for a memory.

No one paid attention to her when she entered the restaurant. She looked around for Eli but didn't see him, so she took the seat closest to the door, at the counter, and waited. She accepted coffee and a menu but touched neither.

When the door opened, bringing with it a burst of frigid air and Eli, she felt such relief that she was afraid she might break down and cry right then.

Eli placed his hand on her shoulder and then took the stool next to her at the counter. Wordlessly, they searched each other's faces as the waitress plunked down another menu. There had been ten years between then and now. Kate didn't count the tussle at her father's funeral—she couldn't even recall if she'd actually taken in his face that day as she had reached for him. Now here he was, looking not that much different than all those years ago.

She reached out a hand to touch him and he smiled and nodded and seemed to know that she was just checking to make sure it was real.

He unzipped his bright blue jacket but kept it on as he said in a low voice, "How are you, Kate?"

She grimaced and he smiled back, although there was a wrinkle of concern in his brow.

"I thought so," he said.

They started safe, talking like old friends catching up on each other's lives. She told him stories about her work, name-dropping just to see him smile and hear him laugh. He told her about the bar/restaurant that he and his wife owned on the Hudson River. His wife was the chef, had gone to the culinary institute in Hyde Park. In the summer they did a brisk business in kayak rentals. Shyly, he mentioned he had two children—a boy, who was obsessed with anything electronic, and a baby girl almost a year old.

Oddly enough, when he talked about the boy, Kate thought of the game her mother had sent her that was now wrapped securely in her trash can—Eli's son probably would have liked it.

It didn't take long to exhaust those subjects. "What do we do now?" she asked.

Eli reached into his back pocket for his wallet and placed a dollar on the counter to pay for Kate's coffee, then he stood and led her out of the restaurant to his car. In the bright sunlight, in full view of the large glass windows in front of the restaurant, Eli pressed her back against his car and kissed her deeply. His jacket was still unzipped and Kate burrowed inside. Frantically, her hands yanked at his sweater and then the T-shirt underneath. She wanted to feel his skin. She was hungry and cold, and being up against Eli had, in a matter of seconds, become a fixation. She wanted Eli, and at the moment she didn't give a damn if he belonged to someone else.

Reading her mind, Eli fumbled in his pocket for his keys and unlocked the car. Their bodies were still connected, and Eli laughed softly and said, "One of us is going to have to go around to the other door. I have bucket seats."

Reluctantly, Kate sidled out from underneath him and walked around to the passenger side. Her legs felt like jelly and she was grateful for the seat. When she turned to face Eli as he got into the car, she caught sight of a car seat in the back. Eli followed her stricken gaze and shook his head in response. "Oh Kate," he said, with his forehead against the steering wheel.

Kate reached up and touched the sliver of skin exposed at the back of his neck. His dark hair curled up along the collar. He was so warm. If she tried hard, she could pretend his skin was warmed from the Mediterranean sun after an hour under the arbor in their little yard in Florence. He was her Eli. In a completely nonsensical way, she reasoned that *her* Eli predated his wife and his children, and so this was okay. She continued to knead the back of his neck and he moaned and looked up at her. How many times had she seen that exact same look from above or below her all those years ago?

The first time they made love on the scratchy sheets and stiff blankets of the motel bed, Kate was not altogether sure she had been in her body. She had responded to Eli as if no time had passed. There was no part of their skin left untouched and Kate couldn't be sure what cries came out of whose mouth when they came. When they were done, they lay shuddering, breathing heavily, sweaty and chilled at the same time. Kate lay between Eli's legs, her head on his stomach. Eli's hands were in her hair. When she recovered enough to lift her head, she traced with her finger the hair that grew in a line from Eli's groin up to his belly button. It was then she noticed the scar on his lower right side. An appendix scar that was still new enough to be pink. She traced that as well and then gave it a kiss. She felt Eli stir again against her and she laughed before she took him in her mouth. She felt greedy. She licked and sucked until Eli cried out again and then he rolled her onto her back and they watched each other's faces as he brought her to orgasm, understanding somehow that it was important to remember everything about this moment.

They slept, and when Kate woke, the room was completely dark and she was naked with Eli curled around her back like an apostrophe. She reached down for the blankets and sheets and pulled them up over their bodies until they were tented. Eli stirred and nuzzled his face into the back of her head.

"Are you okay?" he mumbled.

"Yes . . . no . . . I don't know," Kate admitted, then laughed.

"I'm glad to see counsel is so decisive," Eli joked.

At the mention of her real-life occupation, Kate was quiet. She hadn't told him anything about the offer of Los Angeles. The partner snub.

"Hey," Eli said and tightened his arm around her. "Hey," he said again.

"Why did you come to the funeral?" Kate asked, flinching from the memory of the nearly empty church.

Eli hesitated. Kate could feel it in his body.

"Come on," she urged and nudged him with her hip.

When he hesitated still, Kate rolled away from him, turned on the bedside light, and got out of bed. Naked, she hunched over from the cold and hopped around the room looking for her bag. When she found what she wanted, she ran back to the bed and got under the blankets. Eli blinked at her several times and focused on what she held in front of his face.

He shimmied up and squished a pillow beneath his head against the wall and took the piece of paper she offered. When he was done reading, he peered at her from over the top of the envelope.

"He did call me," Eli admitted.

Kate was surprised. Her father hadn't checked off his name like he had Amy's. But she waited and said nothing. With Eli, she had never needed to spell things out.

"He wanted to know why I didn't fight for you, why I let you go." Eli paused. "When I didn't give him an answer that he wanted to hear, he told me he was sick and that it was too late for regret." He looked down at the note again and frowned but didn't say anything more until a minute later, when he added, "I think he meant for him, though—not me. I'm not sure, although, for me" he shrugged, "it goes without saying."

Kate cleared her throat. She thought carefully about what she should say next. If she admitted to Eli that her father had told her all those years ago that she would be making the biggest mistake of her life should she marry him, that he was weak and without purpose and he would never make her happy, it would serve no one. She didn't know then that one person could never be everything; she'd been too young to understand that there would always be something about the other person that got on your nerves. Surely, she understood now, her father had been wrong. Eli seemed, on the surface anyway, to be making someone happy while Kate hadn't felt a thing since she had left him.

"So, you let him believe that it was your fault?" Kate asked, slightly out of breath.

Eli nodded and avoided her eyes. Kate felt a flicker of the old anger for her father. Why had he questioned Eli, when the dissolution of their engagement had been his seed to plant? What purpose would mucking up all that old pain serve? Obviously, this was her legacy—her father's parting shot at her. Or it could just have been the rantings of a sick man. She'd never know. She asked again, "But why come to the funeral?"

"When I saw the obit in the *Times*, I wanted to see you—make sure you were okay." He paused. "There were so many times . . ."

Kate nodded and looked down at the blankets. She thought but couldn't bring herself to say: *I'm sorry.* Maybe if Eli weren't a husband and a father, she would have the courage to say it out loud and to see where it would take them. Instead, she repeated it like a mantra in her head. *I'm sorry, I'm sorry, I'm sorry.*

Eli laughed a little. "I was more than a little surprised by your greeting."

She elbowed him and blushed, even though, under the sheets, they were currently naked in a motel bed. She remembered the hug that had turned into a kiss, all initiated by her when he'd surprised her in the chambers behind the altar. "How was it that no one saw you?"

He shrugged. "I just didn't make myself known, I guess." He hesitated. "I . . . well . . . after that . . . you know I tried to talk to you but you never took my calls and eventually I figured it was better that way. That I had no right given that I am"—he cleared his throat and whispered the last part—"that I am married and you have a life and we really have no place with each other anymore."

Kate took note of the present tense and turned on her side to face him. "Is that what you really feel?" She had been right, after all, not to apologize for the past.

Eli searched her face. He neither denied nor acknowledged any feelings for her. Instead, he answered her with his own question: "Isn't that how you feel?"

Kate didn't know how she felt about anything lately. She didn't know anything about Eli's life except the absolute basics. Where had he gone when he left their apartment in Florence? How had he come to have the life he led? Had he made the choice or had it been made for him? Did she want him to tell her that he got up with his children in the middle of the night when they called out from a bad dream? That he held his wife's hand and cried as each of their children was born? She couldn't answer that. Instead, she sat up and began searching the sheets for her bra and underpants. Both, she recalled, had been shed in seconds and tossed aside without thought that there would be a later, a *now*.

Eli started to say, "You could stay the night—the room is . . ." But then he stopped mid-sentence.

She was conscious of Eli watching her as she found her clothes and dressed, but he didn't say anything more or move from the bed. Kate couldn't find her bra, so she pulled on her sweater and concentrated on fastening the tiny little buttons. Three of them were missing. That must have happened when Eli had tugged it apart out of frustration. Her nipples, sore from Eli's mouth, ached as they rubbed against the cashmere. Thinking of how Eli rolled her nipples between his teeth caused a rush of wetness between her legs. She wanted to get back into bed with Eli and stay there forever; instead, she pulled on her socks, pants, and then boots, and stood at the end of the bed. She had hours to drive before she got home.

He held her father's note out to her. "You want this?"

Kate shook her head. She had it memorized. She shrugged into her jacket and picked up her bag. With her hand on the door-knob, she turned and looked back at Eli one more time before she left. This was a better ending than the first time. The first time she'd left, he had been begging her to change her mind. They were both crying. The kind of tears that hurt so much that she was sick to her stomach. She remembered retching in between sobs, her stomach in spasms. The ticket back to the States had been in her pocket along with the acceptance letter from Columbia Law School.

That time, the last thing Eli had said to her was "Please don't do this to us."

This time, Kate said, "I may be moving to Los Angeles."

Eli's face registered surprise and then, almost as if he realized he had no right to that emotion, he nodded and quickly said, "Good for you." His voice broke on the word *you*, but when Kate looked up one last time, Eli's face betrayed nothing.

Kate's legs were shaking as she walked to her car. It was dusk. She checked her watch, surprised that it was only just after five. It wasn't until she was back on the interstate heading south that she allowed herself to cry.

It took all her willpower to stay on the road, not to turn the car around and ask Eli to come away with her even if he already had a life that she was no part of—that she had no right to. It was better this way, she knew, better that she would never know what choice he'd make. Better that she'd never really know that this time it wouldn't be her.

seven

THIS IS THE PART WHERE
HISTORY REPEATS ITSELF

*T*here were too many condos to count, although Kate was sure her Realtor, Naomi, was secretly recording the many hours of wasted time in the BlackBerry that was glued to her hand. Since moving to Los Angeles several months ago, Kate had toured multiple units indistinguishable from one another save for the address. They all had a balcony. That balcony, in turn, had a view. Some had a view of the hills, while others had a view of downtown Los Angeles. All views came with a scrim of smog, so, in Kate's opinion, it really didn't matter what was outside the windows. The bathrooms had "spa features" and the kitchens had stainless-steel appliances and granite countertops. The walls were painted in shades of white that were touched with gray or blue but never beige. Whether it was Century City or Mid Wilshire, Kate quickly found out that every preconceived notion she held about Los Angeles was true.

The problem was that now Kate really needed to get out of the hotel. Putting off searching for a home while setting up the office, she'd been living out of suitcases for too long. Five fucking stars and still she avoided going back to her hotel room, instead ordering dinner at her desk and staying so late every night that the security guard insisted upon walking her to her car in the underground garage. The combined hotel bill and her furniture in storage back in D.C. were costing the firm a small fortune. And although Ben would never mention the money, every time they talked he inquired (with just a hint of an edge to his voice) about her apartment search, to which Kate's answers had grown increasingly vague. How could she explain to Ben that she just couldn't make a commitment, when he was banking the firm's success and her future partnership on the Los Angeles office?

Every time Kate went out with Naomi, she saw nothing she could picture herself living in and she didn't know why. She even tried some relaxation technique she had once read about in a magazine in her dentist's waiting room years ago when she had gone for an emergency root canal. She was supposed to close her eyes and breathe deep and imagine herself somewhere safe and loved. But what she saw instead, when she closed her eyes, was her father at his desk, after she came home from school. Often he would be muttering to himself as he read aloud what he had written that day. Sometimes he would repeat a sentence over twenty times. Each time after he did, he would frown, scratch his eyebrow or his scalp, pick up his pen to write, only to put the pen down, and say the sentence out loud all over again. He would never look up to see her standing there, and eventually she would leave and go into the kitchen and make the little kids peanut butter and jelly sandwiches that they ate while she did her homework. The relaxation technique only scared her and made her heart race, so she gave up on that.

Kate was lost. Utterly and completely lost. Although she would rather die than admit it, for once she needed someone to help her figure it out, to offer an opinion. The only person she could think of was Eli, but she would not allow herself to call him, even though he had left three urgent messages on her cell since they'd seen each other and half a dozen other calls she had refused to pick up. Kate needed to be steadfast. He had nothing to do with this life, and dragging Eli into the mix would get her nowhere.

Of course, Kate could tell herself that all she wanted, but Eli, tucked deeply into a pocket of her subconscious, was at least part of the reason she called her Realtor from the side of the road and asked her to find out information on the house for sale behind the gate she was currently staring at. The gate was padlocked with a knot of chain so old it had turned to a nearly unrecognizable ball of rust. The FOR SALE sign was faded and overgrown by vines, but Kate could still make out enough numbers that she could recite them into the phone as she left Naomi a voicemail. Tempted by the locked gate and the bramble of trailing plants, she got out of the car and walked up the drive as far as she could. It was a short, broken trail of gravel and rock at the bend of the road, barely enough to get a car safely over to the shoulder to make the turn unless you knew where you were going. On either side of the gate were boulders that at one time had approximated a stone wall about eight feet high with jagged pieces of glass embedded along the top to prohibit anyone from scaling the wall. Kate could see nothing beyond the forgotten landscaping, and so she got back into the car unsatisfied.

That morning, she had driven north of Los Angeles to an area called Silver Lake. Since she had been in Los Angeles, Kate had probably driven more than she had in all her years in Washington. It was true when they said no one walked in L.A. proper, although here, where it was more residential, Kate could see thin scraps of sidewalk where children zoomed unevenly on bikes and scooters, while adults, draped in brightly colored layers of clothing, stood in clusters talking. There was something familiar about them and yet there was not one specific memory. They reminded her of her parents in those once-upon-a-time years that now seemed like something she must have dreamed.

She had come to Silver Lake to meet a client as a favor to Ben. He had asked that she handle this case personally and not pass it off to one of the junior associates. The client was a widow of an artist whose name meant nothing to Kate but Ben swore was famous. (A quick Google search confirmed that, but still, to Kate he remained anonymous.) The widow was his second wife and was being sued by the son from his first wife. He wanted access to his late father's studio, so she had a guard posted outside (if Kate hadn't seen him, she would have sworn it was untrue). Paintings were involved, as well as an endowment to MOMA in San Francisco. Apparently, Ben was an old college friend of this woman's son from her union with the artist, hence the favor. And Kate wanted to be made partner, hence the acquiescence.

The widow, Shelley, met Kate at the door barefoot, dressed in a pink caftan with little tiny mirrors along the hem that caught the light as she walked. Stringy gray hair fell nearly to her waist and several strands kept getting caught in the bell sleeves of her caftan as she gestured at some paintings she was sure Kate would recognize. They were bold studies of saturated colors, one bleeding into the next in horizontal lines, which Kate failed to understand or see the beauty in, but she did not let on that she didn't recognize them. Then Shelley pointed to the guard out back, on the far side of the pool, policing the building that Kate assumed housed the studio. While Shelley walked Kate to the door of the studio, she did not invite her to look inside. She made it clear to Kate that would be something saved for a later visit. It was obvious to Kate that Shelley viewed her as a member of the sellout generation and was only putting up with the law because her stepson had forced her into this position.

After their meeting, which Kate had left with five boxes of paperwork that the widow said contained her husband's last wishes (Kate had lifted the corner of one of the lids only to find scribbling on the backs of envelopes, takeout menus, and torn scraps of paper), she had taken a wrong turn and ended up on the street in front of the house with the padlocked gate that was for sale.

Ordinarily, she didn't believe in signs. Nothing about her life up until this point had been propitious, left to chance or whimsy. Her sister was one of those people, ruled by desire, never thinking about the consequences. Amy had the moral compass of a Ping-Pong ball. Even agreeing to finally meet Eli after all those years had been a decision Kate agonized over. But there was something about that gate, and even more so about the thought of the house beyond, that made her curious enough to call Naomi. After she left her a second *I really need you to call me back now* voicemail, Kate drove into a more commercial area of town instead of getting back on the freeway and heading south toward downtown.

From the car, she could see several coffeehouses, art galleries, bookstores, and clothing boutiques. She parked her leased Lexus next to a van whose back window and bumper were crusted with socially conscious bumper stickers. Everywhere she looked, there were statements of civic activism ranging from organic farms to impassioned pleas to buy local that rarely entered Kate's speech. She went into the first coffee shop she came to and was never more aware of her black pantsuit and pearls. As Kate sat with her coffee at a table by the window, she fingered the strand of pearls self-consciously. But as she looked around the room, she realized no one was paying any attention to her. Some were reading, some were minding babies and talking, some were scribbling in notebooks. The ages probably ranged from her sister Amy's age to a little older than herself. When she thought of Amy, she fidgeted in her chair. If Amy could see her here right now, she would probably smirk and say: "Who are you kidding?"

She was about to abandon the foolish notion of the hidden house and chalk it up to a lark when her phone buzzed. It was Naomi calling her back.

"What is it?" Kate asked, trying to quell the sudden excitement.

"A dump," Naomi said with a sigh. She paused for dramatic effect. "A tear-down."

Kate heard the word *tear-down* and immediately thought of her childhood home no longer there, a stone-and-glass monstrosity in its place. Had that been the selling point her mother had offered to the people who purchased it?

"Kate? Are you there? Kate?"

She cleared her throat to indicate she was still on the other end of the phone, but she couldn't speak, not yet. If she even attempted to articulate what she was feeling . . . shit, who was she kidding? She didn't even know what the hell she was feeling. Why all this emotion? Why now? Why was she so . . . so . . . so . . . clogged? Clogged. She thought about how she and her siblings had trespassed in the dark like thieves carrying the box of their father's ashes. If she tried, she could still feel the soft dirt at the edge of the bank give way where her heels sunk into the mud. In response, Kate curled her toes inside her pumps as she felt a choking feeling in the back of her throat. She tried to lift her coffee to her lips but her hand was shaking so badly that she put the cup down. My God, she needed to get a grip.

"We've been looking at condos, Kate," Naomi continued. "This isn't exactly move-in condition. And it's in Silver Lake. Have you driven around Silver Lake?"

"I'm sitting in a coffee shop right now."

"In Silver Lake?" Naomi asked. "Really?"

"Yes," Kate said harshly. A girl a few tables away from Kate looked up at her but then looked away when Kate caught her eye. Kate lowered her voice, picked up her coffee, and went out onto the sidewalk. "If you don't want to help me, I'll find another Realtor."

Naomi stammered. "I'm only asking you these questions because you never mentioned anything like this before. You wanted no maintenance and modern, close to the office. That's what I've been trying to give you."

Kate sighed. She had chosen Naomi as her agent because she had been the only one on the entire associates' sheet that had brown hair. The rest had been bleached, blow-dried, and Botoxed, and brown-haired Naomi had stood out as a beacon of sensibility and reason. And now? Of course she was right when she told Kate she had given her what she wanted all along. Yet even as Kate questioned what on earth she was thinking by wanting to see the house, she said, "Well, maybe I've changed my mind."

"Okay," Naomi said. "I'll see what I can do about getting you in there."

Before she left Silver Lake, Kate drove back to the property. She edged the car off the road and parked but didn't get out. All those years of growing up in that run-down house, hating every single minute of it, counting the days until she could escape, and yet, she imagined she felt like her father probably did when he had found that house for them. Kate conveniently forgot the truth: that he bought the house because he had cash and his accountant advised him that he needed a write-off. She forgot that he fancied himself a handyman yet never completed a task. After that initial windfall to purchase the house, there was never enough cash to hire anyone, so things were left to disintegrate. Through the years, the house was overrun by animals in the eaves and the attic, faulty wiring that threatened fires, and windows that didn't open, while her father holed up in his study, pretending to write or worse.

But Kate was nothing if not practical, wasn't she? And practical Kate tried to justify looking at this house by reasoning that her condo in Foggy Bottom had sold before the listing even went public. She had made a killing, so much so that if she didn't buy something to roll over the profits into, she'd be screwed in capital gains alone, come tax season.

She sighed as she turned the key in the ignition. She was getting way ahead of herself. What was she thinking? Was she buying a house for a dead man? Or for the imaginary life she wanted with the man she couldn't have?

The contents of the artist's boxes were strewn across the floor of Kate's office. She had attempted piles according to importance, although most of what was here amounted to incoherent diatribes. So far, only a few passages alluded to art and they were broad at best, mostly about the texture and color of the stucco on his next-door neighbor's pool house. The writing was unremarkable save for the lone exception, a love letter to the black-bean hamburger at a place in the Yucatán where he had eaten a dozen or more years before. He was also a huge saver of receipts, ranging from the absurd (gum, newspapers, tea, the occasional Baby Ruth bar) to the legitimate (film, canvas, paper, brushes, and paint). He probably could have used an accountant. Or maybe he had imag-ined he'd save himself money keeping track of his expenses him-self. Either way, it was a disaster and Kate quickly made a mountain of paper to throw away.

The largest pile concerned his desire—or, more accurately, lust—for Shelley that Kate simply could not bring herself to read anymore. They apparently had voracious appetites for each other, and the artist always seemed to document their encounters on stained Chinese takeout menus. Kate came to the conclusion that MSG must have really rocked his libido. Or maybe Shelley was a lot younger than she appeared. Either way, this information wasn't going to help Shelley (the contortionist) in her fight with the heirs, although it was definitely a boost for yoga practitioners every-where.

Kate was on the floor, crouched over the fourth box, when Naomi finally called with news on the house. Kate had just gotten off the phone with Ben. Their conversation had been terse and unproductive, and because of his love for the final word, when her phone buzzed, she was sure it was Ben again, with one more re-minder. Ben hadn't been pleased with her progress and urged her to look through the papers one more time. He even hinted that perhaps she was too emotional. That the artist's death was too close to her own father's death. It was funny, but until Ben said that, she hadn't even been thinking about her father. Sure, his estate (if you could even use that word) had been in similar disar-ray. But the only thing that was remotely personal that he had left behind was expired coupons and that cryptic laundry list. He was unlike the artist, who obviously recorded every little detail of his life. Of course, by the time her father had probably thought to write something down, the tumor had eaten away at his ability to reason. In order to prove Ben wrong, she had gotten off the phone and attacked the boxes with renewed vigor. She really wanted to ask him what stake he held in all of this—but she bit her tongue. Above all else, she was not stupid enough to jeopardize what she had worked so hard for all these years.

Her heart beat fast as she reached for the phone.

"Kate?"

"Here," Kate said, trying to make her voice appear nonchalant.

"Can you get away this afternoon? Around five?"

She glanced down at her calendar and ran a shaky index finger over the end of her day. She had scheduled a staff meeting for four, but she could push it to a dinner meeting at seven. "Sure," she said, as she stood up from the floor and e-mailed the change to her staff.

"Okay," Naomi said with trepidation, "just don't act like I didn't warn you about the place."

Kate laughed. "I get it—this is ARO: against Realtor's orders."

Naomi returned the laugh and signed off while Kate returned to the pieces of paper on the floor. For once, she was relieved to be numb with busywork.

It had taken a few days to get into the house, because the lock had to be cut off the gate before Kate and Naomi arrived. In its place was a shiny new padlock with buttons that Naomi manipulated until it fell open in her hands. She swung the gate wide and then got back behind the wheel of the car. It was all Kate could do to keep herself in her seat belt as they drove up the rutted path. The first thought Kate had as the house came into view was of the Seven Dwarfs. Hadn't Walt Disney imagined a place just like this?

The steep, sloped roof was covered in so much foliage and layers upon layers of pine boughs that at first it appeared thatched.

There was a broken arbor that had once held a gate, and parts of a picket fence that led to the front door. The windows, those that were not broken, had multiple leaded panes in a diamond pattern with an old iron hardware that latched in the center in the shape of an *S*.

Naomi rattled off the specifics from the sheet in her lap: bungalow built in 1939, two bedrooms, one bath, pool, and a pool house. When she got to the part about the pool, she snorted and then looked at Kate and apologized.

But Kate wasn't paying any attention. She had her hand on the car door handle and stepped out onto what was once a lawn. Rose bushes lined the path and twined across the stones as she stepped over them. Several times she needed to bend down and untangle a prickly branch from the cuff of her pants before she continued on toward the door.

Once she was there, she turned the large iron knob that barely fit in the palm of her hand and was surprised when the door swung open. It was a thick Dutch door, painted black, but now the wood was dull, buffed, and faded like driftwood, and the top latch was rusted shut, so after a brief struggle she gave up trying to separate the doors.

Despite the broken windows that should have supplied adequate ventilation, the air inside the house was like stepping into a litter box. It was obvious from the shredded upholstery of an abandoned wing chair and the multiple droppings on the tiled floors that the house was inhabited, just not by humans.

The room was larger than she had expected; at least twenty feet from end to end. Kate looked down, careful where she stepped. Beneath her feet and the filth were the most marvelous Mexican tiles. She took a water bottle from her bag and spilled some onto the floor. The fanciful patterns were in salmon, cream, and a deeper red with a touch of brown. The walls, she could tell, were once painted a deep salmon as well, although the plaster was flaking so badly they looked like they were infected with a bad case of dermatitis. At the north side of the room, by the wing chair, the tile continued around a simple fireplace and black iron sconces dangled by wires, as if someone had tried unsuccessfully to rip them from the wall.

The main room opened into a dining room with leaded-glass doors that exposed the garden beyond. Mostly, the panes of glass were broken and in their place was wildly overgrown clumps of bougainvillea that pushed pale green tendrils yet to unfurl through the empty framework and into the room and pressed against the remaining intact pieces of glass with leaves. The leaves were so large they looked like something from the plant in *Jack and the Beanstalk*. Kate found herself having nothing to compare the house to save the occasional children's fairy tale. Perhaps the nostalgia was part of the lure of the place.

Next to the dining room was the kitchen, but they couldn't walk very far into the room because a large portion of the ceiling had fallen in. Kate looked up, expecting to see sky, and instead she saw rafters from the attic. She supposed that might be a good thing, although she had nothing to go on other than having lived in an old house. Unable to go into the kitchen, they also couldn't get to the other side of the house, where they assumed were the two bedrooms and the bath.

Naomi had her hand covering her mouth and nose the entire time they were inside. Now, with her remaining free hand, she gestured wildly for Kate to leave the house. Once they were back outside, she let her hand drop and took in a massively large breath before she spoke.

"Oh my God," she cried. "It's worse than I thought."

Kate caught Naomi's expression, but instead of stopping to respond she walked with purpose down the drive. As she picked her way around the house to the pool area, she already knew the house was hers, and that was even before she saw the tiny cottage on the far side of the pool. The pool itself, identifiable only because the paperwork on the property claimed there was one, looked like it had formed its own ecosystem inside the concrete basin after years and years of neglect.

From behind her, Naomi said, "That must be the guesthouse."

Kate stepped over the trunk of a needle-thin pine that had fallen and split in half across the walkway. Actually, the proliferation of piles upon piles of sticks and twigs made the yard look like a series of abandoned campfires in a fantastical gnarled forest where trolls ruled. Sensing Naomi's hesitation, she picked up and moved the largest of the spindle-sized pieces and then cleared a path with her feet. Ironically, unlike the main house, the door to the pool house was locked, and Kate stepped aside and waited impatiently for Naomi to punch in the code.

While she worked, Naomi mumbled something about this being the place they stored the bodies and hadn't Kate seen any horror movies as a child? Now was the part in the movie when all the smart people got back in their cars and drove away.

As the padlock fell apart in her hands, she looked at Kate and said, "Last chance to run."

Kate laughed as she gently maneuvered Naomi aside for a grip on the door handle. She needed to be the first to see the space, before Naomi could say anything and color her impressions. The thing that hit her right away was the sunlight streaming in from above. She looked up, again, like in the kitchen, half-expecting to see the sky. However, this time she was pleasantly surprised by a

skylight. And not just any skylight: one without a single broken
pane of glass. The room was another deceptively long rectangle,
with floor-to-ceiling bookshelves at one end and a fireplace nearly
identical to the one in the main house at the other. Beyond the
main room, there was a rudimentary kitchen alcove with an old
turquoise refrigerator, a two-burner stove top, and a skirted sink
with a cast-iron drain board attached. Kate twisted a spigot to see
if any water would come out, but all she got was a burst of air that
popped and echoed against the porcelain basin. Above the sink
was a window that looked out onto a gnarled tree so loaded with
lemons that they grew double, even triple from the branches, the
skin of the fruit stretched tight, so swollen with juice that the
pointed tips of the lowest-hanging ones rested on the ground. Just
past the kitchen was a tiny black-and-white-tiled bathroom with
a claw-foot tub and a minuscule square of a window above eye
level, which opened to a closet-size room with another window
and a soiled twin-size mattress abandoned on the floor.

Kate returned to the living room. Unlike the main house, this
building was actually inhabitable. There were no broken windows,
and the only glass was a collection of empty liquor bottles on the
bookshelves. The place had been cleaned out except for another
dirty mattress without benefit of a frame on the multicolored tile
floor and a yellowed copy of *Life* magazine from 1956, with Debo-
rah Kerr and Yul Brynner in *The King and I* on the cover.

Kate had it all figured out by the time Naomi caught up to her.
She could live here while the main house was getting worked on.
That way she could get out of the hotel and supervise the construction at the same time. Never mind that her commute to the
office was going to be twice as long as it was now. She would get
the little house wired for Internet so that she could telecommute

if need be. Surely, that would be doable. That café in town had had wireless, as had most of the others on that main street area, and that was less than two miles from here.

When she turned around to tell Naomi her idea, she was surprised that the Realtor was not looking at her with a horrified expression. She shrugged. "Okay . . . so this place at least would probably NOT get condemned."

Kate raised a brow. "You need to work on your sales pitch."

"Ha! I'm feeling like nothing more than a prostitute here . . ."

"I want it."

Naomi sighed. "Kate, do you even have any idea what kind of money it would take to start from scratch?"

"I have money."

"Okay." Naomi bit her bottom lip. "So you have money. But I'm thinking you don't really have time. You need someone, a contractor, someone that can be your eyes and ears twenty-four/seven. Those people are hard to come by—at least the trustworthy ones."

Kate was ready to acknowledge she wasn't entirely thinking straight, but was she crazy for thinking of her brother Finn? He was the first person who popped into her mind. When he was working, large-scale construction but especially carpentry were his areas of expertise. What if she brought Finn out here, gave him a place to live, and he turned his life around by bringing this house back to life? What if? She closed her eyes again and saw the four of them lined up on the bank of the swimming hole, poised to toss their father's ashes. Finn had worn a suit so old and ill-fitting that something in Kate had broken when she saw him. He'd reeked of mouthwash, she supposed, to hide the booze. And his face was raw and nicked to shit because he had obviously taken a razor to it for the first time in months. She didn't know whether to turn away from him or hug him. Then, when they had gone over to their father's depressing apartment and Finn had asked them if it was okay if he had Dad's old leather jacket, Kate had left and gone outside because she couldn't bear to see him put it on. Amy and George had looked at her like she was devoid of any feeling, when in reality she would rather have joined their father in the casket than let them know how hard it was for her to see Finn like that. She would wager a guess that it wasn't out of sentimental reasons that he took that jacket.

Naomi had gone over to the bookshelves and propped open the folder on the house. "You could probably get it for way under half a million . . . it is an estate—and it seems the original owner has been dead over a decade, I have no idea even if the heirs are alive."

Kate was already moved in: she didn't even have to try that hard when she imagined Eli out by the lemon tree, filling a bowl with the fruit and then coming inside to make the limoncello recipe their landlady in Florence had taught Kate all those years ago. And she wanted to go back. Oh God, she would give anything to go back.

Naomi was right, and so the dollar amount Kate paid for a dream was nothing in comparison to its metaphorical worth. On her way to the airport to pick up her brother, she rationalized that the money she was about to dump into the house along with the money it cost to purchase it was akin to all the money she could have wasted on therapy over the years if she had gone.

Kate had been mildly surprised that it had taken so much to convince Finn to come west. As far as she knew, he had gone back to Boston after their father's funeral only to find out that he had been replaced on the job. He'd been living off a friend who hadn't minded, or so Finn believed, so he at first had turned Kate down.

But then, a week later, he called collect to say his friend's new girlfriend wanted him off the couch and he would come to Los Angeles after all. But he wouldn't promise her anything. Maybe it was his pride, who knew? But again, Kate had to stifle the urge to either back away or take him in when he finally got here.

She agreed to meet him at the luggage carousel, and there was a moment, when a glut of people pushed forth from a gate and surrounded her at the previously empty area, when she felt a little panic. What if Finn cashed in the ticket and went on a bender? What would she do?

Then she saw him. He was hunched over, studying the ground as he walked, an olive-colored duffel bag slung over his shoulder. His hair, long at the funeral, was shorn close to his head, as if he were ready to enter boot camp. Save for the unusual tint to his skin, gaunt cheeks, and wasted frame, Metallica T-shirt and faded Levi's, he could be a soldier on leave. Or a crack addict fresh from rehab. Even so, with his bone structure more exposed, there was an uncommon beauty to his fragility, which made him stand out more than blend in with the crowds.

She stayed perfectly still, waiting for him to look up and see her. When he was almost upon her and still hadn't looked up, she said his name loudly. More loudly than she intended but it worked. He stopped and brought his chin up slightly and she saw from the slight movement of his eyeballs that he connected his name to her voice, but still he didn't speak, just continued to move forward until she could smell the peppermint gum on his breath.

"Hey," Kate said, reaching out to touch his shoulder. She pulled back her hand too fast when she felt something sharp. Something sharp that she realized was his shoulder blade. How in the world was he healthy enough to work construction? "How was the trip?"

Finn let the duffel slide off his shoulder to the ground, not bothering to turn around and see if there was room. A girl behind him called him an asshole as she tripped. His cheeks flushed and all of a sudden he seemed embarrassed. He turned away from Kate and picked up the bag and mumbled, "Where's the car?"

Kate gestured to the left and he followed her through the crowd and out the double doors into California sunshine. Finn squinted, and Kate wished she had remembered to pick him up a pair of sunglasses. She was shocked to see that his skin looked even bluer out here than it had inside.

"Are you hungry?"

"I had peanuts . . . and gum."

Kate laughed but Finn didn't seem to think his answer was funny. They found the car and she navigated the parking lot and the freeway entrance in silence. *Please don't let this be a mistake,* she said over and over to herself as she sneaked looks at Finn hunkered down in the passenger seat, a hand thrown across his eyes to shield the sun.

Finally, he said, "Stop, Kate. Please."

They were in the middle of four lanes of traffic. If he meant stop the car, there was no way. She looked at him, alarmed, and he rolled his eyes in response.

"STOP. THAT."

"Looking at you?"

He sighed. "Feeling sorry for me."

"I don't," she half-lied.

"Okay. Then stop looking at me like you think I'm going to break open a beer from my duffel."

"Finn," Kate said as she hit the steering wheel with her palms. "Why did you come here if you're so suspicious and contentious? I really need you. Really."

He slumped farther than she thought possible into the seat and mumbled into his collarbone, "We'll see, we'll see."

Finn didn't speak again until Kate pulled into Shelley's driveway. He roused himself enough to study his surroundings. "This is the house?" he asked.

Kate looked through the windshield at Shelley's and the artist's house. It was a mid-century modern ranch, all one-level glass and wood with a slightly Asian feel. To get to the front door, you had to walk on a bridge over lily pads and gold and black spotted koi.

"No," Kate said as she opened her door. "A client's." She went around to the trunk and retrieved the lone box of paper she saved from the original five Shelley had given her. Inside the box, she had divided and labeled the artist's assorted crap, not even worthy of a memoir or an addendum to an obit. She figured as long as she was out here to show Finn the house, she might as well return this junk to Shelley.

With the box in her hands, she stopped by Finn's window. He'd lowered it down before she had turned off the engine and was resting his head on top of his elbow. Kate found herself hoping that a little sun would change the alarming shade of his skin. "I'll only be a minute."

He shrugged one shoulder. "Okay," he mumbled into the crook of his arm.

Shelley took forever answering the door and Kate was uncomfortable in her dark suit; she was still dressing for D.C. and hadn't yet adjusted to casual Los Angeles. She shifted the box of paper from hip to hip, all the while worrying over Finn in the car and having to go back to the office tonight. She glanced back only once and saw that Finn was in the exact same position as when she had left him. When the door finally opened and she tried to step inside with the box, Shelley, like she possessed a sixth sense as well as double-jointed hips, peered around Kate and stared at her car.

"Who'd you bring?" she asked.

"Oh, oh. That's my brother," Kate floundered, caught off guard.

"Brother?"

"Yes." Kate nodded. Her head and the cords in her neck were killing her. "I just picked him up at the airport." For the first time since Shelley answered the door, Kate realized the woman was wearing a black tank-top without a bra and stretch pants. Her breasts were small, nearly like a boy's, and her body was surprisingly toned. It was definitely not the body that the artist so lustily described in his menu memoirs. Although when you're with someone as long as the artist had been with Shelley, who knew the difference between fantasy and reality? With her gray hair back in a ponytail, she looked younger by twenty years than she had the first time Kate had met her. Her face was shiny with sweat and she gave off the odor of something sweet, but Kate couldn't identify it.

"It's rude to make him stay in the car," Shelley said.

"Oh. Well. Then I'll just hand this to you here and I'll be off." Kate could only imagine how pissed off Ben was going to be when he found this out.

Shelley opened the door wider. "Why don't you come in?" She jutted her chin out in Finn's direction. "Go get your brother. It's hot and I made sun tea."

"Sun tea? Really?" Kate found herself repeating this as if the idea of tea brewing in a jar in a sunny spot was miraculous.

There seemed to be a sixty-second delay between the time Kate motioned to him and the time Finn comprehended what she wanted him to do. Eventually, he got out of the car and shuffled toward the door.

"Not too quick, is he?" Shelley muttered as she turned and went ahead of Kate and Finn. Kate noticed that Shelley's rear view looked more age-appropriate. Low and flat, her ass cheeks seemed to be born from the backs of her thighs.

Finn closed the door behind him. Inside the house it was blessedly cool. Kate heard Finn take a deep breath. She couldn't bear to turn around but she hoped he was at least standing up straight and looking forward, not down.

They were in the room where Kate and Shelley had met the last time. This was where several of the artist's large, presumably famous paintings were hung. Today on the floor was a purple yoga mat, which explained the sweat, and next to that a thin reed of incense, which explained Kate's instant headache from the cloyingly sweet smell. Shelley picked up a towel off a chair and wiped her face as Kate set down the box on the floor between them before taking a seat. She assumed Finn would join her, but instead he wandered in front of the painting with the blue-green blob being birthed from a beige blob. In the upper right corner of the painting, a yellow blob was either descending or ascending, depending upon your view.

"This," Finn said as he pointed, "looks exactly how I feel right before I have my first drink of the day."

Kate bit the inside of her mouth. It was all she could do to not reprimand him, especially as he moved on to the red-blob painting.

Shelley laughed just as Kate was trying to figure out how the hell she was going to get Finn to sit down. "This is a lot quieter," Finn said, pointing to the fiery hellish smear before he sat down across from Kate.

Shelley looked at him admiringly. "Would you like some tea?"

"Sure."

Kate hoped the tea was out of the room so she could fix Finn with a death stare and instead was disappointed to see that Shelley had it set up on top of a white piano that looked like it would be more suitable in Elton John's living room. Shelley served Finn first and then Kate. Before she poured herself a glass and sat down, she looked at Kate and the box and said, "Well?"

"I'm sorry," Kate offered. "There's nothing there that can help your case." She watched as Shelley opened the lid and lifted out the envelopes Kate had labeled, one by one.

As she did, Kate caught the anticipation on Finn's face while he studied Shelley. It was the same look she'd seen on his face a thousand Christmas mornings ago, when he had asked for a puppy and got a G.I. Joe instead. And it wasn't even the real G.I. Joe. It was actually a Ken doll dressed in a soldier's outfit, and her father had laughed nastily when Finn had held it up at his urging so he could call it a sissy toy. Then their father had said it was really meant for George. None of them had even known what he meant, but Kate had gleaned enough to know it wasn't a compliment.

Kate swallowed some tea and squirmed in her seat. She wanted to get the hell out of Shelley's house. The migraine that had been lurking for hours had finally arrived. Between the sunshine streaming in the windows and the smoking incense, she felt like she was going to be sick to her stomach. She was just about to excuse herself when Shelley began to cackle.

Finn looked at Kate and for the first time since she'd picked him up they seemed to share a moment of sibling telepathy: Shelley was nuts.

Shelley was bent over the box, reading labels on the envelopes and tossing them onto the floor all the while laughing so hard she was crying. When she tried to straighten up, she held her side as if a stitch prevented her from doing so.

"Are you all right?" Kate asked, halfway out of the chair. Was Shelley having an attack? Through the haze of migraine, Kate felt helpless as to what to do next, but then Shelley seemed to calm down long enough to motion for her to sit, before she erupted in another uncontrollable fit.

"I just never imagined such attention to detail . . ." she stammered on her way out of the room.

"Shelley," Kate said more loudly than she had intended as she watched the woman retreat. She got up and started to follow Shelley out of the room. She didn't have time for games today. She had to go back to the office after she dropped Finn off at the house. If she left now, she knew Ben would probably kill her. But when Shelley spun around and shooed her back into the living room, Kate complied and flopped back onto the chair across from her brother.

"Patience, Grasshopper," Finn murmured, his lips against the rim of his sun tea glass. "You've been played."

Kate did her best to ignore Finn and looked past him out the sliding-glass doors to the artist's studio. The guard was sitting in a chair tipped back against the door, reading a book. Kate squinted and tried to make out the title but she couldn't see it. She was humiliated. Was Finn right? Had even Ben known the boxes were some sort of test?

Shelley returned, carrying a hardcover black sketchbook the size of a legal pad. Her face and cheeks were streaked with red and her neck and chest were flushed, but she was composed. She handed the notebook to Kate.

Kate hesitated a moment before accepting the notebook from Shelley. Was this yet another joke? As soon as she had it in her hands, she opened the front cover. It appeared to be a diary. Kate looked up at Shelley and tried to raise a questioning eyebrow, but even that slight motion hurt because of the migraine.

Shelley shrugged in response to Kate's facial spasm but didn't seem alarmed. "We lived off the grid our entire lives. We didn't come back here until he was so sick we had no choice. Did you really think I was going to take a chance giving his life's work to someone I knew nothing about?" She paused. "Anyone who could do that," she pointed to the boxes, "could take the care with this." She gestured to the notebook in Kate's hands. "Everything my husband wanted is in there."

"If that's true, why not just show it to your stepson's attorney?" Kate asked, not even trying to hide her skepticism, all the while wishing, for a moment, that everything in life was that uncomplicated. "This would be over."

"I don't trust him," Shelley said simply. "Why should I?"

While they were talking, Finn had risen and gone back over to the red-blob painting. Kate just hoped he wasn't going to open his mouth and offer another critique before they got out of here. She stood and tucked the book under her arm. "We should go," she said to Shelley but looked at Finn, who took her cue and sauntered toward the door.

In the car, Finn smiled and waved at Shelley through the windshield. Through gritted teeth, Kate hissed, "Stop that."

"Huh?" Finn turned to face her as she drove. "What? So she tricked you. Can you blame her, Kate?"

"Finn, please. You don't know anything."

To Kate's surprise, Finn laughed and turned his attention back to the windshield.

"What's so funny?" Kate asked as they turned off Shelley's street.

His face remained impassive as he shrugged.

"Knock it off," Kate snapped. "Tell me what you're thinking."

"Just don't get your hopes up. I mean, seriously, you think the old guy wrote everything down nice and neat in here?" He had reached into the backseat and retrieved the notebook and was thumbing through it.

She glanced sideways at him. "Be careful with that," she admonished, then added, more for her own benefit than Finn's, "she wouldn't do that to me twice."

"Why?" he asked. "What does she owe you?"

The pain behind Kate's eyes thrummed so badly streaks of white crackled at the edges. "Shut up, you don't know anything."

Much to Kate's chagrin, Finn laughed again and said, "So I've been told."

After they toured the main house, the first thing Finn said when he walked into the pool house and saw the mattress on the floor in the living room was "Reminds me of when Dad moved into the barn." He paused and looked around, "You need a love shack, Katie?"

"You're just saying that to get back at me."

Finn looked genuinely confused. "Why would I need to do that?"

"Because of what I said in the car."

"Why would I expect anything else from you?" He didn't look sad or angry, just like a guy making a statement.

Kate was taken aback. So much so that she couldn't speak. She moved into the kitchen, unaware that Finn hadn't followed, and turned the faucet on and then off and then on again. The water started with a thread of bloody rust before it ran clear. She fumbled around in her bag for the bottle of migraine meds, flipped off the lid, and popped two pills onto her tongue. Then she cupped her hands beneath the faucet and swallowed the pills with the aid of the tinny-tasting water. As they went down, she squeezed her eyes shut tight and gripped the edge of the sink to stop her hands from shaking. When she opened her eyes, her vision was so blurry it took several seconds for them to focus on the lemon tree outside the window again.

When she walked back into the room, she said to Finn, "I have to go to the office." She paused and glanced around the room. "I had the electricity turned on and the water. But I don't know that there's anything you can plug in."

Finn watched her without comment.

Kate stepped over his duffel bag on the way out the door. She couldn't even tell him to call her because the phone line hadn't been hooked up. That was next week: phone, computer, wireless. She left him with a backward wave of her hand. She didn't even know if he was hungry or thirsty. There was hardly a place near the house he could walk to even if he wanted. But Kate didn't think of any of these things until she was well on her way back to Los Angeles and it was too late to turn around and do anything about it.

Their father had moved into the barn little by little the fall Kate turned seventeen. It had started off with him needing a place to write away from the house. At least that was the bored announcement their mother had made over a rare appearance at dinner one evening as they watched their father carry a desk chair, a small table, a lamp, several boxes, and the card table from the den, where the same jigsaw puzzle had sat unfinished for the last two years, through the dining room, into the kitchen, and out the back door.

"I don't get it," Amy said as she twirled a massive amount of noodles, too big for the opening of her mouth, around her fork. "He already has a whole room just for writing. What's he need the barn for? Where are we supposed to keep the bikes and stuff?"

She shoved the noodles into her mouth and chewed with her mouth half-open. When she was done, there was sauce all over her chin.

"Can't you even try?" Kate tossed Amy a napkin. "You are so disgusting."

"Kids are supposed to be disgusting your hiney-ness." Amy grinned at her own joke before she wiped her mouth with the sleeve of one of Finn's old sweaters. It was way too big for her but she insisted on wearing it. No one but Kate seemed to think that Amy dressed like a homeless person. Certainly the clothes and feral manners had to be the reason the only person who could stand her was George. Ten was too old to act like this, wasn't it?

While Kate was the de-facto parent for her siblings—forging signatures on permission slips and report cards, writing excuses, making dinner, and procuring groceries and laundry detergent— she knew barely anything about their personal lives. And she didn't care to. What was it to her that Amy had no friends? That George was weirdly attached to his baby sister and that Finn was drunk or worse more than half the time he was awake. Really, what was she supposed to do about them all?

"Maybe if you and George weren't constantly making noise Dad would be able to work in the house," Kate said.

"How did it get to be our fault, Kate?" George asked.

Kate stood up and then sat back down. "None of you understand how difficult it is to be an artist."

Finn snorted and Kate shot him a dirty look. It was obvious to Kate that their father was trying to make a statement, since it would have been easier for him to just go out the wide front door. The kitchen was an odd, narrow configuration, an afterthought to the house, and the outside doorway was blocked by a collection of abandoned sporting goods and a broken old washing machine on the fragile back porch.

But Kate and her siblings weren't gathered in the front rooms—they were in the kitchen. And Kate supposed this was his way of letting them know what he was doing. Although he made a point of not looking directly at any of them as he made his pilgrimage back and forth through the room, Kate caught her mother's eye as she exhaled out of the side of her mouth, surprised by her presence. They behaved as though she was invisible because, frequently, she was. As they ruminated on their father's exit, she had remained characteristically silent. Kate watched her grind out a cigarette, smoked all the way to its filter, in her plate of uneaten spaghetti, and then pour herself another tumbler of wine before she floated away up the back staircase to her room with a vague commandment to "Clean everything up."

Amy and George had been kicking each other under the table the entire dinner and now, after they dropped their plates in the sink, tumbled from the kitchen toward the den. After a few minutes, Kate heard the television. It was Thursday night and that meant *The Cosby Show*, *Family Ties*, *Cheers*, and *Night Court*. They'd be absorbed for the evening in an alternate universe where both parents were present and the problems were solved in less than twenty minutes. She already knew asking them to help her clean was more trouble than it was worth.

She looked at Finn but he pushed back away from the table and said, "I cooked."

Kate nodded. It was true. Finn had dumped the jar of sauce into the pan and boiled the pasta. It had been ready when she returned from cross-country practice. Ordinarily, Finn would have been at practice as well and Kate would have thrown together some sandwiches when she got home, but Finn had been kicked off the team because he'd been caught, after multiple warnings, with another flask of booze in his locker.

As Kate plunged her hands into the hot, soapy water and washed the dishes, her father made several more silent trips through the room. On his last run through, he paused before the stove and thrust a hand into the pot of leftover pasta. Kate tried not to stare as he brought a handful of bloody noodles to his mouth and slurped them up. This was his caveman persona, the one he used on odd occasions when they were little, to make them laugh. She hadn't seen it surface in many, many years. Now, it just made her uncomfortable.

Wordlessly, she handed him the kitchen towel and a fork. He took the towel and swiped at his mouth and then forked the remaining pasta with gusto. When he was done, the fork clattered into the empty pan and he squeezed Kate's shoulder briefly before he disappeared outside. She was the only one who understood him.

That night, when Kate brought the trash to the can out back, a glow from the lamp her father had carried from the house lit up the three small diamond-shaped windows along the side of the barn. Kate knew her father was in there, but without an invitation, she didn't dare go over and see what he was doing. She hopped up and down on the back steps to keep warm, breathing the first puffs of frosty air, hoping for him to turn off the lights and come inside. While she waited, she caught sight of the orange end of a cigarette, and then Finn stepped out into the clearing around the back of the barn. He blew smoke rings that Kate watched drift off. But after a while, she couldn't feel her arms and legs in her T-shirt and shorts, she had physics homework, and she simply grew tired of waiting for something to happen, so she turned and went back into the kitchen without saying anything to Finn.

Over the next few weeks, things disappeared slowly from the house. First, it was the blankets they kept on the couch in the den, then the cushions from the couch, and, eventually, the couch.

Amy mentioned it over breakfast one morning right before Halloween. With her mouth full of Cheerios and a dribble of milk poised on her chin, she said, "I asked Mom why Dad stole the couch, and she said he must have needed a place to sit."

Kate looked at Finn for confirmation but he dismissed them all by walking out the door, so Kate went into the den to see for herself. In the rectangular space where the couch had been was now a shiny swatch of wood—shinier, at least, in comparison to the rest of the scuffed floor. There were clots of dust and hair as if they had a dog (they didn't), a few plastic toy soldiers, a pack of Big Red gum, a lollipop stick, several of the jigsaw pieces from the old puzzle, the requisite spare sock, and lost pencils. He had also, she noticed, taken the coffee table, but nobody seemed to care about that.

Kate wondered how their father had managed to get the couch out of the house all by himself. Surely he had help? But it wasn't like they had another couch to put into the den, so she closed the door and did her best to forget about it. When George and Amy complained they had no place to sit and watch television, Kate had suggested they bring down sleeping bags from the attic. That started the long campout of George and Amy on the floor in the den while their father slept on the couch in the unheated barn. The television was on twenty-four hours a day and Kate struggled every morning to get the two of them awake and out the door for school. Some days she just gave up, and then she would come home in the afternoon to find Amy and George still in whatever clothes they'd slept in, *General Hospital* on the television in the background while they huddled over the old jigsaw puzzle. They'd started working on the puzzle again, since no one had ever picked the pieces up off the floor when their father had taken the card table. It was of the ocean and every single piece was blue.

Kate only knew for sure that she slept in her own bed at night. Finn had always suffered from insomnia; he was lucky if he slept four hours and there was no telling where he would eventually end up. More often than not it had been the couch in the den, but now that wasn't even a possibility. And their mother? Their mother had been more absent than usual, shuttered behind her bedroom door when she wasn't out of the house for hours on end with mumblings of rehearsals or meetings tossed out as after-thoughts if anyone asked. Although, even if she were around, their father's living in the barn with half of the furniture from the house would hardly have been a topic of conversation.

While she waited for her father's invitation, Kate had taken to hiding on the back porch and watching the barn at night to see what was going on. The closest she allowed herself to this new sanctuary was when she left bags of his favorite chocolate chip cookies in front of the door. Surely that would get her inside? But it hadn't, not so far. Yet the cookies disappeared, so she knew he was getting them. Kate deduced that he really must be working on something big, and when he was ready to share, he would come and get her. She was the early reader of all her father's work, from way back, even when she had struggled to comprehend the mean-ing of the words on the page. When she was four, she had sounded out the sentence "I am fucked" across the top of one of his pages, and he had been so pleased that he allowed her to read them ever since.

Once she thought she saw Finn go in and out, but because she had turned off all the lights so she wouldn't be seen, she couldn't be sure. Of all of them, he looked the most like their father and shared his slightly stooped posture and shuffled walk, so it could have been him. If she asked Finn, she knew he would deny it anyway, so she was left with no choice other than to sneak around in the dark.

The first Friday of November, after the track-and-field season had ended and the awards were handed out, Kate went with her teammates to Friendly's. A few of the girls on the team, obsessed with calorie intake, were debating the calories in a Fribble Shake versus a hot fudge sundae. Kate wasn't really participating in the conversation, but she was surrounded by a glut of girls thick into the discussion. It was better than getting stuck with Alison, the best sprinter on the team, who unfortunately had it bad for Finn. From what Kate had surmised during an interminable bus ride back from their last meet, Alison and Finn had hung out and then he never called her again. Take a number, Kate had wanted to tell her. But she kept her mouth shut. With her back firmly in front of Alison's sad face, Kate moved closer to the bigger group. Their high-pitched voices were like cotton in her ears, cramming in useless pieces of information until she was stuffed, until she just couldn't take it anymore. When that happened, their voices blended together in one indistinguishable hum. She was trying hard to stay in that place when she saw her father way in the far back booth of Friendly's, holding hands across the paper place-mats with a woman who was not her mother.

She stood perfectly still and held her breath and willed her father to look her way, and when he did, he smiled as though it was absolutely normal to run into his daughter at Friendly's while he was holding hands with a stranger. The first thing she thought, as he gestured for her to come to his table and she left her friends behind, was that she bet this woman had seen the inside of the barn.

In the middle of the table next to their still-entwined fingers was a platter of onion rings. Funions, Friendly's called them, and Kate wondered why every menu item started with an *F*. Funions and Fribbles. Before Kate could be introduced, she reached for one and popped it into her mouth. The woman laughed nervously and Kate saw all of her teeth. She wasn't that pretty, at least not traditionally. Her mouth was wide and her eyes were almond-shaped, so that when she smiled the corners of her mouth aligned with the far corners of her eyes. It was as if someone had drawn a diagram of a face but forgot to give it any fullness. Although, Kate reasoned, some of the most famous artists, philosophers, composers, and writers of generations past had taken mistresses that were more muse than beauty. This had to be the case with the woman her father introduced as Ingrid.

Her father had done most of the talking, carrying the conversation for Kate and Ingrid as well as himself. After her father had slipped her a twenty to pay for her food, after he bragged to Ingrid about Kate's brilliance, he promised he would soon have some writing to show Kate, because hers was the only opinion he valued. Then he got up, held a hand out to Ingrid, and left. Kate reasoned that her father introduced her to Ingrid because he knew Kate would understand that he needed more from life than the average man, the constrictions of an outdated monogamous society strangling him. No one, especially him, was to blame. It was an overriding theme in every single one of his plays and it didn't take long for Kate to come to the realization that every male character he had ever written was a manifestation of himself.

It wasn't until afterward, as Kate watched him lead Ingrid through the maze of Friendly's tables with a hand protectively at the small of her back, that she realized she had forgotten to ask if he'd gotten the cookies she left and if he had liked them.

Once Kate knew about Ingrid, she was surprised at how nothing really changed. Even in her attitude toward her mother, when she saw her, Kate was unaffected. As Kate saw it, if her mother wanted to make a go of her marriage, she could. But she had obviously chosen not to. So what was her father to do? Abandon his family? The only person she confided in was Finn. Late one night, when she was doing laundry and Finn was at the kitchen table smoking discards from one of their mother's many ashtrays lying about the house, she casually mentioned meeting their father and Ingrid.

Finn smiled, although it wasn't out of happiness, more like instinct over intent. Kate took that to mean that Finn had already known about Ingrid. But when she asked, he looked up at her from foraging through the ashtray, his ash-blackened fingertips poised over a butt, shaking ever so slightly, as he said, "Is she blond?"

Kate shook her head and folded her arms over her robe and waited for Finn to light the butt and take a deep drag. "Then, she's new." His cheeks were concave, distorting the features of his face for a moment before he exhaled. Once he did, he waved a hand in the air, his movements economical yet somehow elegant, before he said, "No one around here thinks I'm paying attention." He paused. "Finn the retard, right?"

There were so many things that Kate could have said to Finn, but she didn't. Instead, when the wash cycle ended, she got up and put the wet clothes in the dryer. She hesitated a second by the kitchen table on her way back through the room. If Finn had looked at her, given in just a little, she might have told him he wasn't stupid. She knew he had problems with reading, with words reversing themselves, yet his struggle in school was only aggravated by his need to be smashed. Dropped from the team, he had

more time on his hands to get wasted. And lately, Kate had noticed, the booze that used to mellow him out was turning him into
something scary. It worried her enough that she wondered what
they would do next year, after she went to college. Would they
eat? Would they have clean clothes? Would any of them even go
to school if she weren't here to make sure they did?

She shrugged in response to the conversation in her head,
even though neither of them had said anything. Kate was on her
way out of the room, resigned to the wall of silence from Finn,
when he said, "So you're okay with this?"

Kate stopped and spun around. "What?"

"With Dad? With Ingrid?" He drawled Ingrid's name out long
and slow, in a mocking way.

"Dad needs different things . . ."

"That he does," Finn said, nodding through a puff of smoke.
"That he does."

"So I get it that you don't agree?"

"What about Mom?"

"He's living in the barn." She made it sound like it wasn't their
father's fault and knew before the words were out that Finn would
rise to their mother's defense.

Finn made a face. "Come off it, Kate. Mom is no idiot either. How
would you like your husband to be fucking someone under your
nose? On your couch? Huh?" He paused. "Where's the great play?
He hasn't written anything in years—anything that could be pro-
duced anyhow. He had one fucking story in him, that's it. If Mom
didn't take any grunt job that came along, we'd have nothing."

"He's brilliant." Kate flinched. "Brilliant. Stop talking about
Dad like that."

Finn tipped the chair back on its back legs as he considered
Kate's statement. "The only thing about our father that's brilliant

is his ability to keep convincing younger and younger women to fuck him."

Kate put her hands over her ears. "Stop," she pleaded.

"Stop?" The chair slammed back down on all fours as Finn leaned forward. "What the fuck is wrong with you, Kate? Don't you care what this does to Mom?"

"If Mom wanted, she could go out there and be with him and support him. But she doesn't."

Finn gave a mean laugh. "Well, what the hell do you think Ingrid is doing for him, Kate? Transcribing his goddamn notes? Huh? I've seen them do it, Kate. Watched right through the windows. She even saw me and she smiled and just kept right on screwing our father. He's a liar and cheat. How can you even defend his fucking, huh? What has he done for you that he hasn't done for the rest of us?"

Kate rolled her eyes. She had never felt such an overwhelming urge to hurt anyone in her entire life, and the only thing she could think of to say was "Alison wants you to call her."

"Who?" Finn snarled.

"A girl I know that you screwed. She'd like a phone call."

"Fuck off."

"What makes you any better than Dad? Seems to me you're a lot worse. You don't even remember their names."

The chair scraped hard against the floor as Finn pushed back from the table and stood up. Before Kate had a chance to say anything else, he slammed the back door and pounded down the stairs.

For a minute, Kate thought he was going to the barn to confront their father. She followed him out onto the back porch but stopped when she spotted Finn in the drive. His body was an angry twisted mass of sinewy muscle as he frantically picked up rocks and hurled them at the barn. In his fury, the rocks mostly missed their mark, landing with a soft thud onto the grass. When his hands were empty, he turned and ran off down the drive toward the road. She watched until she could no longer see his white T-shirt, and Kate knew there was no use following him. Even though she trained every day, Finn was naturally faster. She had asked him once what he did differently, and he had answered that he ran with an empty mind. Her problem, the way he saw it, was that she was thinking too much about running. She needed to just allow it to happen.

Even at seventeen, Kate knew herself well enough to realize that would be an impossible task.

It was close to ten by the time Kate left the office and pulled into a parking lot of one of those overlit, overstocked, perpetually open big-box stores. The tendrils of her migraine wrapped tightly around her brain, the pain appeared to pulse in tandem with her heartbeat, bringing only the briefest of respites before it began again. She'd already exceeded the amount of pills she was supposed to take in a day, and the last time she had gone for a refill the doctor had warned her that the medication would cease to help if she kept abusing it. But she was desperate. It was like a junkie desperation: every thought she had was about getting rid of the pain, and she couldn't help but wonder if this was what Finn felt like when he craved a drink. At this point in the migraine, she would have done anything to make it go away.

Now, all she really wanted to do was curl up into a ball in a dark room. But she was feeling guilty that she had left her brother in an empty house six hours ago with nothing but water, so she ventured into the cavernous fluorescent netherworld in search of bedding and whatever else she could grab.

She squinted against the bright overhead lights, her eyes tearing up, as she piled sheets, towels, pillows, blankets, an air mattress, a lamp, a toaster, plates, mugs, and a coffee pot into the cart. A quick trip down the food aisle yielded a case of bottled water, coffee, crackers, English muffins, popcorn, soda, and cookies, and from the personal-care section she added shampoo, soap, a toothbrush, and toothpaste, because who knew what Finn had in that duffel? Her last stop was in the cleaning-supply section, where she grabbed cans of Comet, bleach, lightbulbs, a mop, broom, dustpan, and bucket.

Traffic was backed up on the freeway and so she got on and off exit ramps in an attempt to outwit her fellow travelers. The last time she took an exit, she picked up a sack of hamburgers and fries from a drive-thru. By the time she pulled into the driveway in Silver Lake, it was nearly midnight and the food was cold, but Finn appeared to still be here. At least there was light coming from the kitchen, one single bulb with a long pull chain that shone out of every window in the small house, casting rectangular yellow shadows across the overgrown yard. The weak light gave the tangle of trees and vines outside a postapocalyptic glow that sent a shivery feeling down Kate's spine and propelled her quickly from the car to the house with the burgers and fries in hand.

Finn, fully dressed, was stretched out on the nasty mattress on the floor, an arm flung across his eyes. His chest, Kate quickly noted, rose and fell evenly. She had so rarely seen him asleep that she reasoned her checking to see if he was alive was a natural instinct and not some maudlin irrational fear. She stepped gingerly around the bed and into the kitchen with the food. She stared at the turquoise refrigerator and stove, not sure what they had to do with the bags of congealed hamburgers and French fries, so she left the bags on the drain board and went back into the living room. Skirting the foot of the mattress, she made her way back out to the car and began to unload her purchases and carry them into the house.

On her final trip from the car, Finn was leaning against the doorframe, peering out into the yard. Lazily, he scratched his belly through his T-shirt as he watched Kate struggle with the last of the bags.

"Some help?" Kate called. If she had to bend over one more time to pick up something she'd dropped, her head was going to split in two. The air was heavy; it smelled like eucalyptus-scented herbal balm. Like the Vicks VapoRub her mother applied to their congested chests when they were young. As she walked, her arms loaded with packages, she felt the gigantic emerald ferns that grew out from beneath the bramble brush against her legs.

When they had everything inside, Kate looked for a place to collapse. She refused to sit on that mattress, and so she leaned up against the bookshelf and closed her eyes. She could hear Finn going through the bags. Her intention was to give him all of this and then turn around and go back to her hotel, but she honestly didn't know if she was capable of that tonight. Or was it already tomorrow? She opened one eye and looked at her watch. It was 12:47 a.m. and she had a nine o'clock conference call.

"You okay?" Finn asked. "I didn't think I'd see you until to-morrow."

As much as she didn't want to, Kate opened her eyes and looked at her brother. "You didn't have food or sheets or . . .."

"I've had much worse than this," he said, although Kate sensed it wasn't for sympathy, he was just relaying the information. Quickly changing the subject, he said, "Wow, you bought a lot of stuff," as he surveyed the mountain of bags. "It must have cost a fortune."

Self-conscious, in her defense, Kate said, "I work hard."

"Listen, I wasn't accusing you."

"Forget it." Kate cut him off. "I just couldn't let you . . ." Suddenly she stopped. She just couldn't what? Be responsible for him living here in squalor? She was surprised after all these years of not taking care of anyone but herself, all the old instincts to make everything right for everyone else came back so easily.

Finn raised his hands as if to say: enough said. He pulled the box containing the air mattress out of a bag and frowned. "That mattress is okay." He gestured to the stained pallet on the floor.

Kate shook her head. "Absolutely not, Finn. I meant to get this place at least cleared out by the time you came but I haven't had a minute so . . ." She shrugged out of her jacket, folded it carefully, and placed it on top of an empty bag she laid out on a shelf. She looked over at Finn and clapped her hands together. "Let's do it."

Finn shook his head at her like she was crazy, but then he picked up a corner of the old mattress and dragged it out the door. When he returned, he said, "You're going to need a Dumpster."

Kate rummaged in her bag until she came up with a notebook and a pen. She tossed it to her brother and said, "Start making a list. That's why you're here."

An hour or so later, the garbage had been bagged, floors had been swept and mopped with bleach, the rust stains on the tub, sink, and toilet scoured, the air mattress pumped, and Kate and Finn perched on top of it eating the cold hamburgers.

Finn had lent Kate a pair of cut-off pants, frayed at the bottom, and a T-shirt, since all she had with her were the clothes she'd worn to work and she hadn't wanted to clean in them. It was strange, wearing her brother's clothes, and she was embarrassed to hesitate before she put them on, to wonder how many people had worn them before her brother acquired them. And although they didn't smell of a specific laundry detergent, they were at least clean. She had felt a twinge in her gut as she watched him unzip his duffel to get her the clothes—right on top was their father's leather jacket.

When they were done eating, Finn balled up the empty foil wrappers and tossed them into the trash pile. He handed Kate a bottle of water, which she drank down in a swallow. The headache meds always left her parched.

"I'm going to stay here tonight, if that's okay with you?" Kate ventured as she set the alarm clock on her cell phone. "It's too late for me to drive back. Unless you mind sharing the bed?"

"It's your house, Kate."

"Right," she said and laughed. "At least you didn't say you'd shared a bed with worse."

Finn stared at her a minute, processing before he got the joke. "I can't remember the last time that you purposely said something funny."

Kate sighed as her head hit the pillow, and she pulled the blanket up around her shoulders. Two bodies on an air mattress were a delicate balance. When Finn shifted next to her, she rolled involuntarily toward the middle of the bed. Her shoulder was wedged against Finn's. He smelled like bleach and something sour but she was too exhausted to move. "Me neither," she mumbled before she fell asleep.

When Kate's alarm went off, she smelled coffee. She opened her eyes. She was alone in the middle of the air mattress clutching all the blankets, with both pillows beneath her head. By the time she registered where she was, Finn had appeared at the bottom of the bed, holding a mug of coffee out to her. She couldn't remember the last time someone had done that for her, and of course all of it circled back to Eli, and she hated that he was the first thought of her day.

So she was a little grumpy when she accepted the coffee from Finn, and he looked pissed by her reaction, but then he said, "I forgot you're not a morning person."

Kate blinked. No headache.

"Do you want an English muffin? I found a package in one of those bags."

She shook her head as she sipped the coffee. "I have to go— grab a shower, change my clothes, and get to the office." Watching Finn, she had a feeling that he had never gone back to sleep last night, which explained how she was alone in the middle of the mattress.

Finn nodded slowly before he returned to the kitchen for his own mug of coffee.

Kate crawled off the end of the air mattress and stood up without spilling her coffee. No small feat.

While she stretched, Finn asked, "Do you still run?"

"Not as much as I'd like, you?"

He frowned and Kate let it drop. Stupid question, she'd admit, although he brought it up. There was an awkward silence between them when Kate picked up her phone to call her assistant and Finn went outside. While Kate talked, she could see him walking the property, coffee cup in hand. His mouth was moving and he appeared to be talking to himself.

When Kate was done on the phone, she went into the bathroom, removed Finn's shorts and T-shirt, and carefully folded them over the towel bar before she dressed, brushed her teeth with one of the brushes from the packet she'd picked up the night before, and washed her face. Finn was still outside when she emerged from the house. He came from behind the pool house just as she was getting in her car.

"Hey," Kate yelled. "I have to go."

Finn nodded and held up the pad Kate had given him. "Making notes," he called back.

She was late and she didn't want to stop and get into things now. She wanted Finn to take control and maybe the note-taking was the first step. Kate shut the door and started the car. Over the engine, she called, "I don't know when I'm going to get back here tonight."

He acknowledged with his coffee mug raised high in the air that he'd heard her, and then turned his back to her before she had a chance to say anything else.

Later that evening, when Kate got home, she and Finn went into town to eat dinner. It was a warm evening and they found a place on the main street, just down from where Kate had coffee that first day she was here, where they could sit at a café table on an outdoor patio. The waiter had seemed reluctant to seat them there, afraid that the sixty-five-degree temperature was too chilly for a California evening in early October. Kate and Finn had surprised each other by laughing at the same time, and he seemed to take that as a sufficient enough answer that they didn't want to move.

When the waiter had left with their drink orders, Finn leaned back in his chair and looked up at the night sky. "I was freezing yesterday morning."

Kate recalled seeing their father's jacket in Finn's duffel. He must have taken it off before he got off the plane, but she said nothing, just nodded and listened.

"Sometimes I forget other places exist, you know? I mean, I guess I just get used to my little crappy piece of the world and that's all I see." He took a deep breath. "It even smells different here."

"You think?" Kate didn't smell anything different about California. If it had a distinct odor, she imagined something akin to burning plastic.

The waiter set down their ice teas and took their dinner orders. While he was still at the table, Kate noticed Finn slip the notebook she had given him out of his back pocket. He flipped open the cover while the waiter finished writing down Kate's order and drummed his fingers on the table.

When they were alone, he said, "Okay—so I took an inventory today and tried to list things in priority order."

"I want to get out of the hotel—soon," Kate interrupted.

Finn held up a finger. "I'm getting there." He outlined a plan where he would attack the pool house first. Make it livable with fresh paint, a rehabbed kitchen, and bath.

"I don't want to spend too much money in there," Kate said, frowning as she reached for a breadstick from the basket the waiter brought to the table. "The main house is my priority."

"Jesus, Kate, can I get through a sentence?"

She crunched down on the breadstick and chewed. When it was obvious that Kate was still chewing, he went on. "The main room just needs paint, the tiles buffed. There's a few pieces of rotten woodwork I need to replace around the sills and the French doors in the dining room, but all in all, I'm surprised."

He paused and Kate waved him on with the end of the breadstick.

"You can keep the general layout of the kitchen. I'll give you a nice slab of wood for a counter. The old fridge works, so that's up to you, but I think you'll need a new stove."

"I don't cook."

"Never?"

"Don't you think I did enough of that when we were growing up?"

Finn didn't answer, just consulted his pad as he sipped his ice tea.

"Can I get away with just a toaster oven and microwave in there?"

"Sure, that's up to you."

Kate nodded. "Get rid of the stove. Add the counter. And I guess I need a new fridge. That one is disgusting."

"Okay," Finn said quietly as he made notes.

"What?" Kate prodded, sensing something was wrong.

Finn looked up. "Nothing. It's your money and your call."

"Is my money bothering you?"

"No, Kate, your money is not bothering me."

"Then what is?"

"Nothing . . . can I go on?"

Kate motioned for him to continue.

"You are lucky that the tile is in such good condition, but the bathroom?" He hesitated. "You can resurface the sink or I can get a new one. The tub is okay—we can add one of those shower attachments if you want and then new paint, fix the rotten sill, recaulk." He looked up from his list to see if Kate was still paying attention.

She smiled at him. "You can do all this?"

"Sure," he answered.

"Really?"

Finn sat up straighter in his seat. "I said yes, didn't I?"

"You did," Kate answered, suddenly distracted by the way the fading light outside illuminated Finn's scalp. Even with his hair cut short, Kate noticed he still drew second glances from women.

Whatever Finn had, even in this state, was undeniable. "Why did you cut your hair?"

Finn's hand flew to his head. He rubbed a palm against the bristle edge on top as if he forgot that his hair was short. But he didn't give her an answer. Instead, he said, "I'll focus inside first, but that brush has to be cut down away from the house. You're going to have all sorts of animals and bugs getting into the walls and up under the tile roof. That tile can harbor a lot of crap you don't want in—"

"Don't touch the lemon tree."

"But it's rotten," Finn said.

"No way. It has a ton of fruit!"

"The branches are black, Kate, with some sort of nasty fungus growing on them. I went to pick a lemon and the entire branch broke off in my hand."

Kate's eyes got wide at the mention of the branch and she felt an unreasonable panic rising in her chest. "Leave it alone, please."

"Whatever," Finn said as he leaned away from the table to allow the waiter to set down his burger and fries. "It's a fruit tree. What's the big deal?"

Kate picked up her fork and stabbed a beet atop her salad. "No deal, okay? Don't you have enough to worry about besides a lemon tree?"

Finn chewed a French fry slowly before he said, "I don't worry."

"I mean," Kate continued, ignoring his statement, "you have to do everything inside. We can get help outside. A gardener?" she offered.

"Sure," Finn said as he took a bite of burger. He hesitated before he chewed, but then he began in earnest, with both sides of his cheeks puffed out. When he was done, he immediately took another bite and started all over again.

Kate moved her food around her plate, unsure of where to go next with Finn when she heard someone say, "I thought that was you."

Kate and Finn turned toward the street at the same time. Shelley was on the other side of the iron fencing, smiling widely in their direction.

"You live around here?" Shelley asked, unable to mask the surprise in her voice.

"Yes," Kate choked out, feeling oddly cornered. Did she want Shelley to know they were neighbors? No, definitely not.

"Huh," Shelley said and narrowed her eyes but seemed to stop short of making what Kate guessed would be a derogatory comment.

She squirmed under Shelley's microscopic gaze but said nothing. At least, nothing came out of her mouth. She was thinking plenty. One: that she wished Finn would stop chewing and staring down at his plate as if this were his first meal out of prison. Fuck.

"So where?"

"What?" Kate stammered, caught unaware.

"Where do you live?"

Reluctantly, Kate gave her the address and watched as Shelley's face changed. Perhaps she was willing to forget that people like Kate weren't a bonus to the neighborhood. "I've always wondered what was behind that gate."

She was waiting for Kate to fill in the blanks, which Kate did, begrudgingly and against her better judgment, explaining that she had brought her brother Finn here to help her with the renovation, that they were, in fact, discussing that right now. She had pointed to Finn's notebook left lying open on the table as if she had to prove to Shelley that she was legitimate.

"Sounds like a big job." She addressed this statement to Finn, who was still, to Kate's dismay, chewing, so he didn't respond.

"Finn can handle it," Kate answered for him.

Shelley smiled like she didn't believe it. Shit, Kate barely believed it. This whole thing was going to be a nightmare. What was she thinking by buying a house?

Then Shelley reached across the fence and touched Finn on the shoulder and he jumped, making her laugh. "Hey, sorry. I don't want to come between a man and his burger."

Stop looking like a crackhead, Kate prayed silently. Please.

"I was just going to say that since you don't know the area I can help you," Shelley continued, "offer some names, places to go for paint and that kind of thing."

"You don't have to do that," Kate said. "But thanks."

Shelley didn't pay any attention to what Kate had said. Instead, she looked at Finn and said, "Really, I don't mind. I have a lot of free time on my hands lately."

Finn mumbled something that sounded like *thanks* and then excused himself.

Kate watched him go, a little nervous to be alone with Shelley.

"So is this going to hold things up?" Shelley asked, not waiting for an answer before she said teasingly, "Or are you holding a grudge because of the box thing?"

In her best professional voice, Kate said, "I am your attorney. I wouldn't hold a grudge."

Shelley laughed.

Kate felt the flush rise from her chest and color her cheeks.

Shelley pointed at Kate's cheeks and said, "Awww, that's so cute. Really. You don't see that anymore."

Kate glanced toward the door of the restaurant. Where the hell was Finn? She couldn't tell if Shelley was making fun of her or not, so she did her best to respond neutrally. "Shelley, your case is a priority, believe me."

"You've given me no reason not to believe you. I'm just asking because according to my stepson's wife, he and his attorney are getting ready to do something big."

"His wife is giving you insider information?"

Shelley shrugged and winked. "What can I say? She likes me."

Kate sighed and toyed with the napkin in her lap as she thought about what to do next. "He knows who is representing you, I assume?"

Shelley nodded.

"Well, I hadn't received anything by the time I left the office this evening." Kate gnawed on her bottom lip. "Or there's a chance he's bluffing?" She felt stupid and unprepared. She wasn't even sure exactly what kind of settlement they were looking at or even, really, what was at stake besides a few sophomoric paintings. She was embarrassed to admit that she hadn't put much merit in this whole case. She saw it as one of Ben's follies, although she was a little afraid of being proven wrong.

Finn returned to the table. He was paler than usual and there was a bead of sweat along his top lip. He hovered next to his seat but didn't sit down. Instead, he looked at Kate and mumbled, "Can I have the car keys?" His fingers shook as he held his hand out for the keys.

Without questioning him, Kate took the keys from her bag and handed them over. His fingers were freezing as they closed over hers. He gave a little wave in Shelley's direction and then he disappeared back into the restaurant.

"I'll get the bill and be right out," Kate called after him, but she was sure he hadn't heard her.

"Hardly a spokesperson for the food here, huh?" Shelley said as she watched him go. "Poor guy. I get sick every time I fly."

Kate wasn't listening. She stood, slung her bag over her shoulder, and started off after Finn. She was halfway through the restaurant when she remembered she had taken off without saying good-bye to Shelley, but it was too late to do anything about it now.

Finn refused to allow Kate to help him out of the car. As soon as she pulled into the drive, he went inside and holed up in the bathroom. He was still in there when she fell asleep and as far as she could tell when she woke, he'd spent the night in there.

She tapped lightly on the door and, when she didn't get a response, turned the handle and pushed the door ajar. She held her breath, fearing the worst, but it was obvious that Finn wasn't in the room. That was when she caught sight of his foot sticking out from the closet on the other side of the bathroom. She swung the door all the way open and stepped inside. Finn was curled on the floor in the closet, wrapped in a bath towel. His eyes were closed and Kate, for the second time in as many days, watched her brother's chest rise and fall in sleep until she backed out of the room and shut the door.

When Kate arrived home that evening, she was surprised that the lights were on in the house, and from the back, she could see her brother standing in the center of the room staring at the wall.

He turned briefly to acknowledge her as she walked in the door and dumped her briefcase onto the floor before he pointed to the dozen or more paint chips he'd taped to the area around the bookcases.

"What's this?" Kate asked as she joined him.

"Paint colors. I pulled what I could from memory—I was trying to match the gold in the floor tiles." He showed her one on the far left. "I like this, but it's got too much of a green undertone." He ripped the rejected paint chip off the wall. "Over here—these are warmer yellows."

Kate shook her head. "Can we back up?" Why did it seem the simplest of things had become a struggle to comprehend? "When I left this morning you were passed out on the floor of the closet."

"I wasn't passed out."

"Okay, sleeping," Kate emended. "How do you feel?"

"Fine."

"Fine? Do you think you had food poisoning?"

"No."

"Do you want to see a doctor? I don't even have one yet but I'm sure my secretary could suggest one."

"I don't want a doctor. I want you to choose a paint color."

Kate turned back to the wall. "Are you drinking?"

"Fuck it, Kate. Was I drunk when we went to dinner last night? I had a goddamn ice tea." He paused and said, "You saw that, right?"

"I was just asking. You could have done a few shots when you excused yourself to go to the bathroom." As she said it, she realized how ridiculous she sounded, but she couldn't help herself.

"I'm broke," Finn said. "How sharp of an attorney are you?"

There was a scratchy feeling at the back of Kate's throat. She felt, without much effort, that tears would spring from her eyes if she didn't get a grip. "So how did you get all these?"

"Shelley."

Kate's stomach flipped. "Shelley?" she repeated.

"Yes," Finn snapped. "Shelley. She came by to see how I was feeling and bring me some soup."

Kate groaned. She could just see her over here with some awful seaweed soup and detoxification tea. "Listen, I am not comfortable with this—she's a client!"

"But she's not mine." Finn adopted a patient tone as if he were speaking to a toddler. "When she saw that I was up and feeling okay, she offered to show me a few of the stores she's done business with in the past. She understands that neither you nor I know where to go or even how to begin. She's lived here forever. What's wrong with that?"

Kate tapped her foot as she considered Shelley invading her space. All of a sudden, she sneezed three times in a row. It had to be because Finn had opened the windows, so now the entire house smelled like Vicks from the eucalyptus.

"How do you think this is all going to get done?" Finn went on. "I didn't have any money, otherwise I would have bought some basic stuff just to get me started. We need joint compound, spackling, putty knives, wood . . ." He trailed off. "I made another list." He gestured toward the chips. "So I figured while I was there I might as well do something useful and I picked up the color chips." He hesitated before he added, "She also showed me a job board where guys looking to pick up construction work leave their cards. Shelley said they are mostly legal. She figured you wouldn't want to use anyone fresh from the border."

As Kate searched in her bag for a tissue, she stopped herself from commenting on Shelley's thoughtfulness. She hadn't thought this through. Finn was right. They didn't know where to go. He didn't have a car, nor had Kate given him money or a phone. All

she had wanted was to bring Finn here and give him a job. Was
that the worst motivation in the world?

"I can tell from your face you've changed your mind about
this."

"What?" Kate said, startled from her reverie. "No. Not at all."

"So what do you want to do?"

"You promise me you're not drinking?"

Finn sighed. "Want me to piss in a cup for you?"

"That's drug testing," Kate corrected him.

"I don't need this from you, Kate." He turned back to the wall.
"Maybe I should just go back to Boston."

"To what, Finn? I thought your friend's girlfriend wanted you
off his couch? It doesn't sound like you have many options."

"Thanks for pointing that out to me."

Immediately, Kate felt bad. What was she doing? "Listen," she
said, "I need you here. Do you feel like eating? If you do, maybe
we could go out and you could show me where some of these
stores are—we can pick up some of the stuff you need? I know it's
not much, but you can start, maybe?"

Finn pulled a wadded-up sheet of paper out of his pocket,
smoothed it out, and held it up for Kate to read. It was the directions to the store. "I'm not hungry," he said as he headed for the
door.

Kate turned back to the wall. Was she supposed to pick one of
these before they left? She was transfixed by how many shades
of yellow there were, and she began to feel an unreasonable sense
of panic. "Wait," she yelled at Finn.

When he looked at her, she pointed to the wall of chips. "What
do I do?"

Finn sighed, clearly impatient. "Those are the yellows with
the blue undertones—they are going to be cooler." He looked at

her to see if she was getting it, before he said, "And those are the yellows with a red undertone. Those are warmer."

"How do you know all this? I mean, the warm and cold stuff. Is that how you knew what to say about Shelley's husband's paintings?"

"I had a girlfriend once who was into modern art."

"Really?" Kate had no clue who that girl might have been and she didn't ask. When they were in high school, there had always been girls, although as far as she knew, they never lasted very long and Finn could have cared less about their interests.

The set of Finn's lips told Kate he wasn't about to elaborate. He pointed at the wall again. "Pick a color, let's go."

"Wait," she called again. "Am I ready for this?"

In response, Finn rolled his eyes.

Kate turned to the wall again and chose the palest yellow on the warm side. It reminded her of the scooped-out flesh of a lemon rind. It seemed the safest choice but one, she saw when she handed Finn the chip, that her brother definitely wouldn't have made.

DREAMS WE MISS WHILE
WE'RE SLEEPING

By Thanksgiving, Finn had been working on the little house for a month and their father had been dead for just over a year, something that neither Kate nor Finn ever mentioned. The rotted wood had been replaced, the skylight and windows cleaned, the walls painted a pale gold (Kate's third choice), and the floors buffed. The stainless steel refrigerator and microwave had been delivered the day before, just as Finn completed the installation of the new porcelain sink and maple countertops.

The little house was as finished as Kate wanted it to be—good enough for her to leave the hotel and start living in it. Finn and Kate were going to be sharing the space for a while longer—at least until a bed and bath could be made livable in the other house; that meant they would need furniture. She had been planning on taking the long weekend to do the shopping and so she was surprised when she returned home on Wednesday evening to find Shelley's truck in the driveway, the flatbed filled to capacity with furniture that looked very much like the mismatched hand-me-down crap they'd grown up with as children.

Finn and Shelley were setting up a round maple table and chairs when Kate walked into the house. They were so involved in

setting the hideously ugly furniture just so that they didn't see
Kate standing in the doorway until she said, "What is that?"

Finn looked up, surprised. "Shelley and I went to a yard
sale."

Kate was speechless. She had opened accounts for Finn at several of the home improvement stores as well as the lumberyard
and the tile guy. She'd also given him a cell phone and was surprised the few times she had heard the phone ring, realizing that
he must have someone he had wanted to give his number to, but
she respected his privacy and never asked. Along with the cell
phone, she had given him a weekly wage that he had tried to argue
against. She reasoned he couldn't go around without money, and
besides, he earned every penny as laborer and contractor. Purchases for the house were what she intended him to use the accounts for, the cash was his to do with as he wished. Certainly
they had never talked about buying stuff like this, but Finn was
clearly pleased with himself.

"A yard sale?" Kate echoed as she took in the colonial-stylized
turnings of the chair. The set looked like Sears catalog circa 1977.
She thought about the furniture from her apartment in D.C., still
in storage until the main house was ready. How long it had taken
her to find each and every piece. How careful she had been before
she made a purchase. She would rather have gone without than
settle for something less than what she wanted. "But why?"

Shelley stepped between Kate and Finn. Today she had on a
deep purple caftan over jeans. Since Kate was able to get her stepson to drop his lawsuit based upon the findings in his father's
diary, and appease the MOMA board of directors with a projected
timetable for the arrival of the artist's endowment, Shelley was
around even more. The only piece Kate had left to negotiate were
the details of the retrospective along with the few paintings

Shelley and her stepson had agreed to sell for profit. Ben had been so pleased that Kate was taking such a protective interest in Shelley that he practically called her partner outright. Still, there had yet to be anything official.

Although the added burden of Shelley made Kate almost wish that the diary had yielded no usable information. She wondered why Shelley's son, Ben's friend, couldn't hightail his ass here to spend some time with his mother so that Shelley would have other things besides Finn and Kate on her mind. But it seemed that apart from her weekly yoga classes and her volunteer activities at the food co-op, Shelley had nothing to do. Right now, Kate was kicking herself for not insisting that the museum hire Shelley to assist in cataloging the contents of her husband's studio.

"Don't worry, Kate," Shelley said, wrinkling her nose like she smelled something bad. "I can tell what you're thinking by the look on your face; we didn't buy anything upholstered."

"Yeah," Finn said as he stepped around Kate. "We got this." He pointed to the table. "A couple of twin bed frames that Shelley said you can turn into couches during the day, some end tables, a coffee table . . . I know you want to save money in here, and they sold me the lot of stuff for a hundred bucks, so I figured, why not?" He stopped, shrugged, and reached around back to scratch his shoulder blade while he thought. "Oh and I got you a desk."

There was something so earnest in the way that Finn announced he got Kate a desk that she could almost forgive him for the truckload of dreadful furniture. And he was right about the money. Kate was adamant that the main house was where the most dollars should be spent. So what did it matter about the furniture, she supposed, as long as it was functional? Still it was horribly ugly and used. She shot Finn a weak smile and retreated to the kitchen for a glass of water. As Finn had predicted, the lemon tree outside the window was definitely ailing. What fruit Kate hadn't picked and used was covered with huge black spots, like bruises only fuzzy, that crept from the trunk of the tree to the branches, leaves, and now the fruit. While she and Finn had worked together outside attacking the eucalyptus and the ferns, pruning branches, mulching bushes, and bagging debris, he asked her repeatedly to let him hack it down. But she couldn't do it. Not yet. She allowed herself to indulge in the fantasy that Eli would get to see it one day.

"Hey, do you want to tell me where you want some of this so I don't break my back?" Finn called to Kate.

She broke away from the lemon tree and followed him outside to Shelley's truck. Once they had everything in the house—the twin bed frames at right angles to each other, an end table at either end, the coffee table in the middle, and the little maple student desk for Kate in the corner near the bookshelves—Finn and Shelley left to purchase mattresses for the new beds/couches but not before Shelley made them promise they would come to her house for Thanksgiving dinner the next day. Kate had been planning on staying in and doing work, clearing out some miscellaneous files now that the house had wireless. But Finn had accepted eagerly and so she reluctantly agreed to go along.

Alone in the house, Kate took a long, hot shower, changed into sweats and a T-shirt, piled her wet hair on top of her head, and covered it turban-style with a towel. She walked around, turning on lights against the dusk; everything was still so new and it was hard to believe that Finn had actually made this little house into something livable.

Kate set her laptop on top of the desk, along with a stack of files and a handful of pens. The pens kept rolling, so she got a mug from the kitchen to contain them. She took the lamp she bought that first night and plugged it into the outlet next to the desk so that she had a functional workspace. When Finn and Shelley returned, she was so immersed in her reading that she didn't even hear them until they were halfway in the door with a plastic-covered mattress.

It occurred to Kate that she shouldn't allow Shelley to carry the mattress and she protested and started to get up, but Shelley, without even a labored breath or red face from effort, told her to sit back down amid claims that yoga had made her strong beyond her years. And, shamefully, Kate complied.

They set up the mattresses on the old frames and Shelley left and finally Finn and Kate were alone. He ripped the plastic off a mattress and then threw himself upon it, bouncing up and down. "Hey, this is nice."

Kate smiled. "No more running out of air."

Finn rolled back and forth. "I forgot sheets."

"You can just tuck in the other ones," Kate said as she finished reviewing a document before she hit SEND.

"Oh," Finn said as he sat up. "I didn't think about that. Okay."

She could tell Finn was watching her and so she finally looked up. "What?" she asked.

He nodded toward the computer. "Why do you like it so much?"

"What?"

"That—your work."

Kate took a deep breath. How would she put into words the beauty of law? Finally, she shrugged and said, "At its best, the order of law eliminates chaos."

Finn stared at her a moment. He appeared to be digesting her comment. She imagined the concept might be difficult for someone who had never followed the rules his entire life.

So she was surprised when he said, "Would you mind if I took the car? Went out for a while?" Finn was casual but wide-eyed and twitchy all over when he asked, as if he expected her to say no.

Kate felt a twinge, a funny, hollowed-out feeling in her stomach that her brother was asking her for permission to go out. Or, if not exactly permission, he was asking for her car. Should she? Finn seemed to be exiled since he got here. And he never went anywhere without Shelley or Kate accompanying him. Was that part of their unspoken arrangement?

She tossed him the keys in what she hoped would appear to be a light response. She wanted to be careful not to make too much of it. He took a shower and pulled on a pair of old jeans and a dark sweater with a hole in the right elbow. She was surprised that his hair had grown so much in the time he was here that it looked like the softer end of a thick-bristled brush and actually reached the top of his ears. He still wasn't eating that much and had been sick two more times while refusing to see a doctor; but he looked better than he did the day Kate picked him up at the airport.

After Finn left, Kate worked bent over her little desk until midnight. When her eyes blurred and she felt the stirrings of a migraine at the base of her skull, she turned off the computer and went to find sheets to make up the bed. She made Finn's bed as well, even turned down the blanket for him before she finally crawled into her bed beneath the thick duvet. She closed her eyes, expecting sleep to be imminent, but it wasn't. Instead, she lay in the dark, staring at the unfamiliar shadows cast by the new furniture. Finally, she stretched out on her back and tried to isolate and relax each part of her body from the tips of her toes to the top of her head. But the concept eluded her because Kate simply could not turn off her brain.

She reached for her cell phone on the coffee table and hit Eli's number. Of course it went to voicemail and she hung up. To torture herself, she called three more times just to hear his voice requesting her to leave a message, which she couldn't, no matter how badly she wanted it, bring herself to do.

When Finn came in, she was drowsy, having dozed on and off for the last hour. She didn't open her eyes, but she heard him drop his jeans and get into his bed with a grunt followed by a long sigh. When she whispered his name into her pillow, she was surprised that he answered.

"Kate?" Finn's voice sounded thick and unfamiliar when he said her name.

"Hey," Kate said softly.

Kate waited but Finn didn't respond, so she said, "I was dreaming. I saw Dad. I tried to talk to him, but I don't think I ever got the words out." She rubbed her eyes. "Now I can't remember."

There was still no response from Finn.

"Maybe it's because of this furniture." She paused. "Remember when you said this place reminded you of when Dad moved into the barn?"

Finn snorted.

"Did you ever get inside there, Finn? I mean, when he was still living in there. Did he ever ask you in?"

"All the time," Finn mumbled.

Kate felt the tears at the corners of her eye. She had waited all that fall and into the spring, but she had never received an invitation from him, never seen what he was working on, even though he had promised more than once. By her high school graduation, he had moved back into the house, but the furniture he had taken, the couch and the tables and the lamp, remained in the barn. A part of her hoped it was still there when the new people bought the house and tore everything down. There was immense satisfaction in believing that every single thing from her past had been obliterated.

For the first time in a long time, Kate woke the next morning without benefit of an alarm. Instead, she heard Finn on the phone repeatedly asking someone why. His voice carried a plaintive tone, tired and ragged. When she woke again a little before noon, Finn was huddled under the blankets, an immovable lump even when she called his name, and so Kate imagined that Finn on the phone must have been another dream.

Her head felt heavy, dreams and reality tangled. She hated that she slept so late, that they were expected at Shelley's for dinner. She made a pot of coffee and carried her mug outside. She walked around the circumference of the old pool, mug in hand, the moist earth beneath her feet, marveling that it was late November and things were still green and she was wearing only a sweatshirt and shorts.

Her thoughts ran to Eli. She imagined him and his wife, the chef, having gotten up early to make the stuffing and prepare the bird for the oven. Their kitchen probably smelled like onions and butter and sage, their son and daughter chattering in the background. Would there be music? Would it be snowing? Would he kiss the sheen of butter off her chin, left over from when she tasted the stuffing?

"Kate!"

Kate looked up. Finn called to her from the doorway of the house, wrapped in his blanket. He was holding her cell phone out to her and he looked pissed. "Kate!" he called again, the hand holding the phone shaking with agitation.

She took the phone from him with trepidation. Eli? "Hello?"

It was Ben. It was business. In spite of Ben's wife and children and most likely a huge Thanksgiving dinner about to be consumed, he had received the files Kate sent him the night before and he just wanted to confirm a few things.

Kate moved back inside and sat at her desk, which looked even uglier in the daylight. She flipped open the lid of her computer and sighed, grateful for something to do other than her current hobby of self-flagellation.

Finn was churlish all the way to Shelley's and his mood improved only slightly once they got there, but Shelley didn't seem to notice. On the way over, Kate asked repeatedly what was bothering him until he told her to shut the fuck up. She complied because she was tired of hearing her own voice—although she was sure Finn thought the victory was his—but not before she reminded him that going to Shelley's had been his idea and that he'd better not screw things up because Shelley was still a client and it certainly had not been her need to encourage this peculiar little threesome.

At her use of the word *threesome,* Finn had raised an eyebrow but didn't reply.

Shelley had decorated the top of the white piano with paper turkeys and carnations; a stark contrast to her husband's paintings that were soon to depart to MOMA. Shelley's taste made Kate wonder if the paintings would be replaced by those black-velvet paintings she had seen for sale at the abandoned gas station right before the freeway entrance. Black velvet, Kate had noticed on more than one occasion as she sat in traffic to get on the ramp, seemed to be suited to the mythical creatures of unicorn and dragon as well as Elvis. What would Shelley choose?

They had drinks before dinner, as well as wine with the turkey.

Finn accepted it all greedily, but no more so than Kate, who was definitely looking for liquid pain meds as well. There was a moment when Finn locked eyes with Kate, a bottle poised over Shelley's glass that had been raised for a refill. She thought she should say something then; as a matter of fact, he appeared to be challenging her to do just that. But she didn't. She hadn't seen him drink since he'd been here. Would one day make a difference? Besides, he hardly seemed affected at all, while Kate's limbs felt all warm and wobbly.

After dinner, Shelley took them into the studio. If she noticed the tension between Finn and Kate, she didn't show it. Perhaps the presence of so much alcohol made it tolerable. But it was only in the studio that Finn's mood lifted a little. He sat at the long worktable that dissected the room and looked through the sketchbooks, making intelligent enough comments that led Kate to believe his knowledge of modern art was more than the osmosis he implied from time spent with an old girlfriend who was into art.

Shelley talked about the estimates the auction house had come up with. Christie's was sending a rep the Monday after Thanksgiving to supervise the crating of the paintings along with other un-stretched canvases and a few miscellaneous items for shipment to New York. The sketchbook that Finn was casually thumbing through bore an estimated price tag of $75,000. This made Kate take a seat at the table across from him and oversee the handling. Her concern wasn't altruistic; she had gotten this far with Shelley and, by default, Ben, and she wasn't about to let anything happen to tarnish her accomplishments. She knew that despite her position as lead attorney in the office, if she screwed this one up, Ben could shuttle her back to defending celebrity sex tapes and cutting deals for fools to go to rehab instead of jail.

Finn had more energy after going through the sketchbooks and his mood had lifted. He mentioned that he was looking forward for the week to begin because that was when the crew he had hired to help with the demo on the main house was to arrive. He seemed anxious but less moody. By the time they'd had coffee and dessert, Kate was sober enough that she felt okay to drive home. She was surprised that Finn retreated back into his bad mood, and as he slumped in the passenger seat, it reminded Kate of their drive home from the airport. He kept checking his cell phone, flipping the lid open and shut, dialing for voicemail, and then disconnecting the call in disgust. She wondered then if she had really heard him on the phone earlier in the day, if it hadn't, as she thought dismissively, been a dream. But she knew that in his current mood he wouldn't answer her, so she didn't even try.

When they got back to the house, Kate announced she was going to take a bath. Finn, stretched out on his bed with an arm flung over his face, didn't comment. When she emerged an hour later, Finn and her car were gone. She tried his cell phone but all she got was voicemail. She sat at her desk and attempted to work, and when that didn't divert her attention, she paced. Where the hell was he?

By four in the morning, Kate felt a little frantic. Repeated attempts to reach him by cell had gone unanswered. She considered calling Shelley but then told herself that was ridiculous. He wouldn't be there and she would just be dragging a client into their personal drama. Kate had worked so hard to put all this behind her that she couldn't believe all it took was Finn taking off to bring it back: flashes of staying up all night taking care of Amy and George when they were really little, putting them to bed and watching the *Tonight Show* and then the *Tomorrow Show* with

Finn until the station signed off with an image of the American flag waving in the breeze, accompanied by an orchestral version of the national anthem. All the while she waited for headlights to crisscross the windows of the den, signaling that either her father or her mother had returned after an argument that had spun out of control, before she'd sneak up the back stairs to bed. She'd be damned if she was going to do that now with Finn.

She took the flashlight Finn had hung on a cord from a hook by the front door and stormed down the gravel drive to the main road. But once she got there, she stood frozen, just inside her gate, peering down the deserted road for the first sign of a car. She wanted to do something, but the idea of risking her life on foot to search the darkened streets of Silver Lake for her brother seemed an unwise choice. While she considered what to do, she noticed that some of her more enthusiastic neighbors had already put up strings of twinkling white Christmas lights along the gates that arched over their driveways and she thought how strange that Christmas came here without benefit of snow or cold.

After a while, Kate made her way back to the house. She was sitting on her bed in the dusky peach light of the early morning when a car pulled into the drive. She twisted around and peered out the window in time to see the driver's-side door swing open and her brother stumble from the car. He had taken a few steps toward the house before he remembered to shut the door, so he had to return, bobbing and weaving, back to the car. He lifted his leg up in the air, nearly falling over, and kicked the door shut.

When he saw Kate sitting up in the bed, he slurred, "Don't give me any of your old shit." Then he disappeared into the bathroom and slammed that door as well.

After a few minutes, during which Kate alternated between wanting to kill him and needing to see if he was alive, she rapped her knuckles against the bathroom door. "Hey, Finn? Finn? You okay?"

There was a mumble of unintelligible words and then she heard the toilet flush. She waited for the door to open but when it didn't she knocked again. This time Finn flung the door open wide before she had a chance to put down her hand. He pushed past her and fell onto his bed facedown.

"Finn?" Kate tried again. The light in the room had deepened to a fireball of orange as the sun rose. "Damn it, Finn?" She walked over and shook his shoulder even though she knew there was no sense in trying.

He rolled over onto his back but didn't open his eyes.

"Where the hell have you been?"

"Does not matter." As he spoke, he spit, but he didn't make any move to clean off his chin.

While Kate realized that Finn was in no condition to reason, she wasn't about to stop. "I've been up all night worried sick. You took my car! Finn!"

His eyes fluttered open and he labored over his words, finally getting out, "You don't own me," before his eyes closed yet again.

"As far as I can see, you don't own anything, including that car. If you're going to fuck yourself do it somewhere else." Kate was shaking. It was anticlimactic to scream at her brother's inert form. She wanted someone to go up against. "Goddamn you, Finn, fight back!" she shouted.

When Finn didn't respond, Kate kicked the bed and felt her toes crunch hard against the wooden frame. Tears came to her eyes and she bent down to massage her foot when she saw Finn's cell phone lying on the floor. She picked it up and began scrolling through the calls. He didn't have anything in his address book, so the unlabeled numbers meant nothing to her. She went over to the computer and Googled a few of the area codes: Boston, predictably, but why Reston, Virginia? New York City, but she didn't recognize it as their mother's number; maybe it was their brother, George? Certainly never Amy. That seemed to be the one thing that Kate and Finn had always had in common.

Frustrated by the lack of information and struggling with the need to know more, Kate realized she could plug the numbers into the computer and possibly come up with names to go with them, but she couldn't bring herself to breach her brother's privacy even further, no matter what he had done to piss her off.

Kate left Finn passed out on the bed and spent the day and most of the evening in downtown Silver Lake. She set up her laptop at a table tucked under the eaves in a coffee shop and was surprised at how easy it was to get work done while Christmas carols thrummed as background accompaniment to the ever-changing clusters of people at the surrounding tables. A change of scenery also seemed to quiet the chorus of voices in Kate's head, which chanted *I told you so* every time she thought of her brother.

When she returned home, the house was dark and Finn was huddled under the blankets. He obviously was sweating out the booze because the entire place smelled like the floor in a bar at closing time, and she went around opening the windows until the air was tinged with eucalyptus. Frankly, Kate didn't know which smell was worse.

She poked his shoulder to make sure he hadn't poisoned himself past the point of no return. When Finn grunted and rolled away from her offending finger, Kate was satisfied that, at least for today, he was alive.

Despite the lack of sleep in the last twenty-four hours, Kate was restless and in search of something—she just didn't know what, so she went into the kitchen and opened a package of crackers. She stood at the sink, messily chewing the saltines one by one, allowing the crumbs to gather in the drain as she inventoried the decline of the lemon tree outside the window.

What was left of the fruit was almost entirely black. The now-leafless branches were crusted over with a foaming fungus that caused them to collapse under the remaining weight. Disease had rotted the tree from the inside out.

Kate went outside and found the handsaw that Finn had left on the bench next to a machete with a bright red handle. The machete reminded Kate of the tool their father once used to mark a path through the grass on the way to the swimming hole. The bench was partially covered by the steep pitch of roof, and even though Finn had purchased a huge plastic bucket to protect the tools, they rarely made it back inside the bucket.

When Kate got to the lemon tree, saw in hand, she reached out and touched a branch and recoiled instantly as her fingers sunk into something soft and smooth, the texture resembling butter only fuzzy and warm. She knelt down and wiped her fingers through the crushed grass beneath her feet, and when that wasn't sufficient, she used the cuff of her pants. Close to the ground, the smell of fermenting lemons was overwhelming. It was a sweet, sick scent that immediately clogged her nostrils and caused her to gag. When she was able, she stood and walked away from the tree in an attempt to gulp some fresh air but it was no use—the smell lined her nasal passageway so that every breath was tainted.

She approached the tree with the saw raised, as if the tree had the ability to fend her off and fight back against her attack. Tentatively, she set the blade against the crotch of a branch and flinched as she felt the first of the saw teeth dig into the bark. The saw seemed to shred the semisoft wood until finally, after several awkward thrusts of the blade, the branch hung by a fine filament of once-healthy bark. With one last pull of the saw, the branch fell to the ground with a swooshing sound. After that, Kate attacked the tree with a ferocity she didn't know she had. The branches fell fast and easy, piling up beneath the tree until in the end a five-foot stalk was left covered all over with the knobs of phantom branches. With her foot and the tip of the saw blade, she pushed aside the fallen branches so that she could get the saw as close to the base of the trunk as possible. The trunk, barely five inches in diameter, was so rotten at the core that the saw blade was covered in drippy black goo. With each thrust of the blade, Kate had to stop and wipe it off in the grass to unclog the teeth.

Eventually, the saw was so gummed up it was rendered useless, so Kate kicked the trunk of the tree where she had made her cuts. It toppled to the left easily and without fanfare, just a slow-motion release as its landing was buffered by a pile of branches. Panting, Kate tossed the saw into the pile before she went back into the house to wash her hands at the kitchen sink.

Blisters had already begun to form where she had gripped the saw and they stung as the water hit them. She looked out the window, surprised by her own reflection and nothing more. She turned off the water, blotted her hands dry on her pants, and crossed the room in the dark, crawling into the cave of blankets on her bed. As she listened to her brother bubble and snort in his sleep, blissfully unconscious, she felt an unfathomably vast, hollowed-out grief for what she'd done.

The next day, Finn acted like absolutely nothing out of the ordinary had happened and Kate was too spent to confront him. If Finn noticed the decimation of the lemon tree, he didn't say anything. They avoided each other, and so the mood was subdued while they involved themselves in separate projects. Finn was up at the main house, getting ready for the work crew, and Kate was back at her stacks of files, when Shelley pulled into the drive, toting a basket of leftover turkey sandwiches.

Kate could sense that she immediately knew something was up between them; she had tried to raise a brow in Kate's direction but Kate had refused eye contact. Finn picked at his sandwich with lackluster attention until finally Shelley packed up the leftovers and placed them in their refrigerator. Finn walked her out on his way back up to the main house. Through the curtainless windows, Kate watched them deep in conversation by the truck. She saw Finn nod several times and then Shelley reach out and touch his arm in acknowledgment of whatever he had agreed to before she engaged the clutch and put the truck in reverse.

Later in the afternoon, Finn came into the house and asked Kate to give him a ride to Shelley's. He had offered to help her with a project, but he didn't add any details and Kate didn't ask. It took all she had left in reserve not to remind him that she was paying him to work on her house, not Shelley's. The woman was wealthy and lonely, which in Kate's opinion was a horrible combination. Years of being usurped by a larger-than-life personality and then a few more spent tending to his illness had left her socially adrift. Kate did not want Finn to be her lifeboat. As they pulled into Shelley's driveway, Kate couldn't help but think that after Finn was done with the house and had gone back to his life, Shelley would be gone as well. Though Shelley was her client, as far as Kate was concerned, it was Finn who fostered Shelley's matronly attentions. Without his presence, Shelley would be forced to look elsewhere.

As Finn unfolded from the passenger seat and shut the door, Kate put down her window and called, "I'm going downtown. Can you get a ride back from Shelley?"

She had just at that moment decided that she could not go back to the house and sit in the stink. The office would be blissfully quiet with everyone gone for the holiday weekend. All of a sudden she felt a rush of fondness for the long evenings she had spent there not so long ago. Kate didn't wait for a response. If Finn could take her car and disappear for hours, he could figure out how to get home.

Around nine, after ordering Thai for dinner, Kate sat slurping the curry at her desk. She had just gotten off the phone with Ben, making sure he knew she was in the office. That kind of information would certainly not hurt her quest for partnership, and whether Ben heard her or not, the subliminal message was almost more advantageous.

Ben was coming into town before the holidays and wanted to have a reception for their clients sometime that week. It would, after six months, celebrate the opening of the firm's L.A. office and Kate hoped, although he didn't come out and say it, her partnership as well. She envisioned by then that at least some of the work would be done on the main house. She was excited to show it off to Ben. A house signified a commitment to California that Kate was sure Ben would appreciate. After all, she had been ambivalent at best when he had offered her Los Angeles. But Kate knew the move had been strategic. If she had insisted upon staying in D.C., she might as well have started looking for a new job. She was always amazed when people acted as if their lives were beyond their control, every move, every job, a whim that caught their fancy. In comparison, Kate's life felt like it played out on a chessboard.

When her cell rang a little after eleven, Kate ignored it. She was deep into a brief by a new associate and she wanted to finish it, post suggestions and corrections, and leave it on his desk to be taken care of first thing Monday morning. Unfortunately, whoever was calling was not taking no for an answer. When she finally got up and walked across the room to pick her cell up off the chair where she had tossed it, she recognized the number as Shelley's home line.

Most likely it was Finn, and she didn't feel like getting into it with him. She tossed the phone down but before she got across the room it began to ring again. She grabbed the phone and turned it off and threw it down on the chair. Just as she made it to her desk, the office line began to ring and she picked it up.

Shelley dispensed with any pleasantries when she said in a breathy voice, "Finn is gone."

"What?"

"Your brother took my truck to the store six hours ago. He's gone." She coughed. "You know what else is gone? Two sketch-books and a rolled-up canvas from the studio. The portrait in blue? That's gone. Gone." Shelley's voice escalated into a nearly nonhuman decibel.

Kate felt the curry rise dangerously in her throat, as if she'd been punched in the stomach. Six hours? Finn could be anywhere by now. "Have you tried calling him?"

"What do you think?" Shelley wailed.

"Have you called anyone else?"

"You mean the police? No. No not yet. But I'm pretty damn close."

"Can you start from the beginning? Please?" Kate tried hard to keep her voice neutral and professional, but it was nearly impossible.

"We were just sitting around, talking, after he hung the lights."

"Lights?"

"Christmas lights," Shelley said. "Does it matter?"

"No, I suppose not."

"Well, somehow we—he—decided more lights were necessary—I really wanted to do it up because I haven't in a few years, you know? And maybe my grandchildren are coming to visit from Connecticut and I just wanted everything to be . . . oh shit." She cried, "Why did he have to steal those sketchbooks? Does he need the money? Do you think this has something to do with his ex-girlfriend getting married?"

Kate didn't know where to go first. She froze at the use of the word *steal* and as far as an ex getting married, she had no idea what Shelley was talking about. "Let's not jump to conclusions."

"Okay, well, the sketchbooks and the painting had nothing to do with him going to the store to get more lights. So what do you think he was doing?"

"I don't know," Kate stammered. "But what makes you so sure he took those things from the studio? That someone else didn't come and take them before? Or maybe you misplaced them?"

"That's where we were sitting and so I left it unlocked. Your brother likes it in there and I guess so do I. It makes me feel like my husband is still around." For the first time since Kate had known Shelley, she sounded old and tired.

"Shelley . . ."

"Kate, I gave him a credit card. If he doesn't show up soon, I'm going to have to do something." Shelley said quietly, "I have to."

Kate cradled her head in her hands as she tried to collect her thoughts. Did last night have something to do with all of this? She jumped up and began gathering her bag and briefcase, shoving in papers as fast as she could. "I'm on my way to you. Promise me you'll wait until I get there, Shelley, please." It took all of Kate's will to add the word *please*. Asking a client for a favor like this? If this hadn't been her brother, her advice would have been to call the police and report the truck stolen. She was just praying that by the time she got back to Silver Lake, Finn would be back at Shelley's with a reasonable explanation. He just had to be.

The Christmas lights Finn had hung outlined the roofline and the low-slung angles of Shelley's California ranch house. She could see where he had begun a row of lights around the large windows, but it was also where he had obviously run short, since only one side was complete. Didn't this signify that his true intention had been to buy lights? Maybe something had happened to him on the way to or from the store. An accident? A robbery? As Kate pulled into the driveway, she found herself praying for any of these scenarios; not so much because she hoped he hadn't gone off on a bender but because she just didn't want to think he'd actually steal in order to finance it, although the romantic notion of a good-natured drunk was as naive as the hooker-with-a-heart-of-gold scenario. She took note of the empty spot where the truck was usually parked as she turned off the car. Shelley opened the front door and met her on the path before the bridge, where just beneath the surface the mottled orange skin of the koi flashed brighter than usual under the reflection from the lights.

Kate ran the idea of an accident by Shelley, and so she agreed to show Kate the way to the store. But the route yielded nothing. The parking lot was empty and the road along the way was clear of overt signs that anything troubling had occurred within the last few hours. While she drove, she hit REDIAL on her cell over and over, hoping that if Finn saw her number, as opposed to Shelley's, he would pick up, but it went to voicemail every single time.

On the way back to Shelley's, Kate swung by her own house, but it was empty and dark, everything just as she and Finn had left it. His duffel was still on the top shelf of the closet, so, at the very least, the lack of premeditation could be argued. But when she pointed this out, Shelley seemed unimpressed with her logic.

Shelley continued to hypothesize that Finn was running off to meet his ex-girlfriend, to stop her from marrying. Kate dismissed the idea. Like their father, Finn was a captivating storyteller. If he had a sympathetic audience in Shelley, she could easily see him embellishing a tale of lost love. She had never known her brother to care intimately about anything for an extended period of time, except a drink.

Back at Shelley's, Kate went into the studio and looked around. Shelley followed close behind, step for step. She had made it sound like she and Finn had only a couple of drinks, but there was a considerable amount of empty beer bottles on the worktable, just shy of a six-pack and a half. Kate would wager a bet that Finn had consumed most of them, considering Shelley's size and her current sobriety.

Kate pointed to the bottles. "That's the problem." This was classic Finn. The drinking started slowly: the night before Thanksgiving, when he had asked to borrow her car, followed by Thanksgiving dinner, and then the night when he took the car and came home smashed. Now this afternoon, into this evening, hence his disappearing act.

Shelley frowned.

"He's a drunk," Kate stated matter-of-factly. "Sometimes he can hold it but other times . . ." She shrugged to indicate that it was out of control.

"Why didn't you say something to me?" Shelley asked, her mouth hanging open in surprise.

Kate supposed she would have had no way of knowing. In the beginning, Finn could be a jovial drunk. "I'm not his keeper, Shelley. This has been going on since he was in his teens." She paused and said, "He's probably off drinking somewhere until either your credit card maxes out or he dies." Kate saw the look on Shelley's face and steeled herself for the reaction.

"My God, how can you be so cold? You allowed him to drink at Thanksgiving dinner—you didn't stop him. You should have told me. You should have told me not to have any alcohol." Shelley ran her hands through her ragged hair, eventually pulling it back away from her face, wrapping it around her neck like a scarf, and twining it around her fingers.

"I am realistic. There's a difference." Unmoved by her insult, Kate shrugged again. "He'd just find a way to get the stuff if he really wanted it."

"But how can you let him?" Shelley let go of her hair as she flung her arms out at her sides as if she were going to fly. "How can you just stand by and watch?"

"I'm here, aren't I?" Kate snapped. "I asked you not to call the police, not yet. Against everything I believe in as an attorney. How much shit do you think I'm in here as well? You are my client and he is my brother." Kate was shaking and she had to turn away from Shelley to compose herself. Everything she worked for was on the line right now if Finn didn't show up. If Ben found out, she was done. Over.

Not wanting to divulge ragged details of her upbringing, enough had already been said at this point anyway, far more than she ever wanted to share, Kate said, "I asked him to come here because I saw the shape he was in at our father's funeral. He's been drifting for a year now, he has nothing." She was astonished by how easily she used her father's death to manipulate the mood.

"Oh," Shelley moaned as she paced the studio. "I'm so sorry."

"Don't be," Kate said just as her cell phone rang.

Shelley stopped pacing and turned to stare at the phone in Kate's hand. Kate didn't recognize the number and her voice quivered when she answered.

"Kate Haas," she said as evenly as she could.

She didn't hear the detective's name, just that he was with the California Highway Patrol. Her brother, as far as they could tell, had been involved in a one-car collision with a guardrail about thirty miles from the Nevada state line. They found him passed out in the truck at the scene of the accident. He had been driving with an expired license.

They were holding him at the hospital for tests. Unfortunately, the truck, which was not registered to him, was totaled.

Kate heard the officer sigh when she explained that her brother had been driving a friend's car with permission. How many times had he heard that excuse?

The officer then gave Kate a series of numbers, which she wrote on her hand. There was the precinct number, his extension, the hospital number, and the impound lot at the tow yard.

When Kate got off the phone, she repeated everything to Shelley, who, at the news of Finn's miraculous reappearance, had sunk down into a chair. She held herself rigid, her posture impeccable, although she appeared diminished: her face as colorless as her hair, the lines around her eyes and mouth a deeper shade of charcoal, as if an artist had deliberately aged her.

Kate could tell she had questions, but before she gave any answers she dialed the tow yard. More than she needed to see Finn,
she needed to know if the sketchbooks and the paintings had
been in the car. Her fingers shook so badly that she had to cancel
the call three times before she got the number right. Once she
finally got someone on the line, she found out that the police removed all the personal possessions. The guy working the office
had no idea what, if anything, they removed from the truck. Although he did add that it was "way beyond drivable" so he couldn't
be sure if anything had been salvaged.

As Kate relayed the information to Shelley, she pulled out a
chair opposite her and sat down. "Obviously, I won't know anything more until I get there." Kate's throat was dry and she
coughed out her words. "I will recuse myself as your counsel due
to conflict of interest. It wouldn't be right. I can't represent both
of you in the same proceeding and, well, I suppose Finn will need
me." She was sure there would be some sort of charges filed
against him. While the officer on the phone hadn't mentioned
Finn being drunk, Kate had a hard time imagining he hadn't been.
Even while she told Shelley that Finn would need her, Kate was
thinking she should just let him drown under a public defender's
care. How was she going to explain this to Ben? She wasn't. What
could she say in her defense?

Kate took a deep breath before she said, "You can tell Ben
whatever you need to about this. I understand."

Shelley sat, stroking the scarf of hair around her neck as she
considered Kate's offer. Kate felt uneasy in the silence, especially
when Shelley reached out and took Kate's hands in both of hers.
Seeing Kate flinch, Shelley opened her hands to examine Kate's.
When she saw the row of blisters, she let them go.

"What happened?"

Kate squirmed as she admitted, "I cut down a tree."

"You cut down a tree?" Shelley repeated but didn't pursue it. She looked all around the studio before she returned her gaze to Kate. "Ben has nothing to do with this. I lent Finn the truck, so I cannot rightly accuse him of stealing it, can I? As far as the sketchbooks and the paintings. If the police have them, I just want them back before the auction people get here."

"Shelley, are you sure this is what you want?" Kate asked. How would Finn ever learn what it was to be accountable?

"Let me tell you something," Shelley said and then licked her lips before she continued, "when I married the artist, I was pregnant and he already had a son." She broke off and gave Kate a wry little smile. "So when I had our boy, I was happy. Two years apart I thought they would be brothers, friends for life, you know? Look out for each other." She leaned forward and said, "It's what every parent wants, I suppose."

Had Kate's parents ever connected the dots between their children? Had they been encouraged to be a tribe? Only through benign neglect, she thought sadly, had they come together at all. And that had been all Kate's doing as she begrudgingly assumed the role of caretaker. A role she recognized now that she had assumed based solely on her belief that her father's dreams had somehow been more important than her own. Considering where she was at this very moment in her life, she would have to concede she had made a very poor choice.

Shelley frowned at her own memories. "They never were. Even as children. I would leave the room for a moment when they were small and have to come back right away because one was always crying in outrage. And you see now," she looked around the studio again, "they are only united in the money their father's legacy will bring and they care about nothing else."

"Shelley," Kate began as she realized how she and Shelley seemed bound to the past by the memories they wanted rather than the memories they actually had.

She held up a hand to silence Kate. "I know you think I'm a fool. But I would never put you in the position to have to choose me over your brother, Kate."

Shelley's generosity where Finn was concerned was enviable, not only because it absolved him but it extended to Kate as well. It seemed quite simply a gift with no strings attached. Although nothing about Kate's emotional state had ever been simple, even in the best of times, and while she accepted Shelley's gift for what it was, she was wary. "What if they aren't there? The books or the painting?" Her chest hurt and she was short of breath. "You heard me say I can't represent you both?"

Shelley rubbed her hand back and forth across the table. "There's no need to make a choice." She looked sorrowful. "You didn't really listen to me. I'm not going to press any charges."

"But—"

"But what?" Shelley asked. "Why on earth are you still here?"

If there hadn't been a pileup on the freeway five miles from where Finn had run off the road and into a guardrail, if there hadn't been a backlog in the usually sleepy emergency room in this border town, Finn wouldn't have lain on a gurney for more than two hours while the triage team, ranking the patients by injury, attended to the most critical first.

By the time Finn was examined and blood tests were administered, his blood alcohol level had fallen a half a percentage point below the legal limit. The police officer that had originally called her had come back on duty just as the reports were in from the lab, and the look he had sent Kate when he found out was barely disguised disgust. But he had no recourse other than to allow Finn to leave. Kate was relieved not to have to fight a DUI, yet she shocked herself by how prepared she was to do that on Finn's behalf. She had paced the hallway outside his room while she waited for the results, readying her arguments in anticipation of manipulating the situation until she won.

Finn's license, while expired, had no outstanding warrants, and so after Kate paid the necessary fines (tow truck, impound lot, ticket for driving without a license), and was handed a large, clear garbage bag with Finn's things (the sketchbook and rolled canvas among them), her knees buckled in relief. If either Finn or the police officer had noticed her reaction, they didn't let on.

Her brother's face and chest were badly bruised from where he had hit the steering wheel on impact with the guardrail. His left eye was swollen shut and his rib cage bandaged with a swath of restrictive cloth that cradled and protected his midsection. Because of this, he couldn't stand up straight, and with his facial expressions limited, Kate was unable to determine just exactly what, if anything, he was thinking.

When she first set foot in his hospital room and peered around the curtain, she had been shocked by how much Finn looked like their father lying there in the bed. How had she not noticed this before? She felt a jolt of adrenaline rush from fear and began to tremble, all because it reminded her of the one and only time she had paid her father a visit in the hospital. Like Finn, he had been sleeping when she arrived, yet she had snuck out before her father or any of her siblings had even known she was there. It was a hard failure to swallow. She couldn't stand seeing her father die in that way, yet a small part of her thought it might be the death he deserved. Afterward, it was nearly unbearable for her to live as his daughter with that realization, to attend his funeral, to scatter his ashes, to ponder what his last thoughts might have been. Had he asked for her? Wondered where she was? She'd never know and she'd never be able to ask her sister.

Because of her freak-out at the sight of Finn in the hospital bed, she had backed out of his room and hid in the cafeteria until he was awake. If running away had been an option, she would gladly have taken it. Especially because it appeared that her presence hardly mattered. When she returned to his room, Finn stared with one good eye at a spot on the wall beyond her head and refused to answer her questions. Kate filled in the blanks and what she didn't know she guessed. Since arriving to clean up Finn's mess, Kate had been forced into doing all the talking; most communication existed out of necessity to relay facts. Nothing personal. She tried to treat her brother as she would any client in crisis and for a while it worked.

It wasn't until she helped him into the car in the parking lot that she felt herself begin to unravel. She never should have come right away. She should have let him spend a few nights in a cell for unpaid fines before she showed up. But then she wouldn't have gotten back the sketchbooks, so she had no choice other than to save his ass. This only made her angrier. When had it become so common in her life to make decisions based upon the absence of choice?

She waited until they were on the freeway until she asked, "Where were you going? Vegas?" She quickly glanced over at him, but his swollen eye was on her side so she couldn't tell if anything had registered. Her craziest guess was that he was headed to Vegas where some pawnshop would probably have given him less than a hundred bucks for the lot of drawings, which he would have spent in some random bar in less than an hour.

He moaned and moved stiffly in the seat. He appeared to be searching for a comfortable way to sit. Kate had forced him to wear his seat belt and she imagined it hurt. Too damn bad.

Inside the closed-in car, the stench leaking from Finn's pores was a combination of the antibacterial gunk they'd swabbed all over the cuts on his face, alcohol, and dirty clothes. It was overwhelmingly sweet, with an underlying dank sour odor that made Kate roll down her window for fresh air. "Hey, you need to say something here," she demanded of her brother as she pressed her foot on the gas and flicked her lights at the car in front of her.

Under her breath, she muttered, "Drive or get out of my way, buddy. Fast lane. *F. A. S. T.*" When the lights didn't work on moving the asshole out of her way, she honked. Finally, the car moved to the right and Kate sped past in the left lane as she continued to berate Finn. "I'm not going to act like you're stupid by stating the obvious, but you have to realize the position you put me in, right? I mean taking off in Shelley's truck was bad enough, but stealing the sketchbooks and the painting? What were you thinking? And don't tell me *nothing*, because I know such an idiotic plan had to have been given some thought."

Finn turned away from Kate so he was facing the window.

She huffed, "I'm not going to stop because you won't look at me. Are you kidding? Seriously?" Kate took a deep breath. "I never should have given you a chance. Never. Never should have brought you out here. I'm the stupid one. Absolutely I am the stupid one. You know, there's a reason I never see any of you. I don't need shit like this in my life. Not any of it. Do you have any idea how hard I work? What it took for me to get to where I am? I have worked forever. I took care of you when we were kids; I'm not doing it as adults. I'm done. The next time you need something try calling Mom."

Finn grunted.

Kate couldn't tell if he was trying to laugh at the absurd notion of calling their mother for help or if he was in pain. Fuck him either way.

"I don't know if I'm going to be able to talk Shelley out of filing charges," Kate lied, trying to provoke a response. "The truck is totaled, the sketchbooks . . ." She banged the side of her hand against the steering wheel in frustration and immediately her hand began to throb. She felt the tears at the corners of her eyes but did nothing to wipe them away as they ran down her cheeks.

"If you're not going to talk to me then I'm putting you on a plane back to Boston. Today. Is that what you want?" She thought the threat of sending him back might get him to talk.

Kate waited. She wanted to hear him say he wanted to stay, that he would work hard to make amends. That he would at least recognize she had saved his ass yet again. In all her years as an attorney, she had encountered remorse, truthful or not, in every manifestation possible. But none was forthcoming from Finn. The silence from his side of the car roared in her ears, giving her plenty of time to figure out exactly what to do next, and that always worked to calm her down.

For Kate, getting to the end was tricky, especially since she had known the outcome at the beginning. Putting her brother on a plane and out of her life was certainly the ending she had envisioned, though she had held out some hope against it. But now she could see that there was no other way, there never had been. And everything she might have hoped or dreamed was simply that and nothing more.

Before she followed through on her intention to send him back to Boston, Kate detoured to Shelley's in order to return the sketchbooks and painting. Finn sat in the car. She asked him if he wanted to do it himself but he sank farther down in the seat and closed his eyes. In hindsight, she should have made him return them, as a parent would have made a five-year-old return the candy bar he stole from the drugstore, but it was too much work. For safety's sake, Kate took the keys out of the ignition in case he got the idea to drive away. She was pretty sure he wouldn't try on foot. He might have been faster than her at one time in his life, but Kate was certain those days were long gone.

Shelley ended up following Kate back to the car. She went around to Finn's side and put her palm against his window. As Kate predicted when Shelley asked if she thought Finn would talk to her, he remained mute.

When they arrived at the house, Kate insisted Finn accompany her inside and sit on the bed while she packed his duffel so she could keep an eye on him. She did it fast so she didn't have to think about the unfinished house and the shitty garage-sale furniture and the way the light came into the kitchen differently now that the lemon tree was gone. Finn remained slumped against the pillows with his eyes closed. He refused Kate's offer of water or anything to eat with the barest shake of his head before they got back into the car for the drive to the airport.

The airport throbbed with people returning back to wherever they came from for the long holiday weekend. Kate had actually forgotten that it was still the same weekend and that Thanksgiving had only been three days before. For all she'd done in the last twelve hours, the holiday seemed like it had taken place a month ago.

At curbside, she requested a wheelchair and generously compensated a skycap to stay with her brother while she parked. At the ticket counter, she argued with the clerk about classifying Finn for emergency medical status. She managed to get him a ticket but she couldn't get them to agree to let her accompany her brother through the gate without a written statement from his doctor. All the while, Finn sat passively in the wheelchair, huddled inside their father's leather jacket. While they waited in the long security lines, Kate tried again to talk to Finn, but he was unyielding. The music piped in over the airport speakers played an unending Christmas rotation. Kate recognized "White Christmas," "The Little Drummer Boy," "The Carol of the Bells," and "Santa Baby" enough times that it caused her to grind her molars in tune as it droned on and on and on.

She bent over and tucked a few bills, whatever she had left in her wallet, into the pocket of their father's jacket and told Finn he could keep the cell phone until his minutes ran out. She had no idea what he was going to do on the other end of his trip once he arrived in Boston.

As the day wore on, the barely twenty-four-hour-old bruises on Finn's face were a startling shade of rotting eggplant. When it was finally his turn in line, Kate saw the security guy's eyes widen along with a sharp intake of breath as Finn unfolded, limb by limb, from the wheelchair and finally looked up, revealing his face as he submitted to the metal detector. The guy even glanced at Kate and gave her a look like she had to be kidding, especially since Finn was hunched over before him, swaying gently back and forth as he tried to stand still. There was blood on the collar of his shirt from the cuts on his face, and his wrist still bore a hospital bracelet. There was no hiding: everyone in line could see that Finn was barely well enough to travel. Still, Kate shot him a stare that dared him to say something.

"Just try me," she whispered, and even though he couldn't possibly have heard her threat, he lifted the wand and waved it in the air around Finn's battered form.

While Kate stood on the other side of security, she was forced to watch helplessly as Finn struggled to put his shoes back on. For all the horrified expressions at his condition, no one offered to help. Instead, people stepped around him as they gathered their laptops, belts, cell phones, and coats. Finn couldn't bend over because of the injury to his ribs and the tight bandages. It took him almost ten minutes, hands shaking the entire time, a line of spittle dangling off his lip as he bit down in what appeared to be concentration, but Kate would venture a guess that it was more like excruciating pain. Finally, Kate had to look away, and when she looked again, he had collapsed into the chair with the jacket across his lap. She could see beads of sweat on his forehead as well as his upper lip as he sunk against the seat in exhaustion and closed his eyes. The guy who had checked Finn through saw that he had finally succeeded in getting his shoes on and wheeled him off to the side. Since the only way they were going to let Kate past security to assist her brother was if she bought herself a ticket, she insisted that someone from the airline meet Finn at security, take him to the gate, and get him on the plane.

When the person finally showed up to wheel Finn down the concourse, Kate was hopeful her brother might turn around to say good-bye; a wave, any tiny, insignificant acknowledgment. When none came, she took a step forward, yet stifled the urge to call out to him. Finn had failed Kate, hadn't he? So why did it feel as if she had failed him? Silently, she mouthed to his retreating form: *I'm sorry.*

She stayed until she could no longer distinguish him from the crowd. As she lost sight of him, it jarred a memory of when they were kids and she and Finn would race each other down their street. Instinctively, he knew how to pace himself while Kate gave it all she had right from the start. Even though she knew she would tire out and lose the race, she did the same thing every single time just for the feeling it gave her. Despite his breath in her ear and the swoosh of air against her side as he pumped his arms faster, for a few precious seconds right before Finn passed her, she was braver, more certain of herself, stronger than she ever could possibly have imagined.

part four

Finn

TO THE BOY WITH
THE RED UMBRELLA WHO
SAVED MY LIFE

Finn did not know where he was the first time he opened his eyes. Then again, it was not an entirely unfamiliar feeling, so he rolled over and went back to sleep. When he opened them again several hours later, he saw a woman with short, shredded dark hair sitting in a chair across the room. Her bare legs were pulled up to her chest and she was staring at something on the floor. Finn looked down. It was a monkey in a green sweater.

"What's up with the green monkey?" Finn asked, his voice hoarse from booze and too many cigarettes. His syntax was off— his brain not yet working. He ran his tongue over the skim on his teeth.

The woman looked at him with a slow smile. She could easily have been mistaken for Miriam. That is, if Miriam hadn't married some doctor last weekend and moved to Virginia. Who the hell moves to Virginia? Beneath the blankets Finn was naked. He reached a hand down between his legs and lazily scratched his balls. He remembered those stupid bumper stickers from ages ago: VIRGINIA IS FOR LOVERS. Who the fuck thought of that? The woman, whoever the hell she was, did not seem at all concerned that Finn was in her bed.

At the mention of the green monkey, the woman picked it up by the arm and hurled it across the room in Finn's direction. He sat up quickly to catch it but he didn't extend his arm far enough. The woman was laughing as Finn fell half out of bed onto the floor in an awkward attempt to save the monkey. It was a stuffed toy. He tossed it onto the floor as he collapsed back onto the pillows and groaned. Fuck. He felt like shit. Nothing new about that.

He threw an arm across his face to block out the light. Vaguely, he recalled this woman wearing a blue wig and standing next to a carrot.

She said, "It was part of my costume—but I suppose you don't remember."

Finn still had his eyes covered but he could hear the pout in her voice.

"You were more concerned with getting my costume off," she added.

So they'd had sex? Finn tried as hard as he could, and still nothing came to him past the carrot and the blue wig. Nothing. It was only because he knew what she wanted from him, the same thing they all (except for Miriam) had wanted from him, that he uncovered his eyes and asked, "Can we do it again?"

So there was no surprise when she got up from the chair and walked back over to the bed. Finn watched as she slowly pulled a peach-colored slip over her head to reveal her body. She put one foot up on the bed and spread her knees slightly, giving him a good long look at her waxed and polished bush—something he didn't really care for and was even more than a little disturbed that he didn't remember—before she commando-crawled up his body to join him under the blankets.

* * *

The doorman at Finn's mother's building on West 91st Street probably knew Finn better than he knew Finn's mother. Just last week he had run into the guy crossing Second Avenue. It was a rainy afternoon and he was holding the hand of a little boy with a red umbrella. His kid, Finn guessed. He had waved and Finn had waved back and said hello to his kid. When he saw Finn in the building, he always felt compelled to shout out to Finn the latest sports scores, as if Finn gave a shit what he was talking about. It probably just made the guy feel alive, because most of the people who lived in this building had nurses and wheelchairs and were totally fucking out of it. Drool city. Finn knew enough of them by sight now from his trips up and down the elevator.

He had been crashing at his mother's place since Kate had thrown him out and he'd been able to stay just under the radar even though his brother, George, lived downtown and his sister Amy in Brooklyn. His mother rarely stayed here and Finn wasn't even sure why she had purchased this apartment to begin with or why she'd given the doorman permission to give him the extra key. But he was glad she had because he had nowhere else to go. When he had landed in Logan from Los Angeles, he had sat in a coffee shop counting out the money Kate had given him. He had just enough cash to buy a bus ticket from Boston to New York. A part of him had hoped his mother would be home. Especially when the doorman caught sight of him and had steeled his jaw to toss him out on the street. It wasn't until Finn explained who he was and offered his license as proof that the doorman gave him the key. Even at that, he had watched Finn warily for the first week the few times he had ventured outside. As his bruises faded, he left the apartment more, and the guy seemed to relent. That was when the barrage of sports scores and useless trivia greeted him as the elevator doors slid open. He supposed it was better than the alternative. Besides, the guy was probably so charmed by Finn's mother that eventually he had to give Finn the benefit of the doubt. His mother was the type of person that people liked to say they knew; it only worked against her if you were related.

Since the mess with Kate, Finn had been trying to be good. Or at the very least he was entertaining the theory of what good felt like. At the moment, he prided himself that there was still a bottle of his mother's vodka in the freezer that he hadn't yet drunk. When he let himself in the apartment, he went to the freezer and bent down and peered inside just to make sure that the bottle was still there. Even if he had drunk so much last night he couldn't even remember having sex the first time with the girl with the green monkey, he hadn't touched that fucking bottle of vodka.

In reality, Finn had been drunk since he found out that Miriam had gotten married. He hadn't talked to her in over a year, and when Kate had given him a phone, the first thing he did was dial Miriam's number. He didn't even think it would be in service anymore. She had threatened as much the last time they'd talked. So when his father died and George had told him to call Miriam, he had lied and told them he had and left it at that. As a matter of fact, he was so positive it wouldn't be her number that, as it was ringing, he forgot to hang up, and then she answered and he panicked and hung up as she was saying hello. Then she called him on Thanksgiving morning and told him she was getting married the following weekend and moving to Virginia. Her voice was timid but resolute. Even though he had begged her over and over again to tell him why, he already knew the answer. She wanted to have babies and a yard with a swing and love a guy who doesn't throw up on her. Who doesn't have the DTs so bad when he's off the shit that he thinks spiders are crawling all over his body and he scratches himself until he's raw and bloody. Who doesn't threaten to kill her if she won't give him the keys to the car so he can go get some more booze. She didn't add those last few things, but Finn knew her well enough to know that she didn't have to; she'd said it all before.

Manhattan was not a place to be without cash and Finn had used the last of the money from his sister just to get to New York. While Finn had always managed to snag a construction job back in Boston where he knew people (eventually that had worked to his disadvantage because too many people got to know him too well), here he was just another person filling up space in a miserable city. New York did nothing for him. It was a cesspool of spoiled rich and filthy beggars. The only thing between him and the guys who constantly hit him up for change in the park was that Finn had a place to crash. Other than that, there was no difference.

There was nothing in his mother's cabinets to eat, and while Finn rarely did so anymore without horrible cramping pains followed by a stream of diarrhea that was incapacitating, he needed to put something solid in his body. With shaky hands, he patted down his pockets for his wallet only to discover it held nothing but a slip of paper with George's phone number and his mother's address. His license had expired a year ago, but it was still in his wallet. He was surprised, actually, that the police and his sister had given it back to him. He thought they would confiscate it. But he'd heard Kate argue that he needed the ID to get on the plane and so maybe that was why they had made an exception. A part of him wished they hadn't because all it did was make him feel like shit. He peered at it sometimes if only to remember how he looked. The picture had been taken years before, when the skin around his eyes wasn't so swollen all the time. And although the photo was too small to really see, he was sure the tiny red capillaries that had started to break around his nose weren't there before. His entire life women had come to him easily and even now there were women who went for his damaged face and charm, and it had become a means of survival or, at best, a way to secure the next drink.

If only he could remember where the green monkey lived. She was into some weird shit in bed but he'd done worse. Maybe he could get a few bucks. He just closed his eyes and thanked his fucking stars that his dick still worked. That and his decaying looks somehow still got him free drinks. There were some days when he woke so hard that he couldn't even imagine that his body had enough blood left in it to go there. Even whacking off was more pain than it was worth lately.

He rifled through his mother's desk and then her closet, looking in old purses and on the table next to her bed. She wasn't here enough to leave anything behind. He came up with a dime, a cough drop, and a card for the laundry room in the basement. With a resignation that at least implied he felt bad about what he was about to do, he unplugged her Bose portable CD player and put it in a shopping bag and headed downtown on foot. A long walk would keep him away from that goddamned bottle of vodka.

In Chinatown, on Pell Street, an appendix of asphalt jammed with restaurants and beauty supply stores, Finn sat hunched over in a corner table way in the back of a restaurant nursing a steaming bowl of noodle soup. He picked out the shreds of pork and tried to chew them slowly without getting nauseated. So far so good.

He'd gotten fifteen dollars for his mother's CD player and he'd have to pay three dollars for the bowl of noodle soup, but the tea was free. Before his food came, his hands were shaking so bad that he had to clasp them together in his lap and hold his entire body rigid just so he wouldn't move the table. He pretended to study his placemat adorned with symbols of the Chinese New Year. So maybe he was wrong and it was already past Christmas. He searched the placemat for some indication of dates, but the numbers and letters swirled in front of his eyes and made absolutely no sense. That had nothing to do with the drink—it was the way he'd always been. School was torture. Being drunk was so much easier. He couldn't even remember the last time he had read a newspaper. And the date? From the lights and the holiday decorations he'd spied in a store window, he guessed sometime in December. A winter wedding for Miriam and her fucking doctor husband. How nice.

At the table across from him, two girls were having lunch. They looked nearly identical with their long blond hair blow-dried straight, tight T-shirts, jeans, and the street vendor's ten-dollar pashmina shawls roped around their necks. They kept stealing glances at him and then looking away quickly—enough times so that he knew that they were interested. From the map spread out on the table between them, they were obviously from out of town, here for a good time, hoping to get his attention, and it seemed to Finn that girls like these were everywhere lately. He smiled weakly in their direction and thought how fucking pathetic they were; if a drunk like him could seem appealing, what the fuck were they expecting out of life?

Finn tightened the scarf around his neck and hunkered down inside his father's leather jacket. He slurped his noodles slowly. So slowly that the girls who had been checking him out ate lunch, had dessert, stalled around, and then paid for their check with one long backward glance at him before they left. He nursed the pot of tea, got up, and pissed, grateful that his stomach was staying steady, and then when he got back to the table he signaled for the check.

The tiny dark-haired waiter rushed toward him, his face all wrinkled like a dried apple. He talked fast in broken English, said Finn was all paid up, and handed him a fortune cookie with a slip of paper. On the paper was a telephone number and below that were scrawled the names Holly and Rose. Fucking-A. The girls had bought him lunch.

He broke the fortune cookie into little pieces, tossed the fortune away without reading it, and crunched on the cookie while he shoved the paper with their number into his pocket and ambled out of the restaurant into the narrow street. With no destination in mind, he allowed the chaos and crowds of Chinatown to carry him uptown toward SoHo. It was colder than he remembered it being when he'd left his mother's apartment. The sky was damp, heavy, and gray. He had no idea what time it was—late afternoon for sure. Just off Broadway, he ducked into a coffee shop near the corner of Thompson and Bleecker Streets. He took a stool at the counter and ordered a coffee. One sip and his bowels let loose, and he tripped getting off the stool in his rush to go to the bathroom. All the sustenance he had gained was lost in the stall as he writhed in pain on the filthy toilet.

When he got back to his coffee, it was cold. He threw a buck on the counter and hobbled out into the street. On his way up Thompson toward Washington Square Park, he passed a pay phone. His fingertips were numb as he fumbled with the slip of paper. The phone rang five times and he was about to hang up when one of the girls answered. Her voice was high, young. He closed his eyes and rested his head against the metal of the phone stand and tried to remember if either of them looked to be over eighteen.

She giggled when he said who he was and thanked her for his lunch. She told him they were shopping a few blocks from where he was right this minute. They arranged to meet in the park, so Finn took his time and walked slowly—although he really had no choice because the stint in the coffee shop bathroom had left him wasted and his legs felt like rubber.

When he finally got to a bench to the right of the arch, he collapsed onto it and stared at the Christmas tree erected below. There were several people taking photographs and a guy with a shopping cart and a boom box blasting what sounded like Latin Christmas carols. Finn closed his eyes for a second but didn't allow himself to go away. When he opened them again, he saw the girls rushing across the square on impossibly high-heeled boots. They each held several shiny shopping bags in their hands, which they swung back and forth as they stood before him.

Finn realized that his position on the bench—legs and arms spread open wide—could be seen as some sort of come-on, but he did nothing to adjust his limbs. Why play games? He knew what they wanted but now just the thought of it made him tired. He was beginning to regret his phone call until one of them—he didn't know who was who—suggested they go for a drink. Exactly what his body needed.

Too many drinks later to count—drinks that were blessedly paid for with a gold credit card (courtesy of Holly's father, who, according to his daughter, owned the good parts of Michigan up into Canada, whatever that meant), they took a cab to the W Hotel in Union Square, where the girls were staying.

Once in their suite, the girls opened the pharmacy. They chattered on about a private club on Gansevoort Street the concierge had told them about and that they'd gone to the night before only to find the boys had been more interested in each other than Holly and Rose. Holly gave a mock pout and said she thought they were going to have to go home without having any real fun. Then Rose climbed onto Finn's lap and bounced up and down until she was satisfied by Finn's anatomical response, obviously proving he was heterosexual. In anticipation, Holly and Rose each took a hit of Ecstasy and then told Finn he could have whatever he wanted from the mini bar while they disappeared into what Finn assumed was the bedroom.

Finn shrugged to himself. So what if he was their second choice for a night of fun. He was a savior, their savior. And the savior shall be duly rewarded. He took every tiny liquor bottle out of the fridge and lined them up on the coffee table in front of him. "Hello, Jack," he said as he twisted the cap and shot the amber liquid into the back of his throat and then tossed the bottle aside and reached for another. "Hello, Grey Goose," he whispered as Rose appeared back in the room wearing only a wife-beater and a thong. He could see her heavy nipples clearly through the fabric and it did absolutely nothing for him. His dick, however, had a mind of its own. Or maybe it was just the Ecstasy.

Holly came up behind Rose and slid her hands under Rose's shirt. Her fingers stroked Rose's nipples, pulled them out until they were long and hard and Rose was writhing and moaning. It reminded Finn of the trip to Amsterdam with his father that summer his life changed. His father insisted he and Finn visit the brothels. Sex had been everywhere—nothing was beyond his reach if he had so desired. His father paid for a room where they stood behind the glass and watched two tired-looking women go down on each other. He remembered looking quickly at his father to see his reaction. He had hoped his dad would laugh and say, "Let's get out of here." Instead, his eyes were glassy and his breath had been coming in short, shallow puffs between his lips. Finn had wanted to run out of there but he didn't want to deal with his father calling him a pussy, so he stayed through to the horrible, staged orgasmic ending. If he could have seen into the future, to what would be happening between them in Italy just a week later, he would never have stayed. But he was the son who never challenged his father—he was a coward. He knew what his siblings thought of him going on that trip with their father. Accepting his bribe. Finn was the weak one.

Finn knew that most likely the porn-star moans coming from the mouths of Rose and Holly were for his benefit. While the show continued, he opened each bottle before him and drank while Holly pulled down Rose's panties. When it was his turn to join in, he allowed himself to be led off the couch and into the bedroom.

He didn't really have to participate, which was just as well. As Holly ground away on top of him and Rose was doing something to his balls, he occasionally reached up to finger a nipple and give a little performance moan of his own, but other than that he drifted.

It had been different with Miriam. Finn had waited. He wanted it to be right. He wanted it to be out of his house and away from the craziness of his family. He had gotten it together for a while then, had a good job out on the Cape working construction, and he had sent Miriam the money for a ticket to join him. It was Columbus Day weekend of her first year of college and Finn was able to get them a room at a hotel on the beach, run by the family of one of his buddies, an end-of-the-season special that he normally would never have been able to afford. The room had a big bed with a bay window overlooking the ocean and a tiny deck. They had curled up on the one lounge chair beneath a blanket and kissed for what seemed like days. He could still remember how his breath caught in his throat when he saw her naked. He had wanted to cry—had, in fact. They both had.

Finn had cried because she was so beautiful and because he knew that no matter how much they loved each other, he would screw it up. He was just beginning his slide but even he knew then he'd be incapable of reversing—even for Miriam.

What should have ended after that weekend went on for years, too many years, too many times that Finn had nearly killed himself or someone else because he couldn't stay sober. And Miriam. She had loved him through everything—was convinced, in fact, that her love was enough to save him. Until one day she just stopped. He had poisoned everyone around him and miraculously he was still alive. Even his bastard of a father managed to get a brain tumor and piss off. Why the fuck was Finn still alive? So that he would know that Miriam had finally left him behind to marry a doctor and move to Virginia? Was that why?

Holly collapsed on top of him with a moan. Obviously, she was done. When she rolled off him, Finn was surprised that he was still hard. Rose seemed to take this as some sort of sign that he wanted her and began to crawl on top of him, but mostly he just wanted this to be over. He rolled her over onto her stomach and took her ass cheeks in his hands and slid himself inside. Each thrust caused him such pain he thought he was going to pass out.

When she finally cried out, Finn withdrew and crawled off the bed and into the bathroom. He got to the toilet just as the liquid shot out of his ass again.

When he was done, when there was absolutely nothing left inside him, he slid onto the marble floor and curled up into a fetal position. Shivering, he reached up and yanked a towel down off the bar and covered himself. After a few minutes like that, he must have passed out because when he woke up, there was vomit on the floor all around his face and in his hair and he couldn't remember puking. He cleaned himself up as much as he could, avoiding the mirror, and slowly opened the bathroom door. Holly and Rose were asleep in the middle of the big bed, curled around each other.

He picked up his pants and shirt and his father's leather jacket from the floor in the bedroom. In the living room, he found his shoes and scarf and Holly's purse—the contents upended across the floor when she had been looking for the drugs. There was a wallet stuffed so tight with cash that it wouldn't close. When he investigated, he saw that they were all hundreds. He helped himself to three bills and then, before he dropped it back onto the floor, he looked at her ID. She had a driver's license that said she was Holly Bliss from Gross Pointe, Michigan. She was twenty-two. He took another hundred and a pack of cigs sitting by his big toe. He and his dick were worth four C notes at least—well, his dick was anyway.

It was snowing when he got outside. Big, wet, juicy flakes that saturated his hair as he started to walk north. He walked up just past West 23rd Street before he hailed a cab. Why not? He gave the hundreds in his wallet a proprietary pat; he was flush.

He was still wasted when he got to his mother's building. The doorman had to run across the lobby to catch Finn by the shoulder as he slipped on the wet marble floor by the elevator.

"Better watch that," Finn slurred and tried to point in the direction of the melted snow. "The old people will break their fucking hips."

The doorman grinned at him, as if he was an old drinking buddy. "I'd say you have more to worry about than they do."

"Nah, not getting old."

The elevator bell rang, signaling that it had arrived on the floor. "Sure you are, bud, we all are."

"Nah," Finn said again as he stepped into the elevator, "not me."

The doorman leaned in and pressed the button for the ninth floor. He held the elevator open a second with his body as he regarded Finn slumped against the back wall. "You okay getting into your place? You want some help?"

Finn waved him off. The doorman nodded, stepped back, and just as the doors slid shut, Finn yelled, "Wait."

The doors slid back open. "What?"

"Was that your kid the other day? With the umbrella?"

The doorman smiled proudly, showing all of his teeth and nodded. "That's my boy, Jonah. He's five."

Finn nodded and closed his eyes. He smelled bile. "That kid saved my life."

"What?"

"Your kid, his red umbrella, saved my life that day."

The doorman shook his head; obviously he thought Finn had gone over the edge and didn't know what he was talking about. "Go sleep it off, buddy."

Finn saluted as the doors shut again. He couldn't find the words to tell him that he had almost stepped off the curb in front of a taxi, and then the red umbrella coming toward him caught his eye and he stopped because he didn't know it was attached to a person—he thought it was floating in the air and he hadn't a clue as to how or even why. When it turned out to be the doorman and his son, all he could do was wave and say hello and then feel an inescapable sadness that the taxi hadn't done its job and smashed his skull to smithereens right there on Second Avenue.

He let himself into the apartment and grabbed the bottle of vodka from the freezer. From the kitchen drawer, he took a book of matches and headed to the bed. Propped up against the headboard, he lit one of Holly's cigarettes and took a deep drag. With the other hand, he twisted the cap off the vodka. The first sip gave him a brain freeze. He took another long, hard swallow and closed his eyes and waited for his liquid salvation.

The morning after the first time he and Miriam had made love, they walked down the beach to watch an old hotel getting demolished. The bulldozer made several passes, ripping off brittle wooden porches until there was a large, gaping hole on the side that faced the beach. Amazingly, there were still beds and chairs and tables in the rooms—they hadn't been cleared out. When he looked at Miriam, there were tears running down her cheeks. When he asked her why she'd been crying, she said she never wanted the memory of their weekend here to be erased just like that. Even though Finn knew he was lying, he took her in his arms and told her that would never happen. Now, the way Finn saw it, Miriam had married the doctor so she could permanently erase all her memories of him. What she had now was a fresh new memory-making start in Virginia. He took another slow drag off the cigarette before he brought the vodka to his lips again. When he closed his eyes, he saw Miriam as she was that day long ago. Her face was so trusting as she opened herself to him beneath their tent of sheets and blankets.

* * *

Before Finn even opened his eyes, he could hear his mother and George arguing. When he was finally able to force his crusty lids apart, he looked to his left. His sister Amy was twisted into a hard plastic chair below a window, chewing at the cuticle on her thumb. He noticed her hair was still blond and short like it had been a year ago at their father's funeral. When she saw that he was awake, her eyes widened but she didn't call attention to him. Instead, she slipped quietly off the chair and bent over next to his bed. She put her head down low near his ear and whispered, "Oh Finny, you've come back to us."

He couldn't lift his arm to touch her even though he wanted to. His hands were tied at the wrists to the sides of the bed. He had no fucking idea where he was or why his mother would not shut the fuck up. The more awake he became, the louder their voices were and the more pain his body was in. Fucking liquid fire shot through his limbs and he had no choice but to moan out loud.

At the sound that came out of his mouth, everything in the room stopped. His mother was at his right side, fussing with the ties around his wrist, and George was at the foot of the bed, frowning. Amy was still hunkered down close to his ear. "Don't say anything," she advised him.

His mother, when she was done fiddling with the ties, reached up and smoothed the hair off his forehead. At the feel of her palm on his skin, Finn cried out again. He had to be on fire and they just didn't realize it. Why the hell didn't they help him? He turned a panicked eye on Amy. She shook her head slightly and made small shushing sounds to indicate that he should relax. When the nurse came in, she shot something into the line that was attached to a bag hanging above his head. He closed his eyes and moments later he started to fly.

He had no idea how long he had been flying in his dreams, but when he woke, he was tired as if he'd been aloft for days with no rest. He wanted to close his eyes again, but a nurse entered the room just then and noticed he was awake. She said, "I'll go get your brother," and left before Finn had a chance to stop her.

When George came in, Finn tried to smile, but something didn't feel right. His wrists were still tied, so he couldn't touch his face to see what was missing. Something had to be missing. He had absolutely no idea of time, or memory of where exactly he was, so when George moved closer, Finn opened his mouth to ask him, but it was so dry his tongue got stuck behind his teeth. He was desperate for some saliva. Some ice. Something.

George pulled a chair up to the side of the bed. He shrugged out of his coat and sat down. There were smudges of blue beneath his eyes, and the corners of his mouth were turned down; he looked as tired as Finn felt. He must be dressed for work, because around his neck he wore a tie, although the knot was loose. Maybe it was after work.

George leaned forward on the bars and said, "I don't know where to start, Finny. You're alive . . ." He shrugged; his mouth was twisted into a sad smile. "If the doorman hadn't checked up on you, you would have burned the whole building down."

Finn closed his eyes. He didn't want to look at George anymore. He wanted George to go away so he could fly again. He wanted the nurse to come back in and put the juice in the bag that made him fly up, up and away.

But George wasn't going to shut up. He was going on about Finn passing out with a lit cigarette. The fire destroyed most of the wall behind the bed and into the closet, but it hadn't reached the common walls, so no one else was hurt. Apparently, the door-man was worried that he had let Finn go up alone. He knew Finn was too wasted to walk and he wanted to make sure that he had gotten into the apartment safely. When he got there, the bed and the wall were already in flames—the fire had spread quickly be-cause of the 180-proof vodka that was spilled all over Finn's clothes and the sheets. They think the thick leather jacket Finn had been wearing had actually protected his chest from really severe burns but the heat had seared the jacket to his chest.

If Finn could have laughed out loud, he would have. His fa-ther's leather jacket saved him? Now that was truly a fucking laugh riot. The last words his father had ever spoken to him were in Italy the summer he and Finn went backpacking. How many years ago was that? Ten? Finn had knocked him to the ground and his father retaliated with the only weapon he had. He had told Finn he wished he'd never been born. He was the mistake that had never panned out. He would always be his father's greatest disappointment.

He tried to concentrate as George cataloged Finn's injuries for him in a tired, mechanical voice. Burns mostly, his hair and the top of his head received the worst, as well as his right hand, where, despite his drunkenness, the doctors think he must have swiped at the flames. He also had burns on his chest and his limbs, as well as his face, but they weren't as bad as the burns to his scalp. Physically, he was already deteriorated before the fire. The doctors said there was severe liver damage and so they were pumping him with super antibiotics because of the risk of infec-tion from the wounds. His body had little to none of the inner resources it would need to fend for itself. Right now, along with the antibiotics, they were just trying to control the pain with morphine. They couldn't do anything about the alcohol withdrawal; he would just have to ride that out. It was a grim prognosis, George said, but he wouldn't lie to him. He thought he needed to hear the truth.

The only time George's voice changed from the robotic was when he got to the ties on Finn's wrists. He cracked when he said, "You were trying to hurt yourself, pull everything out. They couldn't control you when you came in so they tied you down." He paused and continued, "Until they know you won't try again, they have to leave them on."

Finn opened his eyes again and looked at George. George put his hand out to touch Finn but then pulled back. He didn't seem to know what was safe to touch, so his hand hovered there temporarily above Finn's body like that of a faith healer at a revival. Then he closed his eyes and squeezed the bridge of his nose with two fingers. When he opened them, he said, "Mom didn't want to tell you anything. But I thought you should know what you'd done."

Finn could tell George was tired of cleaning up after him. They all were. That's why he wasn't surprised by Kate's absence. She'd told him she was done back in Los Angeles, hadn't she? He tried to nod at George to let him know he understood, but he couldn't. All he wanted was to be left alone. The damn doorman. Fuck him. That was the second time he'd saved Finn's life, redirected his destiny. You couldn't fuck with someone's destiny twice like that, could you? Now he looked at his brother and with everything he had left in him he managed to plead in a hoarse whisper, "Just let me go."

When George realized what Finn had said, the corners of his lips twisted spasmodically and then his entire body jerked as his shoulders shuddered. Finn thought he was laughing until he saw the tears running down George's cheeks. George wiped at his face with the back of his arm and stood up. He didn't say anything else as he swiftly kicked back the chair, grabbed his coat, and moved toward the door. Finn half-expected him to glance back, but he didn't. Through the window on the door, in the hallway, Finn could make out a man with dark brown hair, who pulled his brother into his arms as soon as he saw him.

He remembered that summer after he'd come home from Europe. He remembered how he and George had climbed up the rocks at the swimming hole and had a diving contest. He remembered how silver Miriam's skin had looked in the moonlight as she treaded water below them. He had wanted to impress her, for sure. Especially after the way he saw her looking at him. No one had ever looked at him that way, with an open mixture of curiosity and desire. When they started meeting each other in the kitchen long after everyone had gone to bed, he had tried to act like it was an accident. Until it became every night, and it was all that got him through the day: the thought of tea and cigarettes with Miriam in the kitchen. The way she held her fingers over her mouth when she was unsure of her English, the brush of her hand against his as she pushed a saucer into the middle of the table for ashes, the way her gaze lingered just a moment longer than was comfortable for either of them. A gaze that let him know everything and more was his for the taking but only if he wanted it bad enough.

Wasn't that where he'd gone wrong? He had allowed himself to want it too much when he had absolutely no right to do so?

Finn could wiggle the fingers of his left hand just enough to feel the call button on the railing for the nurse. He pressed it once, twice, three times. When she finally came in, Finn didn't have to say a word. She smiled down at him as she prepared the needle. Thankfully, she seemed to understand that he just wanted to disappear, and she was more than willing to oblige.

epilogue

Marilyn

ten

THE HAAS ARCHIPELAGOES

*M*arilyn Haas watched from the grand old porch of her friend the director's house on the lower Cape as her younger son unfolded from a rental car along with his lover and his lover's teenage son.

Despite her nerves, a wide smile broke out on her face at the sight of the boy. She surprised herself at how much she adored him, almost a man really at sixteen, whom after this weekend she could officially declare her first grandchild. Perhaps her only grandchild. Her remaining three children appeared too frightened to procreate, and in retrospect she supposed she couldn't blame them.

George looked up and saw her watching them from her spot on the swing and, squinting into the low September sun, raised his hand in greeting. Sam was getting the luggage out of the trunk and Asa was coming toward the stairs, grinning at the sight of Marilyn. Theirs was a mutual admiration society. What started out as his starstruck fascination with her as the innkeeper from the *Dead, Again* movies had progressed into a deeply satisfying relationship. One of only a few that Marilyn could count in her life so far.

Asa's own mother had abandoned him when he was three and he had never had much female influence in his life. George had mentioned one recent attempt on Asa's mother's behalf and then silence. So maybe that was why Asa gravitated to her, or she to him. It would be too simplistic to say that after four children, whose upbringing Marilyn and her ex-husband had bungled, Asa was her second chance. But in many ways he was. She saw the way her own children watched her with Asa, tense and distrustful, and indeed in the beginning she could see George waiting for the other shoe to drop every time they were together. Waiting for Marilyn to lose interest, to say the wrong thing, to simply not show up. But she didn't. And slowly she gained Sam's and George's trust. As for the rest of her children? Marilyn sighed. They would all be here soon enough.

Now she jumped from her seat and ran down the steps to greet Asa. Marilyn, at five foot nine, was tall, but Asa towered over her. She stayed on the bottom step to hug him and still he had to lean down into her arms. He gave her such a strong embrace that she lifted up off the step. She laughed and he put her down and Marilyn pushed the hair back out of his eyes and reached up and tweaked his cheeks as she teased, "You're darling! I just want to hold you in the palm of my hand!"

Asa laughed, too, clearly enjoying Marilyn's attention before he turned and yelled to his father that he was going down to the beach. Sam rolled his eyes but was smiling as Asa, not waiting for his response, kissed Marilyn on the cheek and took off in a jog down the shell-covered drive toward the ocean.

Marilyn met George and Sam halfway and tried to take some of the bags, but George brushed her off with a kiss. Sam did the same and Marilyn, empty-handed, was left to lead them into the house.

Saul Tang, whose house this was, came toward them, barefoot and tan, from the back of the house. A trim man seventeen years Marilyn's junior, nearer to her children in age than Marilyn, the same man who had offered Marilyn that tiny part years ago in the first horror movie that got her noticed, had opened his home for George's and Sam's wedding. He greeted Sam and George like old friends and then pointed them upstairs to their room.

When he and Marilyn were alone, he pushed her back gently against the cool whitewashed walls and kissed her on the mouth. Marilyn liked keeping this part of her life secret and had asked Saul to go along with her. He had agreed at the time, but now here he was, kissing her while her son was right upstairs. She kissed him back but hesitantly, before she said, "What was that for?"

Saul grinned. "You're a hot mama," he teased as he let his hand linger a moment on her breast through her thin cotton shirt.

She playfully slapped him away but was secretly pleased with his attention, although she wasn't quite sure what they were really doing yet. During different times in her career, comparisons had been made to the actress Anne Bancroft. She knew Saul was aware of them as well, because when he hired her the first time, he mentioned it during their meeting. It was farfetched, but she couldn't help wondering if he was enjoying his own little Mrs. Robinson fetish. She even thought of doing the whole stocking-and-garter-belt scene with him as a test when they had first started sleeping together, but then she had chickened out. After all, this relationship was supposed to be a diversion during a low point in her life; just sex, was what she told herself every time they got together. And then, over time, Saul became a part of her life. They were together constantly whether it was work or play. And he made an effort with her children, taking an interest in their lives, most of the time handling them better than Marilyn. Although it had taken Marilyn a long time to get used to a man that wanted to have sex with her for something more satisfying than his own needs, it had taken her even longer to trust that Saul was what he said he was: a good man.

"I'm about to become a grandmother," she said softly, proudly. "Shouldn't I act like one?"

Saul fake-pouted at her rebuff but stepped back, allowing Marilyn space to move from underneath his arm and away from the wall. During and after her marriage to Richard, she had lovers, but she used sex as barter for jobs, for favors, to ward off loneliness, and so it was nothing more than physical. Then there had been menopause and what Marilyn had assumed was a natural lack of interest on her part until she met Saul, the surprise of her life. What the hell was she doing? She didn't give herself permission to be happy with Saul until she saw Finn lying in that hospital bed. Everything had changed in that moment. She wanted her children. She wanted Saul. She wanted to be loved, and to be forgiven.

She skirted around Saul quickly and walked back into the kitchen. "Would you like a drink?" she called over her shoulder. "I'm having seltzer with lime."

Marilyn had promised Finn a dry house, even though he didn't ask for one, and George and Sam had agreed, even though it was their wedding. They didn't need to have alcohol. George said it was more important to have Finn alive and sober. Even Saul, with his brand-new wine collection, had, without question, taken every bottle out of the cabinet, tossed them in a box, and driven them to a friend's house across town. He knew what Finn had been through after the fire. Marilyn had been on set with him when she had taken the call from George that Finn had set her apartment on fire and was in a lockdown ward in the hospital because they couldn't be so sure he wouldn't try to kill himself again.

She was most nervous about Finn. The logistics of getting him here had been difficult enough. He had been in a treatment center in Washington State once he got out of the hospital. Nearly four months in the hospital in New York to regain his health, and then the decision to go across the country to spend another six in rehab. Then, once he had been released, he had gone to Seattle. He said he loved the air and the mountains and quiet. Marilyn wasn't so sure. Those things could also drive a person to drink—a person who wasn't used to thinking so much without the aid of alcohol-induced anesthesia could think and think and think and go crazy. But then maybe she just needed to have more confidence in his rehab. Finn was different from the others. As a baby, he had demanded she be present. She attempted what she had thought to be good parenting so many times but had failed more than succeeded. And then he had tried to drink himself to death. After that, nothing bad could happen to him now, could it?

She was nervous enough about seeing all of her children without the added pressure of hoping one of them had regained the will to live. She couldn't remember the last time they had all been together, and this occasion was one she had actually stepped up and orchestrated. George and Sam could not be legally wed in New York. Marilyn had suggested the Cape, since Massachusetts had legalized same-sex marriages, and then Saul had offered his house to all of them. For a woman who had not spent a holiday with any of her children in years, the whole notion of this gathering was so far out there that she was shocked when George and Sam accepted. Now here they were, upstairs, unpacking, and she was awaiting the rest of her family.

Saul entered the kitchen and leaned against the counter. "I'll take mine with lots of ice," he said as Marilyn sliced the limes on the maple counter. She could feel him watching her as she filled the glasses with ice and opened the seltzer. Again she wanted to ask him what they were doing, but she didn't want to start anything right now. Better save that conversation for later—after everyone was gone.

She opened the refrigerator and looked for a place for the seltzer bottle. The shelves were already overflowing with food because the caterers had provided them with a cold supper for tonight, since Marilyn was unsure when everyone would be arriving. There were fried chicken and potato and macaroni salads as well as grilled eggplant and tomatoes for the vegetarians and a low-salt alternative for Marilyn.

Six months ago, Marilyn had started suffering bouts of dizziness and debilitating headaches. Of course, she immediately concluded she had the same brain tumor that had killed her ex-husband, or worse: after all, she had smoked a pack a day for more years than she cared to count. After a barrage of tests, the doctor diagnosed high blood pressure and high cholesterol. Despite her thin frame (for some reason, she had harbored the belief that only fat people had heart attacks and strokes), he scared her enough that she agreed to this health regimen. She was supposed to stop smoking and cut out salt and take medication and get more exercise. Now, to start her day there were pills, patches, and vitamins along with green tea and fresh-squeezed juices. No cigarettes. Just thinking about not smoking made her fingers twitch, and she nervously stroked the patch on her shoulder through her shirtsleeve. What she wouldn't do for a cigarette right this moment; the physical craving was nearly unbearable.

While she stood with the refrigerator open for what seemed

like forever, Saul came up beside her and took the bottle from her hands and slipped it into a slot on the door. Then he closed the doors and handed her a drink. He picked the other one up and clinked it against hers before he raised it to his lips and drank. Marilyn followed his lead. All she had to remember to do was breathe and she would be fine. Just fine.

Marilyn noticed that George and Sam, like any couple, seemed to swing between elation and nervousness in the hours leading up to the ceremony. George had been on the phone since he'd unpacked, making sure the minister from Boston, a close friend, knew the directions to the house, even though they had been faxed to him several weeks before; making sure the caterers knew the time, even though they had provided an annotated sheet of times and foods that currently was taped to the refrigerator. Then there were the other things to make him crazy: the flowers and the cake and the cake topper that Amy was making as her gift to them, along with the possibility that Sam, in a flurry of last-minute packing, had left the rings back in their apartment in New York, although George did eventually find the blue velvet box with the rings in his toiletries bag.

Finally, Marilyn took Asa back down to the beach to give George and Sam some time alone. Sam, she noticed, rubbed George's shoulders or whispered in his ear to calm him. If Marilyn recognized love, this was it, and she was relieved and pleased that someone would care for George like that and that he was capable of caring for someone back.

She tried to remember what she'd felt like marrying Richard. She was a twenty-two-year-old in love with the idea of love and slightly queasy and unsteady on her feet—as if she were standing on the deck of a sailboat—from the beginnings of Kate stirring in her belly. Richard had woken up the town justice in Suffield to marry them, because they were to leave for New Hampshire early the next day where Richard had secured a place at a writers' colony for the summer. The couple who ran it said that he could only bring her there with him if she was his wife, and so, on the spur of the moment, he decided they should marry right then.

It was a warm June, which she remembered because her long-sleeved blouse had been saturated with sweat where she'd tucked it into the waistband of her skirt. The justice's wife had been their witness, and afterward she had handed Richard a pamphlet on keeping their marriage alive with antiquated tips on bringing your wife flowers and thanking her for the meals she cooked. They read it aloud to each other, lying naked in their bed, while on the floor a fan stirred tepid air. She remembered when they got to New Hampshire how Richard kept introducing her to everyone as his wife and how she'd wished he would stop.

She didn't tell Asa any of this as they walked nearly a mile down the beach and back, picking up rocks and shells and horse-shoe crabs that lay tangled in the seaweed. Instead, he did most of the talking about their impending move to a building in Brook-lyn that Owen, Amy's boyfriend, had helped them find. It was a huge space in a former machine factory that would allow Sam to have a studio. They'd have to do a lot of renovation before they moved in, which his father and George seemed excited about. But there really wasn't a neighborhood, and the closest store was about ten blocks away. He'd liked living in the city and didn't seem thrilled with the notion of Brooklyn, but he did like Owen and Amy and was happy to be near them.

Marilyn wondered if it would be strange for Asa at school, but he shrugged and said George wasn't his teacher, since he was in eleventh grade. Besides, lots of kids had weirder home situations than his. Marilyn swung the bag with the shells in her left hand, tucked her other arm in his, and smiled up at him. Times like this she was scared that Asa would find out that she never knew how to be a mother. She wondered how much Asa knew about how George had been raised, what he shared with Sam that Asa may have overheard. Of course there was always the chance that she had exaggerated in her own mind the impact she had on each of her children's lives. Maybe, like Asa had said, once they got out into the world they met other kids whose home lives were weirder than theirs. At least that was her hope anyway.

Somehow she had gleaned from Richard that normalcy was a compromise, and so she never tried for balance, going right for the extreme and damn the consequences, which were, in retrospect, the lives of her children. Loving them was an abstract idea. Raising children was the more complicated task, which she had failed. She was too selfish, too young, had neither the energy nor desire where her children were concerned.

She never held her tongue or hid an emotion or considered that she was the person her children needed protection from the most until it was too late. She smoked and drank and medicated herself with prescription drugs. She drove fast and recklessly without the protection of a seat belt, the children unbelted as well. She matched Richard affair for affair and used sex for all the wrong reasons: lust, loneliness, revenge, and, once, to get a coveted role. She told herself that one day it would all change, but as anyone who has ever deluded himself or herself about that one magic day eventually finds out, it almost never ever comes.

"Hey, you that nervous about tomorrow?" Asa asked with his eyebrows drawn together.

Marilyn shook her head to clear it; she had no idea how long she'd been lost in the past. "No," she said and smiled. "They don't even need us. It'll be a piece of cake."

Asa looked relieved at her response and he laughed. "That's what I keep telling them, but," he said with a shrug, "they seem to want to act crazy."

Marilyn didn't answer him right away. She wanted to hold on to Asa, she wanted to tell him she was more scared to return to the house and face the rest of her children than she was about anything else in the world. She wanted to tell him how sorry she was for everything she had ever done wrong—for anything she might do to him in the future—but of course she didn't.

When they returned, Amy had arrived with her boyfriend, Owen, and several of his bandmates—the cello, fiddle, and bass respectively. They were providing music, including a song Owen had written just for George and Sam, which Amy boasted about to anyone who would listen. Amy and George were side by side in the porch swing: her daughter's feet in silver ballet flats resting on the railing while Sam and Owen reclined on the steps. The other musicians were in the backyard with Saul, checking out the space.

Amy didn't get up when she saw Marilyn and Asa come up the drive, but she smiled in their direction and yelled to Asa, "Hey, geek."

Asa seemed pleased with Amy's greeting as Owen reached up and grasped his hand. Asa bent down and gave him a quick hug, and once again Marilyn was amazed at how generous Asa was with his affection for all of them.

"It's beautiful here," Amy said in Marilyn's direction. She was never sure if her youngest child was directly addressing her, because she hardly ever called her Mom. Marilyn tried hard not to read into it but she couldn't help it. Before she had a chance to answer, Amy added, "Saul was great to do this."

Marilyn nodded quickly. Indeed, it was easier to let them think it was all Saul's idea. They had known Saul from the beginning and had taken to him not because Marilyn acted in his movies but because that was just the kind of person Saul was—people genuinely liked him. Saul publicly claimed he inherited his likability from his grandfather, the number-one pickle-seller on Delancey Street. Marilyn was the only one who knew that Saul was entirely self-made—that his pickle-selling grandfather only existed in Saul's imagination. Perhaps that was why he and Marilyn were so compatible. They each possessed the ability to turn figments of their imagination into reality for the sole purpose of survival.

From behind came the sound of another car pulling into the drive. When she turned around, she saw Kate all alone in an enormous car. For a minute, she hoped that Finn would be with her. Marilyn had asked Kate to wait at the airport for Finn, to try and coordinate their arrival so that Finn didn't have to get out to the Cape by himself. But Kate had mumbled something about time change and flight incompatibility, and so Marilyn had dropped it. In personality, she was the child most like Richard, the one who liked to be in control at all times.

Seeing Kate's face framed behind the glass of the windshield, flushed and grim, reminded Marilyn of the summer when Kate had just turned four and she and Richard argued endlessly about the pigtails Kate insisted he, not Marilyn, put her hair in every single day. Finn was two, and it was the year he seemed to be sick constantly with high fever after high fever, colds that turned into bronchitis, and sore throats that turned to strep. It seemed there was always a bottle of pink medicine in the refrigerator. Finn claimed all the energy Marilyn had to give, so even if Kate had wanted Marilyn's attention, she wasn't going to get it.

Richard had been charmed the first few times that his daughter wanted him, but soon he tired of twisting the bright plastic double-balled hair ties that Kate demanded in her wispy flyaway hair. It was a nearly impossible task for adult fingers, yet Richard was resolute: he would teach her how to do her own hair. Except every session resulted in Kate collapsed on the floor, gulping tears along with the anguished cries of "Daddy do it now, Daddy do it now" coming out of her small, angry mouth.

One afternoon, while Marilyn napped with Finn, Richard did the unthinkable. He took the kitchen shears to Kate's hair and snipped until it was too short for pigtails. After that, Kate wouldn't let anyone near her hair for over a year; to brush it was nearly impossible and often the task went undone. It wasn't until the following fall, when Kate was about to begin kindergarten, that Marilyn was finally able to coax her into a hairdresser's shop to rectify the mess. Kate had agreed on the condition that Richard accompany them. Even after the indignity and humiliation, Kate still adored her daddy the best.

Kate leaned out the driver's-side window and honked the horn several times as she yelled, "Okay if I park here?" She had pulled the imposing black SUV behind the dinged and battered van that Amy and Owen had driven from New York.

When she saw the size of the vehicle, Marilyn couldn't help but feel a twinge of disappointment that Kate couldn't wait for Finn. Having enough room was certainly not an issue.

Owen stood. "I'll pull forward a bit so I can get the equipment out."

After they jockeyed the cars around, Marilyn watched as Kate got out of the car and struggled to slam the heavy door. No one made a move to assist her, probably because they knew she would resist. She had on high-heeled sandals and a beige pantsuit, and over her shoulder a briefcase that was stuffed with multicolored files. Under the weight of the briefcase, Kate listed to the left, causing the skinny heels to sink into the sandy driveway as she lurched toward the porch awkwardly. When she finally reached the bottom step, she looked up at her mother and said, "That was pure hell."

George burst out laughing while Sam looked down at the ground, smiling. Amy said, "Hello to you too, Kate."

Kate retorted, after looking over Amy's thrift-store ensemble, "I suppose I should have gone with bare feet and cut-offs?" She frowned, addressing no one in particular. "Is there anything to drink?"

Amy gave Kate the finger while Marilyn sighed and took her oldest daughter by the arm and led her into the house for lemonade.

Marilyn almost wished that Finn had arrived first. It would have been easier. The waiting only added to her anxiety. As it was, he had called and left a message saying that the plane from Seattle had been delayed in Las Vegas due to thunderstorms and he probably wouldn't arrive in Boston until midnight, and then he still had to get the car that Saul had arranged and drive all the way to the outer Cape. Finn had only recently had his license reinstated and Marilyn was nervous about him driving. But short of going to Boston and driving him back here (something she had given serious thought to), there was nothing she could do to get him here any faster. So they went ahead with dinner, George and Sam at the head of the table, wearing tiaras that Amy had made them out of tinfoil, and Marilyn at the opposite end with Saul to her left. Saul had insisted she take the other end, and there had been an awkward moment when she had wanted to run out of the room.

Dear sweet Saul still thought that if she playacted enough like their mother, it would right the past, but Marilyn knew, while looking at the faces of her children, that no matter the number of occasions she orchestrated or her willingness to be here for them, it would never be enough. And she had made peace with that, she would take what she could get. Still, the head of the table was presumptuous. But then George nodded his head in her direction and she took the seat. She didn't want to cause a scene.

After they ate and Owen and his friends graced them with some music, everyone drifted off to bed, including Saul, who was bunking out back in a half-finished cottage with no heat. He had tried to stay and help Marilyn clear the kitchen, but she had forced him to go. She needed the time alone to think, and besides, she didn't want to have an occasion for sex come up, not tonight.

When she was done, she walked through the downstairs, leaving lights on so Finn could find his way. She wrote a note directing him to his room, and when she went to tape it to the door, she smelled cigarette smoke. She nearly swooned and closed her eyes and inhaled deeply. She wondered if she were dreaming until she saw the red circle in the corner of the porch attached to the hand of Kate, who was curled beneath a blanket in a wicker chair. Her bare toes peeked from the bottom of the blanket, the skinny heels abandoned on the porch floor by her chair.

Marilyn moved toward the smoke and inhaled again. She wondered if the smoke combined with the patch would give her too strong a nicotine infusion and cause a heart attack, as all the paperwork warned, but then she decided to chance it. After all, she wasn't smoking the cigarette, just smelling it.

Kate said, "Saul just left." She gestured with the cigarette in the direction of the stairs.

Marilyn squinted down the dark driveway but couldn't see him. "Smoke a lot, do you?" she asked as she settled into a chair next to Kate.

Kate exhaled away from her mother. "I'm sorry, I'll get rid of it."

She went to grind out the butt and Marilyn jumped out of her seat and said, "Don't, not on my account."

Kate laughed as Marilyn sheepishly sunk back down into the chair. "Okay, Mom, you can live vicariously through me."

Kate had been the only one of her children that even knew that Marilyn had been to the doctor, was on high blood pressure meds, and needed to stop smoking. She was actually surprised that none of them had mentioned that Marilyn, whose fingertips were stained from years of nicotine use, wasn't smoking. Either they didn't care or the excitement of the wedding had their minds elsewhere—she preferred to delude herself that it was the latter.

Now her daughter was asking her, "What are you doing lurking around here late at night? Trying to sneak out back?"

Marilyn blinked rapidly as she looked at Kate. "What are you talking about?"

Kate rolled her eyes. "Pleeease, Mother . . . he practically drools when he looks at you." She paused. "How many years can you use the 'we're just friends' excuse?"

"Kate!"

She laughed. "Hey, enjoy it while you can. You're one of the lucky ones. In Los Angeles every guy I know looks like he's dating a schoolgirl with double-D tits. I don't have a chance." She hesitated. "Saul happens to be a young guy who finds an older woman attractive . . . an anomaly." She screwed up her face, searching for the right words, "To put it in celebrity perspective for you, you're in Demi Moore / Ashton Kutcher territory."

"Kate . . ."

"What?" She smirked. "It could be worse, you could be in love with a married man and waiting for him to leave his wife." She coughed. "Let me tell you that it never happens. You only get one chance."

"Kate . . ." Marilyn tried again. She thought Kate was probably referring to herself, but she couldn't be positive. She knew so little about any of their lives and the things she did know were superficial. Things they'd tell anyone. Things they let slip by accident.

Marilyn shrugged.

"I don't care about any of it," Kate said.

"Sure you do."

"Why? You think everyone needs love?" Kate took a drag on her cigarette. "Love sucks."

"Nice sentiment to have at a wedding," Marilyn teased.

"No one is happy at a wedding save for maybe—*maybe*—the bride and groom." She held up her hand and started to tick things off her fingers. "The wedding party is pissed they spent so much on their dresses and are jealous of the bride no matter how much they claim they adore her; the same for the guests; the couple is second-guessing their relationship no matter how blissful they think they are; the whole reception thing is a total waste of money; and the end of the night sucks because the bride and groom are so smashed that sex is probably a huge disappointment."

"Well, I guess you have it all figured out then. Should we warn George and Sam before it's too late?"

Kate waved her off. "Nah, let them figure it out."

"I think you're wrong—about them anyway."

"Maybe."

Marilyn shook her head; she knew she couldn't change Kate's mind about anything. She studied her daughter's profile. Did Saul find Kate attractive? She could be the younger version of Marilyn. Had they been sitting out here talking while Marilyn cleaned up the kitchen? She didn't want to ask her daughter anything for fear that it would seem that she didn't trust her.

Suddenly, Marilyn remembered the reason Richard had given for cutting off Kate's hair. *She's too old for pigtails* he had said as he swept the delicate swirls of their daughter's hair, probably not amounting to more than an ounce, into a paltry pile on the buckling red-and-black-flecked linoleum tiles of the kitchen floor. Kate's stoic little face had peeked out at her from the pantry where she had fled when Marilyn saw what Richard had done. She had the urge to ask Kate if she remembered that Richard had cut off her pigtails. Then she realized Kate would probably only see it as a desperate attempt by Marilyn to prove that she hadn't been that neglectful a parent—Richard had been worse. So she said nothing.

Kate stood, letting the blanket slip to the floor as she bent and retrieved her shoes. "I'm going to bed." She stifled a yawn and said, "You too?"

Marilyn picked the blanket up off the porch floor and hugged it to her chest. She wanted to sit and wait for Finn, but she knew it would be hours from now and she needed to be awake and functioning for George tomorrow. She looked up at Kate. "Go on. I'm going to stay here for a minute."

Kate hesitated.

"What is it?" Marilyn asked.

"Oh, well. I made partner. Finally."

"Kate! Oh, congratulations . . . you work so hard. Too hard."

She shrugged like she had heard it all before. "Yes, well. About time. Right?"

"Did you tell the others?"

"Why?" Kate looked at Marilyn. It seemed like she wanted to say something more. Marilyn wanted to hug Kate but it just didn't seem right and the moment passed. That's what life with her children was now, filled with missed opportunity and awkward moments. She watched Kate pause at the front door and run her index finger along the note Marilyn had taped to the glass for Finn before she disappeared inside.

When she woke, the sun was streaming through the windows, high enough in the sky already that Marilyn knew it was late. She smelled coffee and bacon, which meant everyone had risen before her. A light sleeper, she had not set an alarm, positive that she would hear Finn come in and then she would just stay up and make breakfast for everyone. But that never happened.

Now she quickly washed her face, combed her hair, dressed, and ran down the back stairs that led directly into the kitchen. She didn't want this weekend to be like it always had been, her children self-sufficient in the morning long before they'd had to be, simply because she never got up early. Just once she'd hoped to beat them downstairs for a Donna Reed moment and she'd missed it.

She smelled burned toast and then she heard George bellow, "Christ, Amy, didn't your mother teach you anything? You can't cook worth a damn!"

Amy laughed. "Well, speaking from the position of caboose," she paused and Marilyn heard more laughter and Amy saying, "I'd say my mother taught me one very important lesson: how to keep my legs shut."

This time the entire room erupted and then she heard someone comment in a dry tone, possibly George, "That true, Owen? You're not getting any?"

Then more laughter and, "Ouch, Amy! You're hurting me! Someone make her stop." More grunts and, "You can't blame me for taking that shot, you left it wide open."

"So to speak," Sam bellowed.

Marilyn descended the last step into the kitchen then and everything stopped. Amy's arm, raised above George's head with a wooden spoon clutched in her fist, dropped to her side at Marilyn's entrance.

Someone snickered and Sam said, "Okay, I feel like I'm five."

Kate, hunched over her files spread all over the kitchen table, said without taking her eyes off the papers, "I got up early to get some work done. Alone. Why the hell can't you people sleep in?"

Asa, from his position at the kitchen counter, looked up from his plate, his mouth stuffed with French toast, and said to Marilyn, "I've been an angel."

Marilyn smiled at Asa, took the spoon from Amy, put it back on the counter, and shook her head. "Is Finn asleep?"

George handed her a cup of coffee but she held her hand up to stop him and put water on for tea. "He's not here yet," he said.

Marilyn stopped what she was doing. All she could think was there had been a plane crash or a car crash on the turnpike. No. She shook her head. Life couldn't possibly be that unfair, could it?

"He was probably delayed again and didn't want to call since it was so late," Saul said from the back doorway as he walked into the kitchen and over to the coffee pot. "I'm sure he's on the way." He looked rumpled still from sleep, and one side of his face had pillow creases. He squinted and pushed his glasses back up on the bridge of his nose.

Marilyn nodded and lit the flame under the teapot. She tried not to look at any of her children's faces and instead concentrated on lining up the vitamins she needed to choke down with her yogurt and granola. Her hands and fingers twitched. She had put a fresh patch on upstairs, but right this moment all she wanted to do was bum a cigarette off Kate. The teapot whistled and she could think of nothing else except how good a smoke would be right now. Just one.

"Look who's a health freak all of a sudden," Amy said from her perch on the counter as she picked at a bowl of leftover pasta salad from the night before.

Marilyn grimaced as the first pill slid down her throat aided by yogurt. She looked over at Amy to see if she was being sarcastic, but Amy's smile looked sincere enough. She was surprised. Maybe Amy was being nice because she figured Marilyn had heard her remark about keeping her legs shut. Still, it was unlike Amy to make amends.

"It sucks," Marilyn said as she choked down more vitamins and accepted from Saul a cup of green tea without milk or sugar.

"Living longer really sucks," Saul joked.

Marilyn smiled. "Says he who is allowed to have a cup of coffee."

Everyone laughed, but when she looked at Asa, he was frowning down at his plate, drawing a line of syrup with his knife. The ceremony wasn't until five, but one by one everyone left the kitchen to shower and get ready for the day. George and Sam were infinitely more relaxed than they had been the day before as they went out to the porch with the newspaper and coffee. Amy went into the dining room with a box that held the cake topper she'd made—there were some last-minute adjustments and she needed space to work. Kate gathered all of her paperwork and jammed it back into her briefcase. Cell phone in hand, she left the kitchen jabbing at numbers on the keypad. Saul and Owen went out back to meet the tent guy and Marilyn concentrated on cleaning up the breakfast dishes, because the caterers would be here soon. She tried not to pay too much attention to the clock or to the phone that hadn't brought word of Finn.

Asa still lingered until finally Marilyn said, "Do you have butterflies?"

He shook his head.

"What is it then?" Marilyn dried her hands on a dishtowel and touched Asa's shoulder. He may be taller than her but his bones still felt fragile beneath his shirt.

He squinted up at her. "Are you sick?"

"Me?" Marilyn shook her head. "It's called growing old."

"You're not that old," Asa blurted.

Marilyn cocked her head to the left. "Oh, but I am in some tribes."

"I don't want to be treated like a baby." His cheeks and neck colored a deep crimson. He seemed embarrassed and worried at the same time.

"I would never . . . if there was something to tell, I'd tell you." Marilyn stared hard at him. There was no reason to tell him all the things that could go wrong. That was one of the great things about being young. Unless there was something specific, you just didn't think about all the what-ifs.

Begrudgingly, Asa said, "Okay."

She rubbed his shoulder. "Now go get into your flower-girl clothes," she teased to lighten his mood.

Asa grinned and slid off the stool. "I think I'm going to go to the beach first. I have time, don't I?"

Marilyn nodded at him and watched as he jogged out of the kitchen. She forgot how boys his age always seemed to run everywhere—their store of energy was tireless. She bent down and put the last mug into the dishwasher. She almost wished she'd jogged along with Asa down to the beach. Instead, she went to find Saul in the backyard. She needed to keep busy.

Later, from her bath, Marilyn could hear the cars as they arrived in the driveway: the caterers, the florist, the baker delivering the cake, and the minister from Boston. Then, as she applied makeup and put on her suit, more cars carrying guests and the voices of Amy, Asa, and Saul as they greeted people rose up through the windows of Marilyn's bedroom.

So it was a surprise then, when she walked into the kitchen to check on the caterers, that she saw Finn in a thin green T-shirt and jeans standing at the sink with his back to her. His shoulder blades jutted sharply through his shirt. His arm was raised, bent at the elbow, and he was drinking a glass of water that he refilled twice. From across the room, Marilyn, hidden by the bustle of the two women from the catering company and their tower of plastic boxes containing food for the reception, watched with her breath caught in her throat.

When she could finally say his name out loud, he turned and smiled in her direction. The skin on the lower right side of his face even nearly a year after the fire was still shiny, pink, and tight. The grafting was evident and causing a crooked smile, which seemed to add to his charm instead of detracting. His hair had grown in enough that he now wore it cut short but enough to cover the scars on his scalp. Instead of the long waves he used to have, his hair now stood up like the thick bristles of a brush all over his head. He ran his hands through it as he waited for Marilyn to make her way across the room to him. He opened his arms to her and she gave him a long, hard hug. She tried to put everything into that hug because she just didn't trust herself enough to say out loud that she was so glad he was alive. She hadn't seen him since she put him on the plane to Seattle all those months ago. Then he had still been so physically and emotionally ravaged that she wasn't positive she'd ever see him again. She had nightmares that he'd find a way to leave the facility in Seattle and just disappear. Now here he was. She hugged him again before she let go and realized, with an incredible sadness, that Finn was the only one of her children that she had really physically touched since they'd all been here.

"Did you just get here?" She noticed the fatigue around his eyes and beneath his tanned face. It looked different from the weariness he'd had when he'd been drinking. This looked more like he just hadn't had a good night's sleep.

He rubbed his eyes. "Plane delays everywhere because of storms. Even Boston is a fucking hailstorm of rain and wind. Unbelievable. It took me hours just to move a mile on the Mass Pike. Ridiculous. I couldn't even get cell reception and I didn't want to pull off and try and use a pay phone. I figured it was hell here as well." He made a face and said, "Then I get here and it's like nirvana. Clear blue sky, warm breeze."

Marilyn rubbed her hand up and down the length of his arm and squeezed. He was real. He was here. "Perfect day for a wedding."

Finn agreed and leaned back against the sink. "I can't believe they're really going to do this." He snorted. "I mean who really thought George would be the first of us to get married?"

Marilyn laughed as she glanced at the commotion going on outside in the driveway through the window above the sink. George and Sam had invited about forty guests. That seemed manageable on paper, but now, as she looked out at Saul's yard, it seemed impossibly huge and out of control. "You don't have long before we start . . ."

"I want to grab a quick shower—do I have time?" He lifted up his arms and sniffed at his armpits and made a face. "Twenty hours in this shirt." Finn started to walk out of the kitchen and then turned back to Marilyn with his eyebrows raised.

She nodded, then added, "But hurry." He looked so thin, but healthy. Yes. Healthy. Strong. There were muscles visible in his arms. He was still her most beautiful boy. She remembered when the doctor had handed him to her all those years ago, his solemn dark eyes against the most amazing porcelain skin. She blurted out, "You look good. Do you spend a lot of time outside?"

"Some." Finn nodded. "Out on the deck. I've got an easel set up and I've been painting some and . . ." Then he added shyly, his words all in a rush, "writing, I don't know if it's anything but yeah, well, I've been writing." He put a finger to his lips like it was to be their secret.

"Writing?" Marilyn whispered. The painting didn't surprise her; long before Amy had found art, Finn used to paint. He stopped somewhere between middle and high school when other things became more interesting. But writing? His struggles with school were rooted in writing and reading, because the letters and the words just hadn't made sense to him. Writing? Now? She thought but didn't add: just like your father.

"It started in rehab. One of the things was keeping a diary. Noting your moods, why you wanted a drink or whatever your poison." Finn hesitated and seemed to read her mind. "Don't worry about me going off like him. I've already been there and it holds no allure, believe me."

She did worry. Early on, she had romanticized Richard's drinking. It was part of his allure as tortured artist. For the longest time she associated sex with the taste of alcohol on her lips.

Then, as the years and professional disappointments took their toll, Richard's drinking made him mean and destructive. As Finn acknowledged, he had already been there. Still she couldn't stop herself from asking, "Are you really okay?"

Finn gave that lopsided grin again. "If you mean can I be trusted not to drink all the cough syrup and mouthwash out of the medicine cabinet? Then yes. Although that's pretty much a strictly hour-by-hour thing." He laughed when he saw the expression on Marilyn's face. "No worries, Ma, okay? I'm kidding."

She smiled back at him. She wanted him to tell her everything. She wanted reassurance. But this was neither the time nor the place.

"About the mouthwash anyway," he quipped as he left the kitchen, but he was smiling, pleased with his joke.

So Finn was writing. Everything good and bad about her marriage had been tangled up with Richard's writing. When the work was good, his appetite for Marilyn had been insatiable—her children were conceived when Richard's career was going well. Even in her ninth month, when Marilyn had been heavy with child, he wanted her and he wouldn't stop until he got her so she almost always gave in to him. No protection, wrong time of the month. He didn't care and he was always able to persuade Marilyn that she shouldn't either.

Yet each time she had told him she was pregnant, he had looked at her like he had played absolutely no role in the conception, even though they were all his. Even Finn, the one pregnancy she couldn't be positive about at the time. But when he was born with Richard's chin, the same stubborn set to his mouth, there had been no doubt. By the time Amy was born, Richard's pursuit of her had stopped. The writing soured and he went elsewhere until he either couldn't find his way back to her or she simply didn't want him to.

She took a deep breath, exhaled, and looked around her at the wedding preparations as though she had just woken up in a foreign land. She blinked once, twice, terrified that she didn't know what to do next—that she had gotten in over her head. Every inclination she had was telling her to run.

"Amy?"

Marilyn looked up. George was standing in the doorway with his tie in his hands. It was true of her children that Finn had needed the most and so he'd had what there was of her limited attention span. But George was the most openly affectionate toward her, seemed to hold the least amount of grudges, even if she didn't deserve it. He, above them all, treated her most like a mother.

"I can't seem to make my hands work." He held a lavender-and-navy-striped tie out to her. "I was looking for Amy to help me."

When she didn't answer him, he said louder, "Mom?" as he walked over and stood in front of Marilyn.

She smiled up at him and took the tie from his hands. "Bend down a little please."

George did as he was told and Marilyn lifted his collar, draped the tie around it, and tied a neat Windsor knot. When she was finished, she scrutinized her knot, straightened it, and patted him on the chest. "Done."

George stood back up. "Isn't this when you give me some last-minute advice about the wedding night?"

It felt good to laugh, to be useful, even if it was just to tie his tie. "Ready?"

He nodded. She took his hand and led him out the back door toward the tent, where Sam was waiting for him.

* * *

Marilyn tried to pay careful attention to the ceremony, but she was distracted. She imagined that if she had the chance to take everything back and find the right place to start her time with them all over again, this would be it. She watched the faces of her children gathered around Sam and George as they exchanged their vows. Amy and Asa had been the official witnesses, and then George had requested his other siblings to stand up there with them as well. Marilyn sat in the chairs with the rest of the guests while Saul acted as photographer.

Amy giggled nervously while they waited for Owen and his band to finish playing and for the minister to speak; a bouquet of orange gerbera daisies clasped in her hands and held up to her chin vibrated along with her laughter. Her short dress matched the daisies—an orange sixties lace in a flower pattern over a slip in the matching color along with high white boots. Sam, George, and Asa wore suits while their feet were clad in old Chuck Taylor sneakers. Sam's in purple, George's in white, and Asa's in red. Every single one of them looked nervous, even Kate, but Marilyn could tell it was a happy kind of nervous, when you realized that something you'd only dreamed of was about to happen. That feeling Marilyn recognized.

Of course, there was an equal amount of discord. While they were united in their happiness for George, she could tell that Kate was avoiding Finn, something was definitely wrong between them. At one point before the ceremony, Marilyn had seen Finn glance in a conciliatory way in Kate's direction, but Kate purposely stepped behind someone else so that she could no longer see Finn or he her. Marilyn realized that any other parent could probably demand outright to know or at the least ferret out enough information to piece it all together, but she wouldn't even begin to insinuate herself like that. She wondered briefly what it would be like if Richard were still alive.

Afterward, as the food was consumed and George and Sam were toasted and the chocolate wedding cake was cut and passed around, Owen and the band began to play. Asa came over and pulled her out of the chair to dance.

She let him whirl her around the floor completely out of time with the music. The kaleidoscope of people around her seemed to all be doing their own thing anyway, and she allowed herself to be passed off to her sons and her new son-in-law until finally she was dancing with Saul.

Marilyn felt sweaty and red-faced, grateful that the music had slowed. She forgot for a moment that she wanted to keep Saul a secret as she slipped into his arms. Thankfully, the cameras around his neck prevented them from getting inappropriately close. "I need to get something to drink, and to sit," Marilyn groaned. Her feet were killing her.

Saul led her to a table and held up a finger indicating that he'd be right back. For the first time, Marilyn noticed that the sky was dark and the candles inside the tent had been lit. Dancing was in full force now and Amy had joined the band, hopping around with a tambourine. Owen grinned at her while he sang about the girl of his dreams dressed in high white boots. Marilyn felt like crying.

When Saul returned, he handed her a pale-red fizzy drink with two cherries and an umbrella.

"What's this?" she asked, taking it from him and bringing it to her lips.

Saul grinned and said, "A Shirley Temple."

Marilyn laughed and drank it, grateful for the cool wetness sliding down her throat. She fished a cherry out with her fingers and offered it to Saul. He raised one eyebrow at her before he plucked it from her fingers.

While he chewed, he said, "You know what I thought when I first met you?"

Curious, she shook her head and urged him to go on.

"Well, I guess I'm really thinking about the time before we were formally introduced. It was at that stupid festival down in Tribeca, remember that?"

Marilyn did remember that stupid festival. She had a cameo in a dreadful small film where every actor had been barely legal and she had felt as old as the universe. It wasn't until two weeks before the premiere that she had found out that her part had been cut, but she had been invited anyway. A mercy invite. She'd gone because she had nothing else to do. Or maybe it was fate. Now she nodded at Saul to continue.

"I let you walk away from me, and as you did, you turned back and looked my way one time and my heart gave a little squeeze, you know?" He made a clutching movement with his fingers and put a palm over the Nikon camera strap and slapped his chest. "And I thought: I'm a glasses-wearing doofus and you are way far out of my league and still"—he paused—"I wished I had said something or everything."

Marilyn smiled at Saul's description of himself. She recalled Saul's funny yet persistent courtship and teased, "You waited a long time for someone you thought was so out of your league."

"I'm always better on my second try," he said seriously and then hesitated. Marilyn was suddenly nervous. What if Saul was going to do something ridiculous, like get down on one knee? Instead, he was looking toward the dance floor as he said wistfully, "I always wanted to play the tambourine in the band."

She followed the direction of his gaze. Amy was still jumping around and hitting the tambourine against her hip, but she was starting to look a little weary. "I think this is your chance. Go for it," Marilyn urged as she stood. Now that she wasn't dancing anymore, she was cold. "I'm going to go into the house for a shawl, you go take that tambourine from Amy." She squeezed Saul's arm and gave him a little shove. He gave her a distracted smile as he moved into the throng of dancers. When he was halfway there, he turned around and gave her the thumbs-up. He was already on his way to claim his place in the band.

Marilyn was surprised how quiet the house was, compared to the tent. She went up to her room and opened a drawer and fished out a periwinkle-colored shawl from a pile of scarves. There was a time she had worn scarves every day—she had fancied them her signature—wrapped in her hair or around her body as clothing. Why she kept them after all these years she had no idea. Certainly it wasn't for the memories.

Most of her clothes were here now because Saul liked to spend his downtime by the ocean no matter the season. The cottage he was building out back was actually going to be an editing studio. The *Dead, Again* franchise was going strong; they were to begin preproduction on number four in two weeks. Saul had invited Asa to the set and the boy was crazed beyond belief at the prospect. His excitement made Saul feel vindicated. There seemed to be no end to teens wanting to be scared out of their minds. Saul liked to say he made movies that helped guys like him get a little. He joked about marketing them with a guarantee: girls will grab their dates every single time.

Marilyn picked up the shawl and started out the door, and then at the last minute she turned back toward the bed, kicked off her heels, curled up, and closed her eyes. She could stay here forever, and not so very long ago she would have given in to this feeling. As she drifted, the music seemed like it was coming from far, far away. She wondered if Amy had relinquished the tambourine to Saul. That she wanted to see. The pull of sleep was so delicious, yet she forced herself off the bed to find her flats; she couldn't bear to shove her feet back into the heels.

As she walked across the shell-covered drive, she could hear the music and when she got closer, she saw, at the far end of the tent, Owen and the band playing on, along with a very exuberant Saul on the tambourine. His hair was wet along the tips as he whipped his head around, dancing like a Hare Krishna who'd just attained the highest level of enlightenment. Closer to her, Amy was laughing as Finn twirled her in his arms, while Kate did the twist all by herself and Asa did something goofy and robotic. Suddenly, Finn stopped, put Amy down, and approached Kate. Marilyn felt the breath catch in her throat as Finn leaned in close and said something in her ear. Kate tilted her head toward his and smiled, not widely but enough that her mouth tugged at the corners. Amy skipped over to them and with a hand on each of their arms tugged and tugged until they relented and fell back into the music along with Asa and Amy, their bodies an indistinguishable jumble of limbs as they bumped up against one another and twirled to the beat. At the edge of the dance floor were Sam and George with their jackets off, ties askew, and arms slung around each other's waists. They watched the dancers and bid good-bye to the guests that were starting to leave. The caterers had begun to clear the tables, and the flames flickered against the glass holders as the candles burned down.

Marilyn took a deep breath and then exhaled. There was a puff of frost in her breath and she pulled the shawl tighter around her shoulders. She looked again at her children, at Saul. It was more than she ever dared to imagine.

ACKNOWLEDGMENTS

For my parents, who never mentioned the word impossible *in* my presence. For my brother, who, in deference to our sibling relationship, allowed me to be the "different" one. For my husband, who never doubted me. For Ellen, gentle reader. For my daughters, Hannah and Tessa, who understood that I was working even if I was still wearing my sweats from the day before and sitting in front of a computer screen muttering to myself. For friends and family who, over the many years I've been doing this, indulged me with the moniker of writer, even when I had nothing tangible to show for it. For Julie Barer, Super Agent, wise, kind, patient, honest, and the best champion of my work that I could ever hope for. For Jeanette Perez, who really and truly "got" this book and embraced the characters and their story as if they were long-lost friends.